Vanished

Peter J. Douros

Paperback ISBN: 979-8-89397-723-3
Published by Solson Publications

Authors note:

The town of Raliegh is made up for the sole purpose of writing this book. Any resemblance to any persons living or dead is purely coincidental. Any resemblance to actual events or locales is entirely coincidental. This book is pure fiction.

Index

Acknowledgements

The author wishes to acknowledge the following people for their encouragement. My wife Janet, my Christian friends Kay and Lowell.

Introduction

The Vanishing of Maya Hahn: A Nick Curtis Mystery In the Shadowed Hollows of the Ozarks

As the clock ticks away the hours, the whereabouts of Maya Hahn is still a mystery—a chilling silence that settles heavily over the small, brick-lined streets of the Ozarks, where autumn leaves spin in restless eddies. In the third novel of the Nick Curtis mysteries by Peter J. Douros, Nick sheds his Brooks Brothers suit and the trappings of city life, disappearing beneath the muted camouflage of a seasoned bowhunter. The precision with which he knots the laces of his high-top boots mirrors the discipline with which he approaches every case, but this hunt is not for trophy or sport; it is for truth, buried deep beneath layers of rural quiet and academic routine.

Under the thin veil of a hunting trip, Nick returns to the college town that both welcomes and resists outsiders. His presence is disguised, his every move calculated to avoid suspicion, for the woods here are alive with secrets and the locals wary of prying eyes. By his side is Emma, a seasoned K-9 officer recently transferred from the metropolis, whose keen instincts are matched only by her steadfast companion, Storm—a sleek black Labrador whose nose is as sharp as her handler's intuition. Together, their partnership is an unspoken language: measured glances, silent gestures, and the shared understanding that, in this landscape, every snap of a twig or distant bark could spell discovery or danger.

The search for Maya Hahn is more than a missing persons case; it is a journey into the heart of the Ozarks, where the land rolls in endless, misty blue ridges and the past clings stubbornly to the present. Here, Douros's prose becomes an invocation of place: the cedar-scented dawns, the lonely farmhouses huddled in clearings, and the watchful stillness of the forest. The investigation winds through abandoned barns, roadside diners, and the labyrinthine corridors of the local college—each location peeling back a new layer of the story, each witness holding a fragment of the vanished girl's life.

Emma's experience in urban investigations brings a new edge to the search, while Storm's tracking leads them to hidden trails and discarded clues—a scrap of fabric caught on brambles, tire tracks washed faint by a recent rain, the faintest scent of perfume clinging to a forgotten scarf. The search party's progress is slow, deliberate; days stretch into nights adorned by the distant calls of whippoorwills, while the townsfolk grow restless, their whispers threading through church pews and general stores.

Yet, as Nick delves deeper, he finds that Maya's disappearance is only the beginning. Shadows stretch long in this part of the country— secrets of old rivalries, jealous passions, and half-told truths that fester beneath the community's polite veneer. The coed's vanishing reveals fractures in the college's insular world: a circle of friends bound by silence, a professor whose interest in Maya was more than academic, a string of cryptic text messages sent in the dead of night.

Douros's knowledge of the Ozarks lends the novel an authenticity that vibrates through every page. The region is not merely a backdrop, but a living, breathing character—its rivers and hollers holding witness to generations of hope and heartbreak. Nick's investigation draws on local legend and contemporary tension, as the woods become both a sanctuary and a labyrinth. Emma's sharp logic and Storm's unwavering loyalty help Nick navigate a world where every friendly face might mask suspicion, and every clue could be a trap.

As the final pieces fall into place, the case takes an unexpected turn—one that entwines the fate of the missing coed with a web of crimes spanning years, implicating not only the guilty, but those who have looked away. The truth, once unearthed, is both painful and redemptive. In the hush that follows, the Ozarks reclaim their quiet, but Nick Curtis, Emma, and Storm know that justice, like the hunt, is never truly over.

Peter J. Douros crafts another masterful tale—a tapestry of suspense, atmosphere, and psychological depth, where the search for one lost woman becomes a meditation on what it means to be found, and what it costs to uncover the truth.

Chapter One

Walking into the office Nick was uneasy with the thoughts that Bobbie had insisted that he twist Kerry's arm to convince him that they could finally take the vacation that he was due. Knocking on the office door of his superior his hands were sweating. Apprehension crept into his body his mouth was dry. He felt he was able to spit cotton. Most of the time Kerry was agreeable but recently he had went through a triple bypass. His health was getting better, but it was slow. His return to work was premature. From the old school his years as an FBI agent had been all that he lived for.

He also thought that everyone that carried that badge should always give the job a hundred and ten percent. Nick could share his feelings, but his two sons were attending a seminar at one of the finest military training schools for the same time that Bobbie wanted to meet her friend from St. Louis.

Bobbie's request weighed heavily on Nick as he stood outside Kerry's office door, rehearsing his words yet again. He couldn't shake the thought of the once-in-a-lifetime opportunity she had described—deer hunting on federal forest land, a privilege granted through a special drawing. Bobbie had been selected for bow hunting during the first two weeks of November, and her excitement had been contagious. She had even gone as far as preparing his favorite meal the night before, a clear strategy to soften him up before pleading her case again.

Nick's hesitation stemmed not only from Kerry's fragile health but also from his own recent break—a three-week vacation he had returned from merely eight weeks prior. Kerry had always expected unwavering dedication, and requesting another leave felt like a betrayal of that unspoken oath. Yet, Bobbie had convinced him that this hunting trip was different. With the ability to include up to four people in their party, it wasn't just a trip; it was an adventure, an experience they might never have the chance to replicate.

Taking a deep breath, Nick knocked firmly on the door, steeling himself for Kerry's reaction. This wasn't just about asking for another vacation; it was about balancing the weight of duty against the pull of family and the rare chance to fulfill a dream. Walking close he knocked on the glass door.

Seeing Kerry turn and motion him to come in held his breath. Kerry spoke "I'm glad you came in I was going to call you. I hope you are ready to get out of the fair city of Toledo. I got a call at the house last night that we got a missing coed down in Missouri. An old friend of mine called me. It is his granddaughter (Maya Hahn), and he feels that the local police are not moving on the case fast enough. She has been missing the forty-eight-hour time line; so, we are going in as soon as you can get there. Have a seat this is not going to be handled only one way. I got a call for D.C. this morning and since she is who she is we are going to do this undercover. I have been thinking about it since last night and I have just not found a good way to get you into this small town without being found out. It's at the small town of Raliegh. The State of Missouri's engineering school. My friend Quan-Lee (Pete) Hahn is the professor of the electrical department. The town has a small police department. Maybe eight or ten men."

"So, you want me to get on this right away? Sounds like I will have to go as soon as I can. Bobbie is going to have a fit. She feels that you owe her a favor since she had you and the missus over for bar-b-que last week. She has had her heart set on going to that bow hunt. You know she was picked out of over two thousand entries. I was coming in just now to try to get off on a vacation. Say how far is it to Raliegh from the Mark Twain Forest land. Have you got a map of that area?"

"Not here, but in the forensic office we do. What are you thinking?" Kerry's tone was curious, his sharp eyes watching Nick intently.

Nick hesitated for a moment, then plunged ahead. "I think that the hunt is close by. If it is, I...we could go in under the cover of bow hunters. We could even rent a Winnebago to live in—pick it up in St. Louis and drive down to Raliegh. Bobbie has already invited her college friend, who just happens to be a St. Louis K-9 officer.

The four of us could bow hunt early in the mornings and work on the case the rest of the day and night. I am sure that if the excessive deer are there, we can bag our limit early and just spend the rest of the time investigating. "

Kerry leaned back in his chair, his fingers steepled as he mulled over the suggestion. "Bow hunters, huh? That's not bad. It gives you a reason to be there without raising too many eyebrows. And with a K-9 officer in the mix, you've got a plausible team. Just make sure the locals don't catch wind of what you're really up to."

Nick nodded, feeling a small wave of relief wash over him. "I'll need to coordinate with Bobbie and her friend to make sure the story holds up. And we'll need to keep everything tight-lipped—no unnecessary chatter ."

Walking toward the forensic room, Nick and Kerry retrieved the map they needed. The Mark Twain Forest land indeed bordered the city limits of Raleigh, confirming Nick's earlier suspicions. Nick traced the boundary with his finger, noting how convenient it would be to move between the forest and the town without raising suspicion.

Kerry straightened up, his sharp tone breaking the silence. "Alright, Nick. Here's the plan. You drive home, pack your gear, and loop in Agent Moore to handle the logistics—the Winnebago rental, and all the necessary cover paperwork. I'll personally call Bobbie to let her know she and you can go on the hunt, but—" Kerry's lips twisted into a faint smirk, "I'll leave it up to you to break the news to her that this isn't going to be the vacation she envisioned. You'll be working alongside Emma-Linh , and this case will come first."

Nick winced inwardly but nodded. "Understood, sir. I'll make sure the setup is airtight, and that Bobbie is on board. We'll coordinate with her friend, the K-9 officer, to ensure the story holds up."

Kerry turned briskly, heading back toward his office. "Keep it professional, Nick. This undercover operation could get messy if the locals catch even a whiff of law enforcement meddling. Make sure everyone sticks to their roles—we don't need any slip-ups."

As Nick stepped out into the morning air, his mind was a whirl of thoughts and responsibilities. He knew the delicate balance between appeasing Bobbie's enthusiasm for the hunt and maintaining the integrity of their covert mission would require all his tact and persuasion. But as daunting as the task seemed, he couldn't ignore the spark of excitement at the idea of blending duty with adventure.

Settling in the front seat of his car, Nick pulled out his cell phone and dialed Agent Moore. "Hey, Roger, do you still have that identity kit we had made up last year? You know, the one for the insurance agent from Toledo Mutual? If you can dig that out and have it handy, I'll need it soon. Also, go ahead and order all the disbursements—the plane tickets, the Winnebago rental—everything charged to my name, just like we did before."

Nick leaned back in his seat, glancing down at the notes he had scribbled earlier. "Make sure Kerry calls the professor to reassure him we're on the way. Be polite, though. I know he's still a little touchy about taking directives from the field, but we need his cooperation to keep this hush-hush. Let him know we'll keep everything discreet."

Roger chuckled softly on the other end. "Got it, Nick. Sounds like you're in for quite the operation. Don't forget to loop me in if anything unexpected comes up."

"Will do," Nick replied. He hung up, his thoughts immediately shifting to the next steps. The plan was beginning to take shape, but the fragile threads connecting their covert mission to the bow hunt, Bobbie's enthusiasm, and the professor's guarded cooperation still needed careful weaving.

As he started his car, Nick reminded himself that every detail mattered. The Winnebago would be their base, blending perfectly into the hunters' scene, but the real challenge would lie in keeping their true purpose concealed while navigating the complexities of the case. With the professor's involvement and the K-9 officer in their team, he hoped their cover would be airtight. He couldn't afford any slip-ups now—not with so much riding on this operation.

Driving home, Nick was still rethinking all of the details. He would bet that Bobbie had already called Emma-Linh and instructed her husband to meet them at the St. Louis airport. The more he thought about her husband, the more he realized he might be the weak link in the plan. A lawyer by profession, Nick had only interacted with him twice and knew he couldn't trust him with the operation's true purpose in the quiet college town they were heading to.

Reaching his house, Nick barely stepped inside before Bobbie swept him into an enthusiastic embrace. Her excitement was palpable, her voice bubbling with energy.

"Kerry called and sounded really strange. What did you say to him? How did you pull this off? He sounded as though he was glad to get rid of you!"

Bobbie exclaimed, planting a kiss on his cheek. She didn't wait for Nick to respond before she continued, her words tumbling out in rapid succession. "I think he should've stayed home for another week or two. Oh well! I've already started packing. Kerry said we're off today to St. Louis, right? Two whole weeks to hunt—this is going to be amazing! Let's get our gear into the car."

Nick managed a wry smile, knowing how challenging it would be to temper her enthusiasm while keeping the mission intact. "Bobbie, I'll grab the rest of the gear and double-check that we have everything. This hunt is going to be... different, but I promise you'll have all the adventure you're hoping for."

As they loaded the car, Nick's mind raced ahead to the layers of deception this trip would entail. Bobbie's boundless energy was both an asset and a liability—her excitement could help sell the cover story, but it also risked drawing unwanted attention. Meanwhile, he couldn't shake the gnawing concerns about how Emma-Linh 's husband would fit into the operation. More than ever, Nick felt the weight of ensuring that every piece of the plan clicked seamlessly into place.

"Bobbie, you go ahead and get in the car," Nick said, his tone both reassuring and authoritative. "I want to swing by and let Mrs. Hickey know we'll be gone for the next two weeks so she can keep an eye on the house."

Bobbie hesitated for a moment, then nodded, her excitement undeterred. "All right, but don't take too long! We've got a schedule, remember?"

Nick offered a quick smile before closing the trunk and heading toward the house next door. Mrs. Hickey, an energetic woman in her late sixties, had always been a reliable neighbor. If anyone could keep a discreet watch on the house while they were away, it was her.

As he stepped onto her porch, Nick paused to pull out his phone and dial Roger. The line clicked, and Roger's familiar voice greeted him.

"Roger, do you have everything ready? The ID kit, the plane tickets, the works?"

"Sure do," Roger replied, a hint of amusement in his tone. "I've got it all prepped for you. If you stop by on your way to the airport, you can pick it up. Oh, and I made sure Kerry is briefed on the cover. He'll be ready if you need to reach out."

"Good," Nick said, his voice firm. "Thanks for staying on top of this. I'll swing by shortly."

"Don't mention it," Roger said. "Just make sure everything on your end runs smoothly. We can't afford any slip-ups."

Nick murmured his agreement before hanging up. Knocking lightly on Mrs. Hickey's door, he quickly explained their upcoming absence when she appeared in the doorway. Her sharp eyes softened with a smile as she promised to keep an eye on things.

Satisfied, Nick made his way back to the car, his thoughts already shifting to the next phase of the operation. Every detail mattered, and as much as Bobbie's unbridled enthusiasm added a certain energy to the trip, he knew maintaining their cover would require careful navigation of each interaction, each story, and each decision.

Nick slid into the driver's seat, catching a glimpse of Bobbie in the passenger seat. Her expression was a mixture of excitement and quiet determination, her gaze fixed on the horizon. There was no mistaking the sparkle in her eyes—she was already imagining herself tracking through the woods, the possibility of bagging a large white-tailed buck in the Ozarks lighting up her features.

Though she'd successfully taken down one in Ohio, this trip stirred a different kind of thrill in her. The dream of encountering a trophy buck with a magnificent rack had been sitting in her heart for years. Nick smiled, knowing how much this meant to her. They had both enjoyed hunting together over the last two seasons, especially after gifting each other new crossbows for Christmas. Hunting was their shared escape, but this trip was about far more than their outdoor adventures—it was about solving the case that had brought them there.

As they approached the office, Nick's mind shifted gears. The missing coed was the priority, but he was determined to make this trip feel special for Bobbie. She had to believe that this was as much about their time together as it was about the investigation.

Hurrying into the office, he found it quiet, with Kerry conveniently absent, leaving him free to finalize the meticulous preparations. Roger's kit was ready, and all the groundwork had been laid, ensuring their cover would hold under scrutiny. Nick slipped in and out with precision, his thoughts already mapping the steps ahead.

Back in the car, Bobbie rested her head against the window, her expression peaceful yet faraway, as though she were dreaming of the forest trails and the hunt ahead. Nick glanced at her, resolving to balance the demands of the case with moments that would make her feel the trip was truly hers. The road stretched ahead, leading them not only to the Ozarks but to the tangled web of clues and the promise of adventure that awaited them both.

Stepping up to the officer stationed near the airport jetway, Nick shifted into his professional demeanor. With a steady voice, he introduced himself, presenting the required credentials and making it clear he was armed. The officer, a seasoned figure with a no-nonsense expression, nodded curtly and directed him to proceed with caution. The exchange was swift but thorough, leaving no doubt that their cover would hold under scrutiny.

Meanwhile, Bobbie stayed a few steps back, her arms crossed as she shifted her weight impatiently. She had no desire to revisit the procedural monotony of check-ins and clearances. Her excitement simmered just beneath the surface, ready to spill over the moment they boarded the flight. The boarding call came like a starting pistol, and Nick barely had time to catch up before she seized his hand, her grip a mixture of joy and urgency.

Walking briskly down the jet bridge, Bobbie's energy was infectious, and Nick couldn't help but chuckle at her exuberance. As they found their seats, she quickly claimed the window, sweeping the curtain aside to take in every detail of the journey ahead. Her anticipation painted her face with an almost childlike wonder that Nick found endearing, even as he gently teased her to rein in her enthusiasm.

"Bobbie," he murmured, leaning closer as the plane began to taxi, "you're acting like a kid on their first roller coaster. We've got hours to go before the real adventure starts."

She turned to him with a mischievous glint in her eye, her voice dropping to a playful whisper. "Maybe so, but you're forgetting something important, Nick. Tonight, there's no forest silence to keep us quiet—just you, me, and a whole lot of gratitude for this trip." Her grin widened, a mixture of affection and mischief that left Nick shaking his head with a warm smile.

As the plane soared into the sky, Bobbie's gaze returned to the window. The sprawling landscapes below seemed to mirror her emotions—vast, untamed, and tinged with opportunity. For Nick, it was a balance of work and life, of duty and joy, but he knew one thing for sure; this trip would leave them both with stories to tell and memories to treasure.

As the plane leveled out and the seatbelt sign flickered off, Nick stretched slightly before rising from his seat. Bobbie raised an eyebrow in question, her lips curving into a faint smile. "Restroom," he murmured in response, his tone clipped but affectionate. With a small nod, she turned her attention back to the view outside, absorbed in the shifting tapestry of clouds and landscapes below.

Nick moved confidently down the aisle; his focus unwavering until he reached the small galley area near the front. Catching the stewardess' eye, he leaned in slightly, his voice low but authoritative. "Ma'am, as you've been informed, I am an agent. However, I'd appreciate it if you kept that discreet during the flight. My wife and I are starting our vacation, and I'd like to enjoy it without drawing unnecessary attention—unless, of course, there's an emergency. Thank you."

The stewardess, a poised professional with a calm demeanor, nodded promptly. "Of course, Agent. Thank you for flying with Ozark Airlines," she replied smoothly, her expression one of polite understanding. Satisfied, Nick gave a slight nod before continuing to the restroom, where he allowed himself a few moments of solitude to gather his thoughts and mentally reset.

Returning to his seat, Nick settled in beside Bobbie, who greeted him with a teasing glance, her fingers drumming lightly against the armrest. He closed his eyes, letting the rhythmic hum of the engines lull him into a state of relaxation. The minutes passed in serene quiet, the occasional murmur of passengers and faint clinking of service carts blending into the background.

Suddenly, the sharp screech of rubber meeting asphalt shattered the calm as the landing gear touched down in St. Louis. The jolt brought Nick fully awake, his instincts quick to assess their surroundings. Bobbie, her excitement undimmed by the abrupt arrival, leaned closer to the window, her eyes sparkling with anticipation

"We're here," she murmured, her voice tinged with eagerness.

Nick glanced at her, a small smile playing on his lips. "Let's make this one for the books," he said softly, the weight of the impending investigation mingling with the promise of shared adventures. As the plane taxied toward the gate, the atmosphere between them crackled with an unspoken understanding—they were stepping into a new chapter, one filled with mystery, challenge, and unforgettable moments.

Waiting for the others to rise up and leave the plane Nick and Bobbie walked off of the plane holding hands like two school kids. Riding the escalator into the first floor. Nick guided Bobbie to the shuttle bus after picking up their luggage. The short trip to the outside basement parking lot was a shock of stifling heat as the concrete structure welcome them to the gateway to the west.ST. Louis.

As they stood in the asphalt driveway the sun was sneaking into the busy trafficway. The structure was a beehive of activity as the passengers rushed to reach their destination. As the hiss of the buses airbrake welcomed them to their ride to the rental office. They sat down and enjoyed the brief ride. The air conditioning in the small bus was refreshing. The harried look on the drivers face suggested that it had been a long day.

As they rode Nick opened the packet that Roger had prepared. Taking out the identification papers and several of the business card and dropping in his Jacket pocket. Bobbie was still busy looking out the window at the bustling activity of the busy airport.

Pulling into the rental lot could see the mixture of rentals, the bright shiny metal covering of the Air-stream parked close to the office was inviting as Nick measure the different styles of recreational vehicles parked on the lot.

Thanking the bus-driver they carried their luggage to the office. Nick reached out his hand guiding Bobbie was they slowly walked to the man who was waiting to greet them.

"Welcome to Missouri Mr. and Mrs. Welsch I opened the Winnebago as soon as I got the call, if you come in to the office, we can fill out the paperwork and get you on the road right away. Just need to see your driver's license and yours too if both of you are going to drive."

Stepping in front of Bobbie Nick spoke "Why don't you go ahead and get in; dear you don't need to drive. It's only a couple of hours to the camp-sight."

Thinking 'no need to let her find out I am on a case; I'll wait until the time is right.'

As Nick handed over his license, he turned to Bobbie with a slight grin. "Maybe give Emma-Linh a call and see if she's on her way. You did call her and tell her we were coming, right?"

Bobbie nodded but frowned slightly. "I thought she'd have grabbed a cab and met us here by now. Good idea—I'll call her and find out where she and Jeffrey are. I was sure she'd be here already."

With her phone in hand, Bobbie stepped out of the office while Nick continued filling out the paperwork, his mind briefly lingering on Roger's detailed packet and the hints of a case that awaited him. He glanced at the shiny Winnebago parked outside, imagining the road ahead—a mix of professional intrigue and personal moments layered with the promise of discovery.

The rental agent chuckled softly, breaking Nick's train of thought. "Looks like you've got a full trip ahead. Hope it's a good one. If you don't I need cash for the food and beer. I stock that stuff myself and it is separate from the rental. You know tax purposes."

Counting out the cash Nick waited for his receipt. Turning his head around looking for Bobbie. The clerk handed it to him after he signed the original contract.

Nick smiled, nodding but offering no details, as Bobbie returned, her brows furrowed. "Emma-Linh says they're running late—it seems Jeffrey had some last-minute errands. They'll meet us at the Elmwood inn across the street instead."

"Not a problem," Nick said smoothly, slipping the completed rental agreement across the desk. He opened the door for Bobbie, and together they moved toward the gleaming Winnebago, ready to embark on a journey that promised more than either of them could fully anticipate.

As Nick maneuvered the massive Winnebago onto the road, the hum of the engine filled the cabin, yet his mind buzzed louder with unease. His hands gripped the steering wheel firmly, and his eyes darted to the rearview mirror more often than necessary. The vehicle felt cumbersome, a far cry from his usual mode of transport, and his thoughts lingered on the delicate balance of keeping his case concealed while navigating this unaccustomed terrain.

The drive to the Elmwood inn was brief, but every moment stretched in his mind as he rehearsed the calm demeanor he needed to maintain. The sight of Emma-Linh and Jeffrey waiting in the parking lot, bags piled with an unmistakable pair of crossbow cases perched atop added layers to his already crowded thoughts. Emma-Linh , sporting shorts that spoke of casual readiness, stood with an air of relaxed impatience. Beside her, Jeffrey—his shirt sleeves rolled up and his suit coat slung over an arm—carried an aura of unresolved business, hinting at his early morning spent at the office.

Nick steered into a spot and killed the engine, its rumble fading into the warm air. Exiting the vehicle, he masked his nervousness with a smile. "Looks like you're armed for more than sightseeing," he quipped, his glance falling on the crossbows.

Emma-Linh grinned, her sharp wit slicing through the tension. "Always ready for what's ahead, Nick. You never know what surprises a road trip might bring."

Jeffrey adjusted his suit coat, his posture suggesting he had yet to fully transition from work mode to leisure. "Not sure how much leisure this trip will allow," he said enigmatically, his gaze flickering toward Nick for the briefest moment.

Nick nodded, feeling the weight of Jeffrey's unspoken words. He was keenly aware that this journey, though wrapped in the guise of personal adventure, carried undercurrents that none of them would ignore for long. Helping Emma-Linh with her bags, he turned toward the Winnebago, its gleaming surface reflecting the afternoon light and the layers of intrigue that marked their start.

"Let's get settled," Nick said with practiced ease, "and figure out the rest as we go."

Nick's mind roved back to Emma-Linh , thinking of her sharp resolve and the unanswered question that lingered about whether the office had managed to contact her. He was eager to discover if she had agreed to collaborate with him on the case—a pivotal decision that could shape the unfolding of their plans. Despite knowing that the office was officially efficient , it seemed there had been precious little time for her to iron out the details with her superiors before their already complex journey began.

Glancing toward the inside rearview mirror, Nick caught sight of Emma-Linh and Jeffrey, now settled at the fold-out table in the back of the RV. Their postures betrayed a rare moment of relaxation: Emma-Linh leaning slightly forward with a beer in hand, her laughter light and unguarded, while Jeffrey, always tethered to the world of business, held his phone to his ear, likely hashing out details with one of his partners. The sight was oddly reassuring—a reminder that even amidst the layers of intrigue, moments of normalcy could emerge.

The hum of the road beneath them offered Nick no reprieve from the questions circling his thoughts. If Emma-Linh had tied up the necessary loose ends, would she finally feel free to immerse herself fully in the task ahead? And if she hadn't, would it complicate their ability to act decisively on this case? For now, Nick chose to keep his concerns buried, focusing instead on the immediate challenge of steering the Winnebago through its next stretch while maintaining the carefully constructed equilibrium he had built within the group.

As the RV rolled onward, the sunlight glinted against the glass, casting fleeting shadows across the dashboard—shadows as transient as the trust and uncertainties that bound the trio together. For Nick, the road ahead was less about miles and more about the delicate unraveling of truths that awaited them at each turn.

As the RV climbed the crest of the hill, Nick felt a chill race up his spine—a mixture of tension and fatigue from the unfamiliar weight and sway of the massive vehicle. The long ribbon of highway unfurled below, shimmering in the sunlight like a path both inviting and relentless. At the base of the hill, a rest stop beckoned, its shaded benches and vending machines promising a brief reprieve.

Nick flexed his fingers around the steering wheel, his joints stiff from the effort of keeping the Winnebago steady. He glanced at the dashboard clock, feeling the subtle tug of time against their plans but deciding that the moment of rest was worth the delay.

"I'm pulling in at the rest stop," he called, his voice cutting through the hum of the engine. He reached up to flick on the directional signal, its rhythmic click mingling with the faint laughter drifting from the back. "If any of you beer drinkers need to stretch your legs, now's your chance."

Emma-Linh's laughter bubbled up again, light and unfiltered. "Beer drinkers? That's bold coming from the guy who just got behind this beast of a machine for the first time!"

Jeffrey, still tethered to his phone, offered a distracted nod, barely glancing up as Nick navigated the RV down the incline. The vehicle groaned slightly as it descended, its weight pressing into the curves of the road.

Pulling into the rest stop, Nick eased the RV into a shaded corner, its engine rumbling to a halt. He exhaled deeply, grateful for the momentary release from the tension of driving. The air outside was warm but breezy—welcoming in its simplicity.

Nick stepped out, his boots resounding against the asphalt. The stretch of his legs sent a wave of relief through him, and he glanced back toward the RV, waiting to see if Emma-Linh or Jeffrey would join him. Sure enough, Emma-Linh bounded out moments later, tossing her empty beer can into a nearby recycling bin. Her gaze swept over the rest stop, her sharp eyes catching the details of their temporary surroundings. "Not bad for a quick pause," she commented, her tone casual but observant.

Jeffrey eventually emerged, phone still in hand, his conversation winding down as he stepped into the sunlight. His posture relaxed slightly, though the faint lines on his forehead betrayed the weight of the business still lingering in his mind.

Nick leaned against the RV, the hum of passing cars filling the silence between them. For now, the journey paused, offering an interlude in the midst of their tangled thoughts and plans. The road stretched ahead, promising answers at each bend and unwavering questions with every mile traveled.

Quickly stepping into the men's room, Nick relieved himself and lingered just long enough to rinse his hands and splash cold water on his face. The chill spread across his skin, refreshing him yet offering a stark reminder of the pressure he had been placing on himself. He had to admit, somewhat begrudgingly, that he'd seen smaller people—half his size, even—casually maneuver RVs twice the size of the Winnebago he had been wrestling with. The thought brought a smirk to his lips, and the faint reflection in the mirror greeted him with a look of humor and concession.

Chapter Two

The smile persisted as a mental note settled in perhaps it was time to ease up and truly enjoy the vacation that stretched ahead with promises of freedom and spontaneity. He adjusted his shirt and pushed the restroom door open, stepping out into the warmth of the day.

Emma-Linh was waiting for him, leaning casually against the RV with a knowing smile. Her sharp eyes met his as he approached. "Since we've got a minute, there's something I wanted to tell you," She began, her voice dropping slightly, as though the breeze might carry her words toward ears they didn't intend. "I know that mum's the word, but I got clearance from upstairs—we're both officially on the job."

Nick raised his eyebrows, the casualness of her tone contrasting with the gravity of what the admission implied. Before he could respond, Emma-Linh continued, her grin widening mischievously. "By the way, I don't envy you when you have to break the news to Bobbie. But hurry—let's not give anyone a reason to think we're conspiring."

Her laughter bubbled out, light yet agreeable, as she turned to glance toward the rest stop benches. Nick chuckled softly, shaking his head. The journey, it seemed, had layers he hadn't fully unraveled yet. For the moment, however, he let her playful tone guide him, relaxing into the brief pause before the road demanded their attention once more.

Stepping towards the door Nick could see that Jeffery and Bobbie were both finished in the restroom and were walking to them.

Quickly leaning close to her Nick said "No more than you will, when it is time for you to tell Jeffery. I can handle Bobbie but pulling him away for the office to go out and solve a crime under the pretext to kill a deer. I am afraid it's going to be a stretch." Gentle slapping her on the back. He began walking to the RV.

Settling back behind the wheel of the RV, Nick felt a familiar weight creep into his chest—the kind that came when the pieces of a puzzle began shifting into place yet refused to align. He gripped the steering wheel, the smooth leather reassuring under his palms. His mind, however, was anything but calm. The professor. He needed to figure out how to contact him without raising questions, and soon. Whatever they were chasing didn't seem inclined to wait.

Outside the RV, Bobbie's determined stride caught his eye as she approached. He could tell by the set of her jaw that she'd already outlined the morning in her mind. She would be out in the forest at the crack of dawn tomorrow, no doubt about it. The hunt, in her eyes, had already begun, and she likely considered today's delays as precious hours wasted. Bobbie's focus was unwavering, a double-edged sword that Nick both admired and dreaded.

He exhaled deeply, brushing the thought aside as the RV rumbled to life beneath him. The road ahead stretched like an unspoken promise, and Nick knew this wasn't just about the hunt or the town they were heading toward. It was about the layers of mystery that Emma-Linh had alluded to, the secrets they carried, and the roles they had to play.

"I hope you're ready for an early morning," Bobbie's voice rang out as she leaned over his shoulder from passenger area behind him. Her grin was sharp, tempered with eagerness. "We've got a lot of ground to cover—and deer don't wait."

Nick returned her grin with a faint smirk, though his thoughts remained tangled in the case and the professor. As the RV eased onto the highway, the hum of the engine filled the cabin, and the journey resumed, carrying them closer to the answers—and challenges—that waited ahead.

Vanished

Nick leaned back slightly in his seat, letting the rhythm of the road ease his earlier tension. The hunt, with all its peculiarities, would take its course; he was certain of that. Yet his thoughts remained tethered to the missing coed—a case with threads too tangled for the locals to unravel. Whatever answers lay hidden in Raliegh, they wouldn't be found in the obvious places. Nick needed a plan, and he needed it before stepping foot in those campgrounds.

Glancing at the dashboard clock, he calculated—with a mixture of relief and apprehension—that the drive ahead could buy him time to strategize. He would make a stop in town, even if it was brief. A simple errand, a casual excuse—that was all it would take to slip away unnoticed. He had to call the professor, not just for the case but to reassure him that his involvement was more than a formality. Kerry had likely already reached out, but Nick knew firsthand how much weight a personal assurance could carry.

As the RV rumbled steadily onward, Nick began rehearsing his rationale for the detour. A convenience store? A hardware shop? Something routine enough to avoid suspicion yet functional enough to keep their timeline intact. He allowed the hum of the engine to steady his resolve, even as Bobbie's words echoed in his mind. She was eager to dive into the hunt, and her determination made her an unpredictable variable. He would have to tread carefully.

The road twisted ahead, stretching out like threads too frayed to weave cleanly. Nick gripped the wheel a little tighter, his thoughts slipping between the case, the professor, and the unspoken layers of the journey. By the time they reached the city of Raleigh, he would need answers—not just about the hunt, but about the roles they all seemed destined to play.

The engine strained to pull the hill of the cloverleaf at the entrance to Raleigh, and Nick was greeted by the glittering display of bright lights advertising gas stations and restaurants. The array of options sprawled out before him like a fleeting promise of comfort, a sharp contrast to the rugged campfire meals that awaited them. He spied several places where they could stop for what might be their last proper meal before immersing themselves fully into the wilderness.

His mind faltered only for a moment as he considered suggesting a stop. Bobbie's focus, unwavering as ever, left him little room for detours. Yet, the idea of a warm meal lingered—something to mend the frayed edges of tension woven into their journey. The glowing marquees blinked at him, each vying for attention, but the RV rolled forward, bypassing their persistent call. The hunt, after all, waited for no one.

Nick pushed the thought aside, tightening his grip on the steering wheel as the city's outskirts unfolded. Raleigh's pulse thrummed faintly in the distance, a city bearing both answers and riddles. His gaze shifted to Bobbie, whose eyes remained locked ahead, her determination a cornerstone of their mission. Nick exhaled subtly, knowing the road ahead demanded readiness—not indulgence.

Bobbie's breath carried the faint trace of the beer she had been sipping earlier as she leaned over Nick's shoulder. Her voice rang with a mix of excitement and insistence. "Look, Nick! There's an Tommys restaurant—right over there to your left."

Her finger pointed across the glimmering lights of Raleigh, guiding his gaze to a glowing sign advertising 'Tommys Oriental Palace.' Without waiting for Nick to respond, she turned to the others seated in the RV. "Hey, you guys! How about Tommys for our last dinner in civilization?" Her call ricocheted through the cabin, injecting a momentary levity into the otherwise weighted silence of the journey.

The wheels in Nick's mind began turning. This was the opening he had been looking for—a chance to make the call to the professor. If he could connect with the grandfather, someone Kerry clearly valued, the gesture might solidify trust and calm any lingering doubts. He didn't need much—just a few minutes to deliver the reassurance he knew would carry weight.

"Alright," Nick said as he flicked on the turn signal, his voice steady as though the decision was made on impulse. "Tommys Oriental Palace it is." Turning into the left lane, he quickly maneuvered to an answer, guiding the RV toward the entrance of the restaurant. Its bright neon lights reflected off the windshield, casting a warm, inviting glow that contrasted with the tension still knotting his thoughts. As the RV rolled into the parking lot, Nick's eyes briefly met Bobbie's in the rearview mirror. She grinned knowingly, triumphant.

The others began to stir, the prospect of a real meal bringing murmurs of approval. Nick, however, remained focused. The moment they disembarked, he would excuse himself—an errand, a quick task outside. That should give him enough time for the call. He tightened his grip on the steering wheel one last time before turning the engine off, his resolve set.

Stepping out into the cool evening air, Nick lingered by the RV's door, his movements deliberate yet unhurried. He pretended to check his phone, the device almost a prop to mask his true intent. As the others meandered toward the restaurant's entrance, their chatter lighthearted and buoyant, he felt a brief reprieve from the tension that had shadowed him throughout the drive. Emma's laughter floated on the breeze, the sound unfurling a thread of relief that made him pause.

Nick's gaze followed her as she moved ahead, her presence steady and unflappable. It wasn't just her smile—there was a quiet confidence in the way she carried herself, something he suspected would be critical in the challenges they were bound to face. He considered how best to approach her, knowing that establishing trust and aligning their strategies was vital. Yet, finding the right moment—one that felt organic and unobtrusive—would require finesse.

As they reached the concrete steps leading to the restaurant's entrance, Nick noticed the easy derie between Emma and Bobbie. Their rapport wasn't surprising; the two women had been in constant contact, their near-daily texts bridging the gaps of physical distance. Still, he couldn't help but marvel at how effortlessly they seemed to slip into their rhythm, their laughter a soft undercurrent to the evening's ambiance.

Nick allowed himself a small smile, knowing that the bond between them would likely strengthen as they shared secrets and updates—the kind of conversations reserved for moments when women felt truly at ease. For now, he would play the part of observer, noting each detail with the precision of someone attuned to the shifting dynamics of the group. The hunt demanded more than just preparation; it required an understanding of the roles each participant played, and Nick knew that every interaction held the potential to shift the outcome.

As they crossed the threshold into the restaurant, the warm aroma of spices enveloped them, a sensory reminder of the comforts that civilization offered. Nick filed away the fleeting indulgence, his thoughts already returning to the call he needed to make. Timing, he reminded himself, was everything.

As they entered the restaurant, guided by a man whose accent carried the unmistakable tones of the Orient, Nick caught a glimpse of the unusual interior. The front section of the space was set one step below the center floor, evoking the charm of a Southern American porch. The architecture felt both unexpected and oddly inviting, blending cultures in a way that mirrored their eclectic group.

Without much fanfare, a petite server appeared, her silk dress flowing with an elegance that spoke of fine craftsmanship from an Tommys boutique. Her youth was striking—she seemed barely old enough to legally serve alcohol, yet her poise suggested she was well-practiced in the art of hospitality. As they settled into their seats, the man who had guided them to their table spread menus across the table with seasoned precision. He paused briefly, allowing the young server to step forward, and introduced her with a cordial yet efficient demeanor. "May Lin will be your server this evening," he announced, his tone warm yet succinct.

Nick glanced at his phone, the glowing screen confirming what he already suspected—they were early for dinner, the time reading only 5:36 PM. Their haste to reach the campgrounds had left them unaware of how the day's rhythm had shifted, and for a moment, Nick felt the weight of their goals pressing against the comforting atmosphere of the restaurant. The others, however, seemed content to take in the surroundings, their attention drawn to the subtle details of the décor and the quiet ambiance that hinted at the potential of a memorable meal.

Nick's mind, however, remained on his true purpose. While the others flipped through menus and exchanged comments about appetizers, he calculated how best to excuse himself. Timing was critical, and if he could step away without drawing undue attention, the call to the professor might unfold as planned. He took a deep breath, allowing the aroma of spices to ground him momentarily, before refocusing on the delicate balance of observation and action.

The server returned, her voice carrying a practiced clarity as she inquired what they would like to drink. Without hesitation, and almost as if choreographed, the group responded in unison, "Hot tea would be good." A ripple of laughter followed their synchronized reply, its warmth cutting through any lingering tension. It was a change from their usual preference for beer, and the novelty seemed to amuse them all.

Emma-Lee spread her menu open saying "Look Bobbie they have two selections of kinds of items both Asian and Vietnamese.

This is the first time I ever saw this; they must do a lot of business. I bet you can mix some of your favorite's on the same plate." The server nodded her agreement.

Nick, however, remained tethered to his thoughts. The unresolved matter of the call to the professor continued to gnaw at him, pressing against the edges of his focus. Clearing his throat softly, he addressed the group with a quiet resolve. "If you will order for me," he began, his tone deliberate yet light, "I'm going to step outside and check the tires on the RV. Maybe stretch my legs a bit. Bobbie, you know what I like. Just order for me, and I'll be back in a minute—if you don't mind."

Bobbie waved him off with an easy smile. "Sure thing, Nick. Go do what you need to do." The others nodded in easy agreement, their attention already returning to the intricacies of the menu. Nick felt a flicker of gratitude for their nonchalance. Without further ado, he excused himself, slipping away from the table with the quiet efficiency of someone adept at managing dual priorities.

As the door swung open, the cool evening air met him with a crispness that was both bracing and refreshing. He took a deliberate step away from the restaurant's glow, his hand instinctively reaching for his phone. This was his moment, the window he'd been calculating all evening. Steeling himself, he dialed the professor's number, letting the first ring echo into the stillness of the night.

Walking behind the RV for cover, he felt a peace fall over him as the phone went through the tiny sound of his number being dialed. The strong voice that answered spoke, "Hello, Hahn here."

"Yes, Professor Hahn. This is Nick Curtis, the FBI agent assigned to look into the disappearance of your granddaughter. My superior, Kerry Gibson, assigned me to this case. I'm here in Raleigh, and I am going to make the best effort we can to find your granddaughter safe," Nick began, his voice steady but filled with quiet determination.

"Let me give you this phone number. Just leave the text 'Updates are ready,' and I will call you back as soon as I can. For the time being, we are not making our entrance to the case public. So please keep my call to you quiet. You can expect Kelly to be available if you need to get any information to me. Thank you. Goodbye."

Nick ended the call, his mind already processing the weight of the conversation. The cool air around him seemed to hold his thoughts, grounding him in the reality of the task ahead. As he slipped his phone back into his pocket, he took a deep breath, steeling himself for the delicate balance of secrecy and action that awaited him inside the restaurant.

Walking around the RV, Nick kicked the tires with a casual precision, his movements deliberate as he maintained the charade of a thorough inspection. Each step seemed to serve a dual purpose—not only as a feigned check of the vehicle's readiness but also as a way to shake off the tension that had taken root in his legs. As he paced across the parking lot, the tightness began to ease, replaced by a subtle sense of relief.

The sprawling lot unfolded before him, and his eyes wandered to the three-story building that housed the restaurant. Behind it, several pickup trucks were parked near the rear entrance, their placement suggesting another layer to the establishment's operations. Curious, Nick strolled closer and caught sight of a basement-level bar bustling with energy—its patrons and the steady rhythm of vehicles pulling in and out formed a lively tableau that contrasted sharply with the quiet of his own thoughts.

Satisfied with his brief excursion and the renewed lightness in his stride, Nick retraced his steps toward the dining room. Timing, as always, seemed to favor him; the server was just placing their meals on the table as he approached. Sliding into his seat with practiced ease, he was met with Bobbie's teasing grin and a playful jab.

"So, old man, did you manage to work out all the kinks in those antique bones of yours?" Bobbie laughed, her good-natured humor breaking through the momentary seriousness. Nick chuckled in response, grateful for the derie that grounded him amidst the weight of his mission.

Sitting down with the others they began eating. Conversation waited as they enjoyed the Asian cuisine. Each ignored the others as they delighted at their favorite meal. Unwilling to share any, only stopping to refill their tiny tea cup. Ignoring the other diners that were beginning to filter in the restaurant. It appeared that the host was shying away from them as he seated newcomers inside the larger dining room. Dinner went quick as they were eager to reach the White tail lodge campground where they would begin their adventure.

Spreading the small brochure from the campgrounds Nick traced tiny description of the route to the campgrounds. "It looks pretty simple. It is just on the other side of town. It looks like the federal forest land surrounds the city limits on the west side of town. The main road leads right to it. We can drive to the main intersection and go veer right and it is just a short piece to it. So let us pay our bill and get going. A quiet night in the woods awaits us."

Getting up they followed Nick to the cash register where Jeff grabbed Nicks bill and said "You are paying for the rental of the RV. The least I can do is buy our first dinner."

The walk to the RV in the cool evening air was a welcome reprieve, washing away the lingering heat and spices from the restaurant. The night, just beginning to settle over the small town, brought a hush to the streets—a quiet that magnified the anticipation in Bobbie's chest. She strolled beside Nick, her pace unhurried, savoring the gentle breeze and the soft glow of distant streetlights.

While the others seemed focused on their upcoming task, Bobbie's thoughts wandered. She knew the hours ahead would demand their attention; every breath sharpened by the urgency of the search. Yet within her, another longing stirred—a desire for closeness, for the warmth of intimacy that had eluded her these past weeks. The prospect of the night ahead—alone at the campground, surrounded by forest and shadow—kindled a hope she barely dared to name.

Bobbie glanced at Nick, watching the way the streetlight played along his features, the determination in his stride softened by the promise of the evening. She wondered if he sensed the same need for comfort, for a moment carved out just for them between the rhythms of duty and responsibility. The air was cool, but her thoughts burned quietly, each step carrying her closer not just to their destination, but to the possibility of something more—a quiet escape from the world outside, if only for a night.

When they reached the RV, the others gathered their things silently, each lost in their own anticipation for the adventure ahead. But for Bobbie, as she measured her steps towards their rolling sanctuary, it was not just the hunt that awaited her—it was the hope of a night where she could let her guard down, where she might remember what it felt like to be cherished, to be seen.

As they made their way along the quiet stretch between restaurant and RV, Bobbie gathered her resolve. With a subtle glance around to be sure they had a moment's privacy, she reached up and gently caught Nick's hand, her fingers squeezing his with a warmth that lingered. She stepped closer, pressing her side to his, and leaned in, her lips just brushing the shell of his ear so only he could hear her words above the hush of the evening.

"I would like it very much if you realized we're not getting any younger," she whispered, her tone tender but edged with playful intent. "And I don't want to sound crude, but I sure do need some real hard loving. Maybe not tonight, but surely, you'll find some time when we can get alone and—well, we could christen this RV, if you get what I mean."

Nick slowed his pace, caught off guard and amused in equal measure. He looked at her, reading the vibrant glint in her eyes, recognizing the gentle mischief, the invitation to escape for a while from the weight of their responsibilities. He remembered, in that instant, all the nights they'd shared—moments of passion, comfort, and laughter, the kind that stitched quiet intimacy into the fabric of their partnership.

He squeezed her hand in return, a silent promise passing between them. Whatever the days ahead might bring, there would be room for them—for moments stolen, for affection kindled beneath the cover of starlit woods or when the world outside grew silent.

By the time they reached the RV, the spell of their exchange lingered. Both carried with them the anticipation of adventures yet to come, and the quiet certainty that, even amid the unknown, they would find time for each other—a sanctuary within the journey, a place to be seen and cherished, just as they'd always been.

Sliding behind the steering wheel, Nick turned and kissed Bobbie's hand, a soft gesture that spoke volumes, his wink sealing the silent understanding they'd just shared. The moment lingered, delicate and electric, before he released her fingers and faced forward, ready to shoulder the next stretch of their journey.

Nick watched as Bobbie headed to the rear of the RV, where the others were already settling into their chairs, each finding comfort in their own familiar way. Her delight was impossible to hide as she flopped onto the overstuffed couch, sinking into its welcoming cushions. With a languid stretch, she kicked off her shoes and tucked her feet beneath her, claiming her place in the little home they'd made on wheels.

Emma and Jeffery exchanged knowing grins, anticipation flickering between them as they waited for the hum of the engine to signal the beginning of this new adventure. The air inside the RV was thick with expectation—of roads untraveled, of mysteries yet to unfold, and of quiet, stolen moments that belonged only to them.

Outside, the night pressed gently against the windows, and inside, laughter and conversation began to rise, weaving a cocoon of derie around the group. Their world, for now, was this rolling haven and the promise of stories waiting to be written—together.

Nick exhaled, steadying his nerves as his fingers curled around the wheel. He started the engine with a low purr, eyes flicking to the rearview mirror to catch Bobbie's reflection, her contentment tangible as she basked in the glow of newfound hope. The dashboard lights cast a gentle glow across his knuckles, grounding him in the moment.

Outside, the city's neon pulse flashed through the windshield—an endless flow of headlights, signs, and urban movement. The RV rumbled forward; Nick's senses sharpening as he approached the busy intersection ahead. When the traffic light finally blinked red for cross traffic, he pressed the accelerator and merged onto the city route highway, the weight of the vehicle settling into a steady roll beneath him.

He glanced at the green-and-gold city signs as they rolled by, trying to shake off the tension that had knotted his shoulders all day. The pressure of the drive, the anxious anticipation of their secretive search, and the knowledge that tonight was another lost opportunity to begin looking for the Professor's missing granddaughter—all of it tumbled through his thoughts. Still, he reminded himself, there was no blame to carry; this secrecy had been at DC's insistence, not his. For now, they moved forward as quietly—and as carefully—as the circumstances demanded.

The RV glided past a parade of illuminated fast-food chains, their fluorescent signs promising comfort and calories, each separated by just a few gas stations with sputtering price boards and clusters of early-night customers. Nick signaled and turned just beyond the last Mobil station, pointing for the others at the big brown sign rising up on the roadside: "Mark Twain National Forest—Whitetail Campsites." The words seemed to shimmer with promise, the prospect of refuge and wild beauty waiting beyond city limits.

Bridge School Road appeared ahead, winding off into the darkness, its shoulders flanked by tall pines and the hush of the unknown. As Nick guided the RV onto the narrow lane, the city's noise faded behind them, replaced with the expectant hush of the woods, the sense of sanctuary growing with every mile. The headlights carved soft tunnels through the night, and anticipation returned to the faces of the group—each of them ready for the adventure, for the comfort of the forest, for the mysteries that waited just beyond the reach of civilization.

The mile-long drive from the highway to the campsites slipped past in a blur, anticipation mounting with every turn of the gravel road. Bobbie, unable to sit still, leapt from her perch on the couch and hustled up beside Nick, bracing herself with a hand on the dashboard as she peered eagerly out the front window.

The headlights washed over a wooden booth and the glint of a conservation agent's badge—a welcoming sentry in the hush of the forest.

Nick eased the RV to a stop, setting the brake just as the Park Ranger strode up to the driver's side window. The man's bright smile was matched only by the warmth in his voice. "Hello, Mr. and Mrs. Curtis, welcome to the bow hunt!" he boomed, his accent tinged with the cadence of the Ozarks. "Had a hunch you were our late arrivals. The rest of the hunters pulled in yesterday and wasted no time— they've already bagged several deer. Don't worry, there's plenty more out here in these fifty-three thousand acres. You'll have your chance soon enough."

He gestured toward the line of campers further on, their silhouettes tucked into the trees, lanterns aglow at a handful of picnic tables. "You'll want to drive past the others to your assigned site—number twenty-three, right in the heart of the park. No need for your ID, sir, but I do need hers—the lucky hunter whose name was drawn from the pot." His gaze flicked to Bobbie, his grin widening with an agreeable wink.

With a quick nod, Bobbie dashed back to the couch, rummaging in her purse until she found her driver's license. She hurried to the window and handed it over, her breath quick with excitement.

"Thank you, ma'am," the Ranger said, tipping his wide-brimmed hat in appreciation. "Best of luck out there—just down the road, site twenty-three!" With another smile and a wave, he stepped back into the night, leaving them with the thrill of possibility and the promise of wild adventure just beyond the next bend.

As they eased past the other campsites, the world outside their windows unfolded in a patchwork of wilderness life. Some lots slumbered in darkness, tents zipped tight, and RVs shuttered against the night; others glowed with the amber flicker of campfires, knots of hunters laughing with bottles in hand, silhouettes animated in the firelight. Bobbie, still on her feet beside Nick, watched with wide eyes—her anticipation bright as the flames they passed.

Nick slowed as they approached their site, careful to angle the RV into what he judged the surest, flattest spot. The motor idled into silence, and the headlights faded, replaced by the hush of the Ozark Forest pressing close on all sides.

He reached for Bobbie, drawing her gently onto his lap as she giggled, surprised but happy. With a soft squeeze, he grinned and whispered, "Well, here we are—the best deer hunting park in the Ozarks." The warmth of the moment seemed to radiate out to the very edges of the forest around them.

He kissed her, laughter lingering at the corners of his mouth. "Let's have that beer together. I bet Emma and Jeffery are as ready for one as we are." The words promised comfort and derie, the kind only found at the end of a long day and the start of a new adventure.

Bobbie returned to the familiar embrace of the couch, stretching out her arms and wiggling her fingers in playful invitation. "Come on, Nick," she called, her voice still shimmering with the afterglow of the drive. Nick grinned, plucked a cold beer from the little fridge, and handed it to her before settling in at her side, pulling close until their knees brushed, and their laughter mingled.

"This is almost the last of the stash," he said, clinking his can against hers. "Tomorrow, someone's got to make a supply run into town. Otherwise, it's early to bed and dry throats all around."

Across the cramped RV, Emma and Jeffery were already gathering themselves, stretching after the long ride. Jeffery glanced over, a crooked smile on his lips. "Well, folks, us die-hard campers are off to pitch the tent and scrounge up some firewood. Emma's idea—she's determined to get as much nature as she can. Says sleeping in this sardine can isn't real camping. But you knew that when you invited us, Bobbie."

Emma laughed, zipping up her jacket with a flourish. "If we get back from the woods before you're up, maybe we'll beat you to that beer run. Or maybe we'll just find a bakery instead."

Jeffery winked at Nick. "You kids enjoy the Oriental Palace. We'll see you in the morning—unless the coyotes carry us off first." With a dramatic shiver and a mock salute, he pushed open the RV door and pulled Emma out into the cool night. Their voices and laughter tumbled through the darkness, mingling with the distant crackle of other campfires.

Inside, the air felt warmer, softer. Nick nestled deeper into the cushions beside Bobbie, the hush of the forest wrapping around them like a thick, woolen blanket. For a moment, neither spoke. The only sounds were the gentle clank of bottles in the fridge and the treetop sighs of the Ozark wind.

Tipping the beer to his lips, Nick took a steady drink, trying to wash away the dryness that had returned since he'd begun driving. The hush inside the RV seemed deeper now, weighted by the darkness beyond the window and the restless thoughts swirling in his mind. He couldn't quite shake the image of the missing coed, the worry lurking just beneath the surface of their laughter, coloring even this quiet moment with unease.

It was hard to think about romance with that shadow hanging over them. Nick caught the faintest flicker in Bobbie's eyes—a knowing look, gentle and bright. She could read him, even in silence.

"It looks like there's more on your mind than the hunt," she said, her voice low and reassuring. "I imagine driving this behemoth out here has worn you down. Getting a good night's sleep is paramount if we're going to do our best in the hunt tomorrow. So, I'll dress for bed, and you finish your beer."

She leaned in, pressing a tender kiss to his cheek, her lips warm against his skin. "Good night," she whispered, the word a small anchor in the drifting hush.

He watched as she padded to the tiny kitchen, dropped her empty can into the recycle bag, and with one last smile over her shoulder, slipped into the back of the RV, leaving him alone with the gentle clink of bottles and the wind sighing in the branches outside.

For a while, Nick sat in the dim glow, listening to the forest and the faint echo of laughter from Emma and Jeffery somewhere beyond the glass. He finished his beer, set the can aside, and let the hush settle around him, both comfort and reminder—a night's promise and its lingering, unspoken fears.

Chapter Three

The shrill wail of the siren cut through the muffled quiet, jarring both Nick and Bobbie from sleep. They hadn't set an alarm—fatigue from the drive and the hush that seeped through the RV's seams had lulled them into a deep, dreamless rest. Now, morning pressed in from all sides: the resinous tang of pine needles filtering through the screen, the faint, lingering smoke from distant campfires winding its way in with the dawn.

Nick blinked, groggy and heavy-limbed, making no move to leap from the bunk. Across the cramped cabin, Bobbie slipped out of the restroom, hair tousled and eyes bright with that sleep-soft mischief she wore so well. "Next?" she asked, arching an eyebrow in challenge.

"Sure," Nick grunted, pushing himself up and sliding past her. He caught her by the waist just long enough for a quick, grateful kiss, a fleeting anchor before he ducked into the tiny bathroom.

Bobbie's bare feet padded over the linoleum as she made her way to the kitchenette. The ritual of morning came naturally: flicking on the little gas burner, measuring out scoops of coffee, the click and whoosh of blue flame catching beneath the battered percolator. She opened the window a crack, letting in a cool, pine-scented breeze that fluttered the edge of her shirt and carried with it the distant sounds—voices, an axe striking, and someone's radio playing a scratchy country tune.

The RV had already grown brighter, sunlight glinting off the chrome faucet and illuminating the tidy chaos of their gear. Bobbie moved through it all with practiced ease, setting two mugs on the counter, humming a half-remembered tune. She heard Nick finish up and soon enough he emerged, hair sticking out at odd angles. They shared a smile—wordless, comfortable, a language built of mornings like this.

Outside, the day was stirring. Emma and Jeffery's tent was still zipped tight, their corner of the site strewn with last night's laughter and half-empty mugs. Somewhere in the forest, birds orchestrated their own sunrise chorus. Bobbie poured two steaming mugs and handed one to Nick as he settled beside her at the makeshift table, both of them gazing out through the window at the world waking up.

Nick took a slow sip, savoring the warmth, feeling the last edges of sleep fade.

"Looks like we survived the night," he murmured, nudging Bobbie gently. He grinned, the memory of the missing coed dancing momentarily behind his eyes but chased away by the familiar comfort of routine and the promise of a new day.

"Let's hope the hunt goes just as smoothly," she said, raising her mug in a mock toast. And as the sun climbed above the pines, the little RV filled with the quiet, steady certainty that whatever shadows the day might bring, they would meet them together.

The unlocked door popped open as Emma and Jeffery rushed in. "Man, that coffee smells good—I hope you made enough for us," Jeffery exclaimed, squeezing in behind Emma as they jerked the door closed with a thump. Their cheerful mood seemed infectious, the RV suddenly crowded and lively with their energy.

Bobbie handed over a cup, picking up the coffee pot, eyebrows raised in mock exasperation. "No breakfast this morning—that whistle you heard means we could already be out there, tracking down our deer. I'm trying to wake all you sleepyheads!" she laughed, pouring generous helpings into their mugs.

Emma rolled her eyes, but grinned, shrugging into a faded flannel over her pajamas. "You've got us up, all right. I heard the siren and thought we were being raided—or maybe the forest rangers were coming for us."

Nick, already halfway through his first cup, glanced at Jeffery with a crooked smile. "You hunting or just here for the free coffee?"

Jeffery raised his mug in salute. "Why not both?"

Outside, the morning pressed in—sharp with promise, brisk with the scent of earth and pine. Inside, the four of them huddled around the table, the clatter of ceramic and the low hum of voices weaving into the fabric of another day begun together. For a moment, the world felt small and contained: just friends, warmth, and the wild waiting beyond the thin RV walls.

They wasted precious little time lingering over their mugs. In a flurry of boots and flannel, the two pairs spilled out of the RV, gathering bows, vests, and packs heavy with thermoses and half-remembered trail snacks. There was an urgency to their movements, but also an agreeable glee, as if each of them secretly believed that today might be the day—the day they outsmarted the legendary whitetail, pride of the Ozarks, whose tracks twisted like riddles through dew-soaked grass.

A late start, Jeffery insisted with a wink, could be the best kind. The other hunters—already deep in the woods—would flush deer from their beds, turning the natural rhythm of the forest to their unwitting advantage. "Let the early birds do the hard work," he muttered, slinging his gear over one shoulder. Bobbie grinned, checking her , her eyes bright with the thrill of the chase.

The woods beyond the campsite still held the hush of nightfall, shadows tangled beneath the pines. But here and there, the sharp scent of disturbed earth betrayed the deer's passage, their hooves having pressed stories into the soft ground during hours of darkness. Now, as the deer sought a quiet hollow to bed down, they would find the forest alive with human scent and sound—a gauntlet they'd have to run whether they willed it or not.

Emma, walking point, paused at the edge of the clearing, her breath visible in the morning chill. "They're out there, all right," she whispered, as a single crow called from the treetops—a warning, a promise, or both.

Together, the four friends set off, weaving through the undergrowth, hearts beating to the quiet pulse of hope and anticipation. The day—so recently begun—now stretched before them, brimming with the possibility of luck, skill, and the wild, living mystery of the hunt.

Nicks mind slipped back to the full instruction that had arrived with the notice Bobbie had been awarded the right to bow hunt. She had been so anxious to open the notice that had preceded this hunt. Twenty awards mailed out, he recalled, each good for a team of four, each team assigned a hundred-acre parcel stitched together by color—red, yellow, blue, green—transforming the wild expanse into a patchwork of private promise.

He'd read the official instructions Bobbie had handed him days before, creased and coffee-stained, the words still echoing in his mind: "Stay within your designated section. Ribbons mark your boundaries. Respect other hunters' space."

For once, he was grateful for the order it imposed. Out here, with the others already swallowed by the woods and no need to watch for strangers beyond that blue border, he could breathe easy.

He let the silence stretch, listening for the distant crack of a twig or the sudden hush when a deer lifts its head to scent the air. Nothing yet—just the slow seep of warmth from his thermos and the faint chirr of waking birds. Confident Nick lingered just long enough to watch his friends melt into the tangled corridor of pines before turning his boots down the faint game trail, the hush of needled earth beneath his feet. He kept within the blue-ribboned boundaries, pausing now and then to check the faded strips fluttering gently from low branches, reminders of the careful planning no one was near enough to overhear.

Nick slipped his phone from a deep pocket, thumbing it awake with cold-numbed hands. The screen's glow seemed foreign beneath the cathedral hush of branches overhead. He dialed the number from memory, the one he'd never thought he'd actually use: Troop I, Missouri State Highway Patrol. The faint hum of signal searching, the automated answering system, then—finally—a live voice cutting through the static. "Sergeant? It's Nick. Yeah, I'm in the section now, just like we discussed." His words were low, clipped, meant for no one but the sarge on the other end and the blue-stitched woods around him.

"I am here at the forest I am afraid that it is going to be harder than I thought to keep this mission on the hush—hush. Is it possible for you to send me a plain clothed officer to pick me up here. I can meet him in the edge of the hunt area. We rushed into this maybe too quickly. All I have here is a trail bike to get me to the town. Once Bobbie gets her deer it will be easier to tell her. Unless she gets it early, I have a couple hours to go into town. I would like to look into a couple of leads that the Raliegh PD gave me. I am sure I can share some of the fact with the ranger."   Nick tucked the phone away, heart thumping a little harder. He set off back towards the start of the marked territory, boots tracing the borderlines with practiced caution. Whatever this day brought—deer or no deer, luck or letdown—he was ready to play his part, watchful and alone, the boundaries clear and the hunt, in more ways than one, just beginning.

The trip back to the RV was interesting; no sooner had Nick reached the boundary road than he spotted one of the early bird hunters, already registering a hefty buck with the park ranger. The antlers—an impressive twelve points—caught the sun, and Nick couldn't resist drifting closer for a better look. He nodded to the ranger, a gesture of quiet admiration, before letting his attention wander to the hunter's broad, satisfied grin.

Glad for a moment's lull, Nick allowed himself to relax, the weight of the morning hunt replaced by a gnawing unease about the missing coed. It was a puzzle that shadowed every step, persistent as the dew lingering in the hollows. Back at the RV, he stowed his bow and tag with practiced care, the act grounding him while his mind churned through half-remembered leads and the scraps of information Raleigh PD had passed along.

When the ranger wrapped up with the victorious hunter, Nick ambled over, his smile curling sly and agreeable—a bit of the Cheshire cat in his eyes. He couldn't help but think, with a touch of regret, that if he'd been less caught up in preparations the night before, he might have sought the ranger out then, shared what he knew under the cover of darkness.

Now, though, in the crisp mid-morning air, opportunity still lingered. Nick approached slowly, weighing what he could share and what would remain tucked away—at least for now—until Bobbie's hunt was through and the day's true work could begin.

Nick caught the ranger's eye, his voice pitched low, "Ranger, any chance we could step inside the hut and have a few words?" He swept a glance around, making certain they were alone, then produced his ID with a quiet gravity. Without further explanation, the ranger nodded, leading him into the dim, wood-scented shelter where morning sunlight slipped in through dusty windows.

Nick waited until the door clicked shut behind them before speaking—his words urgent, edged with a fatigue that came from too little sleep and too much secrecy. "I should have done this last night, but with Bobbie so close... well, I wanted to reap the benefits of both choices. I know her well enough to realize that if she'd caught on to what I was up to, she'd have been thinking about how I tricked her— would have ruined her hunt entirely."

He leaned in, voice dropping further. "Missouri Highway Patrol's sending me a ride. We need to keep this as quiet as possible.

You've been told there's a missing coed, haven't you?" He watched the ranger carefully for any flicker of surprise or recognition. "It hasn't hit the papers yet, and the longer we keep it that way, the better. Sergeant Waters is coming."

He paused, eyes fixed on the ranger's, letting the weight of the news settle. "I'm counting on your discretion. Once Bobbie's hunt is done, I'll be out of your hair. But if you hear anything—someone talking about a stranger, or any odd movement in the woods—I need to know, right away."

The ranger nodded, a solemn understanding passing between the two men. Outside, the world continued on, oblivious to the quiet crisis threading through the morning. For Nick, the boundaries of the hunt had just expanded, the stakes rising on both sides of the forest.

Stepping back into the pale daylight, Nick felt the crispness of the air sting his cheeks, underscoring the urgency gnawing at his thoughts. The forest, so alive just minutes before, seemed to hush around him—branches holding their breath, the distant caw of a crow echoing like a warning. The professor's insistence on secrecy—well intentioned, perhaps, but increasingly fraught—clung to Nick like a burr. He understood caution, the need to keep panic at bay, but with every hour that passed, the scenario shifted from routine to alarming.

He considered the missing coed—her independence, her spirit, the plausibility that she'd simply vanished for a spontaneous adventure. It happened, he told himself; after all, young adults often carved out their own paths, unconcerned with oversight or consequence. Yet in his gut, Nick felt the nudge of doubt grow sharper. There had been no word, no sign, no message to ease the worry simmering beneath the surface. And, as he reminded himself, there had been no ransom note—not the hallmarks of a kidnapping, but still, absence was a language all its own, and silence could be as damning as any demand.

He tightened his jaw, resolve hardening within him. No more gentle waiting on luck or the whims of fortune—a search was needed, one that would turn over every stone and shadow, that would not rest until answers emerged. He would dig deep, chasing every lead and half-whispered rumor, pressing the ranger, the other hunters, the lingering locals for anything out of place.

Too much time had already slipped through his fingers, and Nick was determined to claw it back, one question and one careful step at a time.

Waiting for the trooper became a test of patience that gnawed at Nick as he paced the shaded edge of the roadway, boots crunching leaves and twigs in restless cadence. Seconds stretched, thick and syrupy, until—at last—an unmarked vehicle rolled quietly to a stop, dust drifting in the early sunlight.

Nick halted, the weight of uncertainty pressing on his ribs. What had begun as a questionable missing person case—a college student with the reputation for independence—had now, on the fourth day, hardened into the chilling certainty that something was deeply wrong. There would be no sheepish return, no tidy explanation. The forest's vastness felt suddenly menacing, its ancient oaks and tangled underbrush perfect for hiding secrets, or worse.

When the trooper stepped out, Nick sized him up at once: no routine highway patrol, but someone methodical, sharp-eyed, the sort who carried the weight of more than just a badge. The air between them brimmed with purpose as Nick moved quickly, his nerves visible in the hurried motion of opening the car door and sliding into the passenger seat.

"Let's go," he said, breath tight, urgency sharpening his words as he buckled in. "I'll brief you as we drive. There's not a moment to waste."

As the engine hummed to life and the forest slipped by outside the window, Nick forced his racing thoughts into order, already preparing to recount the fragments of information, the half-seen tracks and uneasy hunches that would form the backbone of their search. With every passing mile, the boundaries of hope and dread pressed closer, but resolve, at least, found a foothold—he would not let the quiet of the woods swallow another soul without a fight.

Nick showed his credentials and grinned, attempting to cut the tension with a note of professional derie. "Do you mind?" he asked, indicating the trooper's own identification. The trooper obliged, pulling out his wallet and laying his credentials on the seat between them.

"Pleased to meet you," Nick said, voice steadier now.

His brows furrowed as he answered Nick "Wish we'd been called in sooner. But I suppose we'll have to work with what we have. I guess you want to go to the grandfather's place first. She lived at a dorm, but the choice is yours. Okay?"

Nick nodded, glancing out at the passing trees. "Yeah, I think anything left at the dorm will still be there in a couple of hours. Grandfather's place first, then the dorm. Pleased to meet you too. We've got one other person to help—she's in the woods, hunting. She'll be ready as soon as we've really established this coed is missing. Funny how this is working out. Call it intuition or a hunch, but I'm afraid this is bigger than just one girl."

Nick's grip tightened on his seatbelt, a chill running down his spine at his own words.

"I have to agree with you... Names Kevin Murdock, they call me 'Doc.' I was moved down here from up in Jefferson City—I work in the lab. Was stationed in Springfield, but as the college grew here and the need came up, well, you know the rest. Know some of the college cops but have very little to do with the RPD. Not that they're unfriendly, but most of my work comes from the Phelps County Sheriff's Department. Their office is in the city—so is the courthouse."

A silence settled, not awkward but heavy with the unspoken knowledge that what they were about to uncover could justify their lives. Outside, the road bent leaving the deeper woods, sunlight flickering on the windshield. The case was no longer abstract; with every turn, it became more real, more urgent, and the sense of alliance in the car—tentative, but growing—felt like the only clear thing in the fog of mounting uncertainty.

Nick settled back as Doc drove, the road humming softly beneath him. The route, familiar yet altered by the morning's tension, traced the same path Nick had taken the day before. He watched in silence as they swept past the Tommys Oriental Palace—the restaurant where they'd dined last night. In daylight, the building loomed even larger: its three stories and attic standing sentry over the squat shops nearby, a patchwork of brick and sun-bleached siding.

The car slowed at the crossing where Rucker met the railroad tracks. Nick's gaze caught on the old steam engine resting in the small park, its blackened iron hull a relic of another era. He smiled, nostalgia flickering behind his eyes as the engine's silhouette cut against the morning sky.

"Now there is a fine piece of Americana," he remarked, voice soft but tinged with genuine admiration. "Interesting."

Doc glanced over, a trace of a grin warming his otherwise analytical expression. "She's a beauty, all right. There's history in that metal—if you know how to look for it."

The car rolled on, tires crunching lightly over gravel as they left the tracks behind. For a moment, the world outside felt suspended—caught between the weight of the past and the uncertain urgency of what lay ahead. Nick's thoughts drifted, gathering details and half-remembered landmarks, each one anchoring him to the case and the strange, shifting landscape of the investigation.

He glanced at Doc, then back at how the Tommys Place stood, thinking how tall it was —wondering if the building was rented out to students. Maybe the restaurant housed one of the many Asian families that were large. The kind that had so many children they felt they could make it better in America. Anything to remove his thoughts about this coed and the thoughts of her peril. That is if she had been abducted. His thoughts wanted to shout out. 'Step on it Doc we are on a case.'

His thoughts were denied as doc spoke. "No easy was to get to old St Judes Road. The professor wanted to build on the only road that was kind of secluded but still in the city limits. Up here on the left."

The sprawling green lawn looked like it ran for miles as the white three rung board fence surrounded the two-story house that sported a four-car garage, and it appeared to be more than six bedrooms. Manicured hedges flanked the drive, and a cluster of ornamental maples softened the sharp edges of the property.

Nick let out a low whistle as they pulled in, the sunlight glancing off the immaculate windows and the gleaming, slate-gray shingles of the roof.

Doc slowed the car and eased it to a stop near the front walk, the tires barely whispering against the gravel. "Somebody's got deep pockets," he murmured, casting a glance at Nick as they both took in the grandeur of the place. The house had a quiet, palatial presence, the kind that hinted at old money or new ambitions—maybe both.

As they stepped out, the air was thick with the scent of cut grass and blooming magnolia. The porch stretched wide, adorned with rocking chairs and a pair of stone lions crouched beside the steps, as if keeping silent vigil. Nick's gaze wandered up to the second floor, where curtains fluttered in the breeze behind tall windows.

Although they had arrived without calling ahead, the door quickly opened, and the aged professor stepped out to greet them. He was dressed in a full pinstriped suit, the lines crisp but his posture faintly unsteady—alert in a way that only sleepless nights and persistent worry could produce. There was an anxious dignity to him, a forced composure that barely masked the strain etched into the corners of his eyes.

"Gentlemen, come on in. Tell me anything that you have, do you have any information?" His voice quavered with hope and fear in equal measure.

Nick moved forward, reaching for his credentials as he spoke. "Professor—Nick Curtis, Federal bureau investigator. This is Trooper Murdock. He's been assigned to help with the investigation of your granddaughter."

"Yes... yes... come on in! Like I said, tell me—have you heard anything at all?" The professor's words spilled out, urgent and pleading, as though he expected answers to materialize out of thin air.

Inside, the house was dim and cool, the entryway lined with family photographs and glass cabinets brimming with porcelain and old books. The faint fragrance of tea drifted from deeper within, mingling with an undercurrent of unease that lingered in the air.

Nick glanced at Doc, searching the trooper's face for any sign of how to proceed. He found himself reflecting, almost unconsciously, on how rare it was to see someone—especially someone from the professor's community—so visibly unraveled. In his experience, most families wore their worries like a second skin, keeping composure even as their world threatened to collapse.

But here, there was no armor—only the raw edges of hope and desperation. "We'll tell you everything we know, Professor," Doc said gently, stepping into the parlor as the professor waved them through. Light filtered in through tall, laced curtains, casting shifting patterns across the floor. "First, maybe you could walk us through the last time you saw your granddaughter? Anything unusual, even the smallest detail, might help."

The professor nodded, already gathering his thoughts, his hands twisting together as he led them further inside, each step echoing his restless vigil.

"She was here last Sunday evening for dinner," the professor began, his voice trembling slightly as he settled into an armchair. "She comes here for dinner several times a month. This week, my wife is in St. Louis for a conference of Christian women. So, as a way of spending more time with me, she was supposed to come and stay the weekend. She had an all-girls meeting at the student center at the college Friday afternoon. I don't know what group it was, so you might make a note of it—the college will have the group and who was there. She is sometimes outspoken about the lack of more protection for women."

He paused, glancing between Nick and Doc, as though searching for reassurance or perhaps simply the strength to continue. The silence that followed seemed to amplify the soft tick of a distant clock and the persistent ache behind his words.

Nick jotted down notes quickly, his mind already weaving through the details: the empty guest room, the mother absent in another city, the mysterious meeting at the student center. "We'll follow up with the college and see who might have attended that event," he said quietly. "And we'll talk to anyone who might've seen her there."

Doc nodded, his expression gentle. "Was there anything unusual that night, sir? Anything she said or did that seemed out of the ordinary?"

The professor shook his head, gaze dropping to his clasped hands. "No... nothing that stands out. She seemed well. Maybe... maybe a little distracted, but I didn't think much of it then."

A hush fell, uneasy and expectant, as the investigation's heavy silence settled once more between them.

Nick cleared his throat, choosing his words with the careful gravity the moment demanded. "I know that you believe, as most parents do, that their children and grandchildren don't do anything wrong—and that's not to infer anything. But..."

He hesitated a fraction, watching the professor's face for any flicker of defensiveness. "Do you know any place she frequents? Maybe somewhere they serve liquor, or perhaps a place where they might dance?"

The professor's brow creased in thought. "No, nothing comes to mind immediately. She's never struck me as the type to—well, to go out much. But I suppose I can't say for certain what the younger generation gets up to, especially at college."

Nick nodded; his pen poised. "Does she have a steady boyfriend, or does she date? Is there anyone she spends time with that we can talk to? Maybe someone who could give us information that might help."

The professor's fingers tightened around the armrests. "There was a boy she mentioned once or twice, someone from her philosophy class, I think. But nothing serious—as far as I know. Her closest friend is a girl named Emily, from her dorm. I can get you her contact information, if you'd like."

"That would be helpful, sir," Doc said softly. "And while you're at it, we'll need a couple of recent photographs of her. Even if you've already given some to the RPD, we'll want our own copies. At the start of this, we're leaving them out of the loop. Since you requested that we do this on the Q.T., we'll wait a few days before bringing them in."

The professor nodded, a flicker of gratitude in his weary eyes. "I have some photos upstairs. I'll bring them down right away." He rose, moving with the slow urgency of a man driven by hope and dread in equal measure.

As his footsteps faded up the stairs, Nick and Doc exchanged a glance heavy with the weight of the case—uncertain leads, a vanished student, and the fragile trust of a family teetering on the edge. The hush deepened, thick with the scent of old books and the sound of longing that seemed to linger in the house's walls.

Walking around behind the large mahogany desk, Nick began looking through the many mementoes behind and beside the desk. The insistent theme of shipping yelled out at him: gleaming brass compasses, a painting of a restless sea, and a handful of model destroyers perched atop a shelf. It was clear that, at one time or another, the professor had served in the navy of his home country.

Nick's fingers trailed along a faded naval cap embroidered with foreign script, its brim shadowed by years of careful dusting. He paused, noting an old black-and-white photograph of young men in crisp uniforms, squinting beneath a tropical sun. Somewhere in the professor's past, the ocean had left its mark.

Walking back to Doc, Nick leaned close and murmured, "What part of Vietnam was on our side? I can never keep that straight."

Doc arched a brow, voice pitched quiet so as not to carry beyond the library's shadowed corners. "What a silly question for you to ask," he replied, half amusement and half chiding, but there was a glint of understanding in his eyes. "South Vietnam was allied with us, remember?"

Nick nodded, feeling the weight of history and the present moment settling together—a tangle of old allegiances, lost places, and vanished people, all pressing in as the professor's footsteps creaked overhead.

Nick hesitated only a moment before accepting the small camera from Doc, its surface cool and reassuringly solid in his palm. "I was just wanting to verify something," he muttered, already adjusting the focus. "These pictures might explain the need for the secrecy in this case. I was just wondering how to tell the Viet-Cong ships from the good guys."

He stepped closer to the shelf, angling for the best light, and snapped several shots of the largest model destroyers and the old black-and-white photograph. The camera's shutter broke the hush— soft, but decisive. He zoomed in on the ships' hull numbers, their distinct silhouettes, the insignia that might mark an allegiance. If there was a hidden story here, perhaps it lurked in the smallest of details.

Doc hovered behind him, watching the methodical way Nick documented each artifact. "It's not always easy, you know," Doc murmured. "Sometimes the only difference was the paint on the bow, or the flag fluttering in a spray of saltwater. But the professor would know. That's his past—etched in steel and memory."

Nick nodded, turning the camera over in his hands, the weight of possibility growing heavier. "Let's see what the professor says when he comes back down," he said softly, glancing up at the ceiling as footsteps began to descend the stairs once more, bearing with them the promise of answers—or new mysteries.

Nick barely had time to tuck the camera away before the professor slipped an envelope from his coat pocket, the corners worn from handling.

"Here are the pictures you requested," he said, his voice pitched low as he descended from the stairwell. "They were taken in January, at the break."

Doc reached out, taking the photographs. He shuffled through them with a practiced eye, pausing at one. A faint, knowing smile touched his lips. "Pretty girl," he mused, tapping a finger against the glossy surface. "Is she the one in the white dress? Standing close to the Christmas tree?"

The professor nodded, a thread of uncertainty tightening across his brow. "Yes, and I think that's the boy I mentioned. She knew him, I'm sure of it." He leaned in as Doc angled the photo toward the slanting library light, the image grainy but unmistakable—the girl's pale dress shimmering in the glow of tinsel and colored bulbs, the boy at her side, half-turned as if caught mid-laughter.

Nick, still half-shadowed by the gleam of the old ships and the echo of their stories, watched as the professor drifted toward the wall of faded photographs.   The professor's hand hovered, fingers trembling ever so slightly as he pointed to the brittle images—a fleet frozen in another era, hulls proud and banners snapping in winds long gone.

"That was another time," the professor said, voice roughened by memory. "Sometime a lifetime ago. I was a captain in the... how shall I say it... the losing side. I was a lot more foolish then. I blame it on my youth." He offered Nick a rueful smile, the lines around his mouth deepening. "I got captured, and that's where I met your superior. He straightened me out. I do owe my life to him. But I babble—"

He stopped himself, urgency spiking in his tone now, all hesitation stripped away. "You need to go to the college dorm. See if Emily has any more to share. Maybe she can help with the boy's name. Maybe even help us with his place—where he lives. Please, hurry."

Nick absorbed the plea, feeling the current of anxiety pass from the professor's words into his own blood. He gave a quick nod, gathering up the camera and the thin stack of photographs. The library's hush pressed in close as he slipped toward the door, heart pounding, the mystery sharpening with every step he took away from the relics of war and toward the uncertain present.

Following the two agents to the door, the professor paused, one hand resting on the worn brass handle, the other gesturing gently back toward the dimly lit study. "As a way of explanation," he began, his gaze flickering to the wall crowded with photographs, "those photos are there to remind me how easy it is for youth to be misled. It is only a hard and silent statement of how we learn from our mistakes."

He lingered a moment, the weight of old regrets pressing deep into the lines of his face. "I did not have any sons, so sometimes they remind me that the danger of oppression is not gone, but just asleep." He dipped his head in a small, formal bow, voice softened by gratitude and sorrow. "Thank you for your concern."

A hush settled as the door opened, letting in a draft of fall air that curled around their ankles. Nick glanced back at the professor—a silhouette among his memories—before stepping out into the uncertain, waiting night. Somewhere beyond, the puzzle stretched onward, its answers just out of reach, but the echo of the professor's warning lingered, as solemn as the faces in those faded photographs.

Nick let the words tumble out, the restless drive behind them growing sharper with each syllable. The campus, that ordinary maze of brick and autumn shadows, now felt charged—every footstep a beat in the quickening pulse of the mystery. He slipped the photos into his coat pocket, the corners pressing against his ribs like a whispered warning.

Doc followed at his side, boots echoing on the marble tiles—a steady counterpoint to Nick's jittery urgency. "You're right," Doc said, voice low. "Let's check in with campus security. Maybe they've seen the boy, or the car he drives. If Emily knows something, they can help us fill the rest in."

Outside, the wind had picked up, catching at their coats and scattering brittle leaves around their feet. Students hurried past, heads bowed against the chill, their laughter trailing like distant music.

Nick found his stride, purpose setting his jaw. "I'll take the lead with the police. We need a reason to be poking around—maybe tell them we're following up on a missing person's report. It's close enough to the truth, and the professor's name carries weight if it comes to it."

Doc grunted his approval, glancing sidelong at Nick. "Let's just hope you come up with a story she'll buy for now. She's sharp, that one. If she starts asking questions, we might have to improvise."

A wry smile flickered across Nick's face. "Maybe she'll land a buck today and be too busy bragging at lunch to notice I'm gone. Otherwise, you might have to back me up."

As they crossed the quad, the sunlight flared against the old library windows, sending shards of gold across their path. The hush of memory was behind them now, and in its place—the quick, uncertain pace of the present, the promise of answers just ahead. Nick could almost feel the case spinning tighter, picture by picture, as they hurried toward the dorm and the waiting shadows of truth.

Stopping at the security office, they were greeted by Officer Jenkins—a tall man whose easy grin and tousled hair made him seem more like one of the students than campus authority.

Nick introduced himself and Doc, offering a brisk explanation of their presence. "We're following up on a young man who applied for a job with the MHP," he said, fishing the slightly creased photograph from his pocket and sliding it across the counter.

Jenkins studied the image for a moment, brows knitting in concentration. "No," he admitted, sliding it back across the cold Formica. "Doesn't ring a bell. But I know the class he's in—at least, according to the notes we've got on file. They'll be letting out any minute now. The building you want is the second on the left, down the lane."

Nick nodded his thanks, already tucking the photo away as urgency ticked in his chest. Doc offered a cordial nod of gratitude. The two slipped out of the warm, fluorescent-lit office and back into the brisk daylight, the wind still driving leaves in frantic circles along the walkway.

They quickened their pace, boots crunching gravel as the old bell in the clock tower tolled the hour. Ahead, a stream of students began to trickle from the entrance of the second building, their voices a low, indistinct murmur blending with the autumn wind.

Nick scanned each face, searching for the boy in the photograph, his pulse thrumming with anticipation. The case, which had seemed so abstract in the professor's crowded study, now pressed close—its resolution so near he could almost reach out and seize it.

Doc fell into step beside him. "We'll have to be quick," he murmured. "If he was just a casual date it might be a waste of time."

Nick nodded; eyes narrowed. "Let's hope luck's on our side, for once."

Together, they moved toward the cluster of students, ready to step out of shadow and into whatever truth was about to spill from the lane of old stone and restless wind.

Waiting on either side of the walk, they scanned the flow of students as it spilled from the doorway, faces flickering in the pale autumn light. Nick's mind roved restlessly, replaying the fragile threads of secrecy still binding the case together. Their alert scrutiny drew a few sidelong glances, but their focus never broke they were searching for the one person who might carry the secret of her disappearance—an unusually tall Vietnamese student, described in hurried whispers and fragments.

Yet as the classroom emptied, disappointment bit at their composure. Not a single Asian male appeared among the departing group; instead, the students were an assortment of non-Asian young men, their laughter and careless conversation swelling and fading as they drifted past. Nick exchanged a glance with Doc, the shared question unspoken.

Trailing just behind, a group of Asian girls emerged, chatting quietly, their bright scarves and dark hair vivid against the gray stone. Nick watched them go by, noting the easy friendship in their voices, the way they seemed at home in the world's small, everyday mysteries. But none of them matched the description he'd received, nor did any pause or linger as if aware of being sought.

Frustration flickered through Nick—a sense of chasing shadows, of answers slipping just out of reach. Doc's gaze lingered on the last departing student, then he shook his head. "No sign," he whispered, voice tight with disappointment.

Still, Nick refused to let the lead die. His mind spun with possibilities—had they missed their quarry, or had the notes in the security file been wrong? He scanned the quad one more time, the wind carrying a hint of rain and the clamor of distant voices. Somewhere, he was certain, the person they sought remained close, a crucial thread still hidden in the tapestry of the crowd.

Chapter Four

As the last echo of footsteps faded and Doc fell into step beside him, Nick spoke in a low, urgent tone. "I think there should be some kind of group for these students—same background, you know? Let's head to the administration office, see if they keep any records. Maybe even a group photo. I've got a hunch: if he knows anything about her, that's our best shot at finding him."

He started off down the walk, casting a wary glance at the slipping clouds above. "Come on, before they break for lunch."

Doc nodded, and together they threaded through the thinning crowd, boots tapping briskly against the flagstones. The air was thick with anticipation now, a sense of momentum building as they left the hush of the quad behind and veered toward the columned entrance of the main administration building.

Inside, the lighting turned cool and institutional. The scent of old paper and floor polish pricked at Nick's senses. He squared his shoulders, determination taut in his voice. "Let's ask about student organizations first—and see if any keep photos for their records."

Doc's reply was a quick nod, his jaw set. "If he's part of something, we'll find a trace. Let's hope your hunch is right."

Nick stepped up to the front desk, ready with the photograph in his pocket and questions on his tongue, propelled by the hope that the next door they opened would finally lead out of the shadow and toward the truth.

Pulling a slim stack of business cards from his pocket—Toledo Insurance Company embossed in crisp blue—Nick slid one across the polished counter. He donned the practiced, disarming smile reserved for uncertain receptionists and bureaucratic gates.

"Good morning. My name's Nick Carroway," he began, voice just loud enough to command attention but not suspicion. "I'm with

Toledo Insurance. We're here following up on a contest—well, to be honest, something of a mix-up in our records. This boy—" He produced the dog-eared photograph, holding it so the light caught the image. "—entered our scholarship program a while back. Somewhere in the mountain of paperwork and the sea of applicants, his address slipped through the cracks. We know only that he's a student here."

He let the photo linger, inviting scrutiny, and leaned in with an agreeable air. "It'd mean a lot if you could help us track him down. I'm sure he'll be grateful, once he hears the news." A sideways grin flashed at Doc, as if to say, See? This is how you grease the wheels.

Doc played along, offering an encouraging nod. "We're just hoping to set things right. Maybe there's a club roster? Or a student organization with group photos? Anything that could help narrow it down."

The receptionist glanced between the card, the photograph, and their earnest faces. Behind her, the gentle hum of the office continued—phones ringing, the shuffle of files, distant voices blending with the faint drone of air conditioning. An uncertain pause hung in the air, heavy with the possibility of revelation.

"We don't want to disturb anyone," Nick added, voice softening. "Just a little help—so he doesn't miss out."

He waited, hope and calculation shining equally in his eyes, poised for the next clue to slip from the depths of administration—or perhaps from the smallest detail overlooked by everyone but the most persistent of seekers.

Nick leaned over, lowering his tone to something agreeable, just for the blue-haired clerk's ear. "There might even be a small reward for you if you can help us."

The clerk's lips quirked in a bemused smile, but she shook her head. "No need—I think I know him. His name is Phong—Paul Tran. He's a last-year student, secretary of the Asian Club. I can let you have his information if you get clearance from campus police. We have a few picky rules about information. But I can show you some photos of the club—they're public." She reached for a battered binder on the desk, then paused, glancing at the phone. "I can call the security office, and they can come over here and help you."

She turned as if to dial, leaving Nick with a moment for calculation. He looked to Doc, eyebrows raised in question. "Well, boss, what do you think? Do we want the campus police in on this... Seems like a lot of trouble for this young man to receive his internship."

Doc's gaze flickered, weighing the risks. "It's your play, Nick. We could make it official and wait or see what those photos tell us first."

Nick considered the options, the hum of the office pressing in. The truth, so close now, glimmered just beyond a bureaucratic threshold—one phone call could open the final door. He nodded to the clerk, voice steady. "Let's take a look at those club photos first. Maybe we'll get lucky and save everyone the paperwork."

The binder landed with a soft thud, pages fanning open to a gallery of hopeful faces and crowded events. Nick and Doc leaned in, searching for the boy whose name had finally surfaced—each image a possible key, each detail a step closer to the truth.

Nick let his gaze linger on the rows of smiling faces, but his mind was already racing ahead. Beneath the surface of the club snapshots and the hush of the office, urgency pressed at his composure. Time, once their quiet ally, was now an adversary—each passing minute dimmed the chances of catching up with the coed, of unearthing answers before they slipped away for good.

He exchanged a quick glance with Doc, the weight of their silent communication clear: the photos might help, but bureaucracy moved at a glacial pace, and the clues were growing cold. Nick straightened up, resolve sharpening his features.

"We appreciate this," he told the clerk, gently sliding the binder back. "But I think we need to move faster. I know a campus officer—tall guy, runs the security desk. If we talk to him directly, we might be able to sort this out right away. No runaround, just what we need." He offered a small, apologetic smile, the kind that asked for understanding rather than forgiveness.

Doc nodded, recognizing the shift in strategy. "Let's not waste the daylight," Doc murmured.

With an appreciative nod to the clerk, Nick tucked the mental scraps of new information—Paul Tran, the Asian Club, the red thread of last-year hopes—into the back pocket of his mind. Then, with Doc at his side, he stepped out of the administrative haze, heading toward campus security. The time for caution had passed; now, every second counted. If the answers they needed could be found behind that familiar desk, with the tall officer and a little luck, they'd be closer to the missing coed—and to the heart of the mystery that refused to let them go.

The walk across campus was brisk, but Nick and Doc moved in mutual, thoughtful silence, each step measured by the quickening pulse of urgency. When they reached the squat, windowed security office, the heavy summer air was spilling in through a propped-open door—a simple invitation, or perhaps an attempt to coax some relief into the cramped space.

Inside, behind a battered desk awash in sunlight, the tall officer looked up, squinting through the glare. Nick didn't waste a second. He stepped in, Doc at his shoulder, and announced with quiet authority, "Afternoon. We've got a positive ID on this student. We need his address—time might be tight. There's a chance we'll catch him at home for lunch."

He passed over his notebook, the name—carefully written, unspoken—centered on the page. Paul Tran. Nick let the gesture speak, aware that names could be fumbled, and that precision now was more urgent than pride.

"We could've had the clerk from admin call you," Nick continued, voice lowered, "but you know as well as we do—the fewer who know, the better. For her sake, and maybe his."

The officer caught the unspoken note of concern, weighing it as he thumbed through the notebook. Sunlight flickered across his badge as he leaned back, the wheels of discretion and duty turning behind his measured expression.

"Just a minute," the officer said, standing and moving to the back office. Nick exhaled slowly, the silence stretching between the three men like a drawn wire. Doc hovered near the door, watchful, while Nick scanned the familiar walls—community bulletins, faded safety posters, the reminders of ordinary days that seemed, now, impossibly distant.

A few moments later, the officer returned, a slip of paper in hand. He hesitated, then handed it over. "This is the address on file. If you find him, let us know. And Nick—be careful. There's something about this that feels off."

Nick nodded, gratitude and resolve mingling in the brief exchange. "We will," he promised.

Then, without another word, they strode back into the relentless light of midday, address in hand, hope and apprehension wrestling for space in their chests. There was no turning back—the heart of the puzzle was close, and with luck, the next door they knocked on would unlock truths long buried in shadow.

The George Wahington residence hall waited at the far edge of the quad, its brick and glass façade shimmering in the noon heat. Nick and Doc quickened their pace, the slip of paper now creased but legible in Doc's steady grip. They slipped through the lobby—past the bulletin boards, the smell of floor polish and old pizza—into the rattle and sigh of the elevator. Nick leaned in, voice low and taut: "Six fourteen."

As the elevator lurched skyward, hydraulics whining, Nick fell back into his thoughts. The facts were clear, but the lines connecting them remained maddeningly faint. Paul Tran, at best, was a footnote in this tangled script—unless, of course, he was more than just a name. The suspicion gnawed at Nick: Was Paul enmeshed in the larger scheme? Did he know more than he'd let on, or worse, was he responsible for the coed's vanishing?

No ransom had come, no trembling demand for cash—just a heavy, hanging silence, and the spreading ring of worry growing wider with each hour. Maybe she'd simply run, Nick thought, hope flickering, but in his gut, he doubted it. If this was a kidnapping, it lacked all the usual trimmings. The biggest question pressed in on him: Why was she gone?

He glanced sidelong at Doc, reading shadows in the other man's eyes. Families had secrets—old wounds and whispered motives—and sometimes the truth was a thing best left undisturbed. If Professor Hahn was involved, the logic tripped and tangled; why not simply snatch the professor, if coercion was the aim? Why her?

The elevator chimed, doors sliding open to a corridor washed in pale fluorescent light. Nick squared his shoulders, pushing aside unease. "Let's see if he's in," he murmured, and together they walked the gray-tiled hall, the weight of answers just beyond the next door.

Nick rapped twice—sharp, measured—then stepped aside, a silent signal for Doc to take position opposite. Doc, practiced and unhurried, melted into the shadow against the wall. The hallway was thick with anticipation, the only sound the hum of distant pipes and a faint, metallic melody seeping beneath the door—some drifting echo of an old Asian ballad, tinny and forlorn.

No answer. Nick's knuckles stung as he knocked again, this time with more insistence. He pressed close, ear nearly to the grain, catching the syncopated rhythm of foreign music tangled with the lightest shuffle of movement inside. He fished his keys from his pocket, tapping them against the frame—a subtle warning or invitation, he wasn't sure.

Suddenly, the door snapped inward. Framed in the threshold stood a large, broad-shouldered young man, face taut and unwelcoming, eyes flickering with suspicion.

"Yes? Can I help you?" The voice was low and guarded, the edge unmistakable.

Nick held his ground, letting the silence hang just long enough to register.   "You're Paul Tran, right?"

Paul's brow furrowed, but his stance didn't shift. Nick measured his words, keeping his tone steady. "We're with the MHP. This is Doc." He gestured, giving Doc room to step forward and display his credentials, the badge winking in the half-light.

"We need to talk—about Emily Dorm. Her car was in an accident, and there are questions only you can answer." Nick's gaze didn't waver.

"Would you mind if we came in? It's a sensitive matter."

Paul glanced from Nick to Doc, jaw setting. For a moment, the music filled the silence again, punctuating the tension. Then, with a brusque nod, he stepped back, swinging the door wide.

"Come in, then," he muttered, retreating into the dim apartment.

Doc entered first, moving with practiced ease, subtly positioning himself so the door couldn't be slammed behind them. Nick followed, noting the lived-in clutter—the faint smell of instant noodles, textbooks splayed across the coffee table, a laptop glowing on the counter. The music, now louder, was coming from an old speaker wedged between stacks of papers.

Paul hovered by the kitchen, arms folded, wary but not hostile. "What's this about Emily? I don't know where she is."

Nick spoke softly, careful not to spook him. "We're not here to accuse you. But time is running thin, and anything you know could help. When did you last see her?"

Doc, sensing Paul's agitation, interjected with a calming hand. "We need your help, Paul, we're just looking for answers."

Paul hesitated, tension ebbing slightly at Doc's measured tone. He gestured toward the worn couch. "Alright. Sit down, tell me what you need to know."

Nick relaxed, just a fraction. The next move was theirs, and with any luck, the shadows in this room would begin to thin.

Nick kept his posture open and calm, masking the thread of tension running through him. "I know—none of this adds up. That's why we came to you. We're trying to piece together her movements that night, and your name came up as someone she trusted."

Doc nodded, leaning forward, his hands laced. "It's important for Emily's sake, and Maya's. Anything you remember, even if it seems trivial, could make the difference."

Paul ran a hand through his hair, pacing the small stretch of carpet between the counter and the coffee table. His brow furrowed, confusion flickering across his face. "I saw Maya at the café on Friday—she didn't mention meeting Emily, but she seemed…distracted. She left early, said she had plans." He frowned, recalling. "Emily texted me later, said she was tied up with something. I figured it was work."

Nick pressed gently, careful not to push too hard. "Did she say where she was going? Anyone she might have been with?"

Paul shook his head, frustration mounting. "No, she was vague. She's always careful, you know?" He paused, glancing at Doc. "If Emily was hurt…does Maya know? Did she reach out to anyone?"

"Not that we know of," Doc said, his tone steady. "Which is why we're worried."

The music had faded into a soft instrumental, the tension in the room now twisting into something sharper. Nick caught Paul's gaze, lowering his voice. "If you think of anything—any message, any call, no matter how small—will you let us know?"

Paul nodded, swallowing hard. "Yeah. I want to help. I just hope she's all right."

For a moment, the only sound was the whirring ceiling fan and the distant hum of the city outside. The web of uncertainty had only grown denser, but a new thread—Paul's concern—offered a faint, hopeful path forward.

Nick frowned, sensing Paul's anxiety spike at the mention of Emily's wellbeing. He caught Doc's eyes, a silent plea passing between them for reassurance or guidance. Moving closer, Nick placed a steadying hand on Paul's shoulder. "She's fine—Emily is okay, and so is Maya," he said quietly, letting the words settle and calm the current of worry in the room.

"We're just trying to understand how well you know them," Nick continued, his tone gentle but searching. "As you know, both Emily and Maya are members of the Asian club on campus, and lately, there's been talk of them being considered for induction into the national Asian magazine club. That's a big deal—a lot of eyes on them, a lot of pressure."

He paused, watching Paul's reaction, hoping for a flicker of recognition or some new insight. "We just need to make sure there's nothing we're missing. Anything you can recall, anything at all—friendships, rivalries, who they spent time with—it all helps."

Paul nodded again, uncertainty giving way to a new seriousness. The air between them shifted, the next piece of the puzzle waiting to be found.

Nick offered a reassuring smile as he stepped back, his tone turning lighter, almost agreeable. "Hey, if anyone asks, we'll make sure both Emily and Maya get a great report to the national office. They've earned it." He let the words hang—a small promise amid the uncertainty.

"But Paul, if Maya does reach out to you," Nick added, keeping his voice soft, "don't mention we stopped by tonight. It's just better that way—for her peace of mind, and ours." He slipped a card into Paul's hand, the inked number barely visible in the dim light. "If she does contact you, could you give me a call? Just so we know she's safe, and we can clear up any confusion."

He hesitated, then leaned in, voice low and earnest. "And about that rumor—about Maya being hurt? It's not true. She's fine. We just want to make sure she stays that way." Nick caught Paul's eyes one last time, a silent message of trust and gratitude passing between them. Then, with a final nod, he and Doc made their way toward the door, leaving behind the quiet hope that the web would finally begin to unravel.

Doc waited until they were on the elevator before he spoke, his voice echoing slightly in the tight space. "You know, I think you win the award for best backpedaling of the year," he said, a broad guffaw escaping him.

Nick rolled his eyes, but a reluctant grin tugged at his lips. "Backpedaling? I was being diplomatic."

"Diplomatic?" Doc snorted, pressing the button for the lobby. "You practically promised the kid a recommendation letter and your firstborn if he kept quiet."

Nick shrugged, the tension ebbing from his shoulders as the elevator rattled downward. "Whatever gets us answers. Besides, I meant it—Emily and Maya deserve a little credit. They've been through a lot."

Doc nodded, growing serious again. "You think Paul's going to talk to her?"

"I hope so. If Maya hears from him, she might feel safer knowing we're not out to get her. Most of all if she thinks that she is going to be recommended to the national club she might even call the grandfather. " Nick leaned back against the cool metal wall; his eyes fixed on the flickering floor numbers. "We just need to keep everyone calm until we know what really happened."

Doc glanced at Nick, the ghost of a smile lingering. "You're a soft touch, Nick."

"Don't spread that around," Nick replied, his own quiet laughter mingling with Doc's as the elevator doors slid open, sending them back into the uncertain afternoon.

Settling into the car, Nick glanced at Doc. "What do you say we grab lunch? Your choice—might even be on me." He flashed his credit card with a flourish, grinning. "Just not Asian. I ate there last night—don't get me wrong, it was great, but two days in a row is asking for trouble. I spotted a Burger King near the campgrounds. I could really go for a large Coke right now. I'm dying of thirst. What do you say?"

Doc shook his head vigorously, the movement almost comical. "I'm with you on the Coke. Ditto on the thirst. But let me ask—did you notice anything weird at that restaurant last night? Rumor has it they're running hookers out of that place. I'll be honest, I wouldn't mind staking it out if we had the time. Not that I've exactly been rolling in fieldwork since I moved down here—this is my first real outing."

He pointed as they neared a squat, familiar building. "Let's go in—here we are. Not that it matters, but I eat here sometimes. That big building we just passed. That's where my lab is. Used to be the troops' old station."

Doc turned the wheel, easing the car into a parking spot. "Well, let's see if this place can solve at least one of our problems. After lunch, maybe we'll have better luck."

Doc laughed, reaching for the door handle. "Come on, let's refuel. We've got plenty of daylight left to chase ghosts and rumors."

Inside, the sizzle of fryers and the low chatter of midday patrons provided a peculiar comfort. They placed their orders—two large Cokes, fries, and Whoppers—and made their way to a battered booth in the back corner. Doc insisted on the seat facing the door, his eyes scanning the entrance with an air of playful suspicion.

He grinned at Nick, mouth twitching as he unwrapped his burger. "I'd recognize the bad guys if they came in… Just kidding," he added, raising an eyebrow. "Actually, I'm expecting someone to meet us here. Had an earlier appointment I couldn't reschedule. Someone you'll be happy to see. In fact, I think she's about to make your day."

Nick's curiosity flickered in his eyes. He leaned forward, elbows on the sticky table, and watched as Doc took an enthusiastic bite from his Whopper.

"She, huh?" Nick asked, trying to sound casual. "You set me up with a surprise guest?"

Doc just winked; cheeks full. "Patience, my friend. Enjoy your Coke. Trust me—this'll be worth it."

Nick eyed the door, the possibilities spinning in his mind as the taste of anticipation mixed with the fizz of cola. Outside, a shadow paused at the glass—hesitating, then reaching for the handle.

The door swung open, and Doc sprang to his feet, carefully laying his food aside in its wrapper. With the same brisk confidence he'd brought to the parking lot, he strode toward the woman stepping over the threshold. She wore her dark hair pulled back and a windbreaker zipped halfway; eyes alert beneath steady brows. Doc greeted her with a warm nod and, with a gentle hand on her shoulder, guided her to the booth.

Stopping in front of Nick, Doc's voice was almost ceremonious. "Nick, this is Clementine Hernandez—she's with Department of Homeland Security. She's here to assist us."

Nick blinked, surprised as he scrambled to his feet, reaching out to shake her hand. Clementine's grip was firm.

"Pleased to meet you, Nick. Don't worry, I already ate." Her voice was low, carrying a hint of mileage and dry humor that suggested she was no stranger to long watches and longer days. "This meeting is about the disappearance of Professor Hahn's granddaughter. I've been—well—hiding out, keeping a watch on him and his family for the last six months."

She glanced from Doc to Nick, reading their expressions. "We're not sure if her going missing ties into the bigger picture, but here I am. Go ahead and finish your lunch—I'll step up and get myself a drink." With a nod, she slipped away toward the counter, leaving the faintest swirl of curiosity in her wake.

Doc gave Nick a knowing look. "See? Worth the wait," he murmured around a mouthful of fries, his gaze following Clementine's path as the booth settled into a new, electric silence.

Although his mouth was full, Nick's mind was racing. He knew that her arrival had just raised the stakes—this wasn't a friendly lunch anymore, it was the opening move in something far larger. Had Clementine's surveillance of the Professor somehow triggered the granddaughter's disappearance? If so, why? The questions battered at him with every hurried bite. Lunch faded into an afterthought, the salty clutch of fries and the last, redolent mouthful of Whopper just mechanical refueling for his brain.

He was relieved, in a way, to see Clementine caught in a short line at the counter—it bought him a precious minute to finish chewing over both his meal and his thoughts. Doc watched him with a crooked grin as Nick stuffed the last fries into his mouth and gulped down his Coke, nerves buzzing. He wadded up the wrapper with a sense of resolve; by the time Clementine returned, cup in hand, Nick was perched on the edge of the vinyl seat, ready.

Clementine slid into the booth, her movements calm but alert, surveyor's eyes flicking over them both before she settled in. Nick tried not to fidget, folding his hands on the table. The case was shifting under his feet, becoming something bigger than just a missing college student. The possibility of international threads—or something even stranger—piqued his curiosity, sending a pulse of adrenaline through him.

He replayed the details in his mind: Kerry's unusual eagerness for him to join the case, the way no one had blinked at including the bow hunt in his cover—details that, in retrospect, felt less like coincidence and more like a silent warning. There was more here than met the eye.

For now, all eyes were on Clementine. Nick held his breath as she took a sip of her drink, ready for her to lay the first card on the table.

Nick cleared his throat, aiming for casual but landing somewhere between nervous and sincere. "Say, Doc, are we going to have any problem with Emma-Lee helping out?" He glanced Clementine's way, hoping to buy her a moment's ease before the inevitable grilling. "Doesn't her authority end when she leaves the city? Not that it matters—I hope she's going to be able to open a few doors for us with her, uh, feminine charms. No offense, Clementine."

Clementine's eyebrow arched ever so slightly, a wry twist playing at the corner of her mouth. She didn't look offended so much as quietly amused, twirling the straw in her cup.

Doc snorted, lips quirking. "Emma-Lee's got enough pull to make herself useful wherever she lands, city limits be damned.

Besides, sometimes it's not about jurisdiction—it's about who answers when you knock."

He leaned back, fixing Nick with a half-smile that didn't quite reach his eyes. "And as for 'feminine charms,' let's just say everyone brings their own tools to the job."

Clementine lifted her cup in mock salute. "Trust me, Nick, the doors I open don't have much to do with charm." Her gaze, steady and dry, flicked to Doc, then back to Nick. "But I appreciate the optimism. I think that the fact that the higher ups allowed her to help should cover any legality."

The tension eased, if only by a degree, as the undercurrent of anxiety gave way to the familiar dance of banter and boundaries. Nick felt the edge come off his own nerves, just enough for him to settle in and wait—because whatever card Clementine played next, it was bound to change the game.

Nick blinked, startled by the sudden weight in Clementine's tone—a gentle warning before she began, as if her words might shift the air between them. She set her drink aside, hands laid flat on the table as she spoke.

"Not to get too deep with the story I'm about to share, but I want to tell you there are maybe three pieces to this puzzle. First, it's still not certain the granddaughter's disappearance has anything to do with the suspicions about illegals staying in the upstairs of the restaurant. That's the first piece." She paused, eyes scanning theirs, making sure they were following her. "The second piece is the rumor that some of the women there are being held against their will. Women brought here thinking they'd become citizens, only to find out otherwise."

Doc's jaw tightened, the banter fading from his expression. Nick leaned forward, the gravity of her words settling in his gut.

Clementine's gaze sharpened. "Any questions so far?"

For a moment, the clatter and hum of the diner seemed impossibly far away, the three of them ringed in the hush of something raw and urgent—a story that was no longer just a case file, but a living thread tying strangers together in peril and hope.

Doc looked at her and asked, "I would like to know is there any reason that her disappearance is the work of just one person or is it part of a group?"

Clementine considered the question, her expression unreadable for a heartbeat. Then she drew in a breath, measured and careful.

"That's what everyone wants to know, isn't it?" she said softly. "Officially, no one's ready to pin it on the restaurant as a whole, not without more. There's too much at stake and too little proof. Some upstairs want to believe it's just one bad actor, something clean and containable. But me—I think the lines are blurred. Maybe someone's using the place, or maybe the place is acting as a shield. Either way, we can't treat it like it's just one person's secret until we know for sure."

She let the weight of that hang in the air; eyes fixed on the condensation gathering at the base of her cup as if answers might swirl up from its depths. "So, for now, we keep watching, keep asking. Because the truth is, it could be bigger or smaller than we think—and that's what keeps me up at night."

Nick broke the silence, his voice threading through the tension. "So, I am sure we want to know how you're going to distribute the investigation. Of course, you're aware that Emma-Lee's the only one who speaks the language, and I'm sure someone higher up took that into account. You will meet her later today."

Clementine nodded, almost as if she'd been expecting Nick's question. Her fingertips tapped once, twice, a silent metronome to the thickening air.

"I will tell you this," she began, her voice steadier now, "about six months ago the city fire chief made a routine check of the building—and he's a friend of the captain, so what he found didn't just get buried. He told him the upstairs has eight bedrooms. But that wasn't the thing that stood out." She leaned forward, her gaze sweeping from Doc to Nick. "All of the bedrooms had padlocks on the outside of their doors."

A hush fell between them. Nick felt a chill unspool down his back.

Clementine went on, "When the chief asked about the locks, the owner said he rented the rooms out, that the occupants liked to keep their things private. But if you think about it, it's obvious—those padlocks weren't for keeping things out. They were for keeping people in." She let them sit with that, her words settling like dust in the empty space.

"The fire chief said the rooms were empty at the time, so he couldn't question anyone. But since then, we've been eager to get someone in there—quietly, carefully. We need to see for ourselves why those doors are really locked that way."

She pushed her cup aside, the gesture final. "That's the third piece of the puzzle. And it's the one that tells me we're already running out of time."

Doc's brow furrowed, the unspoken implications piecing themselves together. "And we're to assume the visit was prescheduled," he murmured, half to himself. "Warned ahead of time, so if there was anything to conceal, they could do exactly that—hide it."

Clementine's lips thinned, a trace of resignation in the curve of her mouth. "That's right. The inspection wasn't a surprise. If someone wanted to make sure certain things—or people—weren't visible, they'd have had ample warning." She let that sink in, her gaze unwavering.

Nick leaned forward, clarifying, "Just to be sure, you mean the doors had actual hasps with padlocks? Not simply that they could be locked from the outside, but that it was obvious they were meant to keep someone in?"

Clementine nodded, her tone grave. "Yes, that's exactly what I mean. Heavy-duty hasps, the kind you buy at a hardware store and bolt to the door. Not subtle, not elegant—just blunt force security." She paused, then added, "And each bedroom had its own bathroom. So, if someone was… kept inside, they'd still be able to take care of themselves, at least in a basic sense. It's the kind of detail that could make a captivity last longer without raising suspicion."

She let her words settle across the table, the unease thickening around them. "That's why every minute counts. The more we learn, the clearer it becomes that we're not dealing with carelessness or coincidence. Someone's gone to a lot of trouble to keep things hidden—and whatever's behind those doors, it isn't meant to see daylight."

"I suppose that a surprise visit from the fire chief would be out of the question?" Doc queried; his words heavy with skepticism.

Nick stood, stretching his legs, the tension in the air seeming to push him from his seat. "Dare I say, I think we need to somehow get someone in that upstairs unannounced and see what we can find out."

They had finished their food, and the last sound Clementine made as she tried for a final sip told them she was as ready to leave as they were. Rising from her chair, concern still etched in the set of her jaw, she gathered her phone, her eyes darting once more around the little diner as if half-expecting someone to be listening.

The trio slipped out into the afternoon. The city's rhythm pressed on, indifferent to their anxiety. As they crossed the parking lot to Doc's car, the signs of the Burger King flickered behind them.

Clementine paused, hesitating at the passenger door. "If we're really doing this, we have to be careful. Whoever's running things up there—" she glanced over her shoulder, "—won't take kindly to surprises. But we're out of time to be cautious."

Doc unlocked the car, the click echoing in the stillness. Nick leaned in, lowering his voice: "We'll need a plan. Something that doesn't tip our hand—or get any of us locked behind one of those doors." For a heartbeat, doubt flickered among them, but it faded in the face of necessity.

The afternoon pressed close, thick with the promise of secrets and the threat of discovery.

Clementine nodded, her face set. "Let's get someone inside. Quietly. And soon."

They slid into the car, each lost in their own thoughts, already assembling the next steps—and hoping they weren't too late.

Glad for the sheltering quiet of the car, Clementine settled into the front passenger seat and left the window rolled up, shutting out the world beyond the glass. She hesitated only a moment, then turned to address Nick, who watched from the rear seat with intent curiosity.

"I—we, the agency—don't know exactly how much you know about the grandfather," she began, her voice low. "But some years back, in the sixties, he was the leader of a defection from the North Vietnamese navy. He stole a patrol boat, commandeered it down the Mekong delta to the south. He's always believed the Reds would want payback."

She glanced at Doc, then back to Nick. "Now, he's convinced they might try to retaliate by going after his granddaughter. It sounds like a stretch, I know—maybe even a little paranoid. But honestly, so does every other theory we've had."

Her hands twisted anxiously over her phone. "If word gets out—about her, about him—it could open doors we don't want opened. There are people with long memories and even longer grudges. That's just one more reason we have to keep this quiet. For her safety. And maybe for all of ours."

For a moment, the only sound was the hum of the car engine, the city's noise held at bay. The shadows seemed to deepen, as if even the afternoon sun understood the weight of what Clementine had shared.

Nick looked at Doc. "So that's what all the pictures of those navy boats in the study were about. It seems like a long time to hold a grudge."

Clementine's lips pressed into a thin line. "Some people never give up," she murmured. "I got a notice from the CIA this morning—apparently the one person who could still want revenge is dying. Maybe this is his last shot before he goes. Old wounds die hard." Her gaze flickered, a note of worry creasing her brow as she studied Nick.

She drew a steadying breath. "That's just a sliver of the story. And now, we have to decide which theory holds water. While I'm in your car, why don't we drive down and talk to Emma-Lee? See if Bobbie's had any luck bagging a buck." The suggestion landed with a subtle weight—half diversion, half strategy.

Nick arched a brow, caught off guard by just how much Clementine seemed to know. The way she'd slipped the details in— the missing coed, the investigation he'd tried so hard to keep under wraps—it all suggested her sources ran deeper than he'd guessed.

Doc started the engine, the car lurching gently forward into the streaming sunlight.

"All right," he said, "The campgrounds it is." The drive was short; afternoon light fractured in the rearview mirror. Inside the car, the three of them sat in an uneasy alliance, each piecing together motives and possibilities, each aware that every place they looked brought them closer to answers—and, perhaps, to danger waiting just around the bend.

Leaning over to talk to Doc, Nick said quietly, "I'd like to soften the blow that Bobbie's going to give me when she finds out we're here on official business. Could you pull over and let me grab some beer? I'm sure it's getting thirsty out there in the woods—a little relief might go a long way."

Doc's mouth twitched with understanding, and he nodded. "Sure, old buddy. Anything to keep peace in the family."

Chapter Five

The car slowed in front of a squat, sun-faded liquor store nestled between a gas station and a bait shop. Nick slipped out, the bell on the door jingling as he disappeared inside. Clementine watched him go, her hands now still in her lap, the hint of a knowing smile playing at the corners of her mouth. She seemed to sense the subtle tug-of-war between loyalty and duty, the unspoken rules that governed marriages and investigations alike.

Nick emerged a few minutes later, two six-packs in hand, the glass bottles clinking together inside the paper bag. He settled back into his seat, the beer resting on his knees, and let out a breath that sounded suspiciously like relief.

As Doc pulled the car back onto the road, Clementine's smile lingered, silent and wry—a quiet acknowledgment of alliances both public and private.

No one spoke for a moment, the only sound the tires humming over sun-warmed asphalt. In that brief hush, the distance between their secrets and their intentions felt just a little smaller, as if an old ritual—cold beer shared around a campfire—might be enough to hold some parts of their world together, at least for an evening.

Driving past the ranger station, they enjoyed the sight of several deer hanging close to the other hunters' camps. The presence animals let Nick relax, and for a moment, even the weight of their investigation seemed to ease in the shared appreciation of the scene.

Clementine turned to Nick; her tone casual but her eyes sharp. "So; tell me, what is this hunt about anyway?"

Nick watched the deer vanish into a stand of birch before answering. "Normally, the government only allows hunting the last two weeks of November that is with rifles and cross bows onto this forest land. It keeps the herds balanced, but sometimes, the numbers swell—too many deer to support, not enough food or space. This is the first year they've tried something different. They opened up certain parts of the forest to a handful of special recipients for the first two weeks of the month, Bobbie ended up being one of them. She doesn't know that the only reason we was allowed to come was because I'm here to find this missing coed. Long story short, Kerry didn't want only the officials in on the secret. We're hoping that, after Bobbie bags a buck, she won't feel so hurt about not being trusted with everything."

Clementine shrugged, glancing out at the sun-dappled forest streaming past the window. "I can see that. But she'll shake it off. She's an agent's wife—she knows secrecy comes with the territory. Sometimes, it's the only way to keep everyone safe in a case like this."

Nick offered a rueful smile, grateful for Clementine's insight. As the car rolled on, the shadows lengthened and the trees pressed in tighter, the day's mysteries gathering around them like the hush before a storm. And still, the promise of cold beer, a campfire, and a few moments of normalcy beckoned just ahead—fragile and necessary, a small comfort against the unknown.

Reaching the Winnebago Nick strained to see if he was going to be lucky. Unable to see his heart quivered in anticipation, eager to get out of the car and find out if Bobbie was successful that morning.

Before Clementine could open the car door, Emma-Lee vaulted out of the RV and rushed across the gravel, her boots scattering dust in her wake. She yanked open the car door with the energy of someone still running on adrenaline.

"You missed it—a fourteen-point buck! I can't believe it—I killed a big buck, early this morning!" Emma-Lee's voice was half-shout, half-laugh, her cheeks flushed with triumph. "They already took it to the freezer locker, and Bobbie—well, she's asleep now. She shot a ten-point, had to drag it up a hill alone until Jeff gave her a hand. She's wore out. But hey..."

Her eyes darted between the unfamiliar faces in the car, her excitement briefly tempered by curiosity and a flash of wariness. "Who are these people... the case?"

Nick looked to Clementine, the question hanging in the air with the scent of dry grass and camp smoke. For a heartbeat, the boundaries—between celebration and investigation, between the hunters and the hunt—felt thin as paper. Doc let his hand rest on the wheel, a silent signal that the next move belonged to them.

Clementine stepped out, her smile easy but her gaze measuring, as if weighing just how much to trust. "We're just here to help, Emma-Lee. Maybe we can catch you up, too. Sounds like you've had quite the morning."

Walking to the RV, Nick waited to say anything, pausing at the door. Leaning in, he could see Bobbie curled up on the narrow bunk, deep in sleep, her hair fanned against the pillow, the exhaustion of the day's effort etched along her brow. He stood for a long moment, the hush of the RV cocooning them both, before quietly pulling the door closed behind him.

He returned to the group with a gentle smile. "She must have tired herself out this morning. Maybe a short afternoon nap will be good for her." He glanced at his watch, then at the cluster of faces— some familiar, some new, all shadowed beneath the brims of their hats and the weight of unspoken questions. "I need to call my boss, and while I do that, you all can get acquainted and get everybody up to speed. I'm sure he was on the phone this morning and part of the afternoon, decoding who's where and what our next step should be. Hopefully, he's got some clarity on where we need to push the hardest. I'll be back in a few."

With that, Nick stepped away, the crunch of gravel under his boots fading as he made his way toward the edge of the clearing, phone in hand. The rest of the group lingered by the RV, the air heavy with the mingled scents of pine, and the distant, tempting notes of woodsmoke.

Emma-Lee tucked a stray strand of hair behind her ear and offered a lopsided grin, breaking the momentary silence. "Well, since introductions are apparently in order—who wants to start?"

Clementine folded her arms, gaze flicking from Emma-Lee to Doc and the others, weighing the others with practiced ease. "I'll go. I'm Clementine, and I'm here to help Nick on this case. But after a morning like yours, Emma-Lee, I think you've earned the best stories."

Laughter trickled through the group, easy and uncertain all at once, bridging the gap between strangers and allies. Outside, the forest waited, shadows lengthening across the clearing as new alliances quietly began to take root, the afternoon ripe with possibility and the faint, ever-present promise of answers just `ahead.

Doc tipped his cap, his voice steady but warm. "Pleased to meet you, Emma-Lee. I'm Doc—work with the MHP, mostly in the forensic lab here in town. Just a regular trooper, but these days, I spend more time under fluorescent lights than out in the woods." He offered a small, reassuring smile before nodding toward Clementine.

"And this is Clementine, she's with Immigration. She's been assigned to assist Nick and the FBI on finding the missing girl."

He glanced around at the ring of faces, the tension in his shoulders easing as the introductions took hold. "There's plenty more to fill you in on, but why don't we all find a spot to sit? Clementine can bring you up to speed—there's a lot to talk through, and I have a feeling your morning's only just getting started."

He gestured toward the nearest picnic table, the kind streaked by sun and softened by years of use, inviting Emma-Lee and the others to settle in. The mood shifted—less wary now, a tentative derie sparking as everyone gathered, the hush of the clearing broken only by the low rustle of wind through the pines.

As everyone settled onto the worn benches, Emma-Lee's fingers drummed lightly against the tabletop, her gaze drifting to the closed RV door before landing back on the circle of faces. The afternoon seemed to pause, suspended between sunlight and shadow.

"Maybe we should take advantage of Bobbie's nap and storm our brains for a direction as to how we are going to find out which theory is correct… that is was she kidnaped for retaliation or was she sold int sex trafficking?" Nick spoke out.

Clementine agreed, her tone light as she leaned forward with an agreeable smile. "We need to divide up into two teams—maybe men against the women." She let out a soft laugh, but her eyes were sharp with purpose. "By that I mean both of the men have already been exposed in the public eye, and the women, on the other hand, haven't. I've just joined the case, and Emma-Lee's been out here in the woods all morning. Meanwhile, both Nick and Doc have been out to see the professor. If he's being watched, then whoever's behind this already knows they're involved."

The group absorbed her words. Doc arched an eyebrow, his lips quirking in reluctant amusement. "So, you're suggesting we use our anonymity as leverage," he said, glancing between Emma-Lee and Clementine. "That's not a bad idea. Keeps the spotlight off you two, at least for now."

Emma-Lee nodded thoughtfully, pulling a twig between her fingers. "If they're watching, they won't expect us. We could visit places or people they'd never let Nick or Doc near right now."

Emma-Lee glanced sidelong at Clementine, a spark of mischief flickering beneath her calm resolve. "I doubt the host from last night would remember me—not with how brief our visit was. If we dressed up like a couple of businesswomen and went in as if we were just there for a meal, we might be able to pick up something about what's really going on upstairs. We could even pose as representatives from the chamber of commerce, or maybe real estate agents scoping out potential properties."

Clementine's eyes lit up, catching on to the plan with eager understanding. "That could work. Two professional women, asking the right kind of questions, blending in—it wouldn't raise any red flags. We'd have the perfect excuse to poke around; maybe even get a look at areas they don't usually show to regular diners."

Doc grinned, a note of admiration in his voice as he said, "I like it. Subtle, but effective. Just make sure you keep your stories straight—folks in small towns remember details, even if they forget faces."

Nick nodded, a hint of hope in his tired eyes. "It's worth a shot. If there's anything shady about the upstairs, someone who works there might let something slip."

Emma-Lee rolled the twig between her fingers, thoughtful. "Then that's settled. Clementine and I will hit the restaurant as soon as Bobbie wakes up. We'll need to look the part—nothing too flashy, but sharp enough to pass for the real deal."

The group lingered in the hush that followed, the plan taking root, silent agreement settling over them like the hush before rain. Outside, the wind whispered through the pines, as if urging them onward.

Nick's brow furrowed as he broke the quiet, his voice low and direct. "But why wait for Bobbie to wake up? She'll want to tag along—she always does. The less she knows about this, the better. We need to keep her in the dark about our real activities and just let her think we're working a routine case. If we're not careful, she and Jeff could become liabilities. Neither of them are involved, and they're certainly not equipped to handle anything if the criminals catch wind of what's going on. They're civilians, plain and simple."

He glanced around at the small group, gauging their reactions. "Trying to protect them is just another job for someone else to worry about. Maybe we can convince them both to head home for now. I'll bet Jeffrey would be happy enough to get back to his law office. Bobbie, though..."

He hesitated, a note of concern in his tone. "She's going to be a tougher nut to crack. Don't forget—she still doesn't know the real reason we're here, that we're investigating the disappearance of the granddaughter."

Clementine nodded; her expression sober. "We'll need to tread carefully. If we push too hard, Bobbie might get suspicious—or worse, try to dig into things herself. But if we let her tag along, she could get caught in the crossfire."

Emma-Lee looked between them, determination settling in her eyes. "Let's keep her out of it for now. We'll go in quietly, do what we need to do, and hopefully get some answers—without putting anyone else in harm's way."

Outside, the wind picked up, rattling the branches, as if echoing their unspoken worries and the weight of the secrets they carried.

Emma-Lee cracked a smile, her tension easing just a fraction. "You've got a point, Clem. Nothing slips past the women at those shops—they know what everyone's up to, and half the time they know it before you do. Might be the best place to pick up a rumor or two, if we play it right."

Nick let out a quiet laugh, shaking his head. "And you both actually want to go clothes shopping? I never thought I'd see the day this turned into a fashion mission."

Clementine's grin widened, her eyes twinkling with mischief. "You can stay outside and watch for Jeffrey's dramatic return. I'll bet he's on some log right now, sending emails and arguing about court filings with a Bluetooth in his ear. Poor guy probably thinks a squirrel's about to serve him a subpoena."

The laughter that followed was a small relief, a shaky bridge above the currents of fear that ran beneath their plans. For a moment, derie dispelled the shadows. But as the wind continued to rattle the windows and the trees whispered outside, the sense of urgency crept back in.

Emma-Lee reached for her bag, determination returning to her posture. "Alright, let's make it count. We'll split up—Clem, you and I will hit the dress shop and see what the ladies have to say. Doc and Nick, keep an eye on Bobbie and Jeffrey. If anything feels off, we regroup at the campsite, no questions asked."

With purpose threading through their movements, the group began preparing for their respective roles—each aware that in a town where gossip moved faster than the river, the right question in the right shop just might crack open the truth they'd all been chasing.

Slipping back to the tent, Emma-Lee grabbed her ID and a few essentials—wallet, notepad, the battered flashlight she trusted more than any phone app.   She paused, letting the canvas flap fall shut behind her, and took a deep breath of pine-laced air. The gravity of the day pressed in, but she felt steadier now, a plan in motion and purpose in every step.

Grabbing the black zipper gun bag, she wrapped it in a tee shirt to carry it with her. The snub nose .357 Magnum inside felt heavy, but reassuring.

She rejoined Doc and Clementine in the unmarked MHP car, sliding into the back seat, her nerves settling into a kind of readiness. Doc gave her a brief, reassuring nod in the rearview mirror, while Clementine shuffled through a stack of maps and handwritten notes, already strategizing. The engine rumbled to life, and the car rolled out along the gravel path, disappearing into the hush of early afternoon.

Back at the campsite, Nick remained on the bench, shoulders hunched, hands clasped. He watched the others depart, a quiet resolve overtaking his earlier humor. The truth about Bobbie gnawed at him—not a lie, not really, he told himself again and again, just the omission of reality. That little difference felt like a lifeline even as it twisted itself into a knot in his stomach.

He let his gaze drift to the winding road leading toward the ranger station, the silence broken by the snap of twigs and a burst of distant laughter. One of the other hunters came into view—a young blond woman, strides confident and powerful, her camo shorts and high-top boots flecked with the morning's dew.   The knee-high socks, the lethal crossbow, the glint of sweat on her brow: all marks of someone who relished the forest's challenges.

She caught Nick's eye and shot him a nod; the kind exchanged between people who'd spent enough time in the wild to speak without words. He watched her disappear behind a stand of trees, the easy athleticism in her movements a sharp contrast to his own restless energy.

Nick exhaled, pressing his palms against his knees. The camp was quieter now, but the current of secrets and suspicion ran just as deep. He rehearsed the words he'd use when Bobbie returned—the calm explanations, the half-truths, the hope that sincerity might be enough to keep trust alive. For now, all he could do was wait, listening to the wind and the distant sounds of the hunt, time stretching taut as a trap-wire.

Sitting alone, the early morning awakening was slowly creeping up on him. The bright sunlight filtering through the pines seemed to coax the sleep to his eyes. His full stomach urged him to close his eyes, the warmth blooming outward from his core. Leaning against his hand, his elbow propped on the bench, he felt the softness of drowsiness coil around his senses.

He let his eyelids flutter shut for a moment, just long enough for the world to blur and the low hum of the forest to fold into a gentle lullaby. The distant trill of a bird, the rhythmic sway of needles in the breeze, the faint smell of earth and sun-warmed sap—all of it pressed in, inviting him to let go.

But somewhere in that space between waking and sleep, Nick's mind circled back to the thoughts that had chased him all morning. Secrets left unsaid, the tremor of uncertainty—each one pulsed like a heartbeat, keeping him perched on the edge of rest. The light kept shifting, dappling over his closed eyelids, and he wondered how long he could let himself drift before the others returned, before questions needed answering and the day's uncertainties demanded his attention.

For now, though, the bench felt like a haven, the hush of the woods a fragile promise that—if only for a few minutes—he could let himself simply be, without pressure, without pretense, and just breathe.

He jerked awake, slow and groggy, disoriented by the sudden shift from dream-thick quiet to the insistent clarity of her voice. His name echoed again, sharper this time, and he blinked up at her—his wife—standing close, sunlight catching in the wisps of hair that had escaped her ponytail.

"Nick... Nick!" she repeated, her voice threading concern and irritation together. He squinted, trying to assemble his thoughts, but they tumbled uselessly against the weight of sleep still lingering behind his eyes.

"Where have you been all morning? You missed the deer we bagged. Where is Emma-Lee—what is going on? Talk to me!"

Her questions battered him like stones skipping across water, each one leaving its own ripple of unease. He sat up straighter, the bench creaking beneath him, and tried to rouse his voice.

"I... I must've dozed off," he managed, rubbing the back of his neck. "Didn't mean to. Emma-Lee's out with Doc and Clementine—they left a little while ago. Said it was important. I didn't want to get in the way."

She frowned, crossing her arms, the smile fading as concern overtook it. "You sure you're alright? You look like you've seen a ghost."

Nick forced a shaky laugh, wishing he could conjure up the easy humor that usually came to his rescue. But the knot in his stomach tightened instead. "I'm just tired, that's all. It's been a long morning."

She sighed, her features softening as she sat beside him, close enough that he could smell the wood smoke in her hair. "Who is Doc and Clementine and where have they gone, please tell me what is going on?"

Nick nodded, silent for a moment as the forest's hush settled back around them. He reached for her hand, grateful for its warmth and the steadying comfort it offered—a small anchor in the current of secrets threading their day together.

"Please give me a minute, I need to think..."

His mind raced as he stared at his wife, searching her face for some footing in the uncertainty pooling between them. Her smile, though tentative, was a small beacon—reassuring, coaxing him toward the right words, though they caught and twisted somewhere between his thoughts and his lips.

"Kiss me. I missed you," he whispered, a plea disguised as affection, hoping any distraction might buy him a fragment of time to gather himself. She obliged at once, her kiss eager, lingering—a soft insistence that told him she was well-rested, but also tinged with a melancholy that she didn't bother to hide.

There was always an edge to her longing when he slipped away into these silent absences, a wondering that went beyond the boundaries of a wife's concern. She wondered about him as a husband, yes, measuring his tenderness against the shadow of his distance. She wondered, too, about the other life he led—the one stitched together with secrets and obligations, the one that sometimes pressed between them like a cold draft through an open door. Today, though, she wondered about him simply as a lover, missing the chance to share the warmth of her body with him the night before.

As she'd lain awake waiting for his return, her mind had circled back to him and all that he never said. She imagined him out there in the hush of the woods, the elusive white-tail always just beyond his reach—or so he'd let her believe. Now, as he sat beside her, still half-lost in dreams and tangled truths, the distance between them felt both impossibly wide and wantonly close.

Nick let his forehead rest against hers for a moment, drawing in the scent of wood smoke and rain in her hair, the quiet comfort of her presence anchoring him as the stories he'd told—both to her and to himself—unraveled softly in the morning light.

He drew a long, steadying breath, emboldened by the trust shining in her eyes. "You know I love you, and I share everything I can with you—especially the love and the trust we have for each other," he began, quiet but certain, the words shaped by both guilt and relief. "I didn't hunt this morning. I'm working on a case. I'm not at liberty to share the particulars with anyone—not even you. I know it sounds like I tricked you, but honestly, it was Kerry's idea. The case is here, in this county, and I'm not working alone."

He squeezed her hand, letting the moment settle between them, hoping she'd sense the sincerity beneath his careful restraint.

"After you went into the woods, I called one of the team, and he picked me up. I've been working with him all morning—a local forensic expert. Emma-Lee is with him, along with another agent, Clementine. They went into the business district for some shopping, and he should be back soon."

He watched her eyes narrow, not with suspicion but curiosity, a little hurt mingling with the need to understand. "The other agent, Clementine, she's with them. And Emma-Lee—she's a St. Louis K-9 officer, but you know that. She's helping with the case; it was all arranged even before she started bow hunting. I don't think Jeff has any idea about all this. He's still out in the woods, and with a charged phone, he'll probably stay there a good while longer. All of this—" he hesitated, searching for her trust in the hush between them, "—it's hush-hush, for now."

He brushed a strand of hair behind her ear, his touch apologetic. "In the meantime, we can stay here and camp. Let Jeffery and Emma-Lee decide what they want, and I'll do what I need to do with Clementine. That's all I can tell you, for now. I wish I could share more. I do."

The confession hung in the air, shimmering with the weight of secrets and the fragile hope that love might be enough to span the unseen distance between them.

He couldn't help but smile, the tension in his chest loosening with the sound of her voice. She recounted her morning with a hint of triumph, a glimmer of the self-reliant woman who could wait out a deer by a hidden stream and wrangle it home as if it were nothing more than a chore at hand. Her words painted a small picture—thick brush, damp earth, the satisfaction of a clean shot, the stubborn weight of her prize. He could see her, crouched and patient, eyes sharp with focus, her body blending with the wild.

"I would have liked to see that," he admitted, his voice low, a soft warmth rising in him at the thought.

"You always find a way to surprise me." He reached for her hand, tracing absent lines along her knuckles, anchoring himself in the moment as she spoke of steaks and quiet dinners, the promise of simple pleasures and the comfort of routine.

But there was more in her smile—a flash of mischief, a sly arch of her brow that revealed her not-so-hidden hopes. In the hush of their shared solitude, she made her invitation, subtle as rain on leaves: the promise of peace, the whisper of silk packed for evenings when the world fell away and only the two of them remained. The suggestion lingered in the air, sweet and edged, teasing him toward laughter, toward longing, toward the possibility of a night unmarred by secrets or distance.

He leaned in, close enough to catch the faintest scent of earth and wildflowers in her hair.

"Maybe you'll show me that secret spot later," he murmured, teasing right back.

"Or the other treasures you brought for me."

Meanwhile, a breeze rustled through the trees, carrying with it the timeless hush of the woods, as if nature itself conspired to keep their secrets. In that cocoon of quiet, he let the rest of the time slip away—the cases, the lies, the weight of what he could not share—until all that remained was her nearness and the fragile promise between them: that here, at least, nothing else mattered.

As she rolled her eyes up at him as she lay against his shoulders she whispered "How long do you think they will be before they come back? Do we have time to lay down in the RV and relax?" Her mood was evident as he voice became husky with the mood advancing. "It could be we could relive sometimes that we shared a long time ago. I don't feel that old; how about you?" She laughed out.

He laughed, a low, easy sound, the kind that bubbled up only when all the barriers between them fell away. "Tell you what—I think that if we go into the RV and find something to drink, maybe in a brown bottle and kept in the fridge, I might be persuaded to go in there."

The joyous look that moved over her face confirmed that they were on the same page. She rose in a single fluid motion, her hand seeking his, fingers entwining with a gentle eagerness that left no room for doubt. With a mischievous tug, she pulled him up beside her, her laughter ringing through the stillness and scattering the last of his reservations.

He followed, letting her lead, the world outside their tiny haven fading with each step toward the RV. Sunlight filtered golden through the leaves, dappling her hair, and he caught himself thinking that peace was not a place, but a moment—this moment, with her. Inside, the hum of the little fridge greeted them, promising simple comforts: a cold drink, shared glances, and whatever memories they might choose to revive behind closed doors. As the door clicked softly shut, the promise of laughter and togetherness hung in the air, as palpable as the summer dusk. In that small, sun-warmed space, the rest of the world could wait.

As they settled onto the narrow bunk, arms woven together in the hush of their retreat, Bobbie's attention seemed to drift, her eyes tracing invisible patterns on the ceiling above. Nick drew her close in the dim amber light, his hand gentle at her waist, lips brushing the soft line of her neck—a silent plea to keep the tenderness between them alive. But her mind lingered elsewhere, and after a few hopeful kisses, she twisted away, sitting up with the covers tangled around her.

A sigh escaped her, equal parts exasperation and longing. "So, what now? I'm just supposed to sit here and watch the campfire all day while you and the others go traipsing around this hick town looking for a kidnapper?" Her words, edged and honest, left no room for pretense.

Nick rolled over, the weight of her question pressing in as he gathered his thoughts. The comfort of their shared bubble was fading, replaced by the cold reality of their purpose here. He reached for her hand, holding it between both of his as he searched her face for understanding.

"No, it's not like that. I just thought maybe we could have a little break from the boys—just us for a while. Besides, if all goes well and we solve this case, we'll have the rest of two whole weeks to lay around and be romantic. Maybe even the coed will turn up unharmed, maybe she'll have her own new romance by the end of it. How does that sound?"

Bobbie was silent, her face placid unable respond.

He tried for a grin, the corners of his mouth tilting up with hope. "No one figured you'd bag a deer so soon. If you think about it, the sooner we find her, the sooner we can get back to being us. Just you, me, and the peace we've earned."

He squeezed her hand, the promise of future laughter and lazy mornings shining in his gaze, as if willing her to believe that the world could wait—if only they could hold on a little longer.

He brushed a thumb over her knuckles, his voice softening as he tried again.   "Come on, you know I love you. This case—it's not just some routine favor. It came down from the top. When DC gets involved, we don't really get to pick and choose. We have to play along, no matter how much it costs us."

He reached up, stroking her soft face, a rueful half-smile growing on his lips. "But hey, look at the bright side. We still have tonight, just you and me. Maybe once the sun sets and the world outside quiets down, we can... reinvestigate each other. If you catch my drift."

A spark flickered in her eyes—exasperation mingling with reluctant amusement. The warmth between them wasn't gone, just buried under the weight of duty and the press of responsibility they could never quite outrun. For now, he held onto the hope that the night would be theirs, even if the daylight belonged to the job.

Nick hesitated, then brightened as an idea struck him. "I'll tell you what—tomorrow, we can have Doc, the local Trooper I'm working with, drive us to the car rental place. We'll get you a car. That way, you'll be free to go wherever you like. If the campsite starts to feel claustrophobic, you can head into town, do some shopping. There's even a college library if you want a quiet spot to read. And the Ozarks aren't all backwoods mystery—there are places worth seeing. You could make a little adventure of it, while I chase down leads."

He watched her, hopeful. "You don't have to stay cooped up waiting for me. This doesn't have to be all about my job." His hand squeezed hers again, reassuring, as if to anchor her to something brighter. "So, what do you say? A bit of freedom, a bit of exploring— maybe we both come back to camp longing for each other."

Nick let out a low laugh, the tension in his shoulders easing as Bobbie's words—half threat, half confession—spilled into the space between them. He shifted closer, looping his arms around her with a tenderness that spoke of apology and relief in equal measure.

"Well, I'll keep you far from Kerry for now, promise... And remind me never to underestimate a woman set on bagging a ten-point buck, again." His grin softened as he pressed his lips against her forehead, lingering there—a silent pledge to make things right.

"I'll get the water running when we get back, and I'll even try not to drink all the margarita's before you're in the shower." He breathed in, as if the scent she teased about was the most familiar, comforting thing in the world. "If anyone's earned a night off, it's you."

He squeezed her gently, letting the sounds outside the RV fade into nothing. "We'll handle the mess. And when the moon's up and the rest of camp is lost in their own stories, you'll have me no shave and all. For what it's worth, I'd pick you and your muddy boots over anyone, any day."

He waited, her warmth pressed close, every worry shrunk to the size of a shared secret. "Just say when, and I'll hold you as long as you want. And don't worry—I'll never forgive Kerry either. At least not until you do."

Outside, the sun began its descent, painting the world in soft gold. For a fleeting heartbeat, Nick let himself believe in the promise of comfort, of laughter, and the fragile peace two people could carve out amid the wild.

Chapter Six

Content to lay close and feel the calmness that was settling over them, Nick was not surprised when his phone rang out, sharp and insistent, disturbing the serene mood like a pebble dropped in still water. He fumbled for the device, its glow stark in the tent's soft gloom. With a resigned sigh and a glance at Bobbie—a silent apology for the interruption—he tapped the screen and set the phone on speaker.

Winking at Bobbie, he exaggerated his accent into a lazy drawl. "Yes sir, boss... Bobbie is here, and she is trying to be calm... She bagged a ten-point buck early this morning while I was talking to that friend of yours about the case. Say hi, Bobbie."

Bobbie shot him a look equal parts amusement and warning, but she couldn't suppress the grin tugging at the corner of her mouth. She leaned in close, her voice smooth, only lightly teasing. "Evening, Chief. You'll be happy to know Nick hasn't let the camp burn down—yet." Her fingers traced idle patterns on Nick's arm, a private anchor in a suddenly public space.

On the other end, the boss's rough chuckle crackled through the speaker, his words carrying the familiar edge of authority softened by distance. "Glad to hear it. I was starting to think you two might not be talking, or at least not talking to me sorry about the trick but if you got a buck that is all that matters. Bobbie, congratulations on the buck... Nick did you hook up with the trooper?"

Nick gave Bobbie an agreeable shrug, voice light. "I did, sir. And He says to tell you thank you for getting him out of the lab. But for now, we're off the clock—well, mostly. I and Bobbie are waiting for Doc to come back."

There was a pause, the silence on the line filled with the hush of Kerry thinking. "No fire, Nick. Just checking in. And tell Bobbie she's got you beat for bragging rights this week."

Nick grinned, squeezing Bobbie's hand hinting for her to leave him alone. "You heard the man. I'm officially second fiddle." Waving is hand for her to leave the RV while he discussed the case.

Bobbie's laughter, bright and genuine, filled the RV, chasing away what little tension lingered. For a moment, even the world beyond their metal walls seemed far away—until duty called again, as it always did. But for now, they smiled at each other and Bobbie went outside with a smile and the understanding not to be upset as the case came first.

"Okay Kerry, I am alone I don't have much to tell you about the case we been to see the Professor and the college. Nothing that we have to tell you except there is still the question of why she is missing. We have two theories, but you can figure that much. Three if you add nothing sinister you know she went somewhere, and it had nothing to do with her being harmed. Like she forgot to let anyone know where she was going to be. Anyway, we are going to split up into two teams and pursue both the women are looking into the abduction angle. Me and Doc are working on the retaliation aspect. If you don't have any questions right now about the case. I might add that Bobbie is just a little perturbed at the way she was held in the dark. I am going to smooth things over so if you see some funny charges on my expense reports don't have a cow." Hearing a slight laughter from Kerry then the phone went dead.

Stepping out into the early afternoon, Nick felt the crisp air wrap around him, the sounds of camp life gentle and grounding after the tense conversation. Across the campsite, Doc and the rest of the team had gathered around the old wooden picnic table, the surface cluttered with some pine cones and pine needles. The quiet hum of voices mingled with the rustle of trees above.

He caught sight of Bobbie right away—her laughter carrying across the clearing as she recounted to the others how Nick was "enduring" one of Kerry's infamous check-in calls. Doc glanced up with a knowing smile, lifting a hand in greeting as Nick approached.

"Well, since I am not privy to all of this cloak and dagger, I'll wait in the RV I have not had a beer all day and I think that it is late enough and no I am not sharing all of you are on duty." Her sneer told them she was not upset with the circumstances. But wanted to make a joke about it.

Emma, always organized even in the wild, turned toward him, her eyes bright with new plans. "I made arrangements—for the training officer I left Storm with. He's going to drive down and join us, He is bringing her with him." she announced, her tone practical but warm. "We had a good day at the shops we went to, picked up some wonderful clothes."

It was then she glanced around, a playful frown creasing her brow. "Have you seen Jeff? Surely, he's not still in the woods."

Nick shook his head, a wry smile tugging at his lips. "Not since early morning. If he's not back soon, we might have to send out a search party—assuming he hasn't walked back and is sleeping in his tent."

The team chuckled, the easy derie settling over them like a well-worn blanket. For a moment, the uncertainty of the case felt pressing as they sat down.

Nick looked at all of the team and spoke, his voice steady but tinged with a hint of humor. "Right now, we need to forget about Jeff. He's a big boy—he probably fell asleep under a tree and didn't hear his phone. Emma, why don't you just call him on his cell and find out where he is when we're done here. No need to fret over him yet."

"I did a long time ago it keeps going to voice mail. But like you say he is a big boy. Tomorrow Clementine and I are going to go to the fire-marshal's office and find out what we can. Maybe we can get some idea why he thought there was something going on. And find out when he was there. Plus, would it be feasible to do a surprise visit."

"Good... Doc and are heading over to the dorm and then to her friend's house, but tonight we are going to sit on the restaurant and find out what is going on in the basement. They are licensed to sell alcohol. We will also rent a car for Bobbie. Don't ask. Plus, I got a call in to the grandfather and he has not called me back. I am sure that we need to talk to him again. Then it's back to here for the night. I need to smooth out my wife and act like a husband for the night." Winking.

Nick stretched his arms, feeling the last notes of tension ebb away. He caught Emma's eye, as she said. "If all of you will excuse me, I am going to try calling Jeff again and walk up to the Rangers' shack and tell him about me bringing Storm into the campgrounds—just a precaution. She's normally fine around the public, but I'm trying to touch all bases. See you later. I'll be where I can see if Storm gets here."

With that, she waved her phone and set off along the gravel path, boots crunching softly as the shadows lengthened through the trees. The others watched her go, their conversation drifting back into low, companionable tones beneath the fading light. She glanced back once, saw the warm glow of sun flickering through the tree limbs, and felt a small surge of gratitude for the team—quirks, worries, and all.

Leaving the group behind she headed to the Rangers' shack, she listened for any sign of Storm's arrival, the gentle dusk settling around her like a promise of things yet to unfold.

Moments later, she looked at her phone no new messages. Calling Jeff's phone, she got his voicemail again. She sighed, pocketing the device, but her resolve did not falter. A squirrel darted across the path ahead, chittering, and Emma found herself smiling at the simplicity of the moment.

As the shack came into view, its door was open. She raised a hand in greeting to the Ranger inside, a figure hunched over a stack of paperwork. "Evening," she called, stepping up onto the wood planks.

"Evening, Emma. Can I do something for you?" the Ranger replied, glancing up.

"Yes, I am a ST. Louis police officer... a K-Nine officer, and I got a call earlier and the person that is keeping my K-Nine 'Storm' has a family emergency and must bring her down to me. Since I already bagged my deer, I just told him to bring her here. She is a black Labrador very well behave, and she is going to be with me. She has her kennel with her, and I will be in and out of the park. But she will be with me anytime I am gone. Be assured that it will be alright. Just be sure that if she is in her kennel don't approach her. If you are on patrol and you see anyone trying to pet her stop them. Hopefully there won't be any issues, thank you."

The Ranger smiled warmly as Emma finished, setting aside a pen and shifting in their chair. "I am glad you came by and told me. Pets are normally allowed as long as they are kept on a leash. I am sure that as a police officer you will adhere to the rules. I am also happy that you found our camping grounds enjoyable."

Emma returned the smile, tension easing from her shoulders. "Thank you, I appreciate your understanding. Storm won't be any trouble, I promise. She's a working dog, after all—well-trained and more likely to help than cause a fuss."

The Ranger nodded, eyes kind but attentive. "That's good to hear. We do get campers from all over, and sometimes folks aren't used to seeing a K-Nine out and about. But I'll make a note for the others on duty, so they know the situation. Just let us know if there's anything you need."

Emma gave a little nod of gratitude. "Will do. And if you see a Labrador trotting purposefully behind me, no need to worry."

With the formalities settled, the two exchanged a few more words about the park's quiet beauty in the afternoon and the gentle drift of campers returning to their campsites.

Emma glanced back out at the pine trees, feeling a little more at ease. She left the shack behind, the faint glow of the sunlight steaking through the trees bringing her into the deep woods and made her way back to the heart of camp—ready for whatever the night might bring.

Turning, she waited, her ears attuned to the sounds of the forest, each breath a quiet invitation for Storm's arrival. The bond she shared with her Labrador was something deeper than the usual tie between handler and dog; it was a thread of trust and devotion woven through countless dawn patrols, late-night watches, and silent moments when the world seemed to hold its breath.

Emma's heart thrummed with anticipation, her affection reaching outward as if Storm could sense her longing across the distance. The last two days had felt oddly incomplete, as though she were missing a vital part of herself—a shadow that should have walked at her side, offering wordless reassurance. She knew, without doubt, that Storm had felt her absence too; the Labrador's loyalty was a constant, steadfast as the mountains hemming in the forest.

A sound on the roadway set Emma's pulse racing, her gaze bright with hope. Soon, Storm would rejoin her, and together, they would stride through the dusk, whole once more—two souls moving in perfect tandem, the woods echoing with the quiet certainty of their reunion.

Hesitating just long enough to be assured that it was indeed an automobile she heard, Emma stopped dead still. Her heart fluttered with cautious hope—a smile spreading as certainty bloomed within her that the distant engine belonged to a vehicle, not some trick of the forest's acoustics. Maybe, just maybe, this was the moment she had been waiting for. Perhaps it was her friend and companion, Storm, arriving at last.

The anticipation was almost too much to bear. Emma's breath caught as she strained to listen, the world narrowing to the subtle shift in wind and the rising crunch of tires on gravel. Every muscle in her body tensed in readiness, that familiar mix of joy and longing washing over her. If it was truly Storm, soon she would see that sleek black form. Her, eyes bright and tail waving—a reunion that would restore the missing piece of her spirit.

Emma stepped forward, unable to help herself, drawn as if by invisible thread toward the road. She felt the hush of the woods gather around her, the last rays of sun gilding the pine needles overhead, as she waited, hope blooming as sure and steady as the dawn.

She hurried back to the campsite cutting through the pines rushing to be at there when the vehicle stopped. Her anticipated reunion needed to be controlled.

Storm was trained to be quiet, to settle into a patient, watchful stillness even in moments of excitement. Yet this was only the second time they had been separated, and Emma couldn't predict how the Labrador would react. Would Storm remember her training, or would the longing of their brief absence overwhelm her composure?

The truth was Emma's companionship had become Storm's world—just as Storm had become the steadfast anchor in Emma's own. Over the last year and a half, they had rarely been apart, their lives knit together by daily rituals and the gentle cadence of mutual trust. Each sunrise, every midnight breeze, had deepened the invisible thread connecting them: handler and dog, guardian and friend.

Now, nerves tingled under Emma's skin as she neared the roadside. She could almost see Storm's eager eyes and the tremor of anticipation running through her sleek frame. Whether Storm greeted her with a quiet, dignified grace or an uncontrollable, joyous flurry, Emma knew her own heart would answer in kind—complete at last, restored by reunion.

The van broke through the pines, a pale silver shape gliding between tree trunks, and Emma held her breath as it slowed near the clearing. The vehicle rolled to a stop a short distance from the weathered picnic table where Bobbie and the others had gathered, their conversation momentarily stilled by the unexpected arrival.

Carl Tremont, behind the wheel, took deliberate care as he parked, his eyes meeting Emma's in the rearview mirror. Understanding passed silently between them—a shared desire to keep the moment gentle, unhurried, for Storm's sake.   Carl exited the van quietly, gesturing for Emma to approach, inviting her close to the sliding doors.

Emma's heartbeat drummed in her ears as she drew nearer, her feet crunching softly in the pine needles. She could sense the restless energy blooming inside the van, the subtle shift and scrape of movement that told her Storm was already aware, already hoping. Carl paused beside the door, his hand hovering over the handle. "You should be the first," he murmured, his voice barely louder than the dusk breeze.

Emma nodded, gratitude warming her features. She steadied herself, summoning a calm for Storm to mirror, and Carl eased open the door. A pause—a single, suspended breath—then Storm's eyes found hers, wide and bright, a universe of recognition and joy compressed into that instant.

Storms tail began to wag as she seen Emma her voice pricked her ears. It was simply a quick reunion. The short separation slipped away as Emma opened her kennel door. Storms body shook in response to the welcome reunion. Stroking her with affection Emma secure her harness in her hand and spoke "Sit"

Silence held them for a heartbeat before Storm surged forward, restrained only by a thread of remembered training. But Emma knelt, arms open, and Storm's restraint melted into exuberant reunion. The woods, the waiting, the ache of separation—all faded as handler and hound found each other once more, the world righted by their bond.

Out of the confinement of the kennel, Storm stepped lightly onto the earth, Emma's firm hold on the leash guiding her into the heart of the clearing. The Labrador shook herself from nose to tail, sending a shimmer of dust and old tension flying, filling her chest with the cool afternoon air. For a moment, time paused—Storm's muscles quivered in the daylight, absorbing the scent of pine needles and woodsmoke, the familiar voices drifting in from the campsite.

Emma bent to rub Storm's flank, fingers kneading gently into her short fur. Storm pressed against her, gaze eager and alert, tail a black metronome marking the rhythm of their belonging. Following Emma's lead, she circled once, twice, then settled at her side, posture attentive and ready for whatever came next. Around them, the pines kept their counsel, and the hush of the woods seemed to echo the quiet relief of reunion.

Together, they walked toward the others—Emma's step lightened, Storm's gait proud and close. In this ordinary act of rejoining the group, there was a quiet triumph, a wordless celebration of their enduring bond and the comfort of return.

As Storm relaxed into her new-old world, Nick moved quietly around the van with Carl, the two working in tandem to slide the wire kennel out and set it beside Emma's tent. Nick carried over Storm's large bag of kibble and her battered water bowl, pausing to fill it from a blue jug before setting it close to the kennel's door—a simple gesture of care that did not go unnoticed. The rest of the team, their energy eased by the calm after reunion, settled along the weathered bench by the picnic table and let conversation drift in lazy circles.

Storm, satiated and content, curled inside her kennel, eyelids drooping as the afternoon unraveled into a golden haze. The rhythm of voices, the gentle clink of a mug, the warm, pine-spiced air—all folded around her in a lullaby of belonging.

Then, with the suddenness of a magpie's cry, Jeff appeared at the edge of the clearing, flanked by two other bow hunters. All three swung beers in easy hands, laughter rolling ahead of them like a tide. They moved with the assurance of old friends, boots scuffing the pine duff, eyes creased with delight at some shared joke.

Leaving Storm to her rest, Emma strode out to meet Jeff, voice pitched louder than the hush. "Where have you been? I called you several times and it always went to voice-mail." Her words floated above the laughter, half chiding, half amused. She caught the flush on Jeff's cheeks, the careless angle of his step, and guessed quickly that this was not their first beer of the day.

Emma's mouth curled in a knowing smile. "So, you found some new friends out here in the pines of Missouri. That doesn't surprise me—never met a stranger, have you?" The other hunters chuckled, nodding in easy agreement. "But you're not the only one. I made a new friend too. Let me introduce you to Clementine Hernandez—she's hunting over in the yellow zone."

The name hovered between them, bright with the promise of new stories. The group shifted, curiosity kindling in their eyes, and the easy derie of the woods seemed to grow. Emma's world, long defined by familiar faces and old bonds, widened with possibility as the afternoon light slipped toward evening, welcoming stranger and friend alike beneath the Missouri pines.

Jeff's voice rang out over the camp, still buoyed by laughter and the easy swing of his beer. "I see you brought Storm down here— are you going to use her to hunt the white tail ?" He grinned at Emma; one eyebrow raised in teasing challenge.

Emma shot him a look over her shoulder, her smile edged with mock indignation. "Storm's got better manners than most hunters I know. Besides, she's earned her rest."

Jeff waved a casual hand toward his companions. "I ran into these guys out at the border of our area—they're hunting in the red zone. We got to talking after I had a big buck run right across the lines, and suddenly these two pop up. Turns out we've got a lot in common."

He gestured with his bottle as he introduced them. "This is Jules, and this is Charley." Both hunters nodded as their names were spoken, relaxed and easy, their faces open to the gathering.

Emma stepped closer, looping an arm companionably through Jeff's. "This is Emma," Jeff continued, a certain pride in his voice, "my girlfriend. And that's Nick—a friend and a damn good shot. Bobbie—Nick's wife, over there by the fire—don't let her quiet fool you, she's tougher than the rest of us put together."

The circle widened just enough to welcome the newcomers. Greetings passed easily, laughter threading through the introductions. Storm, ever watchful from her kennel, let out a contented sigh, her eyes flickering open as she registered the new voices. The afternoon shadows stretched long across the clearing, the scent of pine and woodsmoke curling between old friends and new, as the story of the day settled into the gentle rhythm of belonging and possibility beneath the Missouri sky.

The beer was soon gone, and the new visitors became anxious.

Charley spoke, "It was good to meet all of you guys, but we need to get back to our campsite—our wives are waiting for us. Won't be long until supper time, and we sure need to be there when it's ready. Jeff, good luck tomorrow—maybe that big buck will run across you again."

Jules grinned, hoisting his empty bottle as a parting salute. "Don't let Clementine outshoot the rest of you," he teased, a glimmer of mischief in his eyes. The group exchanged another round of farewells, voices overlapping with wishes for luck and promises to keep an eye out for each other in the woods.

Emma watched as Charley and Jules disappeared among the pines, their laughter still echoing faintly. The clearing felt a touch quieter, settling back into its familiar rhythm, but now richer for the new stories and faces briefly woven into its tapestry.

Jeff walked over to Emma leaning over to kiss her hello. "You are not mad are you. What have you been doing?"

Not drinking beer and sluffing off the day. I bagged a fourteen pointer early on and have already sent it to the freezer locker. Then after that I went into town with Clementine and bought me some things to wear. I have decided that I am going to stay here Bobbie has some distant relative not far from here out by the fort. She and I talked about going out there sometime this week since we both can't hunt. If this is too boring and you want, you can catch a ride back to the city with Carl when he leaves. "Her voice was level unwavering wanting to encourage him to leave. Her thoughts were on keeping the case a secret as she was directed. She thought, 'so much the better.'

"Leave and not get a deer?... No really, I could do just that if you are not mad. I really have plenty of work I could do back in the city. Are you sure that you don't mind?"

Leaning close she pulled him by his shirt kissing him, "Of course not, the buck I got is going to give us more meat than we could eat in a year. If you don't mind missing the thrill of killing a prize buck, then go ahead and go with him. I'll walk you over to the tent and help you get your things together. I got Storm to keep me company. Besides I have plenty of reading material in my duffel bag to while away the hours. Nick still has to continue to hunt until he get his. That is until next Friday gets here."

Emma smiled, her lips curving as she leaned into the warmth of Jeff's whisper. "You old fox. I never said you had to go—I just wanted you to know you have a choice." Her voice softened, barely louder than the breeze.

She tugged gently at his hand, leading him toward the tent with steps that were unhurried, letting the hush of the woods and the fading of the day wrapped around them. "Let's get your things together," she said, glancing up to meet his eyes with a teasing glint

Hearing them talk Carl walked over and picked up one of the bags. "I am glad you decided to go back with me that is not a long drive but just kind of monotonous when you are alone. Storm was good company but just not quite like another driver."

Storm, sensing the shift, gave a quiet huff from her kennel, one ear twitching in the falling day. Emma paused, casting a fond look at the dog. "See? even Storm knows who the best company is."

Their quiet laughter mingled with the wood sounds—a gentle promise that, no matter what night brought, the clearing would still hold space for them, beneath the wide Missouri sky.

Somewhere beyond the trees, the possibility that perhaps the legendary buck—still roamed, waiting for the morning.

As the dust of Jeff and Paul's departure settled and the clearing grew quieter, Nick stepped forward, his voice carrying easily among the small group. The light in his eyes was earnest, colored by the need to restore a sense of order and unity in the wake of so much coming and going.

"With all the disarray created by everyone's arrivals and departures, I'd like to suggest something," Nick began, looking around at the faces turned toward him. "For dinner tonight, why don't we head into town, pick up a rental car for Bobbie, and then have dinner at that Golden Corral steak house? On me—no, not Uncle

Sam this time, just me. I feel like some of the stress today is my fault, and maybe a good meal can smooth things over."

He gave Bobbie a reassuring nod. "While Bobbie takes care of the car, the rest of us can hang back and start laying out our plans for tomorrow. What do you say?"

A gentle ripple of agreement passed through the group, the invitation a welcome anchor after a day of shifting plans. The thought of a warm meal and a few easy hours together brought a renewed ease, as if the coming evening might knit them back into a whole.

Storm thumped her tail in approval, and Emma caught Bobbie's eye, offering her a smile that spoke of fresh beginnings. The woods, watchful and still, listened as the group made their way toward the trucks, the promise of dinner and tomorrow's adventure carrying them forward beneath the gathering dusk.

The rattle of Storm in the kennel made Nick realize, a bit sheepish, that he'd forgotten Storm would be with Emma at all times. He turned toward the kennel and spoke, "My bad!" The apology was half-laugh, half-confession, drawing a grin from Emma and a curious, lopsided look from the dog herself.

Looking back to the group, Nick called, "Clementine, could you drive? Let Emma and Storm ride with you?" His tone was earnest, tinged with that same sense of wanting to set things right, of weaving everyone's needs into the fabric of the evening.

Clementine, already jingling keys in her hand, nodded with a wink. "Of course. The more the merrier, and I'll bet Storm will appreciate having her window rolled down for the drive." She flashed Emma a warm smile, and Emma's shoulders eased, the little knot of tension between responsibility and belonging finally untying itself.

With logistics sorted and the sky deepening to indigo, the group shuffled into vehicles, voices drifting between open doors and the hush of the trees. The engine's hum, the shuffle of feet, and

Storm's contented sigh as Emma settled beside her set the tone—a quiet assurance that, even in the midst of change, they were moving forward together, each one accounted for.

As the two vehicles were loaded, the group found their places with the practiced ease of those who have spent days together, each person falling into a familiar rhythm. The engines grumbled softly to life and, with headlights cutting gentle arcs through the dusk, they rolled out of the campsite's embrace.

The short drive felt almost ceremonial, a quiet respite after the day's turbulence. Conversation was low, the kind of comfortable silence that speaks of mutual understanding more than any words could. As they neared the Ranger shack, both vehicles paused, windows sliding down with a sigh. The ranger, perched on a stool with a thermos in hand, raised an easy arm in greeting and offered a friendly wave-through. It felt like a small benediction—the world outside acknowledging their journey, letting them pass unhindered.

The town's streets wound ahead, a gentle flow against the encroaching traffic. Golden Corral steak house sign, a beacon of predictable comfort, soon came into view. The vehicles pulled in side by side, as everyone exited, they stretched and reoriented themselves to new surroundings.

The others stood waiting outside their vehicles while Emma put Storms muzzle on her. Patting her side reassuring her that it would be alright. Letting Storm with Emma in tow; they all filed into the dining place. Greeted by the hostess as she seated them. Everyone accepted the menus and ordered their drinks.

Nick's expression was easy to read he was hinting that they could order anything on the menu.

When the server returned with a tray of glistening glasses—cola fizzing, water beading, coffee steaming—she gathered up their food choices with practiced cheer, pausing to answer a question about the house special before whisking their menus away. The clatter and chatter of the steak house washed over the table, punctuated by the sizzle from the kitchen and the ringing laughter from a nearby booth.

Left to themselves, the group relaxed further, trading off the day's dust for the comfort of padded seats and warm lamplight. Clementine, turning her iced tea in her hands, broke the quiet first. "I can't say I've ever been someplace quite like this—cowboy boots and neon, steak big as your head." She grinned, her tone half playful, half genuine curiosity.

Bobbie leaned in. "Where I grew up, you got your steak at home, and if you wanted atmosphere, you ate on the porch." Her eyes sparkled. "But I could get used to this."

Emma smiled, glancing around at the wood-paneled walls and the array of ranch memorabilia. "Closest I've come was a barbecue joint with picnic tables. Nothing this... curated." She hesitated, then added, "Though I think Storm would appreciate a drive-through more than table service." Storm, curled beneath the table, let out a contented sigh.

Nick chuckled. "First time for me too. Guess we're starting a tradition?" His voice carried a note of invitation, as if to say: here's something new, and we're all in it together.

Their remarks bounced easily from one to the next, a shared discovery of comfort in unfamiliar surroundings. Each admission, each small laugh, wove them more tightly into the gentle pleasantness of the evening, the unfamiliar restaurant already beginning to feel—if only for a night—like home.

Watching as the server returned with a large tray of food, everyone eyed the procession with a blend of anticipation and reverence. The server, balancing her cargo with practiced grace, announced each dish before setting it gently in front of its eager recipient. Plates arrived trailing ribbons of savory steam—grilled steaks glistening under pools of melted butter, heaps of mashed potatoes crowned with chives, tangles of crispy onion rings, and a bowl of mac and cheese boasting a golden, bubbling crust.

The table, moments ago humming with conversation, fell briefly into a hush as the aroma enveloped them. Clementine let out a delighted laugh, eyes wide as she surveyed her plate. Bobbie grinned, already hunting for the perfect bite, while Emma carefully nudged a piece of steak into her mouth.

Even Nick, usually quick with a quip, paused to take in the sight—a banquet assembled just for them, the kind that filled not only bellies but spirits too. Utensils clinked and murmurs of satisfaction rose, each person savoring that first, long-awaited taste. Around them, the restaurant's din faded into the background, replaced by simple, unspoken gratitude: after the day's trials, this meal together was its own quiet celebration.

With their palates satisfied, the table began to stir from their food-induced reverie. Conversation returned in soft waves, punctuated by easy laughter and the contented shuffle of plates being set aside. Bobbie, her cheeks still rosy from the meal, leaned over toward Nick. To the surprise—and secret delight—of those watching, she pressed a gentle kiss to his cheek and whispered, "Dear, could you have Doc drive me to the car rental office? I'll see you in the RV. I'll be waiting up for you. I saw the showers on our way out and I plan to be nice and clean—I advise you to stop and do the same. Doc will be back in a jiffy, then you can move everyone to that conference room in the back and have your strategy meeting. Don't work too hard. There are no kids to interrupt us tonight."

Her words, half teasing and wholly affectionate, left a ripple of amusement around the table. Nick's face broke into an irrepressible grin as he nodded, the easy understanding between them speaking of long familiarity. Doc, catching the tail end of the exchange, rose with a mock salute and offered his arm to Bobbie, who accepted it with a flourish worthy of a ballroom.

"Duty calls," Doc quipped, and the two disappeared into the gentle chaos of the restaurant, leaving the others with the faintest echo of their laughter.

Nick watched Bobbie go, a thoughtful look passing over his face before he turned back to the rest of the group. "Well," he said, dragging his fork idly through a stray drizzle of steak sauce, "looks like we've got a window for that meeting after all. Who's up for a little early-night strategy session?"

The invitation hovered in the lamplight, greeted by groans and smiles in equal measure. Emma stretched her arms overhead, feigning reluctance but already clearing her space on the table. Clementine gathered her notes, her eyes gleaming with anticipation. Storm, sensing the shift, perked up beneath the table, tail thumping quietly.

As they gathered themselves, readying for the next act of the evening, there was a newfound sense of meaning—born of shared meals and quieter promises, and the unspoken thrill of a night stretching out before them, free of interruption and rich with possibility.

Nick excused himself from the table, weaving through the softly bustling restaurant to seek out the manager. After a brief, genial exchange, he returned with a triumphant grin and a nod toward the rear of the dining room.

"This way, folks," he said, rising to his feet and gathering the group's attention. They trailed behind him, plates and coffee cups in hand, following his lead past the last clusters of diners. At the end of a quiet hallway, Nick pushed open a set of flexible doors and ushered everyone into the empty conference room—a space thick with anticipation and the faint scent of coffee lingering from some earlier meeting.

Once inside, they settled into the cushioned chairs arranged around a long table. Nick closed the doors behind them, muffling the noise of the restaurant and cocooning them in a private hush. Clementine slid her notes onto the polished surface, Emma poured the last of the decaf into mugs, and Storm circled beneath the table, finding a patch of carpet to call her own.

For a moment, the room was theirs alone—a small, bright island carved out of the night, ready for quiet plans and laughter, unhurried and uninterrupted.

Nick went to the whiteboard, grasping the magic marker as he turned with a glint of mock solemnity. "So, I'm going to put the first scenario on the board, and you folks—" he paused, winking at Emma and Clementine—"You guys, girls, anyone—tell me how we're going to tackle it. Anyone?"

He uncapped the marker with a dramatic flourish and, in big looping script, scrawled; KIDNAPPING... He stepped back, letting the word hang in the air as boldly as it did on the whiteboard—a challenge, an enigma, a riddle waiting to be unraveled. "Anyone?" Nick's eyebrows arched with playful insistence. "Why do we think this is a kidnapping? What's the giveaway? No ransom note!"

There was a hush, the muffled clink of coffee cups as Emma sat forward, brow furrowed in thought. Clementine tapped her pen against her notebook, eyes distant as she sifted through details. Storm lifted her head, sensing the group's focus shift, tail giving a tentative thump.

Emma broke the silence first, voice low but certain. "I see that, and we talked about before there was no request for a ransom but that leaves the retaliation angle. That is part one of the theory part two is the human trafficking for sex. So, let's look at the first, retaliation... The professor has not been contacted to inform him that it was for his defection. But that don't discount that theory, maybe the professor has not been honest with us. We need to let me, and Clem talk to him. But not before we make one try and using Storm. I believe that if we take storm to the victim's dormitory and get some of her clothing and get her scent then go to the Tommys Oriental Palace and see what it brings up. If the coed has been there recently, we might get an answer. If she is being held somewhere in the building, we might get lucky. The problem is in the serving area; she is going to be distracted by the many others that have been there. I am hoping that if we can get upstairs and if she is being kept there, we will find her."

"That sound good but how about before we send in Storm, we have Emma go in since she is (No insult intended) of the same heritage, maybe she could try to get next to one of the servers, you know as a friend. Maybe able to get any kind of information. If she is there under duress she might want to get away and help us. Strictly under the aspect that Emma is just a private citizen." Doc suggested.

Instead of speaking out Clementine raised her hand. "Yes?" Nick answered.

"All of this sounds workable but in the meantime this girl is still missing we need to get a better handle on what we can do right away to find her. Time is of the essence; I need to call DC and find out for sure if the CIA has anything that will shed some light on the retaliation aspect."

"Doc, you and I need to drive out to the professors house in the morning and firm up that theory. Surely, he is not being totally up front about all of this. As big as that place is he must have some help, we should talk to them." Nick added.

Doc stood up pacing the floor waiting for it all to settle walking up to the white board. He wrote MHP—St. Louis—FBI—DHS. "Who's left? ...The CIA!"

"You're right since Clem works for the DHS maybe she should be able get them to share some information. Surely if it was the retaliation angle, they must know about it. So, no need to recap but I am going to check at the college. That should cover all of the bases.

Now if Doc don't mind dropping me off at the shower; I want to scrub off all of this woods smell that I didn't get today. "Winking.

While Nick paid the check, all of the others filed out and got into the vehicles. Storm was excited to get out and leave the smell of the food—and not getting any. Emma walked her over to the dog path, allowing her to stretch her legs. Enjoying the night air, she waited until Nick and Doc had pulled away, then joined Clementine with Storm in the car.

In the quiet, Clementine adjusted her seat, glancing in the rearview mirror at Emma and the eager Labrador. "You think she's really up for this?" she asked softly, nodding toward Storm, who had settled in the back, tail thumping against the upholstery.

Emma smiled, still catching her breath from the brisk walk. "She's been itching for something to do. The scent work will be a treat for her." She ran a gentle hand along Storm's flank, the tension of the evening dissolving into anticipation.

Clementine started the engine, headlights sweeping arcs across the empty lot. "We'll drop by the dorm first, like you said. Get her something with the girl's scent. Then...?"

"We could make it a point to question some of the other coeds in the dorm. Somebody might know something... one little piece that would help us."

"Yeah." Emma buckled herself in, eyes sharp in the dashboard glow. "But we play it careful. If anything feels off, we regroup."

The night evening pressed cool and silent as the car slipped onto the road, headlights carving a path through the campus shadows. Storm sat upright, nose pressed to the window, as if sensing the seriousness beneath the quiet. For a moment, all three—the handler, the investigator, and the dog—shared a sense of determined purpose, each ready to follow the clues wherever they might lead.

The buzz of the store's neon sign flickered through the windshield, casting odd shadows over the dash as Doc sat drumming his fingers on the steering wheel.   He watched Nick through the plate glass, the way he moved with that particular blend of purpose and fatigue—a man trying to patch something invisible with small, necessary gestures.

Nick emerged a few minutes later, brown bag in hand, the bottle's neck poking out just enough to catch the light. He slid into the passenger seat with a satisfied sigh, offering Doc a crooked grin.

"Mission accomplished," he said, setting the bag on the floor between his feet. "Maybe tonight we'll actually have a moment to catch our breath, you know? Just a little bit of normal before the next round of questions."

Doc nodded, easing the car back onto the quiet street. The city was winding down, lights dimming, people tucked away behind closed doors. For a while, neither spoke—each lost in the pale hush that sometimes follows a day crowded with uncertainty.

Finally, as they neared the campground, Nick broke the silence. " Don't forget to stop at the showers, I bet that Bobbie has left me a towel and a change of clothes there for me. She has it all planned out. "

Doc let out a low chuckle. "If I didn't have a wife waiting for me at home I might disagree. But as it is I hope you have a good night."

The pine needles crunching under the tires as they pulled into their spot beneath the trees. Nick gathered his bag and paused, looking at Doc with something almost like gratitude. "Thanks for the lift. And for...just being steady."

Doc shrugged, a small smile ghosting across his features. "Get some rest, Nick. Tomorrow's another day."

The door thudded shut and Nick made his way toward the soft glow of the shower, the night cool and forgiving against his skin. For a moment, there was peace—a brief, precious reprieve—before the work began again.

Nick hurried to the primitive shower house, the clothes and a towel with his shampoo and shaving bag was waiting for him with a note. "Hurry. I am all alone"

Chapter Seven

Once again, the shrill sound of the starting whistle woke Nick and Bobbie. reaching over to Nick, Bobbie cooed "Last night was great, the Margaritas were just the right thing to top off an already good night. Beer is alright to pass the day with but when I really want to relax a little hard liquor just seems to do the trick.

Don't get up I will get the coffee and start breakfast. It's only six o'clock I am sure you can rest an awhile. Try to recover from last night. You felt like a teenager, I hope it was the new see through yellow teddy you struggled with getting off of me that seemed to slow you down. I definitely feel that we needed this time together and just think if you solve this case early, we will still have the rest of the time together."

Reaching over and pulling the other pillow and stuffing it under his head Nick grinned letting the memories of the night before slip through his head. "Yes, it was a good night and as you say it would be a good thing that we found the coed safe and sound. I might even get a chance to go out and find that big buck that Jeffery mentioned. That does sound good don't it." Holding back his laugh.

"Whoa...whoa...whoa...who was talking about hunting?" Nickolas Curtis!"

Rolling out of bed he dashed across the short distance in the RV and grabbed Bobbie up and twirled her around holding her close. "My dear wife I was kidding I agree that last night was so hot in the arm for us two old married folks. Something that I am glad that happened. I'll be finished working tonight and we can have pizza and beer. Then we can open another bottle of mix and slowly relax as two lovers, we can sit outside in the quiet of the trees and let nature take its course speaking of nature...duty calls. Hugging her close and kissing her. Rushing to the bathroom.

Nick reemerged, face still damp, and cheeks flushed with the brisk morning routine. The scent of frying bacon and fresh coffee mingled in the close air of the RV, drawing him toward the kitchenette where Bobbie awaited, a hint of mischief sparking in her eyes.

Waiting by the door with a cup of coffee when Nick came out, she handed it to him. "My dear your breakfast will be finished in a shake just sit down after you give me one more of those yummy kisses."

He pulled Bobbie close, feeling her warmth as she pressed against him, the silk of her kimono whispering to the floor in a shimmer of color. Nick's arms found their way around her, balancing the cup of coffee with one hand as Bobbie's fingers traced slow, affectionate patterns along his back. Their laughter mingled with the golden spill of sunlight that dappled through the small window, illuminating Bobbie's graceful form as she leaned in, their embrace both playful and tender. For a moment, the world outside the RV faded to quiet, and time seemed to hover—just the two of them, caught in the gentle hush of morning, wrapped in each other's arms and the lingering glow of affection.

A heartbeat later, Bobbie stepped back, her eyes dancing with the promise of the day ahead, sunlight painting her in radiant hues. "Now, my dear, if you don't sit down, this coffee might end up decorating the floor," she teased, her voice light and full of warmth.

Gratified with the tiny morning Nick sat down, Bobbie turned and bent down to pick up her Kimono. Nick quietly said "Leave it for a while I like the scenery better that way, just something that you can't do at home. Then set across from this wonderful breakfast you have made. You are so beautiful."

Setting the Melmac plate down Bobbie obliged her husband and began sipping her coffee. The pleasant look on Nick face said it all she was happy to sit there and feel loved. Their fifteen-year marriage was working; she was comfortable to be alone in her birthday suit with the man she loved.

The loud rap on the door startled both of them as they were finishing their second cup of coffee. Bobbie jumped up and pulled on her kimono and stepped to the door. Opening it only a crack to answer it, she could see it was Doc, his bright face sporting sunglasses. "Is the old man alive?" he joked.

"Yes, give us a minute, we aren't dressed—be a minute." Bobbie closed the door quickly; her cheeks flushed with a mix of amusement and embarrassment.   Nick grinned, shaking his head as he took one last sip of coffee, savoring the domestic quiet that had just been so sweetly interrupted.

"Well, duty calls for all of us, it seems," he said, sliding into his pants and tossing Bobbie a playful wink. She laughed, gathering her hair up and tying her robe tighter, the easy understanding between them undimmed by the abrupt intrusion. Slipping into a shirt he strapped his revolver onto his ankle. Bobbie threw his tie around his neck sliding it back and forth playfully. Handing him his sport coat she gripped the lapels and kissed him.

Outside, Doc's silhouette lingered by the door, arms crossed and foot tapping impatiently, his posture radiating the kind of cheerful authority that only came with years of being a professional. Bobbie glanced over her shoulder at Nick. "Ready to face the world, Detective?"

Nick straightened, running a hand through his hair before planting a quick kiss on Bobbie's cheek. "With you at my side? Always."

Together they approached the door, the last traces of their private morning lingering in the air. When Bobbie swung it open fully, Doc's grin widened.

"Glad to see you both are still among the living," he quipped, stepping inside. The warmth of shared laughter and the promise of the day ahead drifted through the RV, mingling with the fading aroma of breakfast and the golden light of morning.

Stepping out of the doorway they were greeted by the early morning sunlight as it filtered thru the pines. Emma leading Storm was just coming out of the underbrush over by the largest pine in the area. Making their way to the RV she waved hello. They could see that She was working with Storm as her walk came as a cadence, strictly as a handler. It was not a play day it was a duty day and Emma wanted to keep it strictly business. Approaching the two men she stopped several yards away from them. "STAY! Leaving Storm sitting where they stopped. Continuing to beside them she greeted them

"Morning men are you ready to find this coed and get back to being on

 vacation? I have a favor to ask this afternoon I would like to try to get next to one of the servers at the diner and would like for Bobbie to watch Storm."

Bobbie was still in the doorway watching. Turning back Nick hollered "Hey babe did you hear that?"

Bobbie hesitating to come out dressed as she was stepped out holding the screen door leaning around it, shielding her. Emma walked close and said "Morning Bobbie I want to ask a favor... could you watch Storm this afternoon. I want to see if I can get inside of the restaurant, I am sure she will behave with you she always enjoyed it when you were at the house. But just to make sure can we come in now and you can acquaint her with you."

Nick eager to get to work spoke "You ladies work it out Doc and I need to get going we need to head to the college. If you need me or Doc, just call me or text me. See you later. Walking to Docs car where he was waiting inside."

Waiting until the vehicle had driven away Emma turned and said "Heel" bringing Storm to her feet.

Bobbie stood beside the door as Emma and Storm stepped in, the dog's nails clicking softly against the floor. Once they were both inside, Bobbie gently closed the door behind them, sealing out the morning and inviting a hush into the RV. She moved to the couch and sat down, smoothing her kimono with a practiced hand. "Coffee?" she offered, gesturing to the half-full pot on the counter.

"Yes, please," Emma replied, unclipping Storm's lead. "Let's just let her settle down for a minute—she'll want to sniff everything, it's all new to her. We can relax for a bit." Emma's eyes drifted over Bobbie appreciatively. "I just love your kimono. I can never find one as pretty as that. I'd love to know where you got it."

A hint of color touched Bobbie's cheeks. "It was a gift, actually. But if I ever see another like it, I'll snag it for you."

Emma grinned, leaning back into the RV's worn armchair as Storm began her investigative circuit of the living room, nose twitching at every cushion and corner. "I see the shock of being on assignment has worn off. I hope you two had a good—well, what should I call it?" She broke into laughter. "Not quite make-up sex, since you were not fighting, but whatever it was, you both look fine now."

Bobbie snorted, rolling her eyes in good humor. "Maybe we just needed breakfast and a little honesty,"

She said, pouring coffee into two mugs. "Or maybe it's just the magic of a new day." She handed Emma a cup, her kimono fluttering softly as she moved.

Emma took the mug with a grateful nod, her gaze following Storm as the dog finally settled by Emma's feet, content. "Well, whatever it is, I say we enjoy it while it lasts. There's no telling what the rest of today will bring."

Emma took a slow sip of coffee, letting the warmth settle into her hands. "You know," she began, her voice softer, "let's just forget I mentioned the diner. We should keep you out of any and all of this case, Bobbie. Let's just say you're spending the afternoon with your old friend Storm. She's always liked you—a lot more than she likes most people, honestly."

Storm, hearing her name, lifted her head and wagged her tail, a living affirmation. Emma reached down to ruffle the fur between the dog's ears. "If you like, I can bring her kennel over, set it up by the outside of this house on wheels, so you don't have to be tied down inside all day. Actually, that might be perfect. But not until I finish this cup of joe." She grinned, relaxing for the first time that morning.

Bobbie, a little embarrassed by the way she kept fussing with the hem of her short, silky kimono, stood up and shook her head ruefully.

"Give me a minute to grab something more appropriate for a visit," she said, her tone tinged with self-deprecating humor. "I know we've known each other since college, but somehow it feels different now. We're both grown up and married. Well, I'm just a bit chilly, too."

She flashed Emma a smile and retreated to the small bedroom, the kimono swirling around her knees.

Left alone in the hush of the RV, Emma watched Storm sniff at the edge of a throw rug, her own thoughts turning inward for a moment. The day stretched before them—uncertain, perhaps, but at least for now, there was coffee, friendship, and the loyal presence of a dog who understood more than she let on.

Setting her cup on the kitchen table when it was empty Emma stepped to the bedroom door. "Hey kid I am going to drag her kennel over be right back, I am going to leave storm here just ignore her and she'll be fine." Turning to the outside door she said "STAY" Going out the door.

Storm was as still as a mouse waiting for her master to return, happy to lay on the cool floor out of the bright morning sunlight. Bobbie walked out of the bedroom perking Storms ears making her raise her head long enough to be reassured that Bobbie was welcome.

Picking up her coffee cup she added a bit of hot coffee to her cup and sat down on the couch waiting for Emma to return. Minutes later the door came open and Emma came in. "I brought the kennel over and put it in the shade. Her water bowl is there but you will have to fill it no hurry You won't have a visitor until afternoon. Clementine should be here soon. If you don't mind, I'll just wait in here it is just a tad hot in the sunshine. These dress suits are hot."

Talking about the hunt and the nice camp grounds and other girl talk they waited for Clementine. Storm was drifting off to sleep when they heard a short tap of the car horn. Clementine was eager to go to work.

Storms ears perked at the noise but remained laying down she knew that until Emma called her, she was going to enjoy this quiet place of rest.

"COME" brought her to her feet and the short distance to Emma's side. Emma opened the door, and they went out saying "Thanks" to Bobbie.

Outside the glaring sunlight caused them both to squint as they went to the unmarked police car. As Storm settled in the back seat Emma put her muzzle on, saying "Yes, I know you don't like this nasty thing, but Clementine is just cautious that we might be bothered by someone. You just lay down there and we are going to visit the dormitory where there are lots of pretty girls. But none as pretty as you "Rubbing her under her neck.

Opening the car door and sliding in, Emma took a quick survey of Clementine, curiosity flickering across her features. Had she gone straight to bed last night at the motel, or had she let the evening spirit guide her to a local watering hole? As Emma settled back into the seat, she glanced over in the sharp morning light and caught the faint but unmistakable redness lingering around Clementine's eyes. That answered that question.

"We had a good night, me and Storm," Emma said, her tone light with curiosity as she buckled in. "I took a shower and finished off those two beers you left, then Storm decided the sleeping bag was hers. With Jeff gone back to the city, it was just us girls in that tent— but we managed just fine. How was your night?"

She watched Clementine for a moment, waiting for her to fill in the spaces: the laughter, perhaps a secret, or just the comfort of solitude. Storm shifted in the back seat, her nose pressed to the window, tail thumping softly as if she too was eager for the day's possibilities.

"I am not sure that you knew this but the entire basement of the diner in question is a tavern. After I left you guys last evening I went back to my motel and changed clothes. Put on my slinkiest clothes and went there and had a few drinks. I was sure that they are using that bar to run hookers through it. One of them didn't look old enough to be there let alone drinking. I might have stayed too long as I can feel the effects this morning

Emma grinned, the corners of her mouth twitching upward with both surprise and understanding as Clementine's frank words hung in the air. She could picture her partner at that smoky bar, eyes sharp beneath tired lids, blending in just enough to observe what needed to be seen.

"So, you were staking out the bar while the rest of us were counting stars," Emma replied, her tone admiring but tinged with concern. "Sounds like you confirmed more than we bargained for. If they're running girls that young, we need to move fast."

Storm, hearing the shift in voices, perked up again, her intelligent gaze flickering between the two women as if she understood the seriousness. Emma reached back to give the dog an encouraging pat.

The drive was short as the dorm was only eight to ten blocks from the entrance to the campgrounds. The large six-story building loomed in the sunlight as they drove through the town, windows gleaming and facade casting long shadows across the street. Neighborhood life unfurled on either side—bikes propped against stoops, a jogger pausing to mop sweat from his brow, the faint aroma of fresh bread drifting from a bakery on the corner. Emma kept her eyes peeled for any sign of unusual activity, while Storm's head tracked the shifting cityscape, ears attuned to every honk. Clementine turned off the main road and eased the unmarked car up to the curb, adrenaline threading beneath their anticipation.

For a heartbeat, the three sat in measured silence, gazing up at the building. Every window seemed to hold the potential for secrets, for answers—or for new mysteries.

Clementine's mood remained upbeat, undaunted by the grim details. "I've got a call in to my boss in St. Louis. Should hear back soon about that warrant. But first, let's get Storm a good whiff of the dormitory. Maybe your pretty friend here will find us a scent trail."

"Let's do it," Emma agreed, her energy renewed by purpose. She opened her car door, letting the hot sun spill into the vehicle, and Storm leapt out eagerly, nose twitching for a new challenge. As the trio crossed the parking lot toward the dormitory building, Emma glanced at Clementine, her gratitude unspoken but evident. No matter how rough the night or how tangled the case, she knew she could count on her partner's tenacity—and Storm's nose—to get them closer to the truth.

As it happened, the security guard for the dorms was just coming out of the main office, adjusting his cap against the glare. Clementine caught sight of him first and gently stopped Emma with a hand to her arm, nodding toward the uniformed man.

"Maybe we should check in with security," she murmured, keeping her voice low but firm. "No information about her missing, but we need to get some of her school work for her grandfather. She's staying with him for a while—her grandmother's in St. Louis for the week and she's visiting him. I'll use my I.D., just follow my lead."

Emma gave a subtle nod; her nerves sharpened now with a new direction. Storm circled at their feet, tail still, gaze fixed on the guard with canine alertness.

Clementine straightened her jacket and strode toward the security office, Emma close behind. The guard—a solid man in his early fifties with a clipboard tucked under one arm—paused as they approached, his expression blending professional curiosity with the weary expectation that came from too many uneventful shifts.

"Good morning, sir," Clementine began, flashing her badge with practiced ease. "Detective Clementine Bishop, D.H.S. This is my partner, Detective Emma Lee—and Storm, her K9. We're following up on a case involving a friend of one of your residents. She'll been staying with him for the week while her grandmother's away, but she needs some of her school materials picked up. Would you be able to help us access her room?"

The guard's eyes flicked between the badge, the detectives, and the dog, weighing the gentle authority in Clementine's voice. After a moment, he nodded, reaching for a key ring at his belt.

"Of course, officers. Always happy to assist. Names Gregory Procter." He gestured for them to follow, leading the way across the lobby's tiled floor toward the elevator. Storm fell into step beside them, her nose quivering with the promise of new scents.

As they waited for the elevator, Clementine leaned in, her voice no more than a whisper for Emma alone: "Stay sharp. If anything seems off—neighbors, notes, you name it—let's take it seriously. Something about this doesn't feel simple."

Emma met her gaze, her gratitude renewed. "I'm with you."

The doors slid open with a soft chime, and the trio—plus one keen-nosed companion—stepped into the unknown, ready to let instinct and persistence carry them closer to the heart of the mystery.

Stepping out onto the third floor, they followed Security guard Gregory down a softly lit corridor, the hush of the hallway broken only by the muted squeak of his shoes and the faint jingle of keys. He paused before the resident's door, working the lock with a practiced hand. The door yielded with a gentle sigh.

Clementine slipped smoothly past him, eyes already scanning the interior for anything out of place. Emma followed but lingered at the threshold, lightly pressing her palm against Gregory's arm. "We've got it from here, thanks. We'll lock up when we're done." Her tone was polite, but final.

Gregory nodded, stepping back, and Emma eased the door closed behind them. Storm, nose quivering, gave a soft whine and tugged gently at her leash, eager to inspect the unfamiliar scents.

The dorm room greeted them with the peculiar emptiness of a space in limbo. Bed neatly made, the surface of the chest of drawers clustered with framed photographs—snapshots of family gatherings, summer days, and laughter frozen in time. Clementine's gaze lingered on the group portraits—parents, siblings, a scattering of cousins—the warmth of familial connection radiating from each image.

Across the room, atop a separate chest of drawers, stood only two pictures: one of her mother, the other of her father, both pale-haired, their smiles reserved, distant. The contrast was striking—not just in number, but in sentiment. Where the crowded dresser hummed with the chaos of family, the duo on the far side felt almost like a shrine, private and apart.

Storm, meanwhile, nosed along the bedframe, then sat, tail thumping once, as if announcing she'd found something interesting. Emma knelt beside her, fingers searching along the edge of the mattress, ever attuned to her partner's silent cues.

Clementine moved to the window, glancing at the view outside before returning her attention to the room's silent stories. She sifted through the girl's textbooks stacked beside the desk—Chemistry, a spiral-bound journal with a sun doodled on the cover. She flipped it open, scanning the first page for anything that might help them understand the girl's sudden disappearance.

"Look at this," Emma murmured, drawing Clementine over. Hidden beneath the mattress was a small, navy notebook—its cover worn; the elastic band stretched thin. Inside, cryptic notes and lists, some addresses and names underlined twice, along with a series of dates that didn't match the school calendar.

Emma's pulse quickened. "Let's document everything. Take photos, but don't move anything you don't have to." Her voice was quiet but charged with purpose.

Storm pressed her snout to the floor near the nightstand, intent on something unseen. Emma retrieved the notebook and flipped to a bookmarked page, brow furrowing as she scanned its contents.

"Whatever happened to the Granddaughter isn't jumping out at us. But I think since this note book is not a diary, I think we should take it with us and show it to the grandmother. She is bound to know more than the grandfather. You know kinsman-ship." Clementine said, voice low.

They worked in tandem, the silence of the room stretching between them—an unspoken pact that whatever secrets this space held, they would not rest until every clue was brought into the light.

Throwing back the bedspread lifting the pillow revealed a pair of pajama's neatly folded under it. "That's it," Emma said. Scooping up the soft clothes she held them up to Storms nose. "TRACK!"

Strom's reaction was one of agreement as she gave out a loud bark, they walked out the door locking it and returning to the car. The pajama's in hand along with the navy-blue notebook. Heading to the grandfathers house.

Settling in the car Storm laid down in the rear seat and Emma took out her phone. "I think I need to check with Nick to see where they are; before we go out to the grandfathers house. Then we need to find someplace to get Storm a drink. She can't tell us, but it's been long enough, and I could use a rest room, how about you Clem?"

"Good idea you call, and I'll drive to someplace for both of us." Chuckling.

Emma tapped Nick's number, her thumb drumming a silent rhythm against the steering wheel as the line rang. He picked up with a brisk,

"Nick here, what's up, Emma? We were just leaving the prof's house. The Grandmother was here—nothing new, but she's convinced the past isn't the culprit this time. The last of the players are dead, she says. But she thinks we need to check out the Tommys Oriental Palace. She's got a feeling something's going on there, maybe trafficking. Apparently, she's got some information Clementine should hear. We should meet up. Also, Clementine needs to get that warrant."

Emma exchanged a glance with Clementine, who nodded as she made the next turn. "Okay, pick a place to meet. We could use a break—Storm needs water and I need a restroom. How about that fast food place up the road from the camp turnoff?"

"Works for us," Nick replied. "We'll head there. I'll tell the Doc... No, wait a minute I got it on speaker and Doc says that he talked to his captain, and we can use the conference room in his building. We have to get a warrant from Springfield, and we will have all of the comforts of home. It's that big white building down by the intersection on the same road as the campgrounds. See you there."

There was only one car in the parking lot of the lab building leaving plenty of room for the two cars to park close to the entrance, Doc hurried out of his car first to unlock the door leaving Nick to escort the grandmother into the building. A few minutes later Clementine and Emma along with Storm drove in and parked. Following Nick inside Emma and Storm hung back allowing the others to get settled in the room.

Emma excused herself and led Storm to the grassy area on the side of the building letting her loose to enjoy the freedom of the leash. Minutes later doc came out with a pan of water, giving it to Emma. Storm smelling the liquid rushed over and began drinking. When she was finished Emma clicked on her leash and walked her into the building following Doc to the ladies room.

"Thanks Doc you are a life saver especially for the water, as always Storm comes first. She is a little impatient. I'll just be a minute if you don't mind, please find something to drink for the others." Closing the door behind her and Storm.

In the rest room Emma bent down and rubbed Storm, a small touch of affection for her good behavior. As she sat down Storm sniffed around the room, unsure about the sanitized smell of the room.

Joining the others in the conference room Emma and storm sat close to the door. Slightly away from the others. Emma was concerned that maybe the grandmother might be afraid of storm.

With scraping of the chairs as they all got situated to hear Nick who was in the front of the room. He began I would like to introduce Lan Huu Hahn, the missing girl Maya Van Hahn grandmother." The lady stood and bowed smiling. They could all tell that this was the matriarch of the family, not a sit in the back of the room type but a very modern women of the world.

"Next, I want to introduce Clementine Hernadez from the DHS, and in the back of the room is Emma Lin and Storm from the St. Louis PD. First, I want to thank Mrs. Hahn for coming down here with us so she could her thought's. You can stay seated if we all can hear you. Just repeat what you told us, so we are all on the same page."

"Like I told Nick and doc, the Oriental Palace has been a bad place ever since it opened. The owners are only out to make money; they allow all kinds of things to go on there. Please excuse me but they allow and encourage the young girls to sell their bodies for money. There is one girl that Maya brought to our house that dresses so revealing, well she has to be... how can I say it? You know what I mean any way, we my husband and I had forbid Maya to associate with her. But who knows what they do." Stopping for a minute she waited, taking a drink of the diet coke that Doc had given the women.

Nick spoke "Go ahead and see if I got this straight the week end Maya was supposed to be with your husband why was that? Tell the others."

She was supposed to be with my husband not to visit totally but because she was how do you say grounded. Yes, I know she is nineteen years old, but we are responsible for her as long as she is attending the same college as her grandfather is teaching at. We have some pride. So anyway, about the Oriental Palace not all of the girls that work there are not citizens they have been brought in by some really tough guys. They drive them out to the fort and weekends and well you know"...

"What about the theory that she might be being held because of your husband defecting?" Nick asked.

"No oh no that is not possible the man that Pete thinks might steal her has been dead for some years. I think my husband is ashamed to admit that Maya could possibly be associating with that Lan Tran Hoang girl."

Emma raised her hand. Nick nodded toward her, "Yes, Emma, have you got a question?"

"Not exactly," Emma replied, glancing around at the group. "But I think we should let Mrs. Hahn know that we're currently waiting on a warrant to go into the Oriental Palace. Also, Clem and I have some clothing we believe might belong to your granddaughter. Clem, could you dash out and get them?"

She turned to Mrs. Hahn. "We need to be sure that these items truly belonged to Maya. We found the clothes in what we think was her bed, but since you're here, it would be helpful to confirm they're really hers."

Clementine nodded briskly and slipped from the room, her heels tapping a crisp rhythm down the corridor. The room fell quiet again, all eyes turning to the grandmother, who, after a moment's pause, straightened in her chair, her expression composed but anxious.

Doc refilled Mrs. Hahn cup as Emma continued gently, "It's important, ma'am, because if these are her things, it might help us trace where she's been—and who she's been with—at the Oriental Palace."

A moment later, Clem returned, carrying a clear evidence bag with carefully folded clothing inside. She offered it to Mrs. Hahn, who accepted it with trembling hands. The woman's eyes scanned the garments, her breath catching as she traced the familiar patterns and colors. A tear slid silently down her cheek, and she nodded. "Yes," she whispered. "These are Maya. I bought her these pajama's for her..."

The confirmation hung in the air, laden with both sorrow and a glimmer of renewed urgency. Emma nodded softly, her own voice gentle. "Thank you, Mrs. Hahn. That helps us more than you know.

We'll keep you informed as soon as we have the warrant and can move forward."

Nick offered a reassuring look to the grandmother, and the group, for a moment, felt united in their determination to bring Maya safely home.

Nick leaned forward; his tone gentle but probing. "Mrs. Hahn, is there any reason that you would think Maya might have gone anywhere else and chosen not to tell you?"

Mrs. Hahn, her hands still clutching the pajama fabric, shook her head slowly, uncertainty clouding her features. "She always told me where she was going, even if it was only to the book store. She's a thoughtful girl."

Emma exchanged a glance with Nick, then reached for another evidence bag—this one holding a small, well-worn notebook. She held it up so Mrs. Hahn could see.

"We have this notebook," Emma explained. "We'd like for you to look at it. There are several dates written inside, but they don't seem to correlate with any of the college activities we've checked. Maybe you can help us make sense of them?"

Cautiously, Mrs. Hahn accepted the notebook. Her eyes lingered on the cover before she opened it, her fingers trembling as she flipped through the pages. The group watched in silence, hope flickering across their faces as they waited for any sign of recognition, any clue that might reveal more about Maya recent whereabouts—or the secrets she kept.

Mrs. Hahn thumbed through the notebook, her brow furrowing as she carefully read each page. Her gaze was intent, searching for any detail that might spark recognition. Occasionally, she paused, appearing to sift through her memories for context or explanation. Upon reaching the final page, she closed the notebook with a quiet sigh.

"I do not believe so," she said, shaking her head. "However, I have been quite preoccupied with my numerous appointments. I sincerely wish I could be of more assistance, but I am afraid these entries must pertain to something with which I am unfamiliar." Her expression reflected a deep unease and regret.

Nick accepted the notebook from her, his demeanor composed and earnest. "Do you think the mister might possess further information?" he inquired.

A faint, resigned smile touched Mrs. Hahn lips. "I am afraid not," she replied. "He is extremely absorbed in his current work with the new artificial intelligence initiative and its potential effects on education. At times, it seems as though he inhabits a different world entirely."

A brief, understanding silence settled over the group before the inquiry continued.

Emma pointed to the notebook; her voice steady but laced with urgency. "While we were riding over, I went through every page. There are two more notations this week—one for today, and another dated exactly a week from now. I think we might be rushing things if we act before we know whether the Oriental Palace has anything to do with these dates. And we're still waiting on the judge to rule on the warrant. Maybe we hold our ground and set up surveillance, just in case. I can call St. Louis PD and have detectives here in under two hours—with shotgun mics, telephoto cameras, the works. We could even tap their phone lines if we get the order."

At that, Doc stood abruptly, his voice firm. "There's no need to waste time, Emma. We've got everything we need right here. If Nick calls the captain, we can pull in enough guys from patrol to have eyes on this place in less than an hour."

He fished a phone from his pocket, dialing swiftly, then handed it to Nick.   "Here—you can talk to him directly. Just say the word and we'll be in business." Doc clapped his hands together, anticipation brightening his features.

Nick hesitated for a breath, the weight of the moment settling in. The team hovered on the threshold of action, every second brimming with possibility. Emma's gaze met his, a silent question hanging between them: wait for answers, or move decisively with what they had? The clock ticked on, the promise of the dates in the notebook urging them forward.

Nick took a steadying breath before speaking into the receiver. "Hello, Captain Barton? This is Nick Curtis. Doc's suggested we go all out—do a full court press on the Tommys Oriental Palace. Yes, the one Clementine's been watching." He paused as the captain's voice rumbled on the other end, the tension in the room stretching tight. "Yes, sir. We'll need the whole detective surveillance crew on it. Telephoto, shotgun mics—the works."

He nodded, half-listening, glancing at his team. "I can clear it with my boss, or if you'd prefer, I can get that done myself." Another beat. "All right, I'll call him as soon as I get off. Thank you, sir. We'll be here at the lab. Reach me through Doc. Yes, thank you. Goodbye."

He handed the phone back to Doc, a flicker of purpose in his eyes. "He said for you to call Larry at the phone company—get someone over to set up the wiretap. He sounded excited, like we're finally moving in the right direction."

Doc grinned, already thumbing in the number. "Yes, the phone system here in town is pretty old-school—shouldn't take much to patch us in. I'll tell Larry to keep it discreet. We don't want to spook anyone before we know what we're dealing with."

Emma exhaled, relief mingling with anticipation. "If they're making calls tied to those dates, this is our best shot at catching it. I'd bet that she is still there killing her makes them nothing and if she is there Storm will find her."

Outside, the afternoon was fading—a silver-gray wash over the street. Inside, a sense of momentum gathered, the edges of uncertainty giving way to determination. The group moved quickly, each person slipping into their role with practiced assurance. Surveillance plans were drawn up, equipment lists checked, and a quiet sense of resolve settled over the lab.

Nick studied the notebook's final page, the date looming like a silent promise. Whatever secrets the Oriental Palace concealed, they were running out of places to hide.

"I think that we can let Clementine take Mrs. Hahn home. Thank you for all of your help. You have helped a lot, and we are moving quite fast you were just what we needed. I will let you know as soon as we find her, you will be the first to know. Hurry and by the way both of you mums the word, don't tell anyone where this case is going. Especially your husband, I don't want him doing anything that would hamper this investigation. Remember loose lips sinks ship! "

His comment puzzled Mrs. Hahn but she said nothing.

Turning to Emma Nick's face showed an awaking "Even though it might be thrown out of evidence; I want Emma and storm to meet up with a uniformed trooper and head out to the strip leading to the fort. I want to check out all of those trailers and all of the houses that might have hookers living there. Check all of them with Storm sniffing out every possible place they could be hiding the granddaughter. At this point it is more important to find her alive. With those clothing we have Storm has a good chance of finding her. Going out there and being careful maybe they won't put it together that we are investigating the Oriental Palace.

So, get going Clementine and call me if you two have any trouble or need anything."

Doc's face went into a wide grin as he heard that they were going to use another trooper, and he knew just who they could send.

Stepping aside he called the captain and arranged to have a trooper in uniform to meet them.

Clamping his hand on Doc's shoulder and shaking him Nick said "That's what I like... Teamwork. Thanks."

"Anytime... now let's get the right people to set up the surveillance on the Oriental Palace. The sooner we can nail these guys the sooner she will be safe."

Following Doc out of the conference room they went to the rear of the building. Unlocking the door leading to the equipment room they waited for the troopers that were on their way. Nick could see that all of the equipment stored there would cover all of the help they needed to gather the right information to arrest any of the criminals.

Sitting close to each other at the table enjoying the short breather they sat quietly. Each stirring their thoughts as they sat in the warm room. The room was not air conditioned because it was just a storage room. Within minutes they became aware that the warm room was uncomfortable.

"How about a coke? I am sure that the surveillance team will be here soon but this heat in here we can do without. Come on lets go to the kitchen and see if we can cool off a little. Stopping long enough to relock the room they walked to the kitchen. Satisfied that the actions they were taking were right.

Chapter Eight

The steady hum of the refrigerator in the kitchen presented a steady sound to relax in. Both Nick and Doc waited; their minds calm as the second hand on the clock on the wall measured the afternoon. Nick realized that there was a minute to call Bobbie. Slipping out his phone he grinned at Doc. "I think we have a minute to call my wife and tell her there has been a change in plans. I am sure that she was looking forward to spending the afternoon with Storm and with our change she is going to be disappointed."

"Go ahead, I going to hit the head once this thing gets started there won't be time to take care of it." Walking away leaving Nick alone to call Bobbie.

"Hi Babe!" Nick spoke out as soon as Bobbie answered.

"Hello, Nick I'm glad you called have you heard from Emma I thought she would have showed up by now it's almost after noon. I was all rested waiting for Storm to get here I already filled her water bowl and ate lunch so I could be ready for our visit. Is she alright? I hope she is alright. Do you know what is going on?"

Nick softened his voice, aiming to reassure her. "Yes, dear, she's fine. There's just been a change in plans, that's all. I don't need to go into the details, but she won't be back until she's ready—and I'm going to be busy myself for a while. Like I said, you just need to relax and enjoy the quiet and the calm of the woods. Everything's okay."

He heard Bobbie let out a small sigh, the tension in her words easing.   "Alright, Nick. I trust you. I'll take a walk down to the creek and let the day drift by. Just promise me you'll be careful."

 Nick smiled, even though she couldn't see it. "Always. I'll call when I can, okay? Save a couple of those beers for me."

"I will. Take care, love."

"You too, Bobbie."

As he ended the call, the familiar low murmur of the refrigerator filled the room again, grounding him in the present. Outside, the distant crunch of footsteps announced the arrival of the surveillance team, and Nick felt the weight of the moment settle. The net was tightening, and soon—very soon—the answers they needed would be within reach.

Leaning back, Nick closed his eyes and let the brief hush settle around him, waiting for Doc to return. Minutes ticked by, unhurried, until the sound of car doors being closed, signaled the arrival of another vehicle outside.

Nick sat up, alert once more, and moved toward the door just as Doc appeared, steady hand on the handle, holding it open for the two troopers who strode in with the practiced ease of men accustomed to tense situations.

Doc gave them a quick nod of greeting, then all four men threaded their way through the narrow hallway to the rear room, where their makeshift command post lay waiting. The two newcomers wasted no time—they moved with silent efficiency, gathering up the specialized gear and double-checking each piece with a soldier's attention to detail.

We'll need these for the setup at the Oriental Palace," one of them said, his voice low but decisive as he pointed at a small stack of black cases and a duffel bag bristling with cables and electronics. "If you don't mind, you can carry those out to the van. But wait for us to say what goes where. We're going to be set up in two locations."

Nick picked up some of the items and Doc followed him as they all four of them carried the items out and the tallest trooper pointed where to put it in the van, it was just a short time before they had loaded the van.

The two troopers stopped beside the van, pausing just long enough for Doc to make introductions. "Nick, this is Fred Vickers, and this tall drink of water here is Walter Hauser—we all call him Walt." Walt gave a friendly nod and a quick, practiced handshake, his grip firm and steady. Fred followed suit, his demeanor more reserved but his eyes alert, taking in every detail.

As the introductions finished, Doc got straight to business. "So, where exactly are you two setting up? You mentioned two spots."

Walt stepped forward, gesturing southeast. "Best vantage on the south side is the Raleigh Towers. There's a vacant storage area on the second floor—city-owned, so we've got keys to every door, right up to the roof. Once we're set, I'll be stationed there. Oh, and for discretion, we'll use the fire exit in the rear. Anyone coming or going should use that route—don't want to be seen if we can help it."

Fred nodded, adding, "I'll be across the street, upstairs at Bernie's Auto Parts. There's a private office in front, perfect view of the Oriental Palace. I already spoke to Bernie—he's letting us use it, no questions asked. Known him since we were kids."

Walt clapped his hands, eager to get moving. "Alright, that's logistics sorted. Let's clear out, get everything in place before dark. And Doc—can you arrange for us to be relieved by midnight? It'll keep everyone sharp."

As a matter of fact, Nick is the agent in charge, and he is going to make all of the directions Capt. Said to follow his orders. This is their case, and we are just helping remember that however this turns out Uncle Sam gets the credit and the heart break. No offense. We got a K-Nine officer Emma and Clementine she is with the DHA so to have only one chief Nick is it. I am hoping that we get some more help. To be able to spell each other and still have someone to steer this wagon, Nick is it. Give him a call on his cell number that the Capt. gave you if you need anything."

Nick nodded, feeling the growing sense of momentum. The pieces were slipping into place; now it was just a matter of time.

When the van reached the street, Doc turned, voice pitched just above the noise of the traffic. "Sorry if I was out of line back there, but Corporal Walt's a little used to taking orders from stripes and hardly ever steps out of line—a good man, through and through."

He let out a short breath, as if shaking off the formalities. "I'm going to call my wife, let her know we'll have a visitor for supper. She appreciates a heads-up, and truth be told, I could use a hot meal myself after today."

As good as that sounds, I already told Bobbie I would be there, and she may have decided what she is going to fix."

"I'll tell you what, I can ask my wife to feed her too. I am sure that the ladies would enjoy talking to each other. I am sure that there is not a lot that we can do but wait here until you hear from Emma and Storm and how they made out at the strip."

Walking towards the building Nick chuckled and said "Well if you are going to call her; get on it. I am ready to see Bobbie make this trip a happy one to remember. AS much as it has been slow getting this investigation going, I can see a light at the end of the tunnel. I have a good feeling about this whole thing. I am still not sure that she has went anywhere on her own. Time is against it. She would have popped up by now." Going inside Nick waited for Doc to come in toying with the idea of calling Emma. He walked back to the kitchen and filled a glass of drinking water sitting down at the table waiting for Doc to come inside.

As he settled at the table, Nick's phone buzzed softly against the wood. He slid it out of his pocket and saw Bobbie's name light up the screen. He answered, voice gentle. "Yes dear?"

Bobbie's words came in a rush, a mix of worry and care. "Emma just called me a minute ago and said she wouldn't be back tonight. She told me not to worry about the kennel—that she'd be staying with Clementine at the motel. She sounded a little strange, honestly. Tired, maybe. I know you can't tell me everything, but I am a bit concerned."

Nick listened, quietly searching for a way to lift Bobbie's concern without betraying the boundaries of the case. "How would you like to come in and meet Doc's wife?" he offered, voice warm. "She's invited both of us to dinner. I think it would do us good—and I know she'd love the company."

Looking across the room, Nick caught sight of Doc, who had crept quietly into the kitchen. The mischievous, reassuring smile on Doc's face told Nick he'd made the right call. Doc shook his head, grinning, and came to join him at the table.

Nick ran a hand across his forehead, glancing at the clock above the stove. "I suppose that we had better go outside soon—she'll be here before we know it. I told her we were at the grey building, left side of Prince highway."

Nick pushed up from his chair, stretching his back with a soft grunt. "Not to worry—she's sharp with directions, but you're right, she could drive right on past if we're not watching. Still, we've got time. And you know she'll want to look her best, the way women do." His grin was teasing, good-natured, as he nudged Doc toward the door.

Nick reached for his jacket, eyes drifting to the window where the afternoon had begun to fade. "I noticed the other troopers were wearing protective vests. Might be I'll need to borrow a couple for myself and the rest. Couldn't exactly wear mine and keep this case quiet." He shook his head, a rueful smile flickering. "Bobbie's sharp— sees everything. That's something I've always admired."

Doc grabbed his own coat and opened the door, the bright sunlight sweeping in. "Come on, let's keep an eye peeled for her. I don't want to miss her pulling up. Not tonight."

Together, they stepped outside, anticipation threading through the busy street as they waited for the familiar car to appear.

Looking to the west, the afternoon sunlight washed the roadway, bouncing off the facades of fast-food restaurants and glinting across windshields. The traffic remained sparse, too early yet for the evening dinner rush, and the air hung with a measured, expectant quiet. It was perfect—enough time for the troopers to finish setting up their surveillance without drawing unwanted attention.

Nick checked his phone, the digital numbers glowing with the lateness of the day. A thought nagged at him: they were going to need more agents for this to work. He scrolled through his contacts, pausing at Kerry's name, and pressed call. The conversation was brief—Nick suggested pulling in DHS, maybe even see if Clementine's fellow agent could join them. The circled date on the calendar loomed: tomorrow. It wasn't much time, but just enough to rally reinforcements.

To his relief, Kerry was already one step ahead. "I've called the Springfield office," Kerry said. "Two agents are coming. They'll meet you at the campgrounds entrance in the morning."

As Nick ended the call, a flicker of motion caught his eye—a unfamiliar rental car easing off the main road, tires crunching onto the concrete driveway.   Bobbie had arrived. The anticipation that had been building all afternoon now settled into something more focused, more immediate. Nick signaled to Doc, and together they watched as Bobbie's car rolled to a gentle stop, sunlight glinting off the windshield, the moment between day and dusk stretching on with quiet promise.

Stepping close to her car Nick waited until she rolled down the window. Leaning in he Kissed her on the cheek. "Just follow him I'll ride with him. He is going to stop on the way. He wants to stop and pick up a car part that came in."

Slipping into the front seat of Doc's car they drove out the trip was short Doc lead the way into the parts store. Following him up to the second floor where Walt was set up in the window. The cameras and high-powered Telescope was set up the Venetian blinds were down. Only one slat was holding the line of sight open to the telescope. The circle netting of the shot-gun microphone standing by ready. Nick expressed his compliment of the thoroughness, with a smile and a wink. Doc motioned him close to the window. "See that Standard telephone truck parked at the pole across the street? The step van? Look closer. Right, that's ours Sparks is in there he is our sound and recording man."

"I would suggest that since Emma speaks Vietnamese, I want to place her in the van. All of their talk I am sure is going to be masked. The people that frequent that basement bar are all locals. Except for the trafficker's they could be anyone. I suspect that since this Oriental Palace is right on the interstate highway that is only six hundred miles from the Texas coast, they may be using this place for a stop. All of this is falling into place the pieces are fitting. It looks more and more like they have kidnapped our victim after she discovered the trafficking." Nick's eyes gleamed at his own explanation.

"Yeah, and only two hours to St. Louis and the Mississippi river and all of that barge traffic not to be cute." Doc quipped.

"Yeah, well we better hurry Bobbie is still out in the car. I am sure you will have plenty of time to look at all the criminal aspects that this Tommys Oriental Palace could have." Moving quickly towards the stairs.

Returning to the sales floor of the parts store Doc stopped and picked up and empty parts box that his friend had waiting for him.

Stepping close to Nick as they left the front door, he whispered, "Just in case Bobbie is as much an eagle eye as you are!!! G--Man." Smiling.

Bouncing down the steps Nick agreed "She sure is… sometimes even more."

As they pulled into the garage, the familiar scent of home—oil, cut grass, and something savory—floated in through the open car window.

Marion was there before the engines quieted; her arms already outstretched. Bobbie eased her car in behind Doc's, and Nick caught the warmth in Marion's eyes as she stepped out to greet them.

Marion wasted no time, gathering Doc into a quick, affectionate hug before turning to Bobbie and Nick.

"You folks couldn't have picked a better day," she beamed. "Meatloaf's in the oven, and as usual, I made enough to feed an army. I threw a couple extra potatoes in for the mash, and the salad ought to hold its own too. Welcome, Bobbie and Nick—so glad you're both here."

With an agreeable nod, she added, "I've got a pitcher of martinis chilling. Dinner will be ready in forty-five minutes. Doc, take Nick somewhere—show him the workshop, or get lost for a bit—while Bobbie and I drown a few olives and catch up. Go on now, I'll call you when it's on the table."

She winked at Bobbie, who grinned at the prospect of a quick martini and some time to swap stories. Doc gestured for Nick to follow, the two men stepping into the cool shadows of the house, leaving the welcoming sounds of laughter and clinking glasses behind them.

Seconds in the den, Nick was impressed with the large eight-point buck hung over the broad mahogany desk. Nearby, a Tri folded flag sat in a polished glass case, its presence quietly dignified. Nick felt questions crowding his mind—about the hunt, about the flag's story—but he chose to hold them back, letting the moment breathe.

Doc, with a knowing look, stepped to what appeared to be an ordinary bookshelf. With a gentle push, he revealed a hidden fridge camouflaged among the faux spines and woodgrain. He handed Nick a cold can of Pabst, icy enough to send a pleasant shock through his palm. Nick took it gratefully and continued his survey of the space.

There was no television; Doc's den was, unmistakably, a sanctuary—an office carved away from the world's distractions. To the right of the desk sat a sturdy desktop PC, perfectly positioned for late-night work or quiet research. A long leather couch, worn in the way that only a favorite seat can be, stretched along half the room. It beckoned with the promise of rest when the hours ran long.

Nick settled into the quiet, the hum of the house muffled by thick walls and heavier memories. He took a slow sip, letting the cold beer fill the silence, and watched as Doc eased himself into the desk chair, rolling it back and forth with an absent-minded comfort. Here, Nick thought, was a room built for thinking—a den for a man deeply committed to both his craft and his private rituals.

Nick settled deeper into the couch, letting his shoulders unfurl against the creased leather. The hush in Doc's den was a balm the low light and faint scent of old books creating a private, weightless hour. He closed his eyes for a moment, not to sleep but to loosen the tautness in his mind—a mind lately crowded with the puzzle pieces of a case that, the more he learned, grew only more tangled.   Flashes of possibility churned behind his eyelids: lines of questioning, faces and places, the ache of things unsolved.

True to form, the moment's peace was punctured by the abrupt buzz of his phone. Nick's eyes snapped open as he reached for it, the screen's glow stark in the dim room. Emma's name flashed above the incoming call. He answered with a quiet, "Nick here," and listened as her voice spilled over the line—businesslike, tired, and laced with undercurrents of concern.

"We didn't find anything on the girl," she said, her words clipped for efficiency. "But we did run into two underage girls—both Asian, but neither Vietnamese. No IDs, frightened, probably illegals and definitely not in the system. Clementine is going to stay with them for now—she's tied up processing, making sure they're safe. Troopers are splitting duties: one's bringing me back to the campsite, the other staying with Clementine she will see to the girls and start the paperwork."

Nick stood, the cold beer forgotten, and began to pace, the narrow strip of carpet underfoot cushioning his steps. The news was sobering—it wasn't the breakthrough they'd hoped for, but it was something. At the very least, two kids were out of harm's way tonight.

He pressed the phone tighter to his ear, his voice low and steady. "Tell the troopers thank you. You and Storm wait at the campsite—get her to rest up, too. We might need someone to spell us later. I'll fill you in on the rest when I'm back at camp. Bobbie's with me—don't worry, we're fine. I'll bring you up to speed soon. Good work, Emma."

He ended the call, thumb hovering over the screen in thought before letting out a long, controlled breath. The den felt different now, his moment of quiet replaced with a new urgency. Nick glanced toward Doc, who had watched the conversation with a quiet, unspoken understanding, ready for whatever came next.

"No luck at the strip?" Doc inquired.

"Not really, but I'm starting to wonder if we haven't jeopardized the whole case," Nick replied, rubbing the tension from the back of his neck. "It never even crossed my mind that the suspects might have been using the strip to work those girls. They found two underage girls out there—no I.D., scared, and Clementine's running them through the missing persons database nationwide. It just... makes me wonder if we're missing the obvious."

Doc downed the rest of his beer, the can making a faint click against the desk. He regarded Nick with an earnestness that cut through the haze of exhaustion.

"Cheer up," he said, voice low and steady. "With all the ins and outs of the base, those girls could've been brought out there by anyone. I even mentioned it's only a two-hour drive to St. Louis. Rumor's always been that the big city pimps haul a carload of working girls down here almost every week. Who knows? They might have nothing to do with our case at all. Just have another beer and relax—we're moving as fast as we can."

Doc stood; his steps deliberate as he crossed to the bookshelf fridge. The quiet hum of the hidden appliance filled the silence. He pulled out another can, holding it out to Nick with a nod that was equal parts reassurance and challenge.

Nick hesitated for a moment, then accepted the beer, the cold bite a small comfort. He let out a slow breath, his mind sifting through the swirling uncertainties—a sense of progress, even if the path forward remained blurred.

Doc leaned against the edge of the desk, folding his arms. "We keep at it. Sometimes, Nick, all you can do is keep showing up. The answers have a way of surfacing when you least expect them."

Nick managed a thin smile, the weight on his shoulders ever so slightly lighter, if only for this moment in the sanctuary of Doc's den.

The light tap on the door brought them both back to the real world, away from the what-ifs. A break they both needed. Nick was ready for a home-cooked meal, eager to enjoy something prepared in a home kitchen. In his position and with the varied cases he caught, eating with friends and family was rare.

Doc opened the door wide, his hand reaching out to chaperone Nick to the dinner table. Marrion watched and waited for

Doc; so, she could put her arm around his waist, her love for him shouting out as they made their way to the dining room.

The bright shine of the silver candelabras and the dim lights welcomed them. Marion and Bobbie had brought out the good silver and fine dishes to greet the new friends this taxing case had brought to them.

The table was set with an honest warmth—there was bread still steaming, the tang of roast meatloaf, and laughter lingering just beneath the surface, waiting to be called up. Here, for a few precious minutes, the heaviness of their work could be set aside. Nick caught Bobbie's eye from across the table and nodded his gratitude, feeling, for the first time in days, a flicker of belonging in the golden hush of Doc's home.

Doc helped Marion into her seat, gently scooting her chair beneath her as she settled in, his hand lingering a moment in a quiet gesture of affection. Nick followed suit, sliding into his own chair beside Doc, drawn by the easy derie of two men whose lives had been shaped by the steady weight of commitment.

Once everyone was settled, Doc bowed his head and spoke grace—his voice warm, steady, threading gratitude and hope into the hush before the meal. The moment the blessing ended, he took up the serving dish heaped with the aromatic meatloaf, its steam curling into the golden light. With practiced hands, he passed the platter to Marion, the plates and bowls following in a gentle parade—bowls of buttery potatoes, bright green beans glistening with oil, a pie cooling on the sideboard.

Conversation eased into the spaces between the passing dishes, laughter rising steadily, filling the room with a sense of belonging. Each person, drawn from a different corner of worry and weariness, found themselves momentarily anchored by the ritual of the meal. Nick watched the way Marion filled Bobbie's glass, the way Doc carved a second slice of bread for himself, and felt a small, surprising surge of comfort. For now, the world outside—the bleakness of the case, the uncertainty of tomorrow—faded, replaced by the reassuring clatter of silverware and the hum of shared hunger.

As hands reached and plates filled, Nick relaxed into the warmth of the table, letting the aromas and the company loosen the tightness in his chest. The meal, simple and generous, became a quiet celebration of survival and togetherness, a promise that there were still good things to be claimed, even in the shadow of hard days.

Nick leaned back on his chair, letting out a gentle sigh as his hand found his stomach. "I could not eat another bite," he admitted, a playful glint returning to his eyes. "I have to admit, that meatloaf was just as good as Bobbie's." He cast a sideways glance at Marion, careful not to insult his wife with his praise.

Marion rose swiftly, her laughter ringing as clear as the silverware. "Thank you, Nick, but you should be careful complimenting other ladies' cooking. I'm sure in the small time I've spent with her, she could stand with anyone." She offered a wink, collecting plates with practiced grace.

"Now, you all go into the den and relax while I load these dishes in the dishwasher."

She leveled a pointed finger at Bobbie. "Bobbie, you go with them and make sure these two don't waste this nice evening on work. No, Bobbie, you can't help. You need to be the guardian and keep these two workaholics from talking about this case. In this house, it's leave it at the door—as Doc likes to say. He never talks about work. In this quiet town we live in, he's like a preacher—he does not talk about work, not anytime."

The room rippled with good-natured protest and smiles. Doc pushed back his chair, a small, knowing grin on his face as he gestured for Nick and Bobbie to follow him. Reluctant but amused, the trio shuffled out, leaving Marion in the comforting clatter of the dishes, her voice echoing softly behind them, a gentle reminder that, for tonight at least, they were safe from the shadows of their burdens.

In the den, the lamplight cast a golden glow over the shelves and family photos. Nick sank into an armchair, Bobbie perching close by, while Doc poured each of them a small glass of something amber and warming. They raised their glasses, the conversation drifting into tales of old towns, childhood mischief, and dreams for quieter days. For a while, laughter and gentle voices wove a tapestry of peace, and the outside world stayed, blessedly, at bay.

Settled long enough for Marion to finish in the kitchen, they relaxed, the evening's hush settling over them like a favorite old quilt. Not wanting to waste the time, Doc glanced at Bobbie, a spark of mischief in his eyes. "Nick tells me that you bagged a big buck," he said, swirling his glass. "Did you use one of those new-fangled crossbows? I looked at them, but I'm so used to hunting with my old 'o-6 I think I'll stick with it."

Bobbie grinned, stretching their legs out before them. "Yes, it was a crossbow, actually. I figured I'd try something different this year—less noise, more challenge. Still feels odd not to have the kick of a rifle in my shoulder, though."

Doc chuckled, shaking his head. "Takes all the fun out of it for me, but I suppose it's the way things are going." He glanced at Nick, a smile tugging at his lips. "Maybe next season I'll let Bobbie show me how it's done. Or maybe I'll just stubbornly stick to my ways."

Nick raised his glass, laughter dancing in his eyes. "I'll believe it when I see it, Doc. You're as set in your ways as they come."

Conversation meandered between stories of crisp autumn mornings, deer trails winding through yellowed woods, and the quiet joys of tradition—each memory another thread in the evening's tapestry. The world, for now, felt simple and safe, bound by old stories and the warmth of good company.

Enjoying each other's company and sipping a single beer apiece, they let themselves drift with the quiet rhythm of the evening, time ticking by almost unnoticed. At half past seven, Nick lifted his phone, the glowing screen gently breaking the spell.

"I hate to be the one to break up a perfect night," he admitted, "but if we're going to relieve the others, I should drive Bobbie and myself out to the campsite and get some shuteye. If you're able, Doc, maybe you could swing by and pick me up around four o'clock? By then, those guys will be tired enough to head home, and they can double back this afternoon to relieve them."

Doc nodded, understanding flickering in his eyes. "Four it is. I'll bring coffee and maybe even a donut if I'm feeling generous."

Bobbie, already stretching and stifling a yawn, flashed a grateful smile. "You're a saint, Doc. Just don't eat all the donuts yourself."

The spell was broken, but the warmth lingered as they gathered their coats and goodbyes. Marion reappeared in the hallway, hugging Bobbie. "Drive safe, you,

guys."

With laughter trailing behind them, Nick and Bobbie stepped into the cool night, the day's burdens lighter for having been set aside, even just for a little while.

Nick settled into the driver's seat, the gentle creak of the old truck a familiar comfort. Bobbie slid in beside him, closing the distance between them with a quiet ease. She leaned her head against his shoulder, the steady thrum of the engine and the hush of the night wrapping them in a cocoon of shared warmth. The world outside was hushed and dark, a canvas of shadowed trees and starlit sky, the headlights carving a narrow path through the quiet.

For a moment, Bobbie allowed herself to imagine that this could be a prelude to something more—a night of laughter and whispered promises in the kind of bedroom where nothing else intruded. But she knew better; the RV waited at the end of the road, and Nick's mind, for all its affection, was tethered to the case he carried like an ache. Still, she savored the closeness, the simple comfort of being beside him, and let it be enough.

The drive was brief—a handful of turns and the soft whine of road beneath the tires—and soon the glow of the campground's lanterns appeared through the trees. They passed the shower block; its windows silvered with condensation and promise. Nick broke the companionable silence, his voice low, edged with fatigue.

"No shower tonight," he said, glancing over, a rueful smile flickering. "I need every second of sleep I can get. You don't mind, do you?"

Bobbie shook her head, her lips curving upward. "Not at all. We've both had longer days."

He reached for her hand, giving it a gentle squeeze. "Could you set your phone to wake me at three-thirty? I'm sure I won't hear mine."

She nodded, already thumbing through her phone's settings, content for now just to be near, sharing the quiet hush that lingered between exhaustion and dreams.

As Nick undressed Bobbie searched through her knapsack digging out the flannel pajamas. She was sure that after Nick had left in the morning the cool night would bring her a time of trying to sleep alone in the uncomfortable foam bed that the RV supplied. She knew that she could not sleep in the cool morning if she was foolish enough to wear the skimpy see through lingerie to bed. Eager to take advantage of the early night to bed she jumped into the bed as soon as Nick slid in and pulled up the covers. Snuggling up close careful not to restrict his movement by leaving his arm free, not like usual she made it a habit of sleeping on top of his arm in a cradled position.

Chapter Nine

Grabbing the loud noisy phone that Bobbie had left on the floor on his side of the foam rubber mattress. His finger swiping the face of the brightly lit glass. Turning slowly, he smiled at Bobbie sleeping soundly in her bunny rabbit decorated flannel pajamas. Turning he dropped his legs to the floor waiting a moment measuring his thoughts. Trying to decide what to wear. Nothing said he had to wear the restricting sports coat. His packing had left him little choice.

Deciding to go with the best things he could be comfortable in her put on his baggy cargo pants the ones with the many pockets. Putting his belt on he secured his clamshell holster to it. Dropping two extra clips for his Sieg-Sauer nine in to the leg pocket. Pulling on a tee shirt emblazoned with the large letter FBI on the back. Stooping he pulled on his socks and slipping his Nike's on, he bent to tie them. Standing he slipped on a baggy sweat shirt. Pulling on a Red skins ball cap.

Tiptoeing to the bathroom he unzipped his fly and relieved him-self. Watching out the frosted glass for headlights while he stood there. Rested he was eager to find out if there was any activity at the Oriental Palace overnight.

Trying to leave the small bathroom quietly he slowly opened the door. Stepping close to the small bed he leaned over and kissed her on the cheek. Just soft enough not to wake her.

Going to the door he quietly opened the inside door. The screen door outside was already open. Stepping out into the humid night he could feel the night. The mist in the air smelled of pine, the forest that surrounded them was telling the world hello, welcome come join us. The sounds of lone fox squirrel chattered his greeting.

Walking to the roadway Nick considered the facts continuing to walk hoping to keep the sound of the approaching car that Doc was driving to pick him up. he stopped at the end of the ribbon marked pine. For a moment he admired the thick growth of the fragrant trees. Allowed to grow and not cut down in some places it was hard for a man to slip between them. The beauty of creation made him feel small. The expanse continued for miles. Tree after tree after tree.

His mind was alert, eager to start the day thoughts about how he could break this human flesh machine that he had stumbled on. He had slept soundly and now it was time to turn over every rock and every twig to fond this attractive young Vietnamese girl.

The thoughts that the professors wife had stirred were becoming more valid. Surely an educated girl who was old enough to be almost graduating age was smart enough to tell her family if she was going to be away. He was leaning more to the kidnapping without a ransom. An addition to the stable of young girls that this unscrupulous would bring more that money. A young, educated woman who spoke many languages could be very handy.

The bright light of the headlights snaked through the pines as Doc arrived in the campgrounds. Nick hurried to the door. Easing it open he held his tongue until he was in, out of anyone hearing him. The crisp sound of the white bakery bag was followed by the smell of the fresh baked goods. The greasy stain was making its way up the side of the treasure held paper.

"There is two jelly and two glazed in there. One of each for you and one for me and the front cup of coffee in the console is mine. Cream and sugar is in there too. Go ahead and get started. I didn't bring the others any they are wanting to get some sleep. Those long nights are tough, and we are just beginning." His voice boomed out.

Nick wolfed down the first Jelly donut. Washing it down with a big swallow of the black coffee. Holding the bag for Doc to pull out his. The day was starting just fine. The grin along with the trace of powdered sugar on Doc's face reassured Nick that they were ready for whatever came up. Stopping behind the Raliegh towers. They sat there long enough to finish the donuts and coffee then they quietly went into the fire escape door that led to the concrete and steel stairs.

Making sure that the heavy metal door shut quietly, not wanting to bring any attention to them. Reaching the hidden office door, they went in. Walt and Fred stood immediately as the heavy fireproof door closed behind Nick.

Walt stopped next to Nick and said "No luck, no body from the family was out anytime last night. The crowd from the bar didn't do anything that was against the law. Couple of drunks staggered out they are asleep in those two cars. Well one of them is in that green pick up. None of the girls came out to spend a time with anyone in their car if you know what I mean. No-one went in the door on the first floor from the back." His voice dragging from the lack of rest.

Walt stretched, rubbing the back of his neck, then offered a weary nod. "You got it, Nick. Just call if you need anything. I'll keep my phone on," he muttered, already mentally halfway to his bed. Fred gave a small salute and headed for the door, his footsteps echoing down the hall.

Nick watched them go, letting the silence settle in the dim office. He leaned against the battered desk, considering his next move. The morning sun was clawing its way through the blinds, drawing sharp lines across the paperwork scattered in front of him. He felt the weight of the investigation—too many angles, too many loose ends.

He picked up the phone, dialing Kerry with quick, practiced fingers. As he waited for the line to connect, his mind drifted back to the Vietnamese girl, the missing details, and the faint thread of hope that she was still alive. He knew time was thin, and every minute counted.

"Kerry, it's Nick. Listen, I need two agents from St. Louis as soon as you can spare them. Springfield's office is tangled up with Clementine, but we may have a break on the girls Emma, and she picked up last night. I want to move before the trail goes cold."

A pause, static crackling in his ear. Nick's gaze fell on the half-empty coffee cup, the donut bag now crumpled and forgotten. He thought about Walt and Fred, about the fatigue settling into everyone's bones, and the long day still ahead. He was determined not to let it wear him down, not now.

"Yeah... thanks, Kerry. I'll keep you posted. I'll hold down the fort here."

He hung up, squared his shoulders, and pulled a fresh sheet of paper from the drawer. Notes needed updating. Leads needed chasing. And somewhere, the truth waited, tangled in the shadows and the pine-scented air of the campgrounds. Nick was ready to find it—no matter what the day would bring.

Nick set the pencil down, the rough outline of the Oriental Palace's rear still fresh on the page. His mind worked through the possibilities—hidden stairways, locked rooms, and the subtle glow from a third-floor window hinting at quiet secrets above. He glanced at Doc, whose steady gaze was fixed on the sketch.

"You know," Nick said, voice low, "if someone is living up there, they've either got a way in and out that isn't obvious, or they don't expect anyone to come looking." He tapped the side of the pencil against his notepad, thinking.

"No visible fire escape for the second floor, but someone's making themselves comfortable on the third. That's not by accident."

Doc straightened, his brow furrowing. "It might be worth talking to the building manager. Or the fire chief, if we want a reason to poke around up there without raising suspicions. Maybe we'll find out who's paying rent on those rooms—and why."

Nick nodded, refocusing on the details of the back alley, the shadowed contours of the stairway, the way the boards creaked beneath a light step. "Let's find out if there's a lease—or just a handshake with someone who doesn't want questions asked."

He carefully tore the sketch from the pad and tucked it into his folder. "I'll swing by the station, see if the fire code gives us any leverage. In the meantime, keep an eye on that third-floor window. If someone's up there, it might be they know more than anyone downstairs. And Doc—let's get someone down to the city hall and find out who holds the liquor license maybe talk to the city engineer."

Doc grinned; the morning's light replaced by a glint of anticipation. "You got it, Nick. I'll make a few calls—quiet, like you said. Might be time to shake the tree and see what falls."

Nick watched him go, then return to the window, tracing the lines of the Oriental Palace with his eyes, searching for movement, for patterns, for anything that didn't fit. The day was just beginning, and already the shadows were shifting.

Taking out his notebook, Nick made a quick note to assign someone to surveillance duty that afternoon. He was too tied up to keep sitting here, eyes glued to the building, the detective in him itching to move, to break free from this fixed post and get back into the current of the case. Being in command meant more than being a sentinel; it meant knowing when to become mobile—when to get his boots back on the ground. That was the only way he'd crack this, and maybe, just maybe, save the bright-eyed Vietnamese college student whose hopes and laughter now haunted the edges of his thoughts.

He glanced at the list of clubs she'd joined—or was supposed to have joined. The group of young coeds who gathered every Thursday at the rec hall. But he'd turned her dorm room upside down, and there wasn't a single pamphlet, no meeting minutes, not even a scrap of paper bearing the club's name. Odd. If she were active, why nothing? Why the absence of all the usual handouts and flyers that filled every other student's desk and wastebasket?

His mind flashed back to the whiteboard in the lab, the web of names and dates sprawling in dry-erase ink. He'd been so focused on the Oriental Palace—so set on the shadows and secrets of that old building—that he'd let the young Asians' club drift to the margins of his investigation. Now, the silence in her room felt deliberate, a puzzle piece glaringly absent.

Nick closed his notebook, resolve sharpening within him. He needed to talk to the club advisor, maybe track down a few of the other members. This time, he wouldn't overlook any angle. And as the light outside shifted, he realized: sometimes, what people leave behind says far less than what they choose to hide.

Sitting back down close to the other edge of the table, Nick spread out three pieces of paper torn from his notebook. The lamplight turned each page into a canvas—blank, expectant, hungry for answers.

On the first, in deliberate, blocky script, he wrote: Kidnapped for sex. The words were stark, almost violent against the pale margin, like a wound opened in ink. He stared at it for a long moment, letting the ugly possibility simmer, neither shrinking from it nor shying away. He'd seen enough in his years to know when a shadow might hold substance.

On the second page, his hand moved more quickly: To shut her up about the trafficking she had found out about the Oriental Palace. The letters slanted, urgent. Was it possible the student had stumbled onto something the wrong people didn't want seen? She'd been bright, resourceful—and perhaps, in her courage or naiveté, had poked at secrets that didn't want to be unearthed.

Nick tapped his pen on the third page, hesitating. This time, he just wrote: ??? The blankness beneath was almost a taunt, a mirror for the questions no evidence could yet fill. Was there another motive—a personal grudge, a jealousy, a case of mistaken identity, or something more tangled still?

He arranged the pages side by side, staring at them as if the order itself might conjure a pattern. Sometimes, he thought, the mind needed to see things laid out, the horrors and uncertainties given weight and shape. Only then could you start to see where the lies thinned, where the truth might leak through.   Outside,   the city's rhythms began waking up, the daylight slicing into the stale room making the questions more uncertain.

Nick sat back; eyes narrowed. Somewhere in these three pages—between the names, the silences, and the spaces left purposely empty—was the story no one wanted told. And he would not rest until he had every answer, written in ink that would not fade.

If the investigation into the trafficking ring brought down the whole sordid operation—these merchants dealing in stolen lives— then all the better. But he couldn't, reaching for a fourth slip, he scrawled a single word in heavy, insistent strokes: the Oriental Palace. He underlined it—once, twice, a third time, until the paper threatened to tear. This was a different crime, he was certain. The locks on the doors hadn't made sense, too new for a building so ancient, as if someone had been careful to keep certain people in—or others out.

Nick pressed the pen to his jaw, thinking of whispered rumors, the ones about vanished migrants, about doors that opened and closed without a name entering the ledger. He'd seen enough in border towns and city alleys to wouldn't, let that part of the case swallow the rest.

He jotted a final note, all caps, underlined for emphasis: FIND THE GRANDDAUGHTER. That was the line he refused to let blur, the charge he owed to the family whose hope was starting to fray. Whatever else spun out from the Oriental Palace—whatever secrets or not—it would have to wait. First, he'd find the missing girl. Then, and only then, would he bring the whole house of cards down.

Nick leaned forward, the four pages fanned out, a map of worry, suspicion, and grim resolve. The city's gloom pressed closer, but in this circle of lamplight, he felt the focus that always arrived in the eye of the storm.

Doc continued to circle the table, his steps soft but insistent, eyes scanning the patchwork of Nick's pages as if he might read them by the grain of the paper itself. The quiet was fractured—suddenly, violently—by the metallic crash of the dumpster being hoisted by the truck outside, a discordant jolt that rattled the world and sent a tremor through the room. For a heartbeat, both men were drawn back, their focus wrenched from ink and suspicion to the mundane rhythms of the city beyond.

Doc's gaze lingered on the glass for a moment, as if watching the invisible tide of the world drift by, before he turned to Nick with a rueful smile. "And life goes on... Our worries are not shared by everyone." The words, breezy on the surface, carried a sharp undertow. He tapped a knuckle absently against the table's edge—a habit when his thoughts strayed to places, he didn't trust himself to linger.

"Speaking of worries, Marion was delighted to meet your wife." The remark was casual, almost too much so, but it slipped a hook into Nick's chest all the same. The mention of home, of his life outside these shadows, felt like a hand pressed unexpectedly to an old bruise. Nick's face betrayed nothing, but a slow tension crept into his jaw, the kind that wouldn't easily be eased by daylight or time.

"Was she?" he managed, trying to keep his tone light, but the words tasted foreign. He wondered, fleetingly, what Marion had seen—what anyone ever saw. Did the worries follow him, clinging to his coat like the city's grime, or did he manage to leave them at the threshold, where laughter and the ordinary waited?

Doc shrugged, lips quirking in a way that might have been sympathy or warning—or both. "She said she liked her. Said she seemed... steady." He plucked at one of the slips of paper, setting it straight, as if realigning the world.

"Maybe that's what you need. Something that doesn't vanish in the night."

Roaring, the truck's engine revved, the sound fading down the alley. For a moment, the world felt like it might turn normally again. But inside, the lamplight still drew long shadows, and the pages on the table waited—hungry for answers, for a truth no ordinary day could touch.

Outside, the town was shaking off the last tatters of night. Doc stood at the window, posture tense, scanning the waking streets with the vigilance of a sentinel desperate not to miss the moment when ordinary shifted to strange. His eyes tracked the parade of cars crawling by, glancing off the battered frames and painted signs of the telephone company and street department as their employees trickled up Shissler Road. The city garage swelled and thinned, a tide of uniforms and hunched shoulders. A single yellow school bus, windows fogged and brimming with kids in bright jackets, groaned its way around the corner, the laughter and shouts inside barely muffled by the glass.

Gradually, the rush faded, and a quieter rhythm took over, the city's pulse slowing as the morning found its shape. Doc turned from the window with a thoughtful frown, trading places with Nick at the table. He settled into the seat with a faint grunt, the wood creaking beneath him, and reached for one of the scattered pages, tracing the lines with a callused finger. For a moment, the restless world outside receded; all that remained was the lamplight, the scent of paper, and the heavy promise that, today, answers might finally slip from shadow into day.

The day's first true commotion arrived in the shape of the Crisco food purveyor's truck, lumbering down the street with a groan that set pigeons scattering and broadcasted the undeniable arrival of morning. Doc, glancing at the battered waterproof watch strapped to his wrist, squinted at the silver hands. "About eight-thirty," he muttered, though the early hour still clung to everything like dew. He rolled his eyes, trying to assign meaning, or at least a sense of proportion, to a day that had barely shrugged off the night.

He reached for Nick's phone, which had started its usual morning tremble and chirp, the screen lighting up like an omen. Doc answered him with the careful resignation of a man who expects trouble but refuses to meet it halfway. "Just about seven fifty-two," he said, exaggerating the time as if the day might lengthen or shorten at his whim. "Hey, this thing's alive—here, take it. I think it must be your chief."

Nick, already pacing, snatched the phone away. "Yeah! Kerry, it's me. What's up?" His voice was gruff, carrying more fatigue than irritation, his eyes rolling in a private orbit as he strode the battered floorboards. He listened, pinching the bridge of his nose, while outside, the city continued to arrange itself for another day—trucks rumbling, uniforms shuffling, the last vestiges of ordinary clinging to the light. Inside, Nick's world was measured in shadows and phone calls, the weight of answers still waiting to be found on the table beside him.

Nick's fingers tightened around the phone, the tired lines of his face deepening as he listened. Kerry's voice came through, a rough whisper with the urgency of static—quick, coded, never quite naming names.

"I got great news for you," Kerry began, though his tone held more gravity than celebration. "It seems that DHS has had a Vietnamese agent undercover, living right down near the bus terminal in St. Louis. He's catching the two-forty bus that comes into Raleigh this afternoon. Listen carefully—don't share this with anyone, I repeat, no one."

Nick's eyes flicked to Doc, who was busying himself with a pile of notes but clearly within earshot. He angled his body toward the window, pressing the phone tighter.

"He'll say he's got family in Springfield, could only pay his way to Raleigh," Kerry continued, his voice measured, the words clicking into Nick's memory like pieces of a code they'd used before. "He'll try to get work at the Oriental Palace, see if he can get inside. He's going to pretend he doesn't speak English. Been under for almost two years. He's a good man—we're counting on him to finally crack the secret of the locked doors. Keep up the surveillance, but no one is to know. Not a soul."

Nick grunted softly, the weight of the message settling into his chest beside the day's other burdens. "Gotcha. Anything else?"

There was the faintest hint of a smile in Kerry's reply, the kind that bled through even a bad connection. "Yeah—did Bobbie bag a deer yet? We got so wrapped up in this case, I forgot she was even bow hunting."

An unexpected warmth flickered through Nick's voice. "Yes, Kerry. And I might add, she's forgiven us for the secret... Bye now."

The line clicked dead. Nick let the phone drop to the table's edge, its plastic shell suddenly heavier in his hand. The world outside seemed to pause—the city's usual clamor falling to a hush, as if Raleigh itself were holding its breath for secrets sliding in on afternoon buses. He drew a slow breath, letting his gaze linger on the restless light at the window, and the shadows that kept their own counsel.

Whatever answers today might bring, Nick knew the locked doors was just one threshold among many. And as the morning pressed forward, he would keep watching, waiting, and listening—for footsteps in the hallway, the hiss of static, or the quiet knock that signals a story beginning anew.

Holding back a smile, Nick walked to the bathroom, needing a minute to collect himself. The cracked tile and dulled chrome offered no answers, only the echo of Kerry's words, tight with anxiety. How could Kerry be so afraid of a leak? The question circled, insistent. Why the near-paranoia about keeping the plant's presence a secret? Surely the locals weren't privy to whatever secrets were bolted behind the Oriental Palace's locked door. Surely, Nick thought, the honored MHP wasn't actually aware of the human trafficking that now seemed to snake beneath the Oriental Palace's gaudy lights and cheap glamour.

He twisted the cold-water tap, letting it run until it was icy, then cupped his hands and splashed his face. The shock brought him back to himself, if only for a moment. His stomach grumbled—last night's uneven sleep gnawing at him. There was work to be done, but the body always remembered its own needs.

Finished with the toilet, Nick returned, boots thudding on worn wood, to the cramped office room where Doc was still half-buried in his notes. Nick's voice, hoarse but friendlier now, reached out across the clutter.

"What do you say, Doc? You ready for some coffee? Did that nice wife of yours send enough in that thermos for us to have another cup each?"

He drifted back to the window, cradling the mug as if it were a shield. The city hadn't changed—it was still stretching awake, trucks and sun and the shiver of uncertainty all mingling outside. Yet something in the air felt charged, a pressure building in places no one could see.

Content, just for a breath, that they were moving in the right direction, Nick let his mind slip to the faces left unmentioned—the granddaughter, brave and blameless, whose safety was never far from the back of his mind. He watched the city for signs, the way a storm-watcher reads the clouds, knowing every answer brought its own questions, and the day ahead would not yield them easily.

The sun was making its way to its peak when the backdoor flew open. In bounded Storm, tugging Emma behind; she was well rested and eager to go to work. Clementine followed, holding a bag of burgers and fries, her hair catching the morning light. Settling the cup tray on the table, Emma grinned, sharp-eyed and half-teasing. "Hiding in those civvies, are we?"

Nick tried for a smile, the scent of fresh coffee mingling with the grease and salt from Clementine's bag. Emma crossed to the window, raising the blinds a little higher with a practiced twitch. The room brightened—edges sharpening, shadows thinning.

"That building is tall, isn't it? Must have three floors," Emma mused, squinting at the world beyond the glass.

"Yes," Nick replied, voice low. "Someone's living up there, too. Saw a light up early this morning. Couldn't make out who." He sipped, gaze narrowing at the distant silhouette.

"That could be another piece—if they locked someone up there, no one could hear them, as far up as it is."

Storm pressed close to the window, tail swishing, as if chasing the thread of Nick's thoughts. Clementine's hand paused, paper bag crinkling. The room, for a heartbeat, felt smaller—charged with the hush of secrets about to surface.

Doc looked up from his notes, mouth set. "If someone's up there, we'll need a way in. Quietly. Before anyone gets spooked."

Emma's jaw tightened, her reflection doubled in the glass—one face in light, one in shadow. "Maybe that's why they built it so high. You only put things out of reach if you're afraid someone's coming for them."

Outside, the city pressed on, oblivious. But within these walls, the air felt heavier, as if every word and gesture was another stone in a growing cairn of suspicion. Nick set his mug down, the resolve in his chest settling. Today, they would go think higher—into the locked doors, into the secrets knotted above the city. And whatever they found, he would not let it remain silent.

Eager to satisfy the hunger urge that was growing Nick pulled open one of the bags that were on the table. "Go ahead and eat while it is hot we can wait to hear that nothing of benefit has happened in this part of the town. If we could only get a break...when I think about the possibilities, and they torture that young girl could be going through. Well, no need dwell on bad thoughts."

"At least you gals took those other two girls out of a life of pain; so, to speak."

"Yes, that is one good thing that came from us going out there. So, what's on the deck for us this afternoon. There is two MHP guys over at the auto parts store. I am not sure how long they have been there, but we need to plan on watching this place until we get a break. Maybe those two agents that came down from St Louis are ready to relieve them." Emma asked.

Nick nodded, as if aligning his thoughts with Emma's directive. "Yes, that would be something that Clementine could do while we eat. But when they change with them, I want to have a pow wow here. While we eat, I want all of us to think about something. The circled date in her date book. Why was it circled? Go ahead Clementine it can wait. That is tomorrow I think we need to talk to the professor once again. With Mrs. Professor along with him something about that date seems to be important. Where is that book right now? It should be in the car could you run down and get it. In the briefcase."

While Clementine slipped out, Nick remained at the window, gaze unfocused, mind stretching and folding itself around every unanswered question. The city's skyline was a blur, the traffic below a meaningless current. What were they missing? What piece still lurked, unseen, just beyond the reach of logic or hope?

He turned to Doc, hesitant, struggling not to sound callous but knowing they couldn't afford to dismiss any possibility, however dark. "Doc...I hate to even say it, but—are we missing something?

What if we're dealing with... a sex crime? I mean, even in a small town, it happens. Have we checked the registry? Known offenders?"

Doc's head jerked up; eyes wide—almost a jolt in the hush. "That's a hell of a point, Nick. We never thought of it. Maybe we were too hopeful, thinking she'd just turn up, no harm done." He stood, determination eclipsing his earlier tension. "I'll get right on it. No sense in both of us staring at the walls. I'll call Springfield, see what's in their files—and check with the city, too. Maybe there's something that hasn't made it into our case file."

Nick nodded, a grim sense of resolve settling over him. The air still felt heavy, but at least now, another stone would be overturned.

Clementine returned with the date book clutched to her chest; her face pinched with a private tension. She hesitated on the threshold, fingers tracing the worn leather of the briefcase, her thoughts spiraling through regret and grim clarity. They had talked about sex—but only as a commodity, an ugly transaction at the Oriental Palace, never letting themselves look too closely at the unspeakable. Yet in chasing the big fish, the ringleaders, they had stepped in deep, lost in the scale of it all, the lines blurring between personal and national tragedies. Was it hubris, she wondered, to think that the disappearance of one small girl could be solved by the same tools meant for sweeping up grand corruption?

She crossed to Nick, the weight in her hands matched by the heaviness in her voice. "Nick, I'm sorry. Sometimes I think my case has overshadowed yours—the disappearances, the Oriental Palace, all of it. Maybe I let the mess of the country cloud what should have been our focus. One girl—one family—deserves more than to be a footnote in a bigger storm."

Nick shook his head; jaw set with newfound resolve. "Don't blame yourself. The Oriental Palace is a festering wound, sure, but not at the expense of the professor's granddaughter. From now on, it's wake-up time. No distractions. Back to basics. We owe her that."

The room grew quiet, each of them momentarily lost in their own resolve and remorse. Outside, the day pressed on—unconcerned and ordinary.

Emma sat quietly for a moment, jaw clenched, itching to shout what had been gnawing at her since morning: they'd missed something—missed a chance, when they'd first spoken to Maya's friend. Surely, two girls sharing a background, a friendship, would hold secrets unspoken in front of strangers. Perhaps, in their rush, they'd taken the easy answers, letting the silence between the girls speak louder than any confession.

Suddenly propelled by determination, Emma rose and crossed the room to Nick, her eyes flinty with purpose.

"This afternoon, I want to talk to Maya's friend again," she announced, voice low but urgent. "I think she's hiding something—something she's too scared or too loyal to say in front of all of us. I'd like to go see her alone. Maybe bring Storm along for backup, but that's it. I have a feeling she knows more than she's letting on. Maybe she was with Maya Saturday night—maybe she was just afraid to say. Girls that age, they're chummy, you know? They share things with each other that they won't with adults, or with us, the investigators."

She paused, recalling the professor's wife's earlier remarks. "Her grandmother said she was a little beneath Maya—maybe that's true, maybe not.   But I want to hear it straight from her. If you don't mind, as the agent in charge, I think this is a lead worth chasing."

Nick met Emma's gaze, then nodded. "Do it. Take Storm but keep it low-key. Maybe you can get her to open up—just one girl to another."

Resolved, Emma turned, already planning her questions and the careful, quiet way she'd approach Maya's friend. No more missed chances. The afternoon was shifting—perhaps, this time, they'd catch what had slipped past before.

Emma nodded, the tension in her shoulders easing at Nick's affirmation. "So, then I'll be available in about an hour. The time is right for me to catch her during the class break. She might return to her dorm for the afternoon. So, if it is alright with you, I'll go ahead and take Storm with me and drive over there."

Nick didn't hesitate. "Don't feel that you have to clear everything with me. I will support you whatever you decide to do to help the investigation."

For a heartbeat, the weight of responsibility felt almost manageable—shared, not just hers to bear. Emma offered a small, grateful smile, gathering her things with crisp efficiency. Storm, sensing the shift, straightened from where she laid on the floor, quiet and vigilant.

As the door closed behind them, the room was left in a hush threaded with hope. Outside, the sky had shifted—clouds casting uncertain shadows on the path ahead. But for the first time in days, Emma felt the faintest pulse of possibility, a sense that what had once slipped through their fingers might now be within their grasp.

No sooner had Emma and Storm stepped out than Nick reached for his phone, thumbing Kerry's number with brisk, practiced precision. The line rang twice before a voice answered, wary but familiar.

"Hi, Kerry—Nick here," he began, lowering his tone instinctively. "I know as lead agent I technically have authority to handle and coordinate this investigation, but keeping everything hush-hush is starting to tie our hands. Maya's grandmother insists there's no proof for half of what's being whispered, and frankly, I think we need to pull the city police in. If we want to track down anything on the register of sexual offenders, we need their cooperation. This is bigger than we can handle alone without drawing on some local resources."

He hesitated, choosing his words with care. "If you need to call the professor, make sure it won't cost you a friendship if we loop in the police. But I'm convinced it's necessary. We need to flush out the truth, even if it's uncomfortable."

There was a pause, then Kerry's voice, steady and unflappable, came through. "If you think your hands are tied, then do what you need to do. Bring them in. I'll handle any fallout if D.C. starts kicking up dust about jurisdiction.   Thanks for the heads up, Nick. Call if you need anything else—or if someone tries to run interference from above."

Relief mingled with resolve in Nick's chest. "Will do. Appreciate it, Kerry."

He ended the call, exhaled, and let his gaze drift to the muted light slanting through the blinds. The path ahead would not be easier, but at least they would no longer be walking it alone.

The phone blinked off as Kerry hung up. Nick's mind began to race. Unease coiled in his gut, tightening as he considered the possibility that the missing coed might be close by—frightened, mistreated, even tortured—while the city around him carried on, oblivious. He pressed a palm to the windowpane, tracing the familiar cityscape with troubled eyes.

His thoughts flashed back to the night before. From this very vantage, he'd watched the slow exodus from the bar across the street: two drinkers weaving their way to their cars, choosing to sleep it off in their parked vehicles. Not once had a patrol car rolled by to disturb or even notice them as the hours wore on and the city's pulse dimmed. The silence on the street now seemed more sinister than serene.

It was almost too easy to imagine how, in such a vacuum of attention, an assailant could have stalked the shadows, waiting for someone vulnerable—someone like Maya—to slip through the cracks. The idea that her cries could be swallowed up, unnoticed, gnawed at him. Sure, the city police were likely understaffed and overworked—he knew the reality of small-town departments—but he hadn't seen a single patrol car circle the block all night. That lack of presence was inexcusable. On a street as busy as this, complacency could be deadly.

Nick straightened, resolve hardening within him. They couldn't afford to wait for luck or hope that someone else would step up. He made a mental note: when He talked to the city police, he would make sure they understood—not just the urgency, but the cost of their absence. No more missed patrols. No more blind spots. Not while any hope remained.

Clementine's wry look told Nick that she agreed with Emma— they had not covered all of the bases. Walking close beside her, Nick's voice carried a hesitant edge.

"You choose—you or me. One of us needs to go to the police station, look at the offense reports, the sex offender list. We've got to tighten this net. I'm sure this is something we need to either confirm or wipe off the possibility list."

Clementine didn't hesitate. "You go, Nick. Your badge counts for more in this town. You know how some folks are—think immigrants should be allowed to stay, even if they're here illegally. Go ahead, we need to make some ground. I'll hold the fort."

Her words were pragmatic, tinged with an understanding of the small-town currents that often dictated who was listened to and who was waved away. Nick met her gaze, gratitude flickering across his features. He knew she was right; his credentials carried a certain weight here, a key that might unlock doors Clementine would find barred. Still, the implication stung—a reminder of the subtle, persistent lines drawn through the community, separating insiders from outsiders.

He squared his shoulders, determination settling over him like armor. "Alright. I'll head over now. If you hear from Emma, keep her in the loop. We can't afford to miss anything."

Clementine nodded, her skepticism softening for a moment. "Be careful, Nick. And don't let them stonewall you."

"I won't," he promised, already moving for the door. Outside, the air was heavy with anticipation, every shadow along the sidewalk seeming to watch as he strode away. The quiet between them was filled with all they couldn't say—their shared sense of urgency, the unspoken hope that this search would finally bring answers.

The trip to the city building in Clementines car let Nick have a brief moment of realization. The two-story structure that house the police station, the mayor's office and several department head called out the lack of small-town resources.

Parking on the street He walked to the glass doors that led inside the station.

 Stopping at the glass doors separating the police department from the many other offices. He Leaned in to allow the young civilian woman to hear him. Handing his badge out for her to see He said. Nick Curtis FBI, I would like to speak to the person in charge. The medium size office held two desk pushed together in the center of the room. The Motorola radio sat on the one desk. The white shirted Captain stood up as he seen Nick.

He looked friendly as he walked to the service counter. Sticking out his hand, he responded, "Captain Gordon... Jesse Gordon. How can I help you?" Shaking Nick's hand, he twisted around as if searching for a quieter place to talk. Nick didn't waste time. "I need to see someone about some reports."

"Down the hall—the break room," Gordon said with a nod. He opened a side door, and Nick followed as they made their way to a small room at the back of the building. The break room was utilitarian, the linoleum scuffed and the light overhead buzzing faintly. A worn table and two metal chairs afforded them a place to converse.

"Have a seat. How can I help you? Here about the missing coed, I guess. I thought they'd call you sooner or later." Gordon's tone was matter-of-fact, but a flicker of concern edged his features.

Nick remained standing, not trusting the cleanliness of the tabletop. "You're right. I am here about her. I'd like to see any report you might have from the last two years involving personal disturbance calls."

Gordon's brow furrowed with a mixture of understanding and caution. "That's a pretty broad net—might take some time to pull them all. But I can get you started. Lot of those calls don't make it past the initial file, you know. Folks here don't always want to press things further."

"Still, I need to see them," Nick replied, his tone polite but firm. He watched as Gordon considered, then nodded again. "In the office what kind of offense are you looking for."

"Anything where someone was bothering another person... I know that sounds vague but let me give you an idea. Let's say that a person was complaining that a man was bothering a woman. Maybe with sexual connotations. And he would not leave her alone. Not a civil disturbance like between a husband and a wife. You know maybe bothering a school boy or girl."

Gordon listened, his jaw tightening as Nick clarified the kind of cases he was after.   "Picture this," Nick said, his voice even but edged with something urgent, "a girl goes out for the night, maybe to a bar or a club. Some man asks her to dance—she says no, but he doesn't let up. Keeps pushing, makes her uncomfortable, follows her when she leaves. Maybe he corners her outside, gets insistent, presses her for something more. That kind of harassment. More than just a quarrel, more than drunken persistence—something that crosses a line."

The captain's gaze sharpened, recognizing the gravity behind Nick's words. "Yeah," he said, his voice dropping. "We've had reports like that from time to time. Sometimes they're buried in the noise, dismissed as misunderstandings, but I'll see what I can find." He began to sift through the folders, pulling a few records aside, his manner more focused now.

Nick watched as file after file was thumbed through, the names and dates blurring together, each case a potential thread in a web he was determined to untangle.

As the captain continued flipping through the files, the hum of the building closed in around them—a municipal quiet, punctuated only by the distant ring of a telephone and the muted voices from the outer offices. Nick waited, every muscle tensed with the urgency of his search and the knowledge that, before the night was out, he'd need to find the pattern everyone else had missed.

Nick would have to push past both bureaucracy and prejudice, but he braced himself to do just that. Every step he took was a silent vow: no more blind spots. Not tonight.

Nick leaned in, lowering his voice. "What about convicted sex offenders? Do you have any current names on file? The law says they have to register with the police, right? What about any of those?"

His eyes flicked past Gordon didn't answer immediately Nick, as though checking to see if anyone else was listening. "We do," he said, his words careful. "Registry's not public, you know that. But we keep a list—addresses, last check-ins. Not all of them stay put, and some find ways to slip the net. We do our best to keep tabs."

He set aside the disturbance reports and reached for a smaller, locked drawer, drawing out a narrow folder bound with a rubber band. "There are a few still in town. I'll warn you—most keep a low profile, but a couple have been cited for failing to check in on time. I'll show you what I have, but it stays between us."

Nick nodded his understanding, eyes scanning the scant but telling entries as Gordon flipped through the registry, each name a reminder of the dangers lurking beneath the surface of quiet streets. Every lead, no matter how uncertain, was another avenue to pursue—another shadow to drag into the light.

, Nick would have to push past both bureaucracy and prejudice, but he braced himself to do just that. Every step he took was a silent vow: no more blind spots. Not tonight.

Taking out his notebook, Nick looked at Gordon, intent and methodical. "That's what I need; and listen—I'm here working on the Vietnamese coed who's gone missing. At this point, I'm starting to think it may be someone she knows who took her. Three days have passed since her grandfather reported it to your department. Do you have any leads we can work with? Since I'm here, more or less representing the family, I'm going to make a list—names from the registry, and anyone cited for harassment. If there's anything you need to handle while I work, go ahead. Thank you, by the way. I'll make sure to let the professor know how much help you've been."

Gordon gave a curt nod, accepting Nick's words with a gravity that bespoke both weariness and resolve. He retreated to his desk, phone in hand, leaving Nick to the files. Nick methodically flipped through the reports, jotting names and addresses in his notebook with a practiced efficiency. Disturbance after disturbance, each citation for persistent unwanted attention, every registered offender's latest check-in—he made no assumptions, only careful notes.

The squeak of Gordon's chair and the low hum of his conversation with someone on the other end of the line formed a backdrop to Nick's task. From time to time, Gordon shot him a glance, as if measuring the weight of trust in the room.

Nick's list grew, each entry a possible link in the chain that had pulled the young woman from her life. As he finished, he paused, the names hovering on the page—each a shadow with the potential to become substance. He closed the notebook, resolve hardening.

"Anything?" Nick asked quietly, hoping for even the thinnest thread.

Gordon hung up; his brow furrowed. "Nothing solid yet, but I've got a couple calls out. There's always more noise than signal in cases like this. But we'll keep at it."

Nick nodded, sliding the notebook into his pocket. He knew the hours ahead would be long, but he'd promised the family—and himself—that he wouldn't let the silence swallow another missing girl.

Walking to the doors that led to the street Nick turned to the captain waving his hand "Thanks Capt. Catch you later."

Entering the car, he started the engine pleased that he had come to the station. Driving away from the curb he decided to take the list to the surveillance.

Since he had not gotten any rap sheets, he hoped that they were dealing with a beginner. Only one or two had jumped out at him as he listed the names. His final list of sex offenders was two. The harassment there were a total of six, most were divorce cases that began as arguments.

Climbing the rear steps to the upstairs office when he reached the auto-parts store he was greeted by a county deputy he did not recognize. Clutching the note book wanting to sit down and study the names and the offenses they were involved in.

Raising his hand in a gesture hinting he wanted to shake his hand Nick forced a smile. His action telling the deputy he wanted to welcome him for the help "Nick Curtis with the bureau, been here long?" Shaking his hand.

"Hugh Amos, , pleased to meet you...not long I relieved the other deputy, ready for the night."

"I guess since you are here you must patrol the area close around the city am I right?"

"Yeah, sure right, why do you ask?"

"I have a list of subject's I would like for you to look at maybe you are familiar with. I know sometimes that the sheriff helps out when the city is shorthanded."

His face agreed that Nick was informed making him nod.

Nick sat down and began reading the names off of his list. Watching Hugh's reaction. As he heard the name Wesley Hayes. Hugh reached out to stop him.

"That one I know him not a fighter but thinks he is a lover. You know the answer to all women's needs?"

Continuing to read the names, Hugh stopped him again. "That one Victor Branter. Kind of mean likes to fight."

Nick paused, glancing down at his list, then looked back at Hugh with a probing expression.

"So, what about sex crimes—are there any registered sex offenders in the county?" he asked, lowering his voice as if the question itself might draw attention. "That's something you should remember if you have kids. I talked to Gordon at the city and came up with nothing. But what about the county? That's a bigger area, maybe you remember something?"

Hugh's brows knitted, considering. For a moment, the only sound was the faint hum from the store below. He finally replied, "There are a couple names on the list, but they keep a pretty low profile. The sheriff keeps tabs on them. I'll try to get you more information if you need it."

Nick nodded, jotting down a quick note. The exchange lingered in the silent air, the weight of unspoken concern threading between them.

Nick's phone began vibrating, skittering across the table's surface. He snatched it up.

"Nick here!"

Kerry's voice came through, brisk and urgent. "Hello, Nick, I got it cleared—we can take off the wraps. Get somebody over to the college and interview everybody with any possible information about where she was last seen. We've let this case get too far ahead of us. Shake all the places she could have gone, and everybody she might have met. Talk to everyone. Talk to you later. Take care, Nick."

The call ended as abruptly as it began, the directive hanging heavy in the air. Nick set the phone back down, his mind already tracing the next steps, the sense of urgency pulsing in his veins.

Standing up, Nick began pacing the confines of the cramped office. Resources were thin, and he could feel the pressure mounting with every step. He had to cover too many places with too few people, and it gnawed at him that so much about the missing girl's daily life remained a mystery. The normal questions—her class schedule, her circle of friends, her routines—had slipped through the cracks with her grandparents. It was an oversight that now seemed monumental.

He grimaced, recalling the fragmented details they did have: no steady boyfriend, nothing solid about her women friends, no clear picture of her habits. The possibilities swelled in his mind, branching out in a dozen directions, each demanding attention. He dropped heavily back into his chair and flipped open his battered notebook.

With methodical urgency, he began scribbling out a list—places she was known to frequent, the names of students and staff who might have seen her, corners of campus too easily overlooked. He underlined the need for more photos; every crew member should have a current picture in hand, eyes sharpened by familiarity. If they were going to find her trail, they needed every edge they could muster.

The pen hovered over the paper, then Nick pressed on, jotting down assignments, matching names to locations, dividing the slender resources for maximum impact. The silence was thick with the gravity of the task. There could be no more missed questions.

He exhaled slowly, feeling the shape of a plan take root. Outside, the world spun heedlessly on, but for Nick, time had narrowed to the weight of this investigation and the hope that, if they moved quickly enough, they might still find her.

His thoughts circled back to Lan Tran-Hoang—the friend the girl's grandmother had described with thinly veiled reservations, calling her "kind of trashy," though not quite in those words, more a delicate implication than a condemnation. That stuck with Nick. He knew that sometimes the confidences between friends ran deeper than anything shared with family, and there were truths that would surface only in the soft, agreeable light of friendship. If the missing girl had secrets, Lan might be the keeper of them.

Nick tapped his pen against the page. He would need to approach Lan herself—gently, but with resolve—to press past whatever protective walls she might set up. He suspected she would be wary, perhaps defensive, but he couldn't afford to let politeness stifle the search. There were things a friend might know that no one else did, the kinds of details that could pry this case open.

He began drafting questions, noting the ways he might win Lan's trust, how he might persuade her that this was about helping, not blaming. The logic was simple: if anyone had glimpsed the missing girl's unguarded moments, learned the truth behind the careful façade, it would be Lan. It had to be Nick who asked—the weight of the investigation demanded nothing less from him.

Chapter Ten

For the next half an hour, Nick was glued to the phone, his voice low and clipped as he parceled out new assignments to every crew member he could reach. The troopers and the deputies drew the short straws: they would maintain surveillance at the Palace. Something about that place prickled at the edges of Nick's instincts—a sense that it harbored its own secrets, possibly illicit, possibly dangerous, but he couldn't let that suspicion overshadow the greater task. The missing girl took precedence. Everything else—the rumors about the Palace, the uneasy looks exchanged between staff, even the shadowy reports of late-night visitors—had to wait.

He jotted the last notes, rubbing at his temples. "Keep your eyes open," he reminded his team, "but the girl comes first. We can't let her slip past us because we were distracted by side-shows."

Outside, the campus sprawled in indifferent sunlight, students weaving through their day. Nick tucked his notebook into his jacket and headed for the door. It was time for the next round of questioning, and his mind was already rehearsing how he'd approach Lan Tran-Hoang. He needed her insight, needed to see through the missing girl's facade, needed every thread she might offer. Only then could he hope to pull the case together before time unraveled it for good.

Nick made his way across campus, every step purposeful, his notebook tucked securely beneath one arm. The registrar's office was a relic—oak paneling, an air of organized chaos, and the stern presence of an elder woman whose years behind the desk had taught her to ask more questions than she answered. Before Nick could finish explaining his request for Lan Tran-Hoang's schedule, she had peppered him with inquiries of her own—Did he have authorization? Was this truly urgent? Had he notified the campus administration?

Still, with the soft authority of his badge and just enough urgency in his tone, Nick convinced her to yield the information.

As he left the office, he was keenly aware of the invisible lines of rumor that would already be unfurling across the campus. By the time he reached the building where Lan's next class was held, Nick was certain that a dozen whispered versions of Emily Hahn's absence were already circulating. It wouldn't matter that college students often vanished for a day or two, skipping classes as easily as stones across a pond.

The presence of the FBI was a signal flare—one that would ignite speculation, anxiety, and, he hoped, just enough loose talk to shake a clue out of the campus's stone-faced indifference.

He waited in the corridor outside the classroom, the low murmur of students and the chalky drone of the professor inside drifting through the half-closed door. Nick paced, keeping his movements measured, ignoring the curious glances from other students passing by. When the hour ended, he stepped forward, rapping on the door with two knuckles.

The professor, a thin, precise man with a neatly clipped beard, answered with a look of wary surprise. Nick offered his credentials and explained, in hushed tones, that he'd appreciate a moment to address the class. The professor hesitated—a flicker of concern passing across his face—then nodded and ushered him in.

Nick stood at the front, surveying the sea of young faces, the room brimming with that unpredictable energy unique to university lecture halls. He introduced himself simply, his voice steady but grave.

"I'm here investigating the whereabouts of Emily Hahn. If anyone knows where she is, or has seen anything—anything at all, no matter how small—you could help us find her. Please, if you remember something, come talk to me."

A hush settled over the class, uneasy and electric. Nick could feel the weight of their attention, the gravity of the moment pressing in. He scanned their faces, searching for any sign—a look exchanged, a sudden shift in posture, the narrowing of eyes—that might suggest unspoken knowledge or hidden worry.

Eyeing Lan back at the rear of the class he walked to her. "We need to talk only this time you need to tell me all you know about Emily you know. When was the last time you saw her. " As the rest of the class emptied out of the room Nick sat down in a chair. I know you have another class this afternoon. But you and I are going to stay right here until I say you can go. Now tell me when was the last time you saw her. You are her friend and if you care for her, you should tell me anything that will help. I supposed that you and she were close enough that you shared things that no one else knew. I know that girls talk and that at this age boys come into the picture even if it is only briefly. There seems to be no talk about any kind of recreation surely the two of you must have went some places together. Maybe shopping or got out for a Latte at the local coffee bar. Please I am concerned that she is in danger and anything you can tell me might be the clue we need."

Lan squirmed in her seat feeling the pressure and the seriousness of the inquiry. Her hand shuffling the books on her lap. Nick was not ready to let this opportunity to escape. "You have to help us her safety is paramount; she could be injured or even…" Stopping his voice letting the girl add her own fears to her thoughts. He waited, letting the silence stretch just long enough to signal the seriousness of the inquiry, "I know that girls sometimes share things that they think their family might question. Is there anything that you are not telling us because you think she might get angry with you or just a little something that you two did by yourself. Maybe meeting boys somewhere?" His voice was low encouraging her to answer so only he could hear her.

"Yes, there is something Saturday night we went to the bar up on the hill and had a few drinks. I hooked up with a guy that I was dancing with and"... she stopped.

"Go on... go ahead tell me what." Leaning close so she could whisper.

Her voice hesitated as she spoke almost a whisper. She was talking to some guy in a red flannel shirt when I left with my friend. That was the last time I saw her. It was close to midnight. I texted her Sunday morning, but I never heard back from her. She had told me earlier that she was going to her Grandfathers Sunday for the evening, and I didn't think any more about it. We don't have any classes together on Mondays, so I didn't worry about her. Then you came to my dorm and asked about her, and I had classes the rest of this week and I just was busy."

Reaching out and putting his hand gently on her shoulder Nick leaned close. "The most important part now is you can help us more now. Maybe you can go with some of my people and look at some picture of known offenders and in the meantime, I am going to go to the bar and talk to the people there."

"I still have two more classes this afternoon." Her voice piqued in anxiety as spoke.

Nick stood his urgency rushed out as he spoke, "Right now it is crucial that we find out where she is and any classes you miss, I will make it right. If you can go down to the police station and tell Captain Gordon that I told you to come down. I will call him and clear it. Thank you so much, you don't know how much this helps."

Walking out into the campus his mood was raised. Reaching his car, he drove out to the bar. Unsure that there would be anyone working at this early hour but it was worth a try. Pulling over he stopped and called doc asking him to meet him at the Carriage lounge. Telling him he would explain when they met. His FBI badge would not get the cooperation in this small-town bar he wanted.

Pulling into the bars lot he waited for Doc. Calling Clementine and Emma; he asked them to meet with the others at the lab around four o'clock for a recap.

Nick could see that there was one car parked in the lot, he was hoping it was not one left over from the night before and that it was indeed the barkeepers.

Stepping out of his car as he saw doc drive in. going to him as he parked close to the doorway to the bar. He was eager to relay the information that he had learned from Lan. Doc climbed out of his car his look was one of question. Nick briskly walked to him "She was hiding something that Lan girl she was out here last Saturday night with the victim. She seen her talking to a local. She left her here and has not heard from her since. I want to go inside and talk to the bartender and see if he is any help. Maybe we caught a break, come on I will lead, I want you to back me up. I am sure that he will be more cooperative with you than me."

Inside the brightly lit bar they could see the man behind the bar working. He was the only one there. Seeing Nick and Doc he shouted, "Not opened yet, we don't open until four."

Continuing to walk to the bar Nick held out his identification. "Nick Curtis FBI and this is Trooper Murdock we have some questions we would like you to answer. "

He waited until Doc held out his ID. "Sure I got a minute, but I am pretty busy."

Pulling the picture of Emmie out of his pocket Nick showed it to the man "This young lady was in here last Saturday night; do you recognize her? She was last seen talking to a one of the male occupant in here. He was wearing a red flannel shirt and Levis. Maybe they were dancing. Take your time look at the picture. Do you remember her."

His eyes shifted to Doc, "Say, I know you...you are a trooper. No, I don't remember her. I don't remember her being here but there a lot of college girls come in and out. They are looking for a few dances and drinks. I don't pay them much mind. Every year they change, and I have learned to kind of ignore them. There seems to be more of the Asian kind recently like her."

"Are you sure look again take a good look." Doc said. "Maybe it's time to renew your liquor license soon, I don't know. Step aside let me see."

Nick looked away not wanting to let the typical remark sway his thoughts.

"By the way what is your name?" Nick asked taking out his note book.

"Carl Davis, hey I don't want any trouble I'm just saying that there are a lot of the college girls and men that come in here." The sweat popping out on his face his eyes narrowed as he looked at Doc. Sure that Nick was of no concern, but the local trooper could cause him grieve.

Nick stepped even closer to the bar leaning over so close that he could smell the arid trace of liquor on his breath. "Maybe they were noisy you know like the was fighting. Not just drinking, maybe he was bothering her. Not just friendly. Maybe, you had to speak to him for bothering her. Is that possible? Do you remember them being here and do you know his name. We are just looking for her the family has a kind of a crisis, and we need to contact her."

Doc stepped closer to him "Maybe you know the man, maybe he is one of the regulars that come in a lot. He was wearing a red flannel shirt like Nick said. But that is pretty common. Think about it I am sure that Captain Gordon down at the city would like to know that you were helpful. I even think that the dean at the college would appreciate your cooperation. We are kind of in a hurry, what do you say do you know who the man was?"

Reaching out to lay down the wiping cloth he was holding He leaned close as if to not share his answer he said. "Now that I think about it maybe he was here, Carl, I don't know his last name. Heard him say that he was here for the deer hunt, didn't seem to me that he was any problem. I think they left together she had come in with that other Asian girl that comes in every so often she is in college. I hope you find her. I hope that I have been a help. Would you guys care for a drink. No charge." His grin came from the stress he was feeling.

"No thanks, here is my card if you think of anything else, wait a minute you say he was here for the hunt? He is not a local, someone you have seen before?"

"Yeah, I said that, but I must have meant that he was hunting, but I have seen him in here before. So, I was wrong, he just said he was hunting. Sorry."

Walking out of the bar Nick's attitude shifted to one of satisfaction. As the door closed behind them, he turned to Doc. "Now that's what I like... a helpful witness, now we are getting somewhere. Someone that saw her alive. Maybe she just decided to shack up with this guy and is now ashamed to come out. You know that old thing of falling in love at first sight sometimes it still works."

"What is with the jokes?"

"Not a Joke, I am just glad that we are making some headway at least she was in a safe situation." Continuing to walk aside doc.

"Yes, I understand what you are saying. But we need to put the small piece of the name Carl with a last name and place. You know where we can find him and hopefully her alive. What about the campgrounds. If he is hunting or so the bartender suggested maybe he is right under our noses."

"Great!!! I left my wife in the campgrounds with a kidnapper. Now that is a good story for the FBI annals."

"Chin up that is a stretch even for you, but we should drive down to the ranger station and check the names of all of the hunters. He thought that his name might be Carl. I'll follow you down there."

"Alright you follow me and then we need to meet at the lab. After I swing by the city and check anything they got on their rap sheets. They were not that helpful this morning. This guy could be right here under our feet. Hiding in plain sight."

"Well, I'll see you at the camp grounds. I think the girls are spending the day together at the tennis courts. They have been pretty chummy since you guys were over for supper. She will probably tell you when you see her. They hit it off pretty good."

Not wanting to wait Nick sat in his car and called the city police asking for Captain Gordon. "Hello, Captain Gordon, this is Nick Curtis, could you do me a favor look in your rap sheets and the arrest reports for a perp... names Carl no last name. Yes, I know that is thin but as a favor for me could you look, I am on my way down there and I want to not waste any more time than necessary. By the way how about the NCIC. That would be great. Thank you. Oh, you showed the perps pictures to Lan, and she struck out no luck. He was not in the pictures. Yes, thank you."

The street was full in front of the police station, so Nick drove into the parking lot in back. Walking into the back door he was greeted by the cute little secretary from the police department. Nodding he went to the front desk where he found the captain seated at the radio desk, dispatching a car to investigate a stolen bicycle.

Going inside the office where that Captain was seated Nick smiled, "I guess that you were not able to get those things I asked for?"

The captain waved his hand "I been working here for almost twenty years

And I learned to roll with guys like you that think I have a cushy job. But I have also learned to smile when someone like you comes into town and begins ordering me around. I just do all I can and wait to get to the rest... You can look through those rap sheets on the desk and the NCIC report should be back in a few minutes. I sent in a request after you hung up."

Stopping next to the captain Nick waited as her answered the phone. When he was finished Nick spoke. The bartender said that the guy that was with her Saturday night might have been in the hunt. That is going to stretch the net a long ways."

"Yeah, what was the area of the entry's... Eight states?"

"Yes, all in the mid states area, but most from Missouri as it was. My wife was one of the farthest ones. Special out of state permits for them. I got Doc checking with the ranger getting the names and all of their info right now. When I finish here I and going to run all of the male names through the NCIC."

"Big area, to canvass but then again, he might be from anywhere. Could have moved recently. Didn't have to a regular subscriber could have picked up the magazine at the corner drugstore.

Watching as nick was busy the captain leaned back in the in his chair. "So, nobody has seen her since Saturday night...Time is getting away...That's not good but you know that we never had an abduction. That's a good thing... no ransom note... no money demand, sounds like some kook. Hope she's still alive. Anything you need just give me shout."

"Don't worry, I will and thank you."

Picking up his phone he called Doc, "Did you get a list of the states, we need to check. Yes, so give them to be but slowly I need to write them down, Okay Arkansas, Missouri, got it. Yes, go on, Iowa, Kansas. Then of course there is Ohio where I and Bobbie are from.

No not the ones that were four women, only the ones with men. Thanks. I'll be there in a little while." Hanging up the phone Nick walked to the captain.

"That narrows it down to four states, now let's eliminate by age, we are sure that this guy is not an old geezer."

Stopping by the desk Nick' tone changed "Damn right, there in the trees that son of a bitch could be holding her in the forest where we been hunting. Sorry Captain I have to get down there. He had to show an ID when he checked in and the ranger should be able to recognize him. I am out of here if you don't mind keep checking the NCIC reports for a guy in his mid-twenties to thirties medium build you got my number call me if you get anything."

Rushing to his car Nick carried his phone in his hand, aware that Bobbie was in danger, he had been willing to bring her out here and now she could be in danger too. She was an attractive woman and over friendly. This guy could have approached her when all of the other hunters were in the woods. 53000 acres of trees and brush to hie the body if the girl was not alive. Pushing the gas pedal down a little harder he was getting more concerned by the minute. Doc was supposed to be there but what if...what if? His mind was filled with fear as he reached the Mobil station just before the turn off to the campgrounds. As the traffic coming off the highway continued to keep him stopped, he look to the drive way, there was Doc standing talking to the owner. The short black-haired man, holding what looked like two six packs of beer. Grabbing his phone off of the seat he scanned down to Doc's number. Tapping the phone as the traffic slowed, he could see Doc reach to his hip pocket and heard him answer. "Doc here."

"What are you doing buying beer you were supposed to be talking to the ranger Bobbie is alone there, and the culprit could be there with her." Shouting.

"Relax, Bobbie is fine she has Storm with her and the Ranger is not there, I drove up after I checked, she is fine where are you?"

"Right across the street from you in the black car." Honking his horn.

Traffic slowed down and Nick gunned the engine across the street stopping with a squall of the tires. Leaning out the window he shouted,

"For a minute there you had me going, I thought she was there alone with this guy. Where is the Ranger?"

"Don't know He was gone when I got there, I think he has some rounds to make, give your boss a call and find out his bosses number he can tell you where abouts he is . Come on let's get this beer back to Bobbie before it gets hot. He'll probably be back by then. Stop worrying Bobbie is fine Storm won't let anything happen to her. Besides Clementine and Emma might be back by now."

Pulling his head back in the window Nick twisted the steering wheel and drove out of the station lot. Driving into the campgrounds Nick tried to relax. His heart was pounding with the thoughts of Bobbie and this guy.

The afternoon sun was streaming through the trees as his car reached the ranger station. The door was closed but Nick stopped any way. Bouncing out of the car as Doc pulled beside him, he sprinted to the door. Grabbing the handle, he tried to open it. Shaking the knob, pounding on the door he could see the leg of the ranger on the floor. "Doc!!! He shouted. "He is in there!!! The ranger is in there."

Doc had already jumped out of his car and was coming up on Nick as he shouted. "It's locked. From the inside, we are going to have to bust our way in. I can't see if he is okay or not, quick get something to break in there."

Doc pushed Nick aside and slammed his shoulder against the door, but it would not give. The rough sawed door was made to look rustic and was far too strong for the two men to force it open. Doc rushed back to his car and opened the trunk bringing out a flat tire tool he kept in his trunk. Prying at the lock point as they strained, they wallowed the jamb back and forth finally forcing the door open.

Lurching inside as they fell from the sudden release of the lock. Nick bend down and felt of the rangers pulse. Weak...rolling him over they could see the bright gash on his forehead. Doc shoved his hand struggling to find a pulse on the ranger. Bending closer he could see the blood stain that had crept across the shirt the knife wound just below his rib case. "He's alive call Nine...one...one." Nick yelled as he pressed on the wound.

Jumping up Nick rushed outside leaving Doc to handle the ranger. Striding to his car he jumped inside and spun the wheel around heading for the Winnebago and Bobbie. As he stormed through the trees, the racing car losing traction in the dirt road. Rushing once again his heart was out of control. As he broke through the brush his eyes could see Storm and Bobbie at the wooden bench.

Storm spung up as she heard the racing car approaching. Easing back on the accelerator Nick sighed as the pair appeared to be fine. Stopping inches from them Bobbie stood up Her "Stay" command to Storm stopped the k-nine in her tracks.

Bouncing up off of the bench Bobbie walked quickly to Nick "What are you doing why are you driving so fast. What is wrong?"

Stopping he dialed the Nine. One. One. emergency number.

Holding Bobbie close he relayed the location and the fact that they had a person who was wounded. Identifying himself as an FBI agent. He waited as the line went dead, He turned to Bobbie, "The park ranger has been attacked, Doc is with him I'll need the first aid kit. Stay here with Storm."

Running inside the Winnebago Nick grabbed the first aid kit and drove back to the ranger shack. Doc had removed the rangers shirt and loosened his belt. Still holding pressure on the wound.

Nick pried open the first aid kit careful not to soil the three four by fours he applied pressure on the wound. The shallow breathing of the ranger receded as they held his head upright. Still not awake but his breathing began to become regular.

Nick and Doc remained silent as they waited for the emergency vehicle to arrive, the tension in the small ranger station thick as the fading afternoon light slanted across the floor. Still holding pressure on the wound, Nick could feel the faint throb of the ranger's pulse beneath his hands—a fragile thread tethering the injured man to life. Neither spoke; every second was drawn out in anxious anticipation, broken only by the ragged, shallow breaths of the wounded ranger.

When the medics finally burst in—professional, brisk, and commanding—they quickly assessed the scene. Nick stepped aside looking at the desk blotter scribbled in magic marker the words...'Fire roads', the hard black lines meant to accentuate the words.

The attendants without wasting a moment, they aspirated the ranger and carefully lifted him onto a stretcher, working in swift, practiced harmony. Within minutes, he was loaded into the ambulance, monitors and IVs trailing behind.

As the flurry of activity enveloped them, Nick found himself explaining to the lead paramedic, voice steady despite the adrenaline, "We found him like this—I'm with the FBI, and he's law enforcement too." He gestured to Doc, the implication clear: they were both on the same side.

Doc, concern etched deep in his features, made the decision to accompany the ranger to the hospital. Nick reached over, placing a reassuring hand on Doc's shoulder as he climbed into the ambulance.

"Doc, stay with him until you can find out all you can. Especially what he meant by fire roads. As soon as you can get away, head back to your lab and bring your forensics kit—I'll secure the shack."

With one last look, the ambulance doors slammed shut, siren wailing as it sped down the asphalt road. Nick watched until the flashing lights disappeared between the trees, then squared his shoulders, determination settling in. He turned back toward the ranger shack, already making mental notes of the scene, ready to piece together the puzzle left behind in blood and mystery.

Bobbie waited only a moment as the shrill sound wailed through the trees before She grabbed and hugged Nick. "What is going on Nick. Who stabbed the ranger? Is this part of your case? Never mind just hold me forget that I asked, I can wait until you want to tell me. I have to go back to the camper Storm is going to become anxious."

Knowing that it was safe to shut the door he sat down on the step. Dialing his phone he called the city police department. "Captain Brock please, hello this is Nick again we have an attempted murder at the Mark twain campgrounds the ranger has been stabbed, He is on the way to the county hospital. I can't say how he is. Looked like he is going to survive, I got there close to the time he was stabbed.

Not sure but I think it has to do with the missing girl … He was sprawled on the floor of his shack. Got any idea?"

There was a brief silence on the line, punctuated only by the static hum of uncertainty. Nick pressed the phone closer to his ear, listening for Captain Brock's response.

"Yes, Doc and I were out here to get the list of hunters. Doc's handling the forensics for now—I can call Springfield for backup, but I'd rather let Doc take the first pass. Anything he turns up will give us a head start. He's at the hospital with the ranger now. As soon as he's free—or if the ranger wakes up—he and I will get back to the shack and take another look around. It has to be connected; it's all happening too close together." Nick's words came out measured, determination sharpening each syllable.

There was a pause, then Nick added, "No, still nothing on the girl. We're running out of ground, but I'm not giving up."

He drew in a breath, steadying himself. "Captain, could you put a man on the door at the hospital? You never know with someone like this—whoever did this, they're no amateur." He paused again, listening to Brock's low murmur of assent. "Thanks. I'll keep you posted."

As he hung up, the silence of the ranger shack pressed in—a hush thick with secrets and waiting. The first hints of dusk crept through the trees outside, shadows stretching across the forest floor. Nick pocketed his phone, mind already spinning with possibilities. The next move would depend on what Doc found, and what the wounded ranger—if he regained consciousness—could tell them. For now, all Nick could do was hold his ground and prepare for whatever answers the night might bring.

The air outside the ranger shack felt charged, tense with waiting. Nick rose from his seat, unable to stay still, his boots tracing restless arcs across the creaking porch boards. The day's chaos played over in his mind—the blood, the breathless urgency, the missing girl, and now the ranger's cryptic mention of fire roads. Alone but for the hush of the woods pressing close against him, Nick wrestled with a sense of unease. He needed help—needed familiar voices, sharp minds.

Pacing back and forth, Nick's mind turned over the facts. Sure, that if anything he needed it was help. Reaching for his phone he dialed Clementine's number. When she answered he asked what was she and Emma doing.

"Okay I need you to come down to the campgrounds and bring Emma with you. Yes, I know that I told you we were going to meet at the lab—don't question me now, just get Emma and hurry down here to the campground. No, we are not giving up on the palace investigation but for right now… Please, I am asking you to hurry down here and bring Emma with you. Okay, see you then."

Nick let the phone drop to his side, relief mingling with anxiety. Outside, the forest deepened into twilight, each shadow a question. He braced himself for what would come next—knowing that soon, reinforcements were on their way, and the night's secrets would not stay hidden for long.

Nick watched as Bobbie approached, her silhouette bright against the thickening dusk. The flicker of orange from her pedal-pushers seemed to catch the last rays of sunlight, lending a touch of warmth to the cool hush that had settled around the shack. He felt a smile pull at the corners of his mouth, the weight of tension easing just a fraction as she drew nearer, bottles of beer clasped behind her back in a playful gesture.

She stopped just in front of him, her eyes shining with mischief and a tenderness that made the night's strain recede for a moment. "No beer until I get a kiss," she teased, holding the bottles just out of reach. "Put your work behind us for a minute and be thankful that we're both okay."

Nick rose to meet her, the creak of the step the only sound in the hush between them. He leaned in, brushing away the shadows with a kiss gentle at first, then fierce with gratitude. For a fleeting second, all that mattered was the soft press of Bobbie's lips and the comfort of knowing she was right there—close enough to touch, to anchor him to something safe amid all the chaos.

When they finally parted, she slipped a bottle into his hand, her laughter low and easy. "See? Wasn't so hard to take a break," she murmured, sinking down onto the step beside him.

Nick took a long sip, the cold bite of beer grounding him. Together, they sat in silence, sharing the fragile peace that had settled like a salve. The world beyond the circle of their quiet would wait—at least for a moment longer.

Nick let her words hang between them, the playful caution softening into something more vulnerable as the hush of the Ozarks pressed close. He watched the way the waning light pooled gold along her cheek, catching in the corners of her almost-grin. The truth of her presence, her resilience, cut through the residue of fear clinging to his chest.

"I'll try," he murmured, his hand tightening around the cool glass. "But it's not easy acting like you're just another face in the crowd—especially now."

He glanced away, down toward the darkening curve of the trail where the hush grew deeper, threaded through with possibility and dread. The urge to draw her close warred with the need to keep her distant, safe—shielded from the knowledge of how nearly the night had veered toward tragedy. He was grateful she didn't know, and resolved that, for now, she wouldn't.

Bobbie nudged him gently with her knee, her laughter a hush against the wild quiet. "We'll be boring, then. Just for a while. No one will ever guess." Her eyes sparkled with mischief, but Nick saw the undercurrent of worry there too—a flicker of understanding that some dangers lurked close, just beyond the safe circle of beer and lamplight.

The forest hummed with nightfall, and Nick drew a slow breath, letting the moment settle. He would hold this borrowed peace as long as he could, even if it was fragile—one more stolen grace amid the shadows. And beside him, Bobbie watched the twilight thicken, her hand hovering close to his on the porch step, a promise of warmth he dared not claim but refused to surrender.

Headlights slashed through the trees, sending rivulets of gold lancing across the porch and making Bobbie pull away from the warm, content shoulder of her husband. The tension in Nick's muscles eased as she shifted, the two of them blinking back into the world beyond their tranquil bubble. Doc's car bounced along the rutted track, closely trailed by Clementine's sedan, their arrival puncturing the hush that had settled with dusk.

Engines off, doors clunked open in the deepening dark. Doc moved with a scholar's briskness, eyes alive behind wire-rimmed glasses as he hoisted his battered suitcases from the trunk, eager to set to work. Clementine was at his side before Nick could even rise from the step, her flashlight cutting arcs in the gloom as she helped Doc wrangle his equipment.

Nick, always a heartbeat behind, hurried to the porch and pushed open the shack's door, flooding the inside with harsh light. Doc swept inside without preamble, already sorting through evidence—latex gloves snapped on, vials and brushes arrayed on the warped table. Nick stood back, a bystander in his own refuge, while Bobbie quietly slipped away to gather herself. Emma joined her outside, the two women exchanging a look that spoke of shared burdens and unspoken resolves.

Now, everyone but Nick wore their sidearms openly, holstered at their hips in plain view. The case had shifted: no longer a matter of whispered speculation, but a public investigation. They wanted the world to see, or at least the woods to take note—justice was coming for the one who'd assaulted the ranger. The display was a message, bold as a beacon beneath the watchful eyes of the trees.

Doc paused briefly before stepping back onto the porch, where the gas lantern nailed above the door cast his features into a play of flickering shadow and light. For a moment, his face was strange—part guardian, part ghost—before he leaned in close to Nick, voice dropped low.

"The doctor at the hospital says the ranger's strong. Good chance he'll pull through, but he can't speak yet. No idea who did this, or what those scribbles on the blotter pad mean." He hesitated, gaze flicking past Nick toward the forest. "One of the ambulance crew thinks the markings could be about the fire roads—those old tracks winding through the national forest. Built for the crews to fight fires, mostly ignored by everyone else... unless someone needed to disappear."

His words lingered in the cool night air, heavy with implication. Nick nodded, feeling the boundaries of the evening shift once again, the circle of light on the porch now a stage for secrets brushing dangerously close to revelation.   Inside, Doc resumed his work, instruments gleaming in the lamplight, while outside Bobbie and Emma watched the woods for anything that might emerge from the darkness.

A new phase had begun—one of evidence and vigilance, of open questions and quiet determination. The hush of the Ozarks pressed close, as if the forest itself was listening, waiting for the night's truths to be brought to light.

Nick lingered at the porch rail, phone heavy in his pocket, the urge to call Kerry simmering beneath his skin. The case had twisted overnight—from a missing coed to a battered ranger, from a tangle of worries to something sharp-edged, criminal. Now every breath of wind carried a new urgency: by morning, the woods would bristle with uniforms and search dogs, the hush shattered by the drone of helicopters and the crisp bark of radios.

This was no longer a question of who had vanished, but who had left harm in their wake—who had stalked the national forest's old fire roads and turned prey into predator. It was Nick's case now, and the responsibility pressed hard on his ribs. Soon the headlines would spill from the hilltops to the city, and the state's eyes would sweep over the rugged valleys, hunting a fugitive who had proven themselves both armed and merciless.

In the lamplit gloom, Nick mapped out the morning in his mind. Deputies rousting volunteers, grid maps unfurled across dashboards, checkpoints posted at every backwoods turnoff. The search for a missing girl had become a mutt with teeth, and Nick—steady, dogged, unwilling to let fear shape his resolve—felt the world narrowing to a single point of pursuit. Whatever darkness had crossed that line in the woods, he would meet it head-on. The forest would not keep its secrets much longer.

Nick finally gave in to the weight in his pocket, slipping his phone free from his shirt—right where he'd tucked it earlier while sitting with Bobbie. With a thumb, he found Kerry's number and pressed dial, the quiet on the porch thickening as the call connected.

The line buzzed once, twice, then Kerry answered, their voice taut with worry. Nick wasted no time. "Hi boss there is been a sudden turn everything points to the girl has been abducted by a man she met at a local bar. We were on our way to verify him with the ranger here in the park and when we got here someone had assaulted the ranger. It has to be the same guy we can't find the paperwork that has the names of all the hunters. No...we don't have a positive identification on this guy. No boss we don't know who assaulted him he is still out. Yes, I'll call you. Have a good night." Wiping his phone off. Nick sat down on the step.

Nick's jaw tightened as he ran the numbers, mentally circling the campsites scattered through the dense timber. The missing paperwork gnawed at him—a single, crucial thread that should have cleared the haze, now gone. He imagined again the battered lockbox, the register pad with names and dates, the neat handwriting that ought to have mapped each hunter's claim on the woods. But the shack was empty, the pages vanished. It wasn't just convenience—it was deliberate, and it pointed straight to the careful vanishing act of their suspect.

He pictured the layout: nearest the entrance, the retirees with their quiet fire and well-worn gear—no chance there. Then, just across the hollow, the two young women with the battered Subaru and neat, efficient packs. He'd seen them that afternoon, boots muddy but spirits unshaken by the isolation. Not them. That left the final arc of campsites, four in all, strung along the old road where the forest thickened, and the ground fell away toward the creek. Any one of them could hide a stranger, a man slick enough to slide beneath their notice, dangerous enough to risk everything after dark.

They'd need to sweep every tent and lean-to, talk to every camper left in the woods before sunrise. Nick felt the press of time—a fugitive with a head start, a girl somewhere lost, the forest vast enough to swallow mistakes. He'd have to split the team, keep their wits about them; the man they hunted might turn desperate, might already be watching from behind a curtain of pine.

Nick stood, stretching the stiffness from his legs, scanning the darkness for a hint of silhouette or the glint of eyes. The search had narrowed to a handful of firelit clearings and the thin hope that the clues—however scattered—would finally fit. He clipped his radio to his belt, gathering resolve with each practiced motion. Tonight, the Ozarks held its breath. By dawn, Nick swore, the silence would break.

Nick jumped up, pulse hammering, as a sudden memory flashed through his mind—a stack of maps, rolled and carelessly dropped on the scuffed floorboards, right near the battered wooden case in the corner of the shack. He barely registered the ache in his knees as he bolted across the porch and darted through the night air, boots thudding against the packed earth. He should have looked closer, he thought, cursing his own haste.

He was nearly at the threshold when an arm shot out to block his path—Doc, looming in the doorway, glasses catching the glow from the lantern hanging inside.

"Whoa, where are you going in such a hurry?" Doc's voice was low, wary.

"Maps," Nick blurted, eyes darting past Doc's shoulder to the cluttered room within. "There must be maps of the fire roads. We can narrow down where this guy could be hiding with the maps."

Doc didn't budge. "Stop. I haven't printed all of the items in the room yet. That's way back there, and he probably didn't touch them, but you know..." He trailed off, rubbing his temples. "I need more help if we're going to get this whole place printed before sunrise."

Nick shifted from foot to foot, urgency twisting his insides. The shadows in the shack seemed to pulse with withheld secrets, the silence between them thick as smoke.

Doc stepped closer, dropping his voice to a whisper. "While you're in here, I wanted to ask you something." He glanced over his shoulder, making sure no one else was near.

"Do you think Bobbie saw him come in here and didn't mention it? Maybe she thought it meant nothing at the time?"

Nick hesitated, caught off guard by the question. He thought back to Bobbie's nervous hands, the way they'd lingered by the doorway, gaze flicking over the room with restless energy. Had there been a hesitation, a detail swallowed by shock or uncertainty? The possibility sent a chill down his spine.

"I don't know," Nick said finally, his voice tight. "I... maybe. We'll have to ask, but not yet. Not until we know what to look for. First, let's see those maps."

He ducked past Doc, careful not to jostle the forensic gear scattered across the floor and made his way toward the far corner. The rolls of paper waited for him, thick with dust and the promise of answers—routes to search, roads to block, places a desperate man might run to as the night pressed in. Nick's fingers trembled as he reached for them, ready to pull every path from the forest's memory, determined not to let a single detail slip away unseen.

Doc's shrill voice screamed out "Gloves!"

Grabbing the box of nitrile gloves up off the chair Nick held one up to his mouth blowing the glove up to slip it on his dry rough hand, doing the same with the other he waited while Doc laid the rolled-up packet of maps on the desk.

Spreading them out Doc was eager to see them. He pointed to the key at the bottom of the map "All the black lines are fire-roads. The broken ones are the hard roads. The new campground are not there those that were put in just for the hunt

They will disappear later. They put them up just for this event. You can see the fire roads end at the county roads. There should be a locked gate where the roads meet."

Nick paused; the maps forgotten for a moment as Doc's words caught up to him. The weight of their predicament pressed in, every lead suddenly more vital, every delay more costly.

"If nothing else," Doc said, his voice low but urgent, "the fact that he tried to kill the ranger confirms we're looking for someone desperate. That gives us what we need—if we can just tie a name to it. Do you know if anyone might have a copy of the entrants? That would be key, if he used his real name. Too bad about the time change; we could call the magazine office and get the list."

Nick pinched the bridge of his nose, thinking fast. "Maybe local law enforcement holds a backup from the start of the hunt, or the organizers themselves. Someone's got to have paperwork—waivers, registration, something. We just need to get our hands on it before he slips further away."

Doc nodded, already pulling out his phone. "I'll try the event coordinator. You try to memorize the ones that end up here on the ridge."

Nick turned back to the maps, the lines and symbols swimming before his eyes. Somewhere among these tangled routes and half-remembered names, he was sure, the truth crouched—waiting to be unearthed.

"No answer, go ahead and take those maps outside you will need them to coordinate a search. You might as well go join the others. I will be finished soon. "

Nick nodded, moving to the door. The lantern light by the door seemed dimmer as the evening began to cloud up. A November storm was brewing to the west blotting out the daylight in the west. The tall trees bringing a cloak of darkness to the forest. The forest that held the attacker and maybe the missing girl.

Nick pulled out his phone and tapped in Kerry's phone number. "Me again We are going to need somebody to get us a helicopter down here. I think the girl could be hidden somewhere with the guy that assaulted the ranger. Still don't know who he is nor how he is traveling. We are sure that the ranger stumbled onto this guy somewhere out here and was attacked to cover his tracks. Now that we have a small chance we are going to talk to the other camper. Maybe we will get lucky. Even if he has hidden the girl somewhere here it is still pretty sure she is alive, even if she was hidden here in the woods. But time is definitely running out. You need to pull in some favors and get me some help down here. I'll keep you posted." Swiping his phone, he jammed it in his pocket.

Chapter Eleven

Hearing the sound of a jeep coming from the southern side of the campground, he walked to the road. The two couples that had share a beer the first night were coming up the road. Elated that he had some local help he waited for them to arrive. Stepping into the road way her waved his arms. The driver stopped almost touching him with the front bumper.

Leaning out he yelled. "Hey, get out of the road what are you doing I almost ran you down."

Walking along side he could see that all of the campers had been drinking.

Stepping close he asked " How sober are you guys anyway? You should not be driving if you are going to drink." The sternness in his voice along with his badge he was holding prompted the driver to turn off the engine.

The girl in the back seat leaned out "Hey are you a policeman?" Guffawing.

"No, I am an FBI agent, and I need to talk to you people. We have something serious going on here at the campgrounds and I need your help."

The man in the back, his face shadowed under the brim of a ball cap, met Nick's gaze with the steadiness of someone determined to be useful. "I get it. We'll help—however you need. Just tell us what to do."

Nick nodded, grateful for the shift in tone. "Good. First, nobody leaves the campground unless I say so. Lock your vehicles, keep an eye out for anyone who doesn't belong, and if you see anything strange, call me. I'll need one of you to help look at the map—there's a chance the attacker is using old trails, places only locals or seasoned campers would know. Any of that sound familiar?"

The girl in the back seat, her earlier bravado sobered by Nick's urgency, bit her lip. "There's a cabin out by the east ridge—we saw it on a hike yesterday, looked abandoned. I don't think it is in the forest."

A gust of wind rattled the jeep's doors, sending a flurry of brown needles skittering across the gravel. The storm was nearly upon them, the dark trees leaning into the gathering howl. Nick felt the press of time, each second slipping from his grasp like rain off a slick jacket.

"Alright," he said, voice low and steady, "Let's move. Go ahead and go into town and enjoy your dinner before the real weather hits. And remember—if you see anything, call. We're not just looking for a suspect—we're trying to save a life."

The group drove away, urgency trumping their earlier carelessness. Nick tucked the maps under his arm and started toward the tree line where his RV was parked, the sense of both hope and dread sharpening with every step into the shadowed woods. Reaching the Winnebago, he found that everyone including Storm were inside.

Bobbie was in the small kitchenette fixing something on the stove. Walking to her he leaned over and kissed her on the neck. How long before dinner? I am famished." Wanting to keep the mood light.

We have decided to eat like we are camping so we are having weenies and beans we took a vote, and it won. Have a seat. I know we need to be serious, but we don't need to be afraid. Counting all of the guns and the crossbows we have a pretty good arsenal." Her try at humor fell flat.

Nick wanting to reassure her that they were safe swung his arm pointing to Storm. "But my dear wife you forgot the most important protector of all. The quite well-trained Storm...the pride of the city. Seriously though as long as we stick together, we will all be safe."

"So as to not leave out anything I think we should wait until Doc comes in before we talk about what we are going to do. I called Kerry and I would not be surprised if he didn't show up here by morning. So, to keep everything in perspective bring on the weenies and beans. If you got any peanut butter and grape jelly, I would give you a big kiss in return."

Nick sat down the wheels were turning, "Bobbie have you been in the RV all day? Did anyone drive by while you were here alone?

"No, I came out to wait for Emma to bring Storm to me. A red pickup came by, but not the one that was hunting down in green sector. I was just a pickup but didn't have a camper. The one that you and I saw down there had a camper remember he came back while we were walking. The tall man with long dark hair. We just waved hello, and he waved back and went into the camper. I don't think it was the same truck as I said it was just a truck no camper."

"Okay, so it was not the same truck, is it going to be long on supper? If Doc doesn't come in pretty soon, I want to eat and get that out of the way... We need to get down to the lab and find the girl. "

Emma was listening to them, and she said, "And catch this guy." Walking to the door of the Winnebago looking out into the fading sunlight.

Nick's question hung in the air. The RV seemed to shrink around them, kitchen heat mingling with the rising tension. Bobbie paused, a wooden spoon clutched in her hand, eyes narrowing in thought.

"Could it be that he had just removed the camper and was driving the truck without it."

"I suppose he could have," she said, voice uncertain. "It looked like the same model. The color was right. I didn't see the plates—too much glare. But it didn't have that camper shell, and that's what threw me off."

Emma moved from the door, folding her arms. "If he can take it off and on, then he's a step ahead of us. He could be moving around right under our noses, changing how the truck looks every time."

Nick nodded, the pieces shifting uneasily in his mind. "That's what I'm worried about. He could have hidden her in the camper, dropped it somewhere, and then drove into town as if nothing happened. No one would think twice about a plain red pickup."

A silence settled over them, broken only by the faint bubbling of beans on the stove and the distant call of a bird outside. Nick's jaw tightened.

"We need to get down to the lab as soon as Doc gets here. And keep an eye out for that truck—camper or no camper. If he's changing things up, we can't take anything for granted."

Bobbie forced a small smile, trying to lighten the mood. "Well, at least supper's almost done. We're going to need the energy."

But as they prepared to eat, a shadow of uncertainty lingered in the Winnebago—a nagging reminder that the answer might be right out there, disguised and waiting.

As Bobbie began dishing out the food, the rattle of the RV door brought their attention sharply towards it. Doc stepped inside; his silhouette momentarily framed against the amber dusk. He shucked off a pair of powder-blue nitrile gloves, holding them aloft and glancing pointedly at Bobbie—a subtle hint that he needed a trash can.

Without missing a beat, Bobbie popped open the cabinet beneath the sink and held out the bin, her smile ambiguous—caught somewhere between appreciation for Doc's civility and relief that he'd arrived in time to eat supper while it was still steaming. Doc deposited the gloves with a practiced flick, giving her a nod of thanks.

Turning toward Nick, Bobbie let out a laugh, the tension in her shoulders easing just a bit. "Just in time—now we can get down to the lab." The double meaning wasn't lost on anyone. Nick grinned, and even Emma cracked a smile, the nerves around her eyes softening as the group clung to this brief moment of levity.

Plates were filled, hands passed steaming bowls, and for a few minutes the only sounds were the clink of utensils and the quiet murmur of contented eating. Outside, the light was slipping away, shadows thickening in the trees, but inside the Winnebago, the warmth of companionship took hold—fragile, but real.

When the last spoonful was scraped up, Doc leaned forward, his expression turning serious once more. "I'll get the initial results. We'll want to look at them together." The words seemed to pull them all back to the thread of urgency, reminding them that supper was only a pause—a brief respite before the next revelation.

Dinner finished; Bobbie couldn't hold back her concern. She dried her hands on a towel, heart stilling against the hush that followed the meal, and stepped away from the sink to lean close to Nick. Her voice was low, uncertain but steady. "Do you think I'll be safe here in the RV while all of you go down to the lab?" she asked, eyes flicking to the windows, where dusk pressed softly against the glass. "I'd be lying if I said I wasn't afraid. From what I've gathered, this suspect... he's abducted a young girl, hidden her somewhere out in the woods—maybe even inside that portable camper."

She glanced toward the narrow aisle and the dim corners of the Winnebago, as if gauging the shadows for threats. "If you leave Storm here with me, I can bring her inside. Knowing she's nearby, I'd feel a whole lot safer, no matter what."

Nick considered her for a moment, the weight of responsibility settling on his brow. "You won't be alone. Storm's got a nose for trouble—and she won't let anything get close without a fight." He offered a reassuring squeeze to her shoulder. "But if anything feels off, you phone us. We'll be back before you know it."

The others exchanged glances, the unspoken worry threading through the cozy RV air. Bobbie nodded, taking a slow breath, resolve flickering in her gaze. Outside, night was gathering its forces. Inside, the fragile sense of comfort persisted, bolstered now by the promise of protection—however uncertain the world just beyond the door remained.

Nick's hand lingered on the door handle as the others filed out, jackets shrugged into place, tension sharpening the lines of their faces. A faint blue glow bled from the dashboard, headlights throwing shifting silhouettes across the forest road as the group made their way to their car.

Bobbie stood at the Winnebago's threshold, Storm at her side—the dog's ears pricked, tail low but vigilant, her gaze tracking the departing figures with an almost human attentiveness.

Emma, already dialing her phone, slid into the passenger seat, her voice brisk as she relayed their plans to the station. The Mobil's neon sign would be a beacon in the near-dark—a waypoint where they hoped answers might surface. Dos slid behind the wheel, exhaling slowly, the weight of impending decisions pressing in. "Let's keep this tight," he muttered, half to himself, half to the team.

Nick settled in the back, phone poised but silent for a moment, lost in thought. The engine grumbled to life, its vibration threading through the car as they pulled out, gravel crunching beneath the tires. The forest seemed to press closer now, night's presence thick and watchful. Beside him, Emma caught his eye.

"If the credit card gives us a name, I'll call it in right away. We're not giving this guy another head start."

From the back seat, Nick finally spoke, his tone steadier than before. "The ranger's out of surgery—critical, but stable. They think he might wake up sooner than expected. If we need a positive ID, I'll be ready to go back and talk to him. But—I agree with Doc. We might be chasing more than one set of footprints tonight."

Doc's knuckles whitened around the steering wheel, the stress of the case threading through his veins like cold wire. "We'll split the leads—Emma and I take the Mobil, Doc you stay on the phone with the hospital. If that ranger can talk, we need his story. Fast."

The car hummed along the narrow lane, headlights carving a path through the trees. Each of them, in their own way, watched the shadows for movement, for signs of a fleeing suspect or a terrified child waiting to be found. Behind them, the Winnebago's windows glimmered in the distance—a small island of light and hope, with Bobbie and Storm standing guard.

As the road unwound beneath their tires, the team clung to their overlapping threads of purpose: to protect, to discover, to bring someone home. The night was far from over—and none of them doubted it would demand everything they had before it yielded any answers.

Reaching the lab in a matter of minutes, the group filed in, urgency sharpening each movement. The sterile fluorescence offered little comfort as notebooks were flung open, pens poised for frantic annotation. Nick strode to the whiteboard, fingers tight around the marker, and in a bold hand scrawled the central question: WHY?

"We need to ascertain if the person or persons who abducted the coed is the same as the one who attacked the ranger—and, most importantly, why."

The word hung heavy, suggestion and accusation both, as he underlined it for emphasis.

"Until we talk to the ranger, we have to assume it's the same individual. The missing paperwork at the entry point stands out—

either a slip or a calculated move. Our timeline puts us dangerously close to confirming his identity before he vanished."

Doc, jaw set and voice low, cut in. "If that's true, he's using the hunt as cover—and there's a chance the girl's alive, maybe hidden in the camper deep in the woods. We should go in now: vests on, armed, and sweep for that Winnebago. Keeping her safe is priority one. Catching him is secondary. If she's still alive, her safety comes first."

Emma, never one to hold back, shook her head, concern flaring in her eyes. "But what if we spook him? If we move too fast, he might panic—God forbid, he could hurt her. We have to plan this so her safety isn't compromised."

Clementine jumped up and rushed to the front of the room. "If we do first things first, we need to find out where he is staying. With the fire-roads being in the mix he might have already moved the camper and the girl out of the park. Somehow, we have to get down there and see if the camper is there or not."

" The darkness of the night will be our friend; we have to walk in and use the quiet by walking in on foot for our look see." Doc stopped as if he was thinking.

"Maps that is the key, if I take the county road to the fire-road on the other side of the forest I, We ... I mean I could walk in under the quiet night and see if he is hiding the coed in the camper."

"Wait a minute, Doc!" Emma injected. "Don't the troop have snipers? Maybe even have night sight gear? One or two of them could back you up if you get discovered."

Nick, pacing as he listened, was reminded, "What did the Kansas K.B.I. say about the name on the credit card that was used at the Mobil station? Did it give us anything?"

Doc shook his head. "The credit card came up stolen—probably no use. If we had the registration of the entrants, we could maybe put it closer. The license came back belonging to a Bryant Sloan. Blue springs address, like I said, if that name list was in our hands we could narrow it down."

"Yeah, well I think that Emma has the best suggestion, you call in and get two snipers to go with you. Have them bring in some listening devices and night vision gear for you and them. It might even tell us if the coed is there and if she is okay. By the way call me on your cell as soon as you hear anything... Get on that right away. I am going to secure this lab for a command post."

Clementine still standing spoke to Nick, "I have all of my gear in my car including my vest and a complete tear gas kit. Maybe I would be better off going with Doc."

Clementine gave a quick nod, already moving toward the door. "Don't worry. I'll be careful. And Doc, don't forget to switch your phone to vibrate. We don't need any unexpected chimes out there."

Emma was already rummaging through her bag, searching for her notebook and a spare phone charger as she shot Clementine a tight, grateful smile.   "We'll handle things from here. Just keep your eyes open. If you see anything—anything at all—report back immediately. We can reroute backup if things go sideways."

Doc paused by the threshold, glancing back. "If I'm not in touch every thirty minutes, assume something's wrong. Don't wait. Move."

Nick pulled out his phone, scrolling for Kerry's number, his thumb trembling slightly.

"I'll check in with Kerry. He'll want to be looped in. And Clementine—don't play hero. I want you both back in one piece. That's an order."

Clementine offered a wry grin before slipping out, voice fading as she called back, "I'll do my best, boss. See you soon."

With the team splitting up, tension knotted the air—every eye trained on the clock, every mind racing with contingency plans. The night outside pressed against the windows, thick and watchful, as if the woods themselves were listening in.

Tapping Kerry's contact name on his phone he waited, his thoughts moved to his wife. 'Was it the right thing leaving her alone at the RV the right decision? Of course, she knew where other Glock was, and she could shoot as good as anyone he knew. Beside the well-trained Storm was probably laying right at her feet. Ready to answer any threat that came her way. The other part of the team had not suggested that he was making a mistake at the time.'

"Hello, Kerry not a lot to give you nothing is sure about who we are looking for, no he hasn't been in touch with me."

Nick ended the call, thumb hesitating a moment before he set his phone down. The tinny echo of Kerry's reassurances did little to curb the gnawing doubt rising in his chest. For a few seconds, the hum of electronics and the soft ticking of the wall clock were the only sounds in the command post, their regularity a stark contrast to the turmoil in his mind.

He leaned forward; elbows braced on the table and let the weight of responsibility settle around his shoulders. Bobbie was safe for now—he had to believe that—but as each hour slipped by, the margin for error shrank. The forest outside seemed to press in closer, the kind of darkness that felt sentient, as if it, too, awaited an answer.

Nick glanced at the maps spread across the table, the tangle of radio wires, the hastily scribbled notes. Every decision branched off into a hundred unknowns.   He replayed his recent choices, searching for cracks, for that one thing he might have missed. And always, the unspoken fear lurked: what if this time, it wasn't enough?

Shoving the thought aside, Nick squared his shoulders and focused on the task at hand. There was still time—there had to be.

Seeing the mood on Nick's face Emma stood up walked close stopping long enough to squeeze his shoulder her way of understanding his dilemma.

"How about some coffee? I could use a cup. It's going to be a long night," Nick muttered, in answer mostly to himself, as he pushed away from the command table.   The overhead lights buzzed softly, lending the room a pale, almost spectral glow. For a moment, he just stood there, feeling the fatigue settle deep in his bones.

He found himself thinking of Bobbie—warmth at the edges of his anxiety. Maybe, he thought, a familiar voice would help clear the fog. Sliding his phone from his pocket, Nick dialed her number, a small smile tugging at the corners of his mouth as she picked up.

"Hi honey, do you need something? I was just waiting for my tea water to come to a boil," she said, her voice easy and bright.

It was enough to make him pause, the ache of longing threading through his chest. He hesitated before speaking, pushing back the melancholy threatening to rise

"I just... had a minute and realized that even though you have Storm with you, you might be feeling a little lonely. I feel bad you've ended up babysitting Storm again while I'm tied up with this case." He cleared his throat, searching for levity.

"I promise, when things settle down, I'll make it up to you. If you're still up, I'll try to get home by the ten o'clock news—maybe I'll even stop and pick up something bubbly."

Bobbie's quiet laugh on the other end washed over him, grounding him in the simple reality of connection, even across the night's distance.

"Sounds wonderful," she said. "Storm's guarding my feet, and the Glock is right where you left it. You take care of yourself, okay?"

"I will," Nick replied, his voice steadying. "See you soon."

He ended the call, feeling a little lighter, the weight of uncertainty easing just enough for him to breathe. Refocused, he poured himself a cup of coffee, letting its heat nudge away the chill, and turned back toward the maps—ready to face the night, bolstered by the hope that, if nothing else, there was still someone waiting for him at home.

His phone began dancing across the table where he had laid it down. Grabbing it up he hesitated to answer it. Letting it ring one more time he swiped it.

"Hello, who is this?" anger rising up thinking it was a crank call. "Is this Agent Nickolas Curtis with the FBI?"

"Yes, it is, who is this?"

"You don't know me; Captain Gordon called me and told me to call you I don't know exactly what this is about he was kind of vague about this whole thing but anyway I was supposed to give you the list of the names of the participant's that are in the bow hunt in the woods down in Missouri. My name is not really needed I am the assistant producer of the magazine that sponsored the hunt. If you have a pen and paper, I can read it off to you."

Grabbing a legal pad across the table he answered. "Sure, I am ready."

Putting his phone on speaker he began writing as the names were given.

Emma jumped up grabbing her notepad and began writing the names at the same time. Nick's smile of approval beamed as he scribbled the names down.

Finished Nick leaned to the phone and answered Thank you I appreciate this very much. I'll thank Captain Gordon for being so helpful. Yes, Good night."

"What time is it anyway, surely the captain is not still at work he was there on the day watch, I had better call him and thank him."

"If that won't change your opinion of the old tale that small town won't work with the other departments nothing will." Clicking her tongue Emma sat down.

"Now if we can get someone of the other department to run the list. As Doc said earlier, we can eliminate the couples that were next to us and the two old guys. That's not counting us. So, let's see. I am sure that we can "

Emma hesitated, tapping her pencil against her notepad. "I would also note that there have been two of the men that left because they bagged their deer. What does that leave—five?" Her fingers flicked as she counted off the entrants.

"So out of the original bunch, that leaves five," Nick repeated, pacing once again towards the whiteboard. The wrinkle of his brow showed the strain, his mind racing through possibilities.

He strode to the whiteboard and, with a quick glance at Emma, began copying the remaining five names, marking each one as he spoke.

"We need some way to eliminate each of these. Damn... I wish it was daytime—everyone who could help is closed." His frustration was readable, a hand raking through his hair as he spoke.

"The military records center in St. Louis is closed. If they were in the service, we could eliminate some of them."

He paused, the marker poised midair.

"I need to call the captain and thank him—and see if he's willing to run the names through NCIC for any hits. Maybe we'll get lucky, and something will shake loose before morning."

Stopping at the table where his phone was laying, Nick slid it over to the edge. Tapping the contacts, he let the phone ring until he heard the Raleigh police pick up.

"Hello, this is Agent Nick Curtis with the FBI—could I speak to Captain Gordon? ... Oh, he's gone for the day. So, have you got any brass there—no, I mean, could I talk to the person in charge? Yes, I'll hold."

A brief silence stretched between the click of the hold music and the next voice.

"Sargent Salter here, how can I help?"

Nick introduced himself and explained what he needed, reading off the list of names with careful precision. He thanked Salter and left his number, then hung up.

Laying his phone aside, he turned to Emma, his lips threatening a smile but settling instead into a line of weary patience.

"Now we can just wait... you know... now we wait."

Emma exhaled, tapping her pencil lightly on the table, the faint ticking echoing the hush that fell over the room—the suspense hanging as heavy as the night air outside.

Picking up his coffee cup, Nick held it up. "Any of that coffee left? My mouth is dry."

Emma sprang up from her chair. "I think so. If not, I can make another pot."

"No, don't bother," Nick said, the fatigue softening his features. "By now, Doc and the other troopers should be in place. With any luck we'll be hearing

something soon. We might even get back to the campgrounds and settle in for the night. You and I could use some sleep—and I need to put my phone on its charger. I'd have thought you'd be missing Storm by now. You can crash with us in the Winnebago tonight. I'm pretty sure there's enough room to pull Storm's kennel in too. Looks like it's going to rain before morning."

He tipped his mug to drain the last swig of coffee, the taste just sharp enough to stir his senses as he sat back down. Emma hovered in the dim light, glancing toward the windows as if she could already hear the whisper of rain approaching, her pencil stilled at last. The room settled into another hush—the kind that comes just before the news breaks, or the storm rolls in.

Quickly grabbing his phone off of the table Nick started towards the door.

"The more I think about it the more I realized it that we would be closer to the suspect if we went back to the campgrounds. It is the straightest way to him, and I am sure that the main road runs right down to his spot. If we stay here, it is far longer of a trip by the way of the county road. Grab you gear and follow me in your car back to the campgrounds."

Stepping out of the lab door Nick was greeted by the loud clap of thunder coming from the west. As he surveyed the large four-lane intersection where the two main streets merged, he shook his head, conceding to himself that he'd been right all along—'the storm was indeed moving in from the southwest. Relief bloomed in him, for the weather would lend Doc and the other troopers a much-needed cloak of noise and darkness. The approaching tempest would mask their movement, letting their boots and voices blend into wind and rainfall as they slipped closer to the suspect's hideout.

Lightning stabbed the clouds, illuminating the slick pavement as Nick hurried to his vehicle. The tactical advantage wasn't lost on him: if the suspect was on edge, the deluge and rolling thunder would distract and confuse, making it easier for the troopers to get close— close enough to see if the missing coed was truly there, and if she was, whether she was unharmed. In the hush between thunderclaps, even the faintest cry could carry. Nick tightened his grip on the door handle, mind racing ahead to every possible outcome.

Behind him, Emma exited the building, her jacket pulled tight against the gusts that heralded the downpour. Above them, the sky churned, promising a long and wild night. All they could do now was drive into the storm and hope that, before dawn, silence would be broken not by disaster, but by a message of safety.

Easing into the car seat, Nick turned the ignition and listened as the engine came to life beneath him. The wipers thudded gently, clearing arcs through the mist that clung to the windshield. He glanced in the rearview mirror, just in time to see Emma's headlights blink on behind him—her silhouette a quiet reassurance in the downpour. Satisfied she was following, he guided his car out of the parking lot, double-checking in his mind that he'd locked the lab door behind them. He wondered, suddenly, if that had been the right call. There were spare keys, of course, but if they needed to get back in for any reason, the detour would cost them precious time. Still, the decision was made, and he tried to shake the thought loose.

Slowing as he reached the turn-off to the park, Nick's eyes drifted across the rain-streaked road to a low building nestled down to the left—the headquarters for Troop I, where Doc's fellow troopers were stationed. Just a few minutes' drive from the lab, and now a world away as the storm closed around them.

He took the narrow road into the pines, headlights shimmering with each curtain of rain. The main highway fell away behind them, replaced by the soft hush of tires against wet gravel and the whisper of wind in the trees. The potholes forced him to slow, each jolt softened by his steady grip and the knowledge of what lay ahead. His breath began to fog the glass, and for a moment, he couldn't help but remember winters past—when breath on cold windows meant scribbled hearts and laughter, not the tension that now wound through his chest.

But tonight, there would be no such warmth. Not until they found the missing coed, whose fear hung in the air, invisible yet understood, coloring every thought and every mile. Somewhere up ahead, past the tangled arms of pine and the wild dance of rain, answers waited—along with Bobbie's embrace and, perhaps, a fragile sense of hope for dawn.

Passing the ranger station Nick was reminded that there was already another person who had been pulled into the crime. He could only hope that he would be a survivor and his wounds would heal. His headlights lit up his campsite illuminating the shadow of his wife struggling to carry the kennel. The place that would let Storm settle down for the night ignoring the storm outside.

As she reached the doorway to the warmth and the anxious Storm standing in the doorway, she acknowledged the approaching car. The slightest wave of her free hand told Nick that there was no need to hurry she would be able to pull the kennel inside and be ready to greet him with a kiss when he stopped.

The dash from the car to the RV was a blur of rain and adrenaline, every step punctuated by the hiss of water on gravel. Bobbie, efficient as always, had already settled Storm in her kennel, her arms outstretched as Nick burst through the door. For a moment, the world outside—the storm, the search, the fear—fell away, eclipsed by the simple comfort of a tight embrace. Warmth radiated through him, chased off the chill that had seeped into his bones, and he let himself breathe, if only for a second.

Emma entered minutes later, lingering at the threshold, her presence gentle and considerate. She caught sight of the reunion and quietly steered herself toward Storm instead, leaving Nick and Bobbie their fleeting moment together. Closing the door behind her, she crouched at the kennel and reached through the wire grate, fingers seeking the familiar patch of fur. Storm's tail thumped an eager rhythm, her body wriggling with joy. Even in the shadow of uncertainty, that happy greeting was a comfort—an unspoken reminder that, for now, they were all safe inside, together against the wild night.

Emma scratched Storm's head, murmuring soft words so only the dog could hear. The storm outside battered the RV, but within, there was a hush, punctuated only by Storm's little huffs and the sheltering sound of rain. Whatever

waited beyond the pines, it would have to wait a little longer—inside, for these brief moments, hope was allowed to catch its breath.

Bobbie settled on the couch wiping the raindrops from her face her lips curled holding back a smile, "Unless I was seeing things I would swear that the day that you stopped and bought beer. You sneaked in a bottle of Wild turkey and put it in the cabinet when I wasn't looking, is that possible?"

Nick following Bobbies humoristic attempt to hide her desire to wash away the chill that her dash outside to bring in Storms kennel had brought.

He yelled out, "Glasses I need glasses!!!"

Bobbie rolled her eyes, but the warmth in her expression outshone the lingering chill on her cheeks. "Glasses, he says, like I keep the good crystal tucked next to the marshmallows." She ducked to a cabinet under the sink and rummaged, emerging with three squat tumblers—one chipped, two mismatched, each a veteran of campfire evenings and long, uncertain nights like this.

Emma flopped onto the bench seat beside her; feet tucked beneath her and hair dripping little rivers onto the cushion. "I'll take whatever you've got. If it holds whiskey, it's fine by me."

With a flourish, Nick twisted off the cap and filled the glasses—a little more generous than usual, amber liquid catching the lamplight and promising a heat to stave off more than just the weather. He handed one to Emma and one to Bobbie, pausing just long enough to toast,

"To dry clothes, safe company, and mornings that always come, no matter how rough the night."

The three of them raised their glasses, clinking them together in a soft chorus. For a moment the storm was nothing but a distant percussion, a wild and rhythmic backdrop to the hush that settled in the RV. Bobbie leaned into Emma's side, laughter warming her voice as she nudged,

"Next time, you're on bottle duty."

Emma grinned, tilting her glass in agreement.

"Deal—provided we're not running rescue missions in the middle of a monsoon."

Nick settled onto the edge of the couch, feet planted, tracing the rim of his glass as if the motion could smooth the edges of his worries. The whiskey burned, sweet and sharp and necessary. Around them, the small space glowed with quiet agreement, the world whittled down to the comfort of four walls, three friends, and a dog dozing in her kennel. For tonight, that was enough.

Putting the bottle back brought no objections; they all knew that drinking tonight still standing was victory enough. Nick slipped off his holster, the familiar weight of the Glock replaced by a fatigue he could finally acknowledge and tucked it in the cabinet beside the bottle—a ritual of setting burdens aside. With a sigh, he gathered his dry pajamas, the fabric cool in his hands, and nodded toward the back of the RV.

"Guess it's time we all settle in," he said, voice softer now, the edge of vigilance blunted by warmth and whiskey.

Emma stretched, her limbs sprawling in content defiance of the rain's drumbeat. Bobbie flicked off the main light, letting the soft glow of the lantern pool around them, and began hunting for her own sleep shirt in the cluttered bag at her feet.

The RV shifted gently in the wind as Nick ducked into the bathroom, the click of the door a signal—a gentle suggestion that the storm outside could have the night, but inside, they'd claim their peace. Soon, the only sounds were the quiet shuffle of cotton, the settling of bodies into makeshift beds, and the steady, reassuring breaths of a dog dreaming in the dark. For a little while, the world was small and safe, and the promise of sleep was enough.

The scream of the ringtone shattered the hush, slicing through the tranquil cocoon they'd drawn around themselves. Emma jolted upright, pulse spiking, while Bobbie's hand flew to her chest, breath caught somewhere between annoyance and alarm. For an instant, the storm outside seemed less menacing than this new intrusion.

Bobbie grabbed the vibrating phone from the table—Doc's name flashing on the display—and hurried down the narrow aisle to the bathroom, wrapping on the door with the urgency of someone desperate to hand off bad news. Nick emerged; towel draped over one shoulder and worry already gathering in his eyes. He took the phone, his expression tightening as he listened.

"It's Doc," he reported, voice low, so as not to rouse the fragile calm. "They checked the camper—the one we thought might be the kidnapper's hideout. Place was empty. No one there, but... signs a woman had been staying there. Nothing conclusive. No one home when they swept it."

He paused, the weight of disappointment settling on him, but pressed on. "We've got a listening device planted at least. And Doc says I'm relieved for the night—two new troopers are covering until I can get there myself."

Emma let her breath out slowly, her tension warring with exhaustion. Bobbie sank onto the edge of the couch, running a hand through her hair, gaze fixed on a point somewhere far away.

"Well, it's something," Emma said finally, a note of hope threading her words. "We'll know if anyone comes back."

Nick nodded, tucking the phone back into Bobbies hand and slipping once more into the quiet bathroom of the RV. Outside, the storm pressed on, indifferent. But inside, the three friends drew their circle of light a little closer, Nick and Bobbie settled on the bed and Emma slept on the couch.

Chapter Twelve

The clouds were slipping away as the starting whistle shocked everyone awake. Bobbie was in her favorite place laying in Nick's arms; his hand was covering her breast. He was unable or unwilling to move, just a grin at her as her eyes smiled back at him. The quick glance to see where Emma was hinted to them that a quick kiss might be alright but anything more intimate would be inappropriate.

Raising up on one arm Nick stretched out trying to find her. A sudden noise from the tiny bathroom satisfied him. Slipping his hand under the silky feel of her gown he satisfied them both. His gentle touch brought Bobbie fully awake.

It was a tempting gesture, as if they were two youngsters stealing a quick touch. Bobbie's longing grew, mingled with the thrill of being nearly discovered. Throwing caution aside, she drew the covers higher and pressed her lips to Nick's—a kiss deep and vivid, sending a current through both of them as she shifted closer. Her hand guided his, each movement electrifying, though restrained by the gentle boundaries they both honored. For a moment, the world outside faded, replaced by the soft hush between them and the morning's golden light filtering through the curtains.

Nick caught a glimpse of Emma, already up and letting Storm out of her kennel, the dog stretching and prancing in anticipation of her morning treat. That window of private bliss shrank as reality rustled nearby, but neither Bobbie nor Nick let go of the sweetness. They savored that fleeting connection—a shared touch, a whispered laugh, the intimacy of two hearts finding each other in the calm before the day's demands.

They were wise enough to cherish it for what it was: a brief, gentle romance, bright and real in the soft hush of morning. And when Storm's exuberant bark sliced through the ecstasy, both smiled, their moment tucked safely away, ready to greet whatever the new day might bring.

Emma slid open the kennel, allowing Storm to trot back in, the dog's tail a signal of morning enthusiasm. Turning, Emma crossed to the kitchenette, her movements purposeful as she filled the coffee pot and set it to brew, the faint clatter and hum sending a gentle signal to the others that the day had begun.

Bobbie, catching the cue, straightened the covers around her and arched her back in a long, luxurious stretch, reluctantly bidding farewell to her cozy haven.   Beside her, Nick reached for his pants, discreetly slipping them on beneath the covers. He leaned in, cupping Bobbie's face with both hands, his touch warm and lingering as he kissed her softly on the lips.

"To be continued," he whispered with a mischievous grin, before vaulting from the bed and making for the tiny bathroom, the curtain fluttering in his wake.

Left in the golden hush, Bobbie sank back against the pillow, a lazy smile curling at her lips. The languid, dreamy mood of awakening still clung to her like a second skin, and she watched Emma move about the kitchen, grateful for the brief lull before the day's bustle began. The smell of brewing coffee mingled with the gentle patter of Storm's paws, and for a moment, Bobbie allowed herself to savor the peace—the warmth of the bed, the gentle promise in Nick's parting words, the comfort of friends nearby.

She knew soon enough she would rise to meet the day, but for now, she clung to the fleeting magic of the morning, letting it fill her with a quiet optimism, ready for whatever awaited them beyond the sanctuary of the RV.

The quiet didn't last much longer. Searching his phone as he returned, Nick glanced at both Emma and Bobbie before dialing Doc's number. The call slipped straight to voicemail. With a sigh, Nick set his phone down on the table and strode over to Emma.

"Doc is still out of it, so we've got a few moments before we need to hurry over to the troop," he said, voice low but purposeful. "I want to get with the man in charge over there—see if he'll contact the county sheriff for some backup. We need to keep eyes on that camper and start searching for this guy."

He paused, gathering his thoughts before turning to Bobbie. "Meanwhile, the RPD needs to run those three guys through NCIC. See if anything pops up. Emma, could you get on the phone and contact all the cities those men have lived in? Ask about any reports of criminal activities involving them. I can't shake the feeling this isn't the first incident—maybe he just hasn't been caught yet. Even cases where they were only questioned. Anything."

Emma nodded, already reaching for the notepad by the coffee pot, jotting down the names and making a checklist of calls to make. Bobbie, catching the drift, gave a brisk nod as well.

Nick glanced at the slim laptop tucked near the dinette. "I'd like to sit down and run through everything on the computer, but first—maybe one of us could volunteer to fix breakfast? It's going to be a long morning."

Bobbie grinned, already sliding out of bed and reaching for the skillet. "I'll handle breakfast. You two focus on the case—I'll keep the coffee coming."

The RV buzzed to life: keys clacking, coffee gurgling, the sound of eggs cracking against the rim of a bowl. Outside, the morning sun brightened, casting the day in honest gold as their small team set to work—each focused, determined, and united by the sense that something much larger than themselves was about to unfold.

Breakfast was a blur as they hurried through their plates, the once-leisurely atmosphere dissolving into a focused urgency. Nick, already dressed and zipped into his jacket, slipped the Glock from its cabinet and threaded it onto his belt—his movements quick but steady, the ritual familiar. Satisfied, he leaned over to press a kiss to

Bobbie's temple; she was still perched at the dinette, cup half-full of the last of the coffee, her gaze trailing the sunlight through the window.

Storm, her keen eyes following every movement from her kennel, let out a soft whine, paws shifting anxiously on the thin mat. Emma caught the signal, crossing the narrow aisle to kneel beside the cage. She longed to run her fingers through the dog's sleek, dappled coat, but the wire mesh pressed between them.

"Say, Nick," Emma called, glancing back, "I think we ought to let Storm come with me today. She's getting restless cooped up in here. I know you figured she'd keep anything from happening to Bobbie, but for now—why don't we drop her at Doc's place? It's sudden, but I'd like her to have a change."

Bobbie raised a hand, agreeing before Nick could even respond. "That's a good idea. Doc's wife said I'm welcome anytime. She and I can figure something out—just give me a minute and I'll be ready." Her smile was reassuring, warm as she began to gather her things.

Nick hesitated only a moment, considering both women and the eager dog. Finally, he nodded. "All right. We'll swing by Doc's before heading over." He paused, surveying the small, determined group—each with their own part to play. Outside, the sunlight sharpened, and the day beckoned with the promise of revelation.

Emma gathered Storm's leash and Bobbie's spare jacket, the air in the RV now vibrant with anticipation. They moved with purpose, their footsteps echoing quietly across the floor, ready to step beyond the threshold and into whatever the day would bring.

As they stepped outside, the crisp morning air brought a flush to their cheeks, the promise of the day settling over them like a gentle cloak. Bobbie slid in beside Nick, her movements easy, familiarity settling between them with the comfort of long partnership. She glanced sideways, catching his eye, a wry smile tugging at her lips—

there was a mischievous spark there, born more of affection than intent to aggravate. How many mornings like this had they shared, she wondered—how many more would come before routine crept back in, softening the edges of adventure?

She let her thoughts wander as the road rolled beneath the tires, her mind tugged in two directions: the steady pulse of duty, and the lingering memory of weekends when life was unburdened, and laughter came easily. She missed those moments—their rare, untamed escapes from the careful patterns the world expected of them. But she also knew the price of loving someone called to work beyond the ordinary. The quiet nights, the waiting, the pride mingled with longing—these, too, were woven deep in the fabric of her days.

Bobbie leaned back, letting the engine's hum and the sun's rays through the

Windows their love for each other and the care that came with it—was enough.

She wanted to at least warn Marion, so she dug through her purse, fishing for her phone beneath a tangle of keys and markup. Marion picked up almost instantly—her voice bright, a note of amusement slipping through: "Funny you should call. As Doc was getting dressed, I asked him what you were up to while Nick was working. He shrugged, said he didn't know, but promised to let Nick know I'd inquired. And now here you are, calling—right on cue."

Bobbie laughed, the sound crackling across the line. "Hey girl, if you'd give me a chance, I'm actually on my way over to your house. Wanted to give you a heads-up." She could almost see Marion grinning on the other end, already half-planning the morning.

"Well, I'm glad you called. I've found plenty for us to get up to—two wives left alone to entertain themselves."

Bobbie smiled, settling back against the passenger seat as the car moved along the quiet road. "I'll be there in a minute. Just pour me another cup of coffee—I think I'll need it to keep up with that caffeine high you've got going this morning." Laughter bubbled between them, easy and familiar, weaving through the air as the day stretched open, filled with new plans and the comfort of old friendships.

"Will do, I am ready for a new pot myself, Doc left a minute ago. It will be ready and waiting see you."

Passing the lab as they followed the street to the tee, Nick could see that Clementine was already there—her car parked close to the entrance, gleaming in the pale morning sunlight. He pulled into the lab parking lot to drop Emma and Storm off. After they were inside the lab. Back on the roadway He turned right, easing past the donut shop whose doors were propped wide, the sweet, yeasty scent of fresh pastries spilling onto the sidewalk and mingling with the cold air. The familiar aroma tugged at something warm inside him, and he rolled the window lower, letting the chill help shake off the remnants of sleep.

Without a word, he reached over and squeezed Bobbie's knee—a silent touch, equal parts reassurance and gratitude for her steady presence by his side. She acknowledged him with a soft smile, content to let the gentle melancholy that wrapped around them linger a little longer. There was no need to fill the easy silence; the comfort of their connection, unhurried and unforced, was enough as the quiet neighborhood rolled by and the day quietly gathered momentum.

Stopping in the driveway, Nick caught sight of Marion in the doorway, holding it partway open, her body angled in anticipation, eager to greet Bobbie.   The exchange between the two was swift and familiar—a quick, warm kiss on the cheek, a squeeze of hands, then Bobbie bounded out of the car with a lightness that belied the heaviness she sometimes carried. Nothing more was needed in that moment; their silent parting spoke of trust and of all that was understood without words.

Nick lingered a moment, his gaze following them before he let out a long, measured breath. 'His day pressed in around him—urgent, fragmented, paramount. So many details to coordinate, each one demanding its piece of his attention. The investigation had become a puzzle, clues scattered like breadcrumbs at the edge of his thoughts, and he felt the weight of responsibility settle in his chest.

He replayed the latest reports in his mind—the discovery of a trace of females being there, in the abandoned camper had struck him like a lightning bolt, quickening his pulse and cementing the suspicion that had been gnawing at him for days. The evidence was finally aligning with his instincts: the kidnapper had made a mistake, left a trace, and now the path, though tangled, was becoming clearer. Nick's mind sifted through the possibilities, assembling the fragments into a pattern only he could see, urgency sharpening his focus.'

As he gathered his thought's and Bobbie stepped from the car, the crisp morning air braced him for everything still to come. Today, he would have to be sharper than ever—firm, unyielding. Too much rested on the choices he'd make in the hours ahead. He squared his shoulders, one last glance at Bobbie and Marion, then turned toward the street, already rehearsing the questions he'd ask, the people he'd call, the ground he'd need to cover before the day was done.

His busy mind made the trip to the donut shop seem short. He wanted to have a small snack to tie them over as they spend the morning at the lab; sorting through the tasks that seemed to be growing and the hands on the clock moved. His time seemed to be on an accelerated schedule. His mind was aflutter with the tasked that lay ahead.

The stop was a blur as he hurried into the shop; the white clothed man with floury hands smiled and gladly sacked up the donuts. Turning away so to help the no conversation he wanted he handed him the money and looked across the street in hopes he could leave and hurry to the lab.

The one thing he needed today was focus; he needed to focus and narrow down the leads that they were stymied with now.

Reaching the lab Nick breezed in the door holding the big white bag in front of him as if the ward off any onslaught of unfriendly effects that were waiting.

Emma was seated turning pages of the stack of reports that were accumulating. Her harried look made Nick hold off any talk. Stopping at the counter he sat the donuts down and pulled out a seat on the side beside the large table.

Storm laid back down ignoring Nick and the others that were in the room.

Walking out of the rear room Nick was greeted by a new trooper in civies.

"You must be the agent in charge, Names Evan Bogg's Captain Hovel sent me over he wants me to help you out any way I can; just tell me what you need. I can do just about anything you need been an investigator for about four years."

"Good! Nick Curtis, that sounds great I need for you to contact the PD,s in the towns of these three guys and see if they have anything on them. Any brush with them and especially any kind of questionable arrests, even if there was no prosecution. Anything that would red flag them for this missing coed. Find out if there were any missing young women in their area. Thanks."

Swiping his phone Nick taped Doc number... two rings later Doc answered "Doc, here what's up Nick."

Did you get down to the hospital this morning? What's the news? "

"Some good some bad!" He mumbled.

"Tell me the good."

"The ranger is the good, he is going to recover. He did not see the assailant. He was stuck from behind and was out cold until he woke up in the hospital."

"Glad to hear he is okay, not happy with the rest. I'm at the lab are you coming down here soon?"

"On my way should be there in ten. Talk to you later."

Settling back to the key board Nick began running the state wide adductions for the last year. Hoping to find anything that would give him a clue as to who the kidnapped was. Scanning the screen his thoughts were still rolling.

'So, if she was not there last night and there was signs of some female being there it still might be her. If he had taken her someplace else ...where?' Rubbing his temple, he could see that Emma had stop working and was staring at him.

Turning to her, Nick motioned Emma over to his table. "Tell me, what do you think about us playing dumb?" He paused, scanning her face for any hint of hesitation. "What do you think about this—what if we drive you and Storm back to the campgrounds, and have you, with Storm, walk down to the campsite where we think the abductor is staying? Give Storm a whiff of the camper shell that he's in. Just act like you were out for a morning walk with your dog."

Emma frowned slightly, the lines of worry deepening around her eyes. Nick continued, "If you keep the pajamas away from Storm until after you go down there, then see what happens... If he's injured her, and she's buried near there, Storm should be able to pick up on it. If he's actually there when you arrive, we can close in and capture him. But if he turns out to be innocent, well, we're back to square one."

Emma mulled it over, her gaze flicking to Storm, who sat obediently by the door, tail twitching with anticipation. "It's risky," she said softly, "but it's also the best way to get Storm as close as possible to any trace of her. If there's any scent at all, Storm will find it."

Nick nodded. "Alright then. Let's run through the details once more before we head out. I want every angle covered." As he spoke, he felt that familiar surge of hope, cold and bright, that maybe—just maybe—they were closing in on the truth.

As Nick reviewed the plan aloud, Evan leaned in, absorbing every detail. He set his phone aside, glancing between Emma and Nick before speaking up.   "Not that I have any thoughts that Emma isn't able to take care of herself," he began, his tone both respectful and practical, "but if we want another witness—someone to confirm where everyone was, and that all the evidence is accounted for—I could go with her. One good thing to mention is that I'm stationed here and know the court system inside and out. If anything comes of this, it might even save you a trip back here to testify later on."

Nick considered this a moment, recognizing the weight of Evan's offer. Emma, too, seemed to relax slightly at the proposition, her posture easing as she exchanged a quick glance with Storm. The idea of an extra set of eyes—and an ally who understood the local legal landscape—added another layer of reassurance to an otherwise precarious plan.

"Alright," Nick said, nodding, "that actually makes a lot of sense. The more solid our chain of evidence, the better." He drew in a breath, feeling the atmosphere shift as the plan took on firmer shape. "Evan, you'll shadow Emma and Storm, keep an eye on everything. If anything, strange goes down, you call me. Agreed?"

Evan's steady nod confirmed it, and for the first time that morning, Nick felt the uncertainty of the situation give way to a new sense of control. The pieces were aligning—now all that remained was to see if Storm would lead them to the answers they so desperately needed.

Grabbing up his phone, Nick dialed Doc's number, his fingers steady despite the tension threading through his muscles. When Doc answered, Nick didn't waste time.

"Say Doc, we are going to take Emma along with Evan and Storm down to the site of the camper. I would like to give the camper if it is still there the once over. Giving Storm a good sniff to see if it will bring us any closer to finding this girl. If nothing else, we can find out if he is still there. We need to push this case hard. Time is Running out on her being alive if we don't find out something concrete about where she is. While we are coming in from the west side, I want you to drive down to the county road where the fire road joins it."

"Will do," Doc replied, his voice calm over the line despite the gravity of the moment. "I talked to the captain earlier, and the two troopers who were there overnight have been rotated out—replaced by two more. They're both in camouflage, no transportation, dropped off at first light. We'll need to make sure they know you're making a move on the camper. Glad to see you're pressing forward on this case."

Nick paced a tight circle; phone pressed to his ear. "Has anybody confirmed if this guy's actually from around here? Is he on his home turf or not?"

There was a pause, filled only by the faint silence. "No, we're still trying," Doc admitted. "But no luck so far. We don't know—he could be, so we're keeping it tight."

Nick's jaw tightened. "Alright, Doc—keep your head on a swivel. Make contact with the troopers as soon as you reach the site. If anything shifts, call in, but keep chatter to a minimum."

Doc grunted his assent. "Copy that. Good luck."

As the call ended, Nick turned back to the group. The tension in the room was rising, but so was a sense of resolve. Storm whined softly, as if sensing the urgency that filled the air.

"Let's move," Nick said, his voice low but unwavering. The moment had arrived—every second counted now, and whatever happened next could mean the difference between hope and heartbreak.

The drive to the campsite wound through a corridor of silent trees, the early morning light filtering in soft ribbons across the hood of the car. As the familiar, U.S. Forest sign for the campsite appeared through the windshield, Emma leaned forward between the seats, her eyes sharp with purpose.

"Nick, could you stop by my tent I want to change my clothes, maybe put on something a bit more enticing. Maybe distract this guy a little I think it is warm enough that shorts and a halter top might do the trick. Really the more I look like I belong out here knocking around in the woods the better. In fact, I think Evan should join me. I have some of Jeffery's clothes that he left here. We will surely fit in better. Being discovered is going to be part of the fear that we should have."

"Okay you convinced me, just be sure that you stay safe. This guy may be dangerous. He has already attacked the ranger, by the way Doc told me that the ranger was going to be okay. But he could not identify his assailant."

Nick stopped outside the Winnebago, gravel crunching beneath the tires. He paused, glancing at the battered white-and-gold stripes running the length of the RV, its windows reflecting the cautious morning sun. Turning to Evan, he lowered his voice.

"If you want to change into your disguise, you can come in—this is my RV. It may give us a better chance to approach him and surprise him."

Evan nodded, the tension in his jaw betraying his nerves. He followed Nick up the narrow metal steps, the door groaning open on its hinges. Inside, the familiar scent of coffee grounds and pine-scented air freshener mingled with the faint memory of last night's rain. Nick tossed his keys onto the chipped counter and gestured to the back. "You can hang your things in the closet by the bed. Take your time—no hurry. If we're going to do this, we need every edge we can get."

Emma stepped out of the car; Storm's leash looped firmly in her hand. The dog, sensing a rare reprieve, stretched out her legs in a languid arc before setting off at a brisk trot alongside Emma. The air behind the RV was cool and thick with the scent of dew-soaked grass. Emma stooped, unclipping the collar to let Storm roam, her tail wagging as she bounded into the tall grass, nose twitching at every hidden scent. Trained but exuberant, Storm darted in quick, looping circles, never venturing far from Emma's watchful eye.

Emma let herself breathe, just for a moment, watching Storm revel in a brief spell of freedom. The morning sunlight caught in the dog's fur, and for an instant, the world seemed to pause—quiet, suspended between anticipation and action. When Storm finally returned, her energy spent and tongue lolling, Emma gave her an affectionate pat. Together, they made their way to the tent pitched on the edge of the clearing.

Inside, Emma rummaged through her knapsack, fingers brushing past notebooks and survival gear until she found what she needed—shorts, a halter top, sturdy boots. She changed quickly, listening to the low murmur of voices by the RV and the distant caw of a jay overhead. Once she was ready, Emma led Storm to the small travel kennel beside the tent, coaxing her in with a treat and a promise of more adventure soon.

Back at the RV, Nick was deep in conversation with the captain, his voice low and urgent as he relayed their plan. Evan, out of sight, was changing into his borrowed disguise, the tension in the morning air thickening with each passing minute. Emma waited, checking and re-checking the contents of her phone, steeling herself for whatever came next. The woods seemed to hush around them, every leaf and shadow holding its breath.

A moment later, the RV's bathroom door swung open, and Evan stepped out, tugging at the hem of a faded T-shirt that barely skimmed his waistband. The borrowed jeans clung to his legs with an almost comic stubbornness, the cuffs hovering too high above his boots. He tried to suppress a grin, the corners of his mouth twitching as he caught Emma's eye across the clearing.

"Just a little tight," he admitted, a dry amusement threading through his voice. "This guy must buy custom clothes—either that, or he's never met carbs. I guess I'll have to let the shirt hang out to cover my Glock anyway. What do you think—too tight?"

Nick glanced over, eyebrows arching as he took in the ill-fitting ensemble.   "You look fine, hopefully he will be more interested in Storm," he deadpanned, but his smile softened the words.

"Honestly, you'll blend right in. Nobody out here's going to care what you're wearing—as long as you are quiet."

Emma, emerging from her tent with Storm trotting at her heels.

Evan flexed his shoulders, making a show of adjusting the shirt.

A brief, shared smile punctured the tension, drawing them all a little closer to the task at hand. Outside, the hush of the woods pressed in again, heavy with expectation, as they eyed each other's, in the RV, running through final thought's before stepping into whatever waited among the trees.

Nick stood alone in the doorway of the RV watching as two members of the team walked away. A twinge of regret rushed through him. Before he could think better of it, Nick sprang from the RV, his feet thudding against the metal step. "Hey! Wait a minute!" he shouted, slicing through the hush that hung over the clearing.

Emma and Evan halted, startled, the soft gravel crunching under their boots as they turned. Nick jogged up, breath quick, his words tumbling out.

"We need to change this—I need to be the one to go with Emma. I don't know why I let you get this far," he said, voice urgent, eyes darting between them. "Your clothes aren't the reason, Evan. I just realized—if he saw us earlier, he'll remember Emma and I were together before. It makes more sense."

For a beat, the three stood ringed by morning sunlight, the brush of wind in the pines the only sound. Emma's brow furrowed, searching Nick's face for certainty, while Evan's mouth curled in a wry understanding. There was a shift beneath the surface—a new current in the plan, as obvious as the sky overhead.

Storm, oblivious to the change in tactics, nosed Emma's hand, her dark eyes bright with anticipation for whatever would come next.

Nick joined Emma, pausing just long enough for Evan to stride by, shoulders set with the relief of someone briefly let off the hook.

"Go ahead and sit down in the RV," Nick called softly after him. "We shouldn't be too long. If he's out there, we're going to at least find out who he is. Storm will help if there's any sign of the coed."

He glanced at Emma, his hand unconsciously settling on Storm's head for reassurance. "If he tries to run, Doc's there to intercept him." A rueful smile flickered. "Sorry I slipped up. Trying to be in charge, I almost forgot—I needed to wrap this case up myself."

Nick tugged at the edge of his shirt, revealing the faint outline of a vest beneath the riot of floral fabric. "Put my vest on under this, just in case," he confessed, tone caught somewhere between sheepish and determined. The sunlight filtered through the trees, dappling the ground at their feet, and for a moment the world narrowed to the three of them—Nick, Emma, and Storm—alone with the hush of the pines and the uncertain promise of what lay ahead.

Emma offered a steady nod, eyes sharp and ready, while Storm leaned into Nick's side, already alert to the coming charge. Together, they stepped away from the safety of the RV and into the breathless, waiting woods, every sense attuned to the possibility that today, at last, the case would find its ending.

For the first two thousand yards, they moved in near silence, the world distilled to the crunch of boots and the dry whisper of needles underfoot. Then, abruptly, Nick began raving, his voice cracking the quiet just a little too loudly, adrenaline bubbling up in a torrent of words.

"Boy, did you see that buck I bet he was a fourteen pointer. That one that we saw earlier would not hold a candle to that one. They must still be stirring them up; what do you think." His voice loud wanting the next campsite to hear him talking ahead of his arrival. He wanted if there was anyone in the target site to hear him.

Passing the next campsite, they could see that the couples that had been camped there were gone. Nick sighed with relief that they had left and had not encountered any problem with the supposed abductor. The were pretty drunk the two nights back and he had just a small feeling that they might have trouble.

Midway between the now-abandoned campsite and their next destination, Nick angled to the far side of the path, his eyes sweeping ahead with a sharpened intensity. Through a break in the trees, he caught the familiar shape of the camper nestled in the clearing—but the pickup truck was gone. He flashed Emma a fleeting, hopeful grin—perhaps this time, the site would be empty, a silent answer to at least one worry.

Storm moved in step with Nick as they approached the opening, the dog's muscles taut and ready, nose twitching at scents on the breeze. Nick's exhale slipped between his teeth, a quiet sigh of relief as nothing stirred—no voices, no movement—just the subdued hush of the woods. Emma, her pace quickening with purpose, strode ahead, boots crunching the brittle needles as she headed directly for the camper.

Every step closer to the camper, the air seemed to thicken, expectation straining in the hush that followed their approach. Emma's boot scuffed a stone, the sound sharp and abrupt, but nothing inside the camper moved. The forest pressed in around them—no birdsong, no wind—only the soft pant of Storm and Nick's measured breaths.

Emma motioned for Storm to stay at her heel, then gave Nick a quick nod. Nick squared his shoulders and advanced, the adrenaline braiding his nerves with alert determination. The sun slanted over his shoulder as he stopped in front of the door, the world shrinking to that battered threshold.

Unsnapping his Glock then peering into the camper through the window.

He could not see any danger in the camper turning to Emma he motioned for her to send Storm in. Storm leaped into the camper her ears pricked . Her nose began her work.

Emma followed close behind, Nick right at her shoulder as they entered, eyes sweeping the vacant interior. The camper was emptier than they'd imagined—one crude frame of a bed, every angle visible, nothing to partition off space for a bathroom or a kitchen. The morning light slanting through a grimy window threw the mess of wrinkled bedding into sharp relief, dust motes drifting in the still air.

Emma unzipped the plastic pouch she'd carried tucked beneath her arm and drew out the coed's pajamas, sealed tightly against the forest's persistent damp and any contaminating scents. She knelt by Storm, calling her quietly. "Seek."

Storm's nose dropped to the linoleum; she moved in deliberate, practiced circles, nostrils quivering as she mapped invisible trails. She made a slow circuit of the cramped camper, then arrowed toward the heap of bedclothes, tail twitching with the certainty of a true find. A sharp bark broke the hush—a signal unmistakable.

Patting storm on the ribs she said. "Good girl." Clipping on the leash Emma let her tow her around the camper leading her back to the door. Going outside Storm pulled Emma out of the camper following the scent. Still tracking Storm stopped midways to the roadway like she had lost the trail.

Nick stood in the door way watching as Storm stopped tracking. "Looks like the coed was here and she has been taken away. Probably in the red pick-up I am going to call Evan and have him come down here and start a forensic check of this place. We need to find out if she could possibly be alive. It looks like we need to run over this place before he gets here. For anything that might hint that she has been here just to confirm it."

Emma led Storm back to the camper door. "Say, Nick, do you think you could call Doc and see if the red pick-up has come to him? I'd be curious to know if we missed him this morning, or if he pulled out of here before we even made the move on him."

Nick thumbed his phone from his pocket, expression tightening in thought. "Yeah, good idea. If Doc's seen that truck, it might give us a heads up." He stepped away from the camper's shadow, signal hunting with his phone held high, the sunlight painting his features with anxious resolve.

Happy with the four bars he called Doc, "Yeah, Doc has the red pick-up came out where you are?" No, he is not in the camper did you check with the other troopers when you went over there.? No, he isn't here in the camper, but we have proof that the coed has been there so give everybody a heads up the girl could be with him, and he is wanted . Yes, just arrest him I'll figure out the charges if he is alone. No there was no sign of weapons. Except his crossbow, that's funny I guess he forgot it. Yes, stay put until I let you know where we are, Good bye."

"Nick, I called Evan, and he is on his way here with the car and there is a kit in the trunk so he can start the forensics investigation on the camper."

"Thanks, we need to drive the road out to the county road on the fire road and keep all of the troopers in place. We are missing something... I thought we had him trapped here in the park."

Leaving Evan to run the forensics, Emma hustled Storm into the back seat of the car and Nick slid behind the wheel. With Emma in beside him, Nick drove through the forest, slowing as the road narrowed and gravel grated beneath them, the green shadows pressing close. The air was tense, heavy with urgency and frustration.

A half mile in, the fire road branched abruptly, a rough, barely visible track veering off to the left beneath leaning pines. Nick's jaw clenched as he recognized what they'd overlooked. He slammed the brakes, dust spiraling up around them in the shafts of sunlight. "Damn!" he barked, hands tight on the wheel. "That's it—there's another road, another way out. How did we miss that?"

Chapter Thirteen

Emma stared down the newly discovered track, her mind already racing with possibilities. The deep tire ruts and broken branches hinted at recent passage. Storm, restless in the back, pawed at the glass, picking up the urgency in the air.

"Do you think he took her this way?" Emma pressed, her gaze flicking from the tracks to Nick.

He nodded, lip curling with a mix of anger and admiration for their quarry's cunning. "He must have. It's the only explanation. He knew this place better than we gave him credit for. We need to follow—now—before he gets too far ahead."

Without another word, Nick spun the wheel, sending the car bouncing onto the rough track. Storm whined in anticipation; nose pressed to the gap at the window. The world narrowed to the rutted path and the jostle of the chase, the forest rushing past in streaks of sunlight and shadow. Emma clung to the door, heart pounding as they tore deeper into the unknown, every sense straining for a sign— any sign—that they were on the right trail.

Soon the road became less visibly as they drove suddenly as it appeared the road stopped and the barbed wire-fence with the familiar national forest signs appeared.

Getting out of the car Nick began pacing, the thoughts that they had let the abductor with the coed slip through their grasp.

Walking around to the side of the car where Emma sat, Nick tapped lightly on the window. She rolled it down, breath quick and eyes still searching the tangled forest. "Can you see if you can turn this car around?" he asked, pitched low so Storm wouldn't pick up his rising sense of urgency. "I'm going to walk back the way we came. There has to be something that I missed."

Emma nodded jaw set in determination. As Nick stepped away, she shifted into reverse, careful to avoid the creeping limbs and dense undergrowth threatening to snag the tires. Storm gave a short, anxious bark, pacing in the backseat, but Emma spoke softly to calm him, inching the car around with measured precision.

Meanwhile, Nick retraced their route along the less-traveled road, boots crunching over gravel and fallen needles. Each step was deliberate, eyes scanning for out-of-place scuffs, tire tracks, or any break in the underbrush that might reveal the abductor's movements. The hush of the forest pressed in on him, broken only by the distant rumble of the car's engine and the restless call of a jay hidden in the pines.

Somewhere behind them, the mystery gnawed at him—what had he missed? His pulse thudded in his ears as he searched for the thread that would unravel the fugitive's escape, determined not to let another clue slip unnoticed in the dappled shadows of the old fire road.

Continuing to walk slowly back toward the fire road, Nick kept his eyes low, every instinct taut. Emma followed at a crawl, the car's engine a quiet reassurance behind him. The forest's silence pressed closer, broken only by the subtle crackle of gravel and the car's careful progress.

They had nearly covered a quarter mile—almost back to the original fire road—when something caught Nick's eye. He stopped abruptly, raising a hand to halt Emma. There, just beside the faded edge of the main track, the grass was crushed in a haphazard line, only a couple of car lengths from where the old road merged. It was so subtle, a break in the neat tangle of green, that he realized with a sinking feeling he'd already driven past it once, missing the faint trace entirely.

Nick knelt, brushing his fingers over the flattened stalks. Tire marks, faint but unmistakable, pressed into the soft earth—evidence of a hurried turn, someone slipping off the obvious path in a bid to disappear. He signaled Emma, who rolled to a gentle stop, Storm's head darting eagerly from window to window.

"This is it," Nick said, voice low and urgent as Emma stepped out beside him. "He didn't stay on the main road—he doubled back and cut in here. We were right on top of him."

Emma's breath caught, hope flickering in her eyes. Nick's heart hammered. The game had shifted again, the trail opening—narrow, challenging, but suddenly visible—just when he was certain it had vanished. Together, with Storm dancing in anticipation, they prepared to plunge into the hidden track, the forest holding its breath as they pressed onward, every sense braced for what lay ahead.

Slipping his phone from his pocket, Nick tapped through his contacts and dialed Doc. The line buzzed twice before a familiar voice answered, gruff but alert.

"Doc, it's me," Nick said, keeping his voice low as he eyed the faint tire tracks disappearing into the undergrowth.

"I'm on the trail that I believe the kidnapper has taken. For now, I need you to drive down the county road and wait. There's a spot where two large oak trees stand close together, right by a sharp bend. You can spot the old fire road from there—it's been abandoned for years. Park there and stay put until I call. Don't go wandering, not yet."

Doc's answer came through, edged with worry, but Nick heard determination behind it. He ended the call and tucked the phone away, glancing at Emma and Storm, both poised at the shoulder of the path. The forest seemed to lean in, every branch a dark silhouette against the dimming sky. With the backup in place and the next move clear, Nick led the way into the narrow break, boots silent on the mossy ground, senses sharpened for the chase that was only just beginning.

Nick leaned into the car window, giving Storm an affectionate scratch behind the ears as she thrust her muzzle eagerly toward him. "Emma, I think that driving further down—where we might be seen—could tip him off. The engine could carry through the woods and give us away." He glanced back along the track, wary. "We're going to need binoculars. Hand me the keys so I can check the trunk—there should be some gear, maybe even a shotgun or a rifle."

While Nick opened the trunk Emma decided to let Storm out to enjoy the freedom of the woods. Unplugging her phone from the car charger she opened the door. Taking her leash loose, Emma stretched her legs walking back to the open trunk. Pulling on her shorts legs, shaking off the sitting in the car.

She leaned around the opened trunk "Well Nick any luck? I can see there is a high-powered rifle, and it even has a scope on it. If you can't find a pair of Binoculars that will do."

Nick nodded; his face set with a grim sort of gratitude. "That'll do, more than we could've hoped for." He quickly inventoried the contents Emma had spotted—tear gas canisters snug in their holster, a battered but stocked first aid kit, and two thick wool blankets folded beneath a tangle of rope and a flashlight. Each item felt like a lifeline, insurance bought by years of preparation for contingencies just like this.

He hefted the rifle case and the box of shells. Slinging the rifle over his shoulder, Nick handed the first aid kit and one of the blankets wrapped around the large flashlight to Emma. Then he closed the trunk with a quick click.

"Keep these handy," he said, pausing as Storm circled them, nose close to the ground.

"If things go sideways, we might need to make a quick camp. Or help someone who's hurt."

Vanished

The woods pressed in with their own quiet urgency, shadows stretching long over the path. Nick glanced at Emma, reading the same determined glint in her eyes that steeled his own resolve. Together, they set off—Storm leading, nose to the earth, Nick behind with the rifle, Emma close with supplies. The hush of the forest and the distant echo of their own steps made the threat ahead feel closer, more real than ever.

They followed the faint impressions of tires and broken twigs, hearts racing, every sense straining for a sign—a sudden movement, a snapped branch, or the hush that sometimes falls before something breaks loose. The chase was on, and the night, with all its secrets, waited just beyond the next tangle of brush.

Walking along the winding track. Storm's eager leaps the sun streaming down was dazzling, almost disorienting in its golden persistence as they followed Storm through the high grass sent seeds flying and left serpentine traces in the dew. She bounded ahead, nose twitching, tail high, relishing the freedom after so many hours cooped up or waiting at Emma's feet.

Emma watched her with a small, relieved smile, remembering how restless Storm had grown during the long days of waiting—how her paws would pace the floor, ears pricked at every promise of movement. Busy days and tense nights had disrupted their routine, leaving both dog and companion hungry for motion and purpose. Emma had always been careful to make sure Storm had plenty of exercise, but lately, every outing had felt rushed, shadowed by worry.

Now, though, something of that worry eased as Storm threw herself into the wilderness, forging ahead with joyful abandon, leaping at the scent of adventure. The tall grass, wild and uncut, forced her to spring above its stems, and her exuberance lightened the tension that had been building in Nick's chest. He traded a glance with Emma, their resolve strengthening in the shared moment—a reminder that, even in pursuit, there was room for hope and for small joys.

With Storm as their scout and the day brightening around them, they pressed deeper into the unknown, following the invisible thread she traced through the wild grass and tangled undergrowth. Each step drew them further from certainty and closer to answers, guided by sun, instinct, and the steady rhythm of determined hearts.

As the terrain began a slight downhill grade, Storm slowed, then stopped entirely, her ears pricked and head turned, waiting for Emma to catch up. Emma trudged through the tall grass, bits of dried stalks clinging to her shins, a faint line of scratches marring her calves. Nick watched her, a pang of guilt flickering across his features before he reached out and gently placed a hand on her shoulder.

"I think I owe you an apology," he said, his voice low and wry. "I shouldn't have insisted on those shorts. Looks like the high grass is chewing your legs up pretty good."

Emma glanced down at her scuffed knees and grinned, shrugging off the discomfort with practiced ease.

"Not to worry," she replied, brushing a stray blade away. "I've had worse things happen to me on the job. I just hope we get to stop soon—I think we're going to need a drink before long."

Nick chuckled, the tension between them eased by her resilience. "Deal. First clearing we find; I'll dig out the canteen. Maybe even break out the emergency chocolate."

Storm, catching the renewed lightness in their voices, wagged her tail and padded back to nuzzle Emma's hand, as if in silent approval. Together, they resumed their descent, the air growing cooler as the sun dipped behind a fringe of pines ahead. Every step brought them closer to whatever lay waiting in the shadows, but for now, there was the job and hope—and the promise of a rest, however brief, just up ahead.

Suddenly, the ground dropped away before them—a sharp, unexpected dip that announced the hills of Missouri had finally caught up with their weary steps. Here, the sheltering tall grass thinned, giving way to a raw openness where the sun bore down unhindered, painting sweat across their brows and lending everything a washed-out brilliance. Shade was a memory; the sparse vegetation offered only the faintest promise of cover as they emerged, blinking, into the open.

Nick shielded his eyes, scanning the horizon. Laid out before them, scarred into the earth, were the unmistakable tire tracks of a truck—fresh, their edges still crisp where the grass had been flattened and the dirt churned by heavy wheels.   The path angled down the grade, carving a determined route toward the hollow ahead.

Emma followed his gaze, her heart quickening. Off to the left, nestled across the shallow dip in the land, stood an old cabin—its weathered boards silvered by years of sun and storms. The structure seemed to hunker into the hillside, half-hidden except for the battered red pickup parked just to its side, its paint dulled but still vivid against the muted tones of the landscape.

For a long moment, the world narrowed to the scene before them: the abandoned tracks winding down, the promise—or threat—of shelter beyond, and the silent invitation of the cabin's darkened windows. Storm, sensing the change in mood, pressed closer to Emma's leg, her tail still, ears pricked forward in anticipation.

Nick exhaled, slow and deliberate, the significance of what lay ahead settling over them like a second shadow.

"Looks like we found the truck. You need to call Storm back here and we need to move back into the woods I ... we can't be sure if he has seen us," he murmured, voice barely above the hush of the wind. Emma nodded, eyes fixed on the red truck, a thousand possible futures flickering behind her steady gaze.

With renewed caution, they moved back to the cover of the woods.—each step measured now, deliberate—following their tracks carved into the land, drawn back by the danger and mystery waiting just across the hollow.

Wanting Storm to be rested, Emma spread out the blanket and took the canteen from Nick. Cupping one hand, she poured a drink for Storm, who lapped at the water gratefully, pink tongue flicking in and out with quiet contentment. When Storm was satisfied, Emma lay down beside her, letting herself sink into the hush beneath the outstretched branches of a hickory nut tree. The shade here was thin, variegated, but it softened the glare enough for them to feel hidden, at least for now.

She turned to Nick, her voice low, intent. "We're going to try to become invisible right here in the shade. I'm sure you're going to have to make a lot of decisions soon, so we'll watch the cabin while you decide what the next move should be."

Nick nodded, grateful for Emma's calm. He knelt, pulling closer, and peered through the leaves toward the silent cabin. Every heartbeat felt magnified in the hush, the only sound Storm's steady breathing as she settled between them, dark eyes fixed on the distant red pickup.

For a while, they simply watched—three figures hidden by leaves and distance, poised between caution and necessity. The hollow ahead shimmered in the late sun, the suspect truck and silent cabin waiting, as if holding their breath for what would come next.

Nick mind was flooded with thoughts as he looked across the road.

They were separated by the narrow asphalt county road and the unknown. Was he the kidnapper or was it all still to be proven. Sure, the traces of her scent that Storm had sniffed out seemed to prove she had been there. Was it the same red truck in this world of the Ozarks where pick-up's almost outnumbered the population.

There was no proof that it was the same pick-up. Only traces of the bent grass that led across the road. They had not even reached the barbed wire fence to see if there was an opening to allow passage.

The cabin was nestled in the middle of the almost u-shaped turn in the road, a perfect spot to remain unseen until you were nearly past it.

But maybe that was to their advantage if Doc approached from the west, he could park his car aways to the west and walk close to the hollow. Remaining unseen until he reached the thicket of tree and move up alongside of the hollow being directly across from the cabin. His line of sight would be perfect to take aim.

Taking out his phone Nick tapped in Doc's tapping in his message. "Silence from now on we are too close to be using voice message. I am reassured that the way the hollow is situated he can hear us. I want you to move in as close as you can without being seen. Did you think enough ahead to change into your camos?"

Doc texted back "Sure did and I have my vest on. Marion insists that I come home tonight."

Nick texted back "Ten-Four"

As the afternoon light slanted lower, the shadows from the oaks stretched like patient sentinels across the hollow. Nick waited, his eyes shifting between Storm's relaxed form and the narrow ribbon of road that separated them from the cabin. The faded blanket beneath them muffled the ground's roughness, offering a rare comfort among roots and rocks. Every so often, Nick sipped from the battered canteen, offering Emma a drink. His mind ticking through contingencies, gauging how long they might need to remain invisible.

Storm, feeling the gentle tension in the air, only moved her head to watch the sunlight drift closer to her paws. Her steady presence was grounding—her breathing calm, her body relaxed but always alert. Emma kept her hand on the shepherd's fur, fingers absently tracing familiar patterns, an anchor for both of them. She watched the cabin, but her mind remained on Nick's plan, the silent codes they'd rehearsed for moments exactly like this.

The minutes passed, measured by the slow arc of the sun and the distant hum of summer insects. From their vantage, Nick could just make out the glint of Doc's vehicle as it eased off the shoulder, hidden by brush and a gentle rise in the road. There was no sound— no crunch of gravel, not even a door shutting. Doc moved with practiced stealth, his form blending into the tangle of green and gold beyond the barbed wire, the camouflage catching dapples of sunlight.

Nick reached out; fingers light on Emma's shoulder. He tipped his head, indicating the movement across the hollow. She caught the signal instantly, her gaze sharpening as she caught sight of Doc's careful approach through the underbrush. Emma gave a quick, silent nod, her lips pressed together in determined understanding. She reached for Storm, stroking behind the dog's ear—a small reassurance, a gentle reminder to stay settled, should the dog catch the faintest whiff of the approaching ally.

Time seemed to contract and stretch, every sense tuned to the world beyond their leafy cover. Nick pressed his body lower, ears straining for any break in the hush—any crunch of a footstep, any sign of the cabin's occupant. The plan, simple in outline yet precarious in practice, hinged on patience and quiet. For now, the only movement was the languid shifting of shadow and the measured breaths of three companions, poised on the edge of action.

Waiting until Doc was slowly moving out of sight as he made his way into the thick brush of the Ozark hill, Nick stretched and closed his eyes, slowly rubbing his eyelids. Shifting, he tried to ease the cramping creeping into his legs—the squatting position had stiffened his muscles, but still he resisted the urge to move more than necessary. Every sound carried in the hush of the hollow and he wanted to remain as invisible as the tree he leaned against, its scaly hickory bark rough beneath his shoulder blades.

His eyes, gritty from strain and nerves, flickered open and settled again on the face of his phone, anticipation tightening his grip as he waited for Doc's signal. Each second crawled by, slow and syrup-thick, a test of patience and nerve. Just then, the crunch of tires—a ghostly sound, barely there—drifted across the hollow. Nick tensed until he caught sight of another unmarked car, sliding quietly to a stop behind Doc's vehicle. Relief swept through him. The other two troopers were here, shadowing Doc, their presence a silent promise of backup should things turn.

Nick let his breath out, slow and careful, feeling the subtle shift in dynamics. The odds, at least for this moment, had tipped ever so slightly in their favor.

Still, uncertainty pressed in around Nick like the thickening dusk. He and Doc had discussed it in clipped exchanges—no one was truly sure they had identified the right man. The figure in the red pickup, while suspicious, was proof only of presence, not of guilt. At best, it placed him at the hunt, and little more. All their evidence, Nick reminded himself, was circumstantial—whispers in the dark, patterns that might unravel under scrutiny.

Nick's thoughts spun as he weighed the slender threads tying their suspicions together. The muddy boot prints outside the cabin, the odd timing of the truck's comings and goings, the overheard fragment of conversation—none of it was solid, not enough to name a perpetrator outright. Even the backup, reassuring in its presence, couldn't transform hunches into hard proof.

He glanced at Emma, saw her jaw set with the same tension he felt. Storm shifted beside her, the shepherd's ears pricking as a breeze stirred the leaves. Somewhere between hope and apprehension, Nick pressed his phone to his palm and let silence fill the hollow again, the weight of unanswered questions settling over the trio as they waited for the night to deliver its verdict.

Only one thing, Nick knew, would truly settle the gnawing uncertainty—a clear sign of innocence, unmistakable and unforced. If the man in the cabin emerged, unarmed and cautious, and walked out to the tree line, waiting there quietly until Doc could step from cover and cuff him without resistance, it would be the first honest breath of hope. Even then, the real answer would remain locked inside the cabin's four shadowed walls. Only once the troopers entered, searching for any trace of the missing coed—once Storm had swept every corner and found nothing—would Nick allow himself to believe in the possibility of not guilty.

Nick's stare hardened on his phone, nerves ricocheting between hope and dread. He waited for the text, the one that would confirm all the pieces were in motion: that Doc and the backup troopers were poised, that the moment had come to leave the hush of their hiding place. He pictured Doc slipping to the fence line, pressing his shoulder to the rough trunk of an old oak and calling out to the man within the cabin—his voice carrying across the hollow, a summons and a test in equal measure.

A single text. One movement in the dusk. The whole case, all its doubt and desperate hope, hung suspended in that breathless pause between strategy and truth.

Doc's moved steeled Nick's eye's as he seen the trooper step close to the tree as he shouted out "Hello in the cabin. Missouri state police, come out where we can see you...You are surrounded . Come out with your hands in the air.!!!"

As Doc's command cracked through the evening hush, the world seemed to contract to a single tense moment, as if the trees themselves were holding their breath. The only motion was the restless shifting of the backup troopers, their silhouettes dissolving into the undergrowth, swallowed by the mottled twilight until only the faintest suggestion of movement betrayed their presence.

Nick's pulse thudded in his ears, loud against the sudden, oppressive quiet. The cabin remained dark and silent, its windows reflecting the last bruised light of the day. No shadow moved behind the glass; no footsteps answered. Even the birds seemed to have fled from the charged air, leaving the hollow suspended between anticipation and dread.

Doc rocked on his heels, impatience etching lines across his face. The authority in his voice was edged with something raw and urgent—fear or hope or maybe both. For a moment, Nick saw the uncertainty in Doc's eyes, flickering beneath the stern professionalism. He wondered if, beneath the uniform, they all felt the same gnawing doubt.

Then, snapped twigs—a sound too heavy for a squirrel, too deliberate for a deer. Nick tensed, his muscles burning from holding so still. Storm, beside Emma, let out a low, warning whine, hackles raised. The troopers drew in, tightening the net, every sense straining toward the cabin.

A door creaked within the gloom. It was so soft, so tentative, that Nick almost doubted he'd heard anything at all. But then a figure emerged, silhouette wavering at the threshold—lean, hunched, hands high and trembling. The man stepped into the failing light, eyes wild with fear or guilt or simply the shock of being found.

It was as if a large bell had signaled the start of a race. Instantly one of the troopers moved. Doc rushed the man. The one trooper busted out of the brush running to reach the man before he had any time to run or change his mind.

Cuff's in one hand and his rifle in the other doc waited. The other trooper reached for Doc's rifle. The other trooper in ready with his rifle up waited. As Doc cuffed the man's right wrist. Emma and Storm rushed across the asphalt road; their target the cabin.

The cabin loomed ahead, its rough-hewn door yawning open to the hush that had fallen over the clearing. Emma's grip tightened on Storm's leash as the shepherd surged forward, tail rigid, every muscle quivering with the urgent discipline of purpose. Storm circled the porch, nostrils flaring, her paws whispering over warped boards as she searched for the invisible threads of scent that might unravel the mystery locked within.

Nick's only hesitation, his sole deterrent, was his wish for Storm to have a clean scent to lead her all the way to the missing student. But there was no more time for caution. He followed Emma and Storm inside, stepping into a darkness thick with the stale tang of fear and old wood.

In the stifling darkness, Emma's voice wavered, soft yet steady as she called out, "Is anyone here?" Storm's nose led them unerringly down a narrow hallway, past scuffed boards and empty cans littered across the floor—a silent testament to nights spent in desperate waiting.

When Emma pushed open the bedroom door, the scene inside made her heart lurch. Both girls were huddled together on the sagging mattress, arms wrapped tightly around each other, shivering though the air was heavy and close. They wore little more than thin T-shirts and shorts; pale limbs knotted together in a shared attempt at warmth or comfort. The stench of urine was sharp, mingling with the acrid undertone of fear and the stale, breathless press of too many hours cloistered away. The corners brimmed with shadows and scattered food tins, some empty, some half-crushed—remnants of frantic, uncertain days.

Emma crouched low, her hands open and visible, Storm pressed to her side, a living shield and promise. "Are you all, right?" she asked, keeping her tone gentle, the words carefully measured as if she feared the syllables might shatter the girls further.

One of the girls, her hair tangled and eyes red-rimmed but fiercely alert, nodded. "Yes," she replied, her voice so small Emma barely caught it above the drumming of her own pulse.

Emma's gaze flicked to the second girl, whose wide, wary eyes darted from face to face. Her lips parted but no sound came; the confusion and terror on her face spoke more eloquently than words. Maya—Emma realized belatedly—leaned forward, her own voice a tremulous lifeline.

"She doesn't speak English," Maya explained, glancing anxiously between her companion and the officers now crowding into the tiny space.

Understanding dawned in Emma's expression. She knelt closer, keeping her movements slow, her palms facing upward.

"It's okay. You're safe now," she repeated, first in English, then in halting, hopeful phrases of the other language she remembered her parent's spoke so easily in their home.

Storm nosed gently at the girls' knees, tail wagging with a restrained hope, as if sensing the shift—from terror to the tentative beginnings of relief.

Behind them, Nick and the others moved with new urgency, clearing the rooms, calling in the ambulance, voices low but efficient. The clearing outside soon filled with the chatter of radios, the crunch of boots, and the quiet, steady hum of hope, fragile but fiercely present, as two girls emerged from the darkness at last.

It seemed like hours before the scream of the ambulance cut through the

dense forest and the hollow's while they stood waiting outside, siren wailing as medics hurried to the battered porch.

The two girls, now swaddled in a coarse blanket, sat close together on the stoop, eyes wide and unfocused as paramedics gently checked them over. Emma hovered nearby, her hands trembling with the aftermath, feeling the weight of their survival woven with the memory of that room—its shadows and stifled fear.

Across the clearing, the man was being searched, his wrists bound, then led toward the troopers' car that had joined Nick and Doc. The rigid lines of the officers' uniforms, the mirrored sunglasses and clipped commands, drew a flicker of panic from the girl who didn't speak English. She shrank back; gaze fixed on the troopers as if expecting them to transform into something even more terrifying.

Emma caught the look, her heart twisting; she recognized the uncertainty, the uncertainty that came from unfamiliarity with these modern rituals of justice.

While the troopers shepherded the arrested man toward the waiting vehicle, voices low and urgent over the radio, Nick stood aside, his phone pressed to his ear. "Kerry, we found her," he said, the relief roughening his voice to a husky rasp. "She's safe—they're both safe. The medics are taking them to the county hospital now." He paused, struggling to explain, to make sense of the unexpected. "There's another girl. She was with her—no, I didn't know either. No one did."

The words hung in the thick October air as Kerry's voice tumbled through the line, a mixture of disbelief and gratitude. Nick watched as the ambulance doors closed with a decisive sound, Emma's silhouette momentarily framed in the blinking lights. As the vehicle pulled away, carrying the girls into a new chapter of uncertain promise, the clearing seemed to exhale. Above the grass and the rutted tracks, hope flickered—fragile, battered, but alive.

Nick sat down, his mind whirling—it was not over. The most important part had been completed: the girl was safe, and for all obvious signs, all right. Now came the tedious task of collecting the clues that would ensure the right punishment for this one bow hunter—someone who had clearly been hunting more than deer.

He glanced over to where the officers were marking the ground, flagging items half-buried in the loam: a battered thermos, a torn piece of flannel, a single piece of a dress half-shrouded in mud. Every detail mattered now. The case had shifted from frantic hope to the slow, relentless pursuit of justice—a process as painstaking as piecing together the fragments of a shattered window, sharp edges glinting in the afternoon light.

Storm hovered at Emma's side, nose twitching at the scent trails that lingered in the air. The woods felt altered, the hush between the trees deeper, as if the land itself was holding its breath, waiting for answers.

Nick forced himself to focus. He pulled out his notebook, fingers stiff, and began to jot down the sequence of events as best as he remembered them, his words forming a record that would stand against forgetfulness and doubt. The evidence gathered here would be the echo of truth in the weeks ahead—a truth not just about what had been done, but about how fiercely they had fought to bring the girls back to the light.

The bow hunter/kidnapper, now silent in the back of the troopers' car, was no longer a shadow slipping through the underbrush. Justice moved slowly, steadily, weaving its net from the fibers of patience and perseverance. And so, as the clearing emptied and the day faded into dusk, Nick remained—vigilant, determined, unwilling to let hope be the only thing left unclaimed.

At last, Nick rose and squared his shoulders, the mantle of his role settling over him with renewed certainty. For a moment, he surveyed the fading scene—the officers in their slow, methodical dance, the girls now miles away under fluorescent hospital lights, and the deep woods pressing close on all sides. He found Doc across the clearing and caught their eyes.

"Good job, you guys," Nick called, his voice carrying a warmth that threaded through the exhaustion and landed as relief on those who heard it. Then, turning to Emma and Storm—a pair bound together by courage and instinct—he nodded with sincere gratitude. "And you ladies. I couldn't have wished for a better ending than this."

Under the hush of the trees, the words lingered, drawing out a small, genuine smile from Emma. Storm pressed closer, tail sweeping the ground. For a fleeting second, the weight of the day felt lighter, buoyed by the knowledge that sometimes, against the gnaw of darkness, hope and humanity could win.

As Doc approached, Nick's mouth twitched with the unmistakable urge to smirk—a moment of levity threatening to crack the solemn veneer. "And as I am the senior agent in charge," Nick declared, doing his best to sound both official and magnanimous, "I'm going to have to ask you, Doc, for the keys to your car."

Doc, caught mid-wipe, looked up, brow raised in mock suspicion. Nick pressed on, "I'd like to take Storm and Emma back to town myself. Naturally, I only do this for Emma's safety. Besides, I think you deserve the privilege of extricating that black trooper car from wherever it's wedged out here in the wilds of these Ozark hills— back out to the county road."

He extended his hand, palm up, feigning grave authority while his eyes danced with amusement. Storm gave a little whine, as if in on the joke, and Emma's faint smile grew, emboldened by the gentle teasing in Nick's tone.

Doc snorted, tossing the keys in a lazy arc that Nick caught midair. "Just don't scratch the paint, chief," Doc replied, but the edge of their voice was softened with understanding.

Nick grinned, giving Doc a salute, and motioned for Emma and Storm to follow. The three set off toward the vehicles, the hush of the woods behind them replaced by the soft crunch of gravel and the distant hum of possibility. For a brief and shining instant, the world felt restored—a little battered, yes, but stitched together with kindness and the wry spark of hard-won good humor.

Reaching the car parked on the county road, Nick paused, the keys cool in his palm. The hush of the woods seemed to lean in one last time, as if listening. He turned and handed the keys to Emma, the gesture gentle but deliberate.

"How about you drive?" he suggested, voice easy now, the tension of the day beginning to unwind.

"I'd like to call Clementine—let her know the good news. I'm sure she'll be happy to hear it. She can get back on the palace investigation full time. That is, if you don't mind."

Emma's fingers curled around the keys, a quiet confidence sparking in her eyes. Without a word, she strode to the driver's side and, with a practiced motion, opened the rear door for Storm. The dog leapt in, settling onto the back seat with a satisfied sigh, the furrow of worry eased from her brow.

Emma slid under the wheel, the keys fitting into the ignition as if they'd always belonged there, then glanced sideways to watch Nick circle the hood and climb into the passenger seat.

The car doors closed with twin, solid thuds, muffling the world outside. For a fleeting heartbeat, everything stilled. Gravel crunched beneath the tires as Emma guided them away from the double-trunk oak, the woods receding in the rearview mirror— shadows giving way to the promise of open road and the starlit certainty of relaxing.

Nick pulled out his phone, thumb hovering over Clementine's number, a rare smile flickering at the corner of his mouth. In the back, Storm pressed her nose to the glass, watching the world slip past—three companions carried forward by relief, hope, and the knowledge that, tonight, the darkness had not won.

One buzz on the phone and Clementine answered immediately, her tone brisk with concern. "Hello, Nick. Where are you? We drove to the lab, and nobody was there."

"We're on our way there now, and I have great news," Nick replied, glancing at Emma as relief threaded through his words.

"We found the missing student—Maya Hahn. And we arrested the kidnapper without a single shot fired."

There was a pause, the hum of the road filling the silence.

"That's incredible," Nick Heard.

Nick hesitated, then added, "Funny thing. She wasn't alone. There was someone you might want to meet—a young Vietnamese girl. They were both held in a cabin off County Road KK. Both are safe now—at the hospital."

On the other end, Clementine's tone softened, heavy with relief yet sharpened by urgency. "I am going out to the hospital I want to talk to them."

"Okay, yes, go ahead out there. I'll talk to you later, but hurry back to the lab—we still have a lot to do. You're right, we need to build a strong case against this guy. Hopefully these two are the only ones."

Nick nodded, even though she couldn't see him. "Yes, talk to you soon."

He ended the call, sinking back against the seat, the weight of the day eased by the knowledge that, for once, hope had outrun the dark. Emma's eyes met his in the shifting glow of the dashboard, and for a moment, the open road ahead felt like more than just a way home—it felt like the promise of a beginning.

"Now for the good news." Dialing the grandfathers home he waited looking at the slight smile on Emma's face.

"Hello Professor Hahn, this is Nick Curtis I have good news. We have found your granddaughter, and she is fine. Yes, she is at the county hospital, and you can go see her. If they will let you, she will able to go home with you. I will need to talk to her myself right away. Yes, thank you. Talk to you later."

As they neared the lab Nick relaxed stretching back on the seat. As they pulled into the parking lot and stopped at the door Nick looked at Emma with a quizzing look,

"I have a question for you, and I would like you're take on it? Where did the other girl come from... why no missing report. She has got to belong to someone. She can't be much older than twenty or even younger. I didn't really get much of a look. What do you think?"

"I think that she will talk to me if I go out to the hospital and talk to her maybe find out all of those things. You are right she is not of legal age."

"I would appreciate it if you would go out there. I know you are tired."

Emma smiled, a flicker of gratitude passing through her tired features. "No, I don't mind at all. Honestly, that's probably the best idea I've heard all day. She definitely looked like she could use a decent meal—and a friendly face who can understand her."

He checked his watch, rubbing the back of his neck. "You know, sometimes it's the small things that make the biggest difference. Let her know she's safe here. And if you think she'll talk, see what you can find out—especially about how she ended up here, who she might be connected to. Anything could help."

Emma offered a brief, encouraging nod. "I'll take Storm too—she has a gentle way with people. Maybe she'll help her feel a little at home. Don't worry, I'll stop at Burger King and get the food and head right over after I drop you off. I'll text you any updates as soon as I have them."

The car idled in the soft wash of the lab's floodlights. Nick gathered his things, feeling the pressure of too many unanswered questions, but also the first stirrings of hope. "Thanks, Emma. I owe you one."

She grinned. "Just keep pushing in the lab. We're close—I can feel it."

Nick stepped out into the night, watching as Emma and Storm drove away toward the fulfilling promise of Burgers and Fries, and then beyond, to the county hospital where answers—and, perhaps, a new path forward—waited in the quiet company of a warm meal.

Chapter Fourteen

Nick hurried into the lab, the promise of good news stirring beneath the surface, yet he found himself walking softer than usual, careful not to disturb the hush that had settled over the worktables. Doc's chair sat empty, his usual cup—untouched. Even if he were here, Nick knew, he'd have to keep his excitement on ice. The arrest wasn't public knowledge yet, and until all the pieces fit, secrecy was another burden to juggle.

He let himself drift through the familiar clutter: the tang of alcohol, the gentle whir of centrifuges, the half-lit whiteboards scrawled with half-answers. His thoughts circled restlessly. The girl—no name, still a cipher—was with Maya now. That alone complicated everything, made every next move feel precarious. But maybe, if the gears aligned, if Thursday brought clarity or even a sliver of resolution, Nick could finally disentangle himself from the knots of the week.

He caught himself daydreaming—of the Winnebago parked under the sweep of a generous sky, of evenings spent unwinding time with Bobbie, unspooling the quiet joys they once knew. Maybe, if luck allowed, they'd string together enough calm nights to remember how good things could be, the hush between them filled not with questions, but memories and the gentle, persistent hope of old romance rekindling.

For now, though, he returned to the present—the lab, the unanswered calls, the weight of secrets—and reminded himself that sometimes hope was a question of patience, and the promise of rest was reason enough to keep going.

Sitting down at the table, Nick leaned back, giving himself permission—for just a moment—to let his mind wander and storm through the tangled mess of leads and half-formed theories. Where to begin? The board was littered with evidence, but the real puzzle was whittling it down to what truly mattered.

He pressed his palms flat on the surface, feeling the cool laminate ground him. Emma was out there, doing what she did best—unraveling the truth with patience and a kindness that seemed to coax answers from even the most guarded. If she had any luck, by dawn they'd know who the new victim was, and maybe, just maybe, the chaos swirling around the case would start to settle. The questions ricocheting through everyone's thoughts—Who was she? What happened to her? Was she the thread that would pull the whole knot apart?—all seemed to converge on Emma's efforts tonight.

Nick frowned, glancing at the clock above the door. Evan had still not returned from the county jail. The silence dug at him. He hadn't expected answers to fall into his lap, but the waiting gnawed at his composure. Outside, the city's pulse continued obliviously—sirens in the distance, the hum of fluorescent lights, the slow creep of exhaustion. Here, the quiet seemed to magnify everything: the weight of responsibility, the ache of uncertainty, the flicker of something that might be hope.

He picked up Doc's mug, thumb running along the smooth edge, and stared at the whiteboard, searching for patterns in the mess. He knew from experience that when a case grew this tangled, clarity rarely arrived all at once. It came in fragments—a phrase, a photograph, a slip of paper, a name whispered in the right ear at the right time.

Tonight, all he could do was trust his team, trust the process, and prepare himself for the moment when those fragments finally clicked into place. Until then, he'd keep his vigil at the table, mind churning, ready for whatever news the night might bring.

He pulled out his phone, thumb hesitating a second before he found Doc's contact and pressed call. The line rang and rang, a hollow sound that only seemed to deepen the stillness in the lab. No answer—just the distant click of voicemail.

"Hey Doc, it's Nick," he said, trying to sound casual, though the edge of worry slipped through. "Give me a call when you get this. Not to press you, but I wondered what was going on. I thought you'd have made it back to the lab by now. Not to pry—just, uh, let me know you're alright. Call me."

He ended the call and let the phone rest on the table, the unanswered message lingering in the air. For a moment, Nick listened to the quiet, half-expecting the door to swing open, for Doc to stroll in with a sheepish grin and some offhand explanation. Instead, there was only the faint humming of machines and the gentle rattle of his nerves. He stared again at the whiteboard, its mass of clues and questions, hoping that somewhere in all this silence, Doc would reach back out and help piece together whatever the night was trying to tell them.

Still wondering about Doc Nick walked to the outside window looking out the window he could see the afternoon traffic bunching up at the traffic signal at the intersection. Turning away he seen the donut shop and the empty parking lot. Jogging his memory, he went into the kitchen and saw the full sack of donuts on the counter were he had placed them earlier that day. Stepping over, he pulled one out. His thoughts returned to the morning; he was going to take the donuts to the surveillance team across from the Palace.

The day had sped by and the return of the coed and with the arrest of the suspect he had been gone all day and had not deliver the donuts. His mind felt a twinge of guilt when he realized that the surveillance team had been completely left his mind.

Walking back into the other room, Nick noticed his phone skittering across the table, vibrating insistently. He snatched it up just as Doc's name flashed on the screen.

"Hello? Where are you?" Nick tried to keep his tone even, relief threading through his words.

Doc's voice came over the line, calm but with a background murmur of voices.

"No, nothing urgent," Nick continued, waving aside his own concern, "I was just starting to wonder what happened to you."

He listened as Doc explained, the words piecing together the night's movements: at the surveillance with the troopers, the team still holding their post. Nick nodded, moving restlessly around the room.

"Yes, keep them in place. Clementine is at the hospital—yeah, I know, it's her call. Right, I can meet you there." He paused, glancing at the cluttered board one last time, then back toward the window where the city's pulse continued in indifferent waves.

"No, I'm at the lab. You remember—just down by the intersection. I'll head out in a minute, just need to lock up."

Ending the call, he strode to the kitchen, grabbing the forgotten bag of donuts. They felt heavier than before—maybe from the passing hours, maybe from the weight of all he'd missed. Still, they were something to bring, a small peace offering for the team bracing against the slow grind of the night outside. With one last look at the evidence-laden board, he flicked off the lights, locked the lab door behind him, and stepped into the neon-streaked shadows, ready to bring what answers—and donuts—he could to the people still out there watching, waiting, holding the line.

The short drive to the Palace kept Nick alert, the wheels turning as he remembered just how much of their time had been spent circling this block, watching and waiting. Doc's voice echoed in his mind—Raleigh Towers. That's where he'd said he was posted at. As Nick pulled around the corner, the old neon sign of the Palace flickered to life, casting wavering blue and pink streaks over the sidewalk. He could see, through the large windows, that the basement bar was already filling up for the night.

Stopping behind the tall brick building out of sight he shut off the engine and exited the car. He felt the cool night air seeping into the small Ozark town.

Walking he could hear the live band floating out into the evening air. The sound of the peoples voices and laughter filtered through. Hurrying up to the building he quietly let the steel fire door close slowly.

The trip up the concrete and steel stairwell resounded as he walked up the two floors. The echo of him trying to be quiet. His thought were stymied as he tried to think about the emptiness he made in the stairwell. The smell of the many trips to the trash can by the residents wafted as he walked. The crunching sound of the white donut bag was amplified. Stepping to the second-floor door he quickly jerked it open, wanting to shake the strange feel the solemn well had brought on. Inside, the corridor was lit by a single, bright incandescent light bulb at each door, throwing uncertain shadows onto walls and faded emergency exit signs. The scent here shifted— bleach, distant frying onions, the faint smells of old cooking. Nick paused, listening for voices, but only the far-off hint of music and laughter drifted up from the bar below. He pressed forward, shoes soft against decades-old carpet, each step erasing a little more of the unease from the stairwell.

He rounded the corner toward the end unit, where the door to the makeshift surveillance room stood ajar. Warm lamplight spilled over the threshold, painting a golden invitation across the worn tile. Nick rapped softly, then slipped inside, the donut bag in hand.

Within, the surveillance team was hunched over radios and notepads, their faces drawn and focused, illuminated by the glow of equipment and a half-dozen empty coffee cups. Doc looked up first, offering a weary grin that crinkled the corners of their eyes. Nick set the bag on the table with a gentle thud, drawing a ripple of appreciative murmurs.

"Long day?" he asked, voice low, not wanting to break the fragile calm.

Doc nodded, gesturing to the board on the far wall, a new pattern of strings and photos crisscrossed since morning. "Longer than most. But we're close, Nick. Real close."

Nick smiled faintly, glancing around the room at his team—his people—holding the line through another day. He found a seat, extracting a donut for himself at last, letting its stickiness melt away the last of the stairwell's chill. For a moment, time slowed, and the watchful waiting felt almost bearable.

Nick grinned, mid-bite, a sprinkle of sugar trailing down his knuckles as he looked over at Doc. "One donut, scout's honor," he said, mouth half full and keeping his voice friendly.

"The wife's have gotten together and decided that we along with them are going to the Bar-B-Que shack for dinner—real Ozark barbecue, even if we have to stop work for the evening"

A sit-down dinner if the wives had their say—hit him with a welcome jolt of anticipation. He glanced down at his jeans, spotted with dust and evidence of the day's long unraveling, and gave a sheepish shrug.

"I could use a change," he admitted, making a face as he brushed what might have been a cocklebur from his pant leg.

Doc waved away his concern, a dry chuckle scraping through the fatigue.   "You'll fit in just fine—besides, the sauce covers a multitude of sins. And the girls, well, they're just happy to see us walk in on two feet, not twenty-four cups of coffee and a prayer."

The mood in the surveillance room lightened, the promise of good food and familiar voices shifting the mood from tense to almost jubilant. Nick felt the exhaustion settle just a little less heavily on his shoulders, the room's glow warming him as much as the donut had. He tucked the last bite into his mouth and rose, clapping Doc on the back.

"R-N-R, huh? Think you can remember how to relax?"

Doc grinned, eyes twinkling behind tired lids. "With the girls running the show? You better hope we're up for it."

Doc eyed the other troopers in the room, a sly smile flickering. "Yes, if we can remember, we'll bring you folks some barbecue on our way back. Just don't get antsy—remember, the wives are the ones who need to enjoy the meal. You all are secondary tonight. Keeping them happy is top priority, and besides, they serve beer at the pit. So, we are going to have to take our time."

A chorus of mock groans and grins answered him, the retreat easy as worn denim. Someone scribbled a reminder about "beer at the pit" on the board beneath the case files, and another tossed a balled napkin in celebration.

For now, at least, they had a little bit of peace, and the promise of slow-cooked ribs waiting somewhere down the line.

The team laughed, gathering their notes and the night's business jumping at them as easily as the city's neon behind a closing door. For now, at least, they had a little bit of peace, a change of clothes, and the promise of slow-cooked ribs waiting somewhere down the line.

Nick headed for the rider's side of the car, pausing to let Doc slip behind the wheel. He leaned an elbow on the roof, a lopsided grin quirking his lips.

"Since this is your town, I'm going to let you drive. Don't want the local LEOs getting too curious about my identity," he said, voice low but playful, scanning the lot as if expecting a deputy to materialize from the shadows.

Doc chuckled, the sound mingling with the road noise outside as he settled into the driver's seat.

"A wise move," he replied, reaching across to unlock Nick's door.

"Last thing we need is you getting side-eyed by someone's cousin on the force, not when the barbecue's got our names on it."

The car's engine came to life, and with the air humming with the promise of a night unburdened by duty, the two eased out of the lot—leaving behind, for a moment, the glow of the laboratory and the weight of the day.

As they rode, the chatter of night faded into a humming quiet, the wheels turning both on the cracked city asphalt and in their own minds. Nick broke the silence, his words stretching to fill the thoughtful dusk. "I think it's kind of strange that the other girl this guy abducted is—or at least seems to be—the same nationality as the coed. Or is that not strange?"

Doc's face was half in shadow, the late sun glaring in from the west and painting his features in broken gold. For a moment, he didn't answer, eyes on the road as if the lines themselves might spell out a solution. They passed the glowing sign of the Oriental Palace, bathed in neon and the perfume of old secrets. Doc nodded toward it, a quick tilt of his head. "There's the place that might hold the answer," he said, his voice measured. "Too many coincidences."

The city's pulse seemed to quicken as they turned the corner, the world outside the windows shifting into a blur of possibility and suspicion.

The wives were waiting as they rolled into the driveway, their laughter rolling out into the dusk, a bright counterpoint to the hush that had filled the car.   Even after a whole day spent side by side, their conversation danced on, lively and unbroken—the shorthand of those who share not just a home but a life's rhythm.

Though not identical, the resemblance between them was unmistakable, two branches from the same sturdy tree: twins, fraternal but fiercely close.

Tonight, they were dressed for mischief and memory—a pair of terry cloth tops and shorts that made them look like they'd just returned from some sunlit, impossible summer, twenty years younger and twice as bold. Their heels—five inches, at least—caught the last of the sunlight, scattering it across the drive like handfuls of confetti. It was clear to anyone with eyes: these women were out to claim the night, and woe to whatever dull routine got in their way.

Nick stepped from the car first, straightening up and letting out a low, appreciative whistle that curled through the air like a playful dare. He paused just long enough for Bobbie to reach his side, the two falling into step with the easy confidence of old accomplices. Playing along, his voice dropped into a teasing, agreeable register— soft, but carrying just enough through the gathering dark. "Hey, little girl—does your mama know you run around dressed like that?"

Bobbie's eyes flashed with laughter, her lips quirking in a mock-scandalized smile as she tipped her head.

"Wouldn't you like to know?" she shot back, glancing over at her friend, who was already rifling through her bag for house keys— and maybe a bit of lipstick, just for good measure.

Doc, leaning out his window, shook his head fondly. "If you two are trying to relive your college years, I hope you remember how to out-run the sheriff," he called, his tone half warning, half invitation.

The evening's promise shimmered between them: a good meal, the warmth of friends, and the heady sense that, for a few hours at least, time could be coaxed into running backwards.

A quick kiss—light as laughter—was exchanged, and the wives, all mischief and anticipation, slipped into the car. Bobbie lingered at the rear door, her stance both poised and playful, waiting for Nick to perform the old-fashioned courtesy.   With   a theatrical flourish, he stepped aside, granting Marion a regal passage as she slid past, her movement a flash of practiced elegance. Nick's gaze, never quite as subtle as he imagined, stayed briefly with Bobbie, a silent challenge in his eyes—a game they'd played for years. If he'd dared to sneak a look at Marion derriere as she bent to enter, Bobbie's knowing grin would have caught him red-handed.

But tonight, Bobbie's returning smile was something different—brighter, agreeable, as if she carried a secret the evening itself had whispered to her. This was her night, and she wore readiness like perfume. She slipped inside with a glance that promised trouble, the door closing softly behind her.

They had worked at this—their outfits, their timing, the sense of occasion. Their entrance was no accident; it was a performance, rehearsed and refined, meant to upend the dull cadence of any ordinary Friday.

Beside Marion, Doc slid behind the wheel, his thoughts spinning with the improbable image of two police wives plotting a night of revelry, scheming to outfox the very routines their husbands enforced. The idea was both hilarious and strangely endearing.

As the car pulled away, laughter and anticipation mingling in the air, it struck Nick that maybe the real heart of the night's adventure wasn't where they were headed, but the brazen, joyful way they'd decided to begin.

It felt, for a moment, as if the world had shrunk to the warm cocoon of the car—the city lights blurred by dusk, the radio humming softly in the background, and the gentle arc of Marion's laughter. Nick's arm draped comfortably over Bobbie's shoulders, his thumb tracing quiet circles as she curled into him, her perfume rising faint and sweet above the scent of sun-warmed upholstery. In the front,

Marion shifted closer to Doc, their hands finding each other with the easy confidence of long-held affection.

The ride to the Bar-B-Que shack was a study in contented silence. No one felt the need to fill the air with words; everything necessary was spoken in a gentle squeeze, a shared look, the hush of anticipation that settled as the neon sign drew near. When they arrived, the lot was already full, the heat of the day giving way to the golden glow of string lights and porch lanterns.

Inside, the place pulsed with familiar voices—neighbors waving from crowded tables, a chorus of hellos and quick nods from friends who knew exactly whose night this was. A state trooper, uniform crisp but smile easy, caught Nick's eye and offered a fraternal wink before leading their little party through the maze of laughter and clinking glasses to the very back of the dining room.

They took the last booth in the house—a spot that gave them a commanding view of the entrance and a measure of privacy at the edge of the revelry. Instinct and custom dictated that the men linger, letting their wives slide into the booth first, settling with a rustle of movement and a shared, expectant grin. The menus arrived, but there was no rush; the ritual was familiar, each page a prelude to the evening's real feast.

No one spoke at first. The quiet was companionable, tinged with mischief and the low hum of the crowd. A pitcher of beer arrived—cold, foaming, promising—and glasses were filled without ceremony. All around them, the din of the restaurant swelled and receded, a living backdrop to an evening that felt suspended, charged with the possibility that anything might happen, and that—just maybe—the best parts of themselves thrived in moments exactly like this.

Nick knew that he should be glad he'd stopped at one donut that afternoon. Already, watching Doc pull on the thin plastic bib—the kind meant to guard against the most enthusiastic of eaters—he suspected the ribs were going to be as good as they were messy. The sauce, glossy and deep red, would be everywhere before the hour was out.

As they all settled on the Ozark Special dinner from the men and nursed their beers, anticipation humming anew, Doc was the first to break the companionable silence. His hands, deft from years of shooting and driving, finished tying Marion's bib before he leaned in, voice pitched just above the crowd.

"I hope the preacher doesn't decide to have barbecue tonight," he said, grinning as his gaze flicked to Nick and Bobbie. "He'll think we've been out to the strip and brought a couple of the girls back here for dinner."

Marion stifled a laugh, her eyes dancing with mischief. "Well, if he does show, we'll just have to save him a seat—and a bib," she said, twirling a lock of hair and giving Bobbie a wink.

Bobbie raised her glass in a mock toast. "To scandalizing the righteous and surviving the sauce."

Nick, feeling the warmth of laughter and friendship buoy him, leaned back as a server swept by, arms laden with platters of ribs, fried okra, and thick slices of white bread. The feast was delivered with a flourish, and soon the table became a happy chaos of passing plates, sticky fingers, and the kind of contented grins that only come from good company and better food.

There, in the amber-lit haze of the Bar-B-Que shack, with sauce smudged on his knuckles and the echo of his friends' laughter rising above the clatter, Nick found himself hoping the night would linger just a little longer.

The noise of the shack was tolerable as the two couples ate away at the ribs, the stack of bones glistening from their cleanliness. Nick leaned back, shifting in his seat to make room for just one more rib, already half-lost in the languid, satisfied haze that only good food and easy company could bring. Sitting beside him, Bobbie had called it quits, laying her napkin on the table with a soft sigh, resolving that any extra indulgence tonight would find its retribution on her hips by morning.

Marion, having finished well before the others, cradled her beer, taking measured sips and watching the men with an amused glint—her appetite sated, her spirit content. For Doc and Nick, the count of calories was a non-issue, a distant worry meant for other times and other places. Doc leaned back, stretching his legs under the table and dropping the last rib bone—picked clean—into the communal pile. The bones stood as a quiet testament to the feast, a monument to the pleasure of the moment.

The buzz of voices, the scrape of forks, and the faint twang of country music spilled around them, blending into a backdrop that made the booth feel like a small, private universe. Here, among friends, the outside world could wait. Nick wiped a smear of sauce from his chin, caught Bobbie's eye, and grinned helplessly, feeling the fullness of both his belly and his heart.

Doc tipped his glass in a lazy salute, the gesture saying all that needed to be said. For a long moment, the four sat quietly in the golden light, the wreckage of their meal between them, savoring the pause before the slow unraveling of the night.

Watching with a keen eye, Nick waited for the server to bring the bill. It was his turn tonight, and he was determined to claim it—last time at Doc's house, the memory of fine food and warmer company still lingered, and though he could repay the meal, trying to pay back the friendship felt like a debt without end. As the server finally set the check on the table, Nick swooped in, snatching it before Doc could even reach. Bobbie's smile sparkled with understanding; she was attuned to Nick's gestures; her new companion having been the very picture of generosity all day.

Doc, ever the observer, caught their exchange and grinned into his glass. He could sense the gratitude in both Nick and Bobbie—a subtle current that ran beneath the laughter and sticky hands, something honest and rare. As the four stood and began to make their way out through the crowded shack, Doc sidled up beside Marion, dropping his voice for her alone.

"I think you need to insist they stay in the basement apartment tonight," he murmured, a playful glint in his eye. "After all those ribs and all those hard rolls Nick put away, they need somewhere to sleep it off. Besides, it's about time that place saw some use."

Marion laughed, eyes crinkling with delight. "You're right. That concrete-encased bedroom is as silent as a tomb. Bobbie will love it—it's soundproof enough for dreams or secrets."

Nick and Bobbie walked ahead; the large white sack emblazoned with the familiar Rib Shack logo shining in the night air. The sight of it seemed to make their steps lighter, the comfort of leftovers a small assurance as they navigated toward Doc and Marion's car. Both relaxed, knowing the troopers at the surveillance post would appreciate their good memory—nothing smoothed a late-night checkpoint like the promise of barbecue.

As they stepped into the cool, forgiving night, Nick and Bobbie exchanged a glance—one of those wordless questions that pass between new friends leaning into the promise of more. The world outside felt softer, the air fragrant with cut grass and distant honeysuckle, their limbs heavy with good food and contentment.

The trip to Doc and Marions house was spent with Nick and Bobbie cuddled in the back seat. Like two lovers they held each other close. The evening and the food taxing them. Silence stayed with them all the way to the house, both were filled with the contentment of the dinner. Secure in his arms Bobbie marveled at the way the simple plan of the two new friends had bolstered their mates away from the world outside.

Doc leading the way into the house showed Nick and Bobbie to the apartment in the basement. Pointing out the bathroom and shower. This was the end of a long day for them. A full stomach and a relaxed night topped with a hot shower would grant them a peaceful night of rest.

Bobbie thanked Doc and slowly led Nick to the bedroom. Pushing him towards the bed to rest while she showered. The trip was long as she stayed in the hot stream of water long enough to filled the appetite of her body. The long fatiguing day was washed away as she enjoyed the steam and soap. Remembering the last lukewarm shower she had at the campgrounds.

Nick slipped quietly into the cozy bathroom, the thick steam on the glass shower door obscuring Bobbie from view. He tapped gently, a playful signal that he was ready for his turn beneath the warm cascade. When Bobbie peeked out, he was waiting—a large towel draped across his arms, offered with a tender smile. She stepped from the shower, the air rich with lavender and heat, and Nick averted his eyes, gentlemanly to the core, as she wrapped herself in the towel.

For a few moments, their hands brushed—one reaching for the towel, the other steadying her shoulder—and the intimacy was gentle, familiar, easy. The simple choreography of caring for one another after a long, shared day was a comfort in itself. Bobbie pressed a quick kiss to Nick's cheek, a silent thank you, before disappearing into the bedroom with her hair damp and her spirit lighter.

Left alone in the steamy hush, Nick let the hot water erase the fatigue from his body, lingering until the last of the day's burdens melted away. When he emerged, the apartment was silent but for the faint sounds of Bobbie moving about, the quiet rustle of fabric and distant hum of her voice as she settled in. They dressed in the soft, borrowed clothes Marion had left for them, finding small solace in the kindness of friends and the promise of rest.

Soon, they slipped beneath the cool sheets, Bobbie curling close, her breath evening out as sleep claimed them both. The basement apartment, with its peaceful hush and sturdy walls, became their refuge—a pause in the world's unraveling, a space for dreams untroubled and hearts to mend. In the gentle dark, wrapped in warmth and each other, Nick and Bobbie surrendered to rest, the memory of the evening carrying them softly, quietly, into morning.

Chapter Fifteen

Shaking off the remnants of sleep, Nick trailed quietly behind Bobbie as she ascended the stairs, the hem of Marion's borrowed kimono brushing her knees, the fabric shifting just enough to hint at the shape of her beneath. Even after years of marriage, Nick found himself endlessly captivated by her presence—by the ease with which she inhabited a room, the quiet confidence in her stride, and the way she could make even this borrowed garment look like something meant only for her.

He felt the old, familiar tug—a gentle ache of longing mingled with deep affection—and steadied himself, content to let desire simmer beneath the surface. There was a tenderness in his restraint, a silent vow not to spoil the fragile peace that lingered from the night before. As they made their way toward the kitchen, the scents of brewing coffee and toasting bread greeted them, weaving the promise of a new day through the air.

Doc and Marion were already at the table, hands curled around steaming cups, their faces alight with the easy brightness that comes only with good sleep and the anticipation of another morning among friends. The gentle clatter of dishes, the low murmur of voices, and the golden spill of early sunlight through the window made the kitchen feel like a sanctuary, a space suspended between memory and possibility.

For a moment, Nick paused in the doorway, taking in the scene—Bobbie slipping into the chair beside Marion, the two women exchanging a smile that needed no words. He felt the weight of the case recede, replaced by the quieter joys of routine and shared company. It was enough, he thought, to begin again with full hearts and emptied plates, moving forward into whatever the day might bring.

Nick lingered in the doorway, savoring the gentle rhythm of coffee and quiet conversation, but Doc's voice soon drifted from the hall, his tone brisk but warm: "I'm going to get dressed while you and Bobbie have breakfast. Take your time—it's early, and you need a minute to direct your thoughts to the second part of this case. I'm sure you know you're still on the job."

Nick nodded, letting his words settle. The case—never far from his mind—pressed in with a familiar weight. He waited until Marion had disappeared up the stairs, the soft tread of her feet fading, then turned to Bobbie with a rueful smile. "I know I need to wait until we get breakfast out of the way and call Kerry. Not sure if he's up yet, but we have time. This investigation isn't quite as important to keep quiet as before. I have a feeling the paper's going to splash it all over the headlines."

Doc, ever attuned to the undercurrents, set down his cup and leaned in.

"Yeah, I'm afraid you're going to have to take the back seat on this one. Hopefully your order to keep word of the second girl quiet is obeyed. Sending Clementine and Emma down to the hospital might keep a lid on things—for now."

Doc rubbed his brow, thoughtful. "Clementine isn't used to people ignoring her orders."

Nick's lips quirked, amusement flickering in his eyes. "She'll manage," he said quietly, his hand finding Bobbie's on the table. The room, with all its warmth and morning light, offered a brief reprieve—a chance to gather themselves before stepping back into the churn of the world outside.

Nick stepped away from the table, phone pressed to his ear, the bustle of the kitchen fading behind him as Clementine picked up, her voice sharp and already laced with the day's impatience.

"Good morning, Clementine." He caught the faint rustle of papers and the muted echo of voices in the background—she was clearly already at work. "How's the new victim holding up?"

There was a pause, a sigh. "Restless, but stable. Huh? I've got Doc with me—we're on our way down to the lab now. Where am I ?"

Nick glanced over his shoulder, watching Doc and Bobbie in quiet conversation, sunlight dappling across the table. "I'm still at the house, but we'll meet you down there. I'll call Kerry and have him touch base with St. Louis, see if we can bring in a couple more agents. With the way things are shaping up, we'll need the extra eyes."

Clementine barely skipped a beat. "That call to your boss—he'll approve it. Just tell Kerry to keep it discreet. The last thing we need is more attention."

Nick allowed himself the ghost of a smile. "Understood. We'll see you at the lab. And Clementine—"

She was already moving, her words clipped and final. "Save it for when you get here, Nick."

The line clicked off, and Nick stood for a moment in the hush that followed, the weight of the day settling on his shoulders. He drew in a steadying breath, squared himself, and turned back toward the kitchen, the promise of action—and answers—waiting just beyond the morning's fragile peace.

The short trip to the lab proved tense, the silence between Nick and Doc broken only by the sound of tires on cracked asphalt and the intermittent, clipped breath of anticipation. Clementine's earlier tone still echoed in Nick's head—a rebuke sharp enough to sting even after the call had ended. He gripped the steering wheel a little tighter, uncertain whether to voice the tangle of questions crowding his mind. Beside him, Doc sat taking in the morning air, lost in his own thoughts.

Nick's phone buzzed in his pocket, breaking the silence. He hesitated, then fished it out and answered, his voice pitched low and urgent. "Hello, Kerry. Sorry for the odd hour, but the sooner you can get DC on the line, the better. We need all the help we can get—Clementine's working with someone from Homeland Security."

On the other end, Kerry's reply came with a dry chuckle. "You're a little late, Nick. Her boss in DC rang me at five-thirty this morning. And, for the record, you're staying put. Three agents are already enroute to Raleigh as we speak."

Nick let out a slow breath, the edge of responsibility pressing deeper.   "Copy that. Just keep it off the radar as much as you can. We can't afford a circus down here."

"Already on it," Kerry assured, tone softening. "I'll loop you in the second I hear anything else."

Nick hung up, glancing sidelong at Doc. The soft morning light outside was shifting, gray clouds rolling in overhead as the city came alive. Somehow, the world felt changed—tilted into a sharper, more uncertain focus. He wanted to ask Doc what he thought of the new agents, of Clementine's clipped urgency, of the whole spiraling mess. But the words stuck, unformed.

Instead, they drove on in silence, the lab drawing closer, anticipation and questions riding unanswered all the while.

Still, a thread of doubt wound through Nick's thoughts, a quiet skepticism about the urgency swirling around the new girl. Clementine's intensity on the phone had left him unsettled, but it wasn't just that—there was something about this newcomer, the absence of answers, the way everyone seemed to expect gravity where he saw only fog.

Nick entered the lab, the sterile hush amplifying the tension coiled in his chest. He sat, the chair cold beneath him, and leaned forward, elbows on knees, eyes fixed on the door as if he could mentally bring it open. The emptiness of the room pressed in, filled only by the low hum of the building waking up for the day, and the relentless tick of seconds stretching out.

He hadn't heard a word from Emma, nor from Clementine, since the chaos of the rescue. That silence gnawed at him, each minute passing sharpening the blade of worry and what-ifs. Was the new girl truly as important as everyone claimed? What had they gotten themselves into? The questions pulsed, relentless, pressing against the inside of his skull. Every footstep in the hallway set his nerves on edge, every muffled voice outside the door sent his mind racing.

Nick forced himself to breathe, rolling his shoulders, trying to shake off the edginess. He couldn't afford distraction now—not with so much at stake and the unknowns multiplying by the hour. He waited, the silence growing heavier, bracing himself for whatever revelation Clementine would bring through that door—if she came at all.

Looking at his phone, Nick hesitated, thumb hovering over the screen, fighting the urge to call Emma and demand to know where she was. The minutes dragged by, each one a pebble tumbling through his nerves. Frustration simmered under his skin—a feeling he hated, a sense of powerlessness turning his thoughts sour.

Turning at last to Doc, he broke the silence. "Do you have Evans's phone number? I think he could shed a little light on the questions gnawing at me."

Doc nodded, already reaching for his own phone.

"Sure, but he's probably at the troop right now. I think he and the other troopers who were at the cabin were told to report back there this morning." Doc scrolled through his contacts, the glow from his screen reflecting in his eyes.

"Want me to give him a heads-up, or do you want to call yourself?"

Nick weighed the option for a beat, then shook his head.

"Let's not spook him with too many calls. Just text him, ask if he's free to talk. Tell him it's important."

Doc obliged, fingers flying over the keys before the message whisked away into the ether. The quiet stretched again, taut and uneasy. Nick closed his eyes for a moment, listening to the faint tap of rain against the window, the world outside growing grayer by the second. He tried to picture Evans at the troop, maybe trading notes with the other troopers, maybe already piecing together things Nick didn't yet know.

All he could do now was wait—wait for Evans's reply, wait for Clementine to reappear, wait for the next piece to fall into place. The questions didn't fade, but for now, at least, he wasn't alone in asking them.

Walking to the window, eyes fixed on the shifting veil of rain, Nick caught himself grinning in spite of everything as Clementine's familiar grey, unmarked car nosed up to the front door. The world outside blurred and shimmered, the street haloed with reflected headlights, but he recognized her vehicle instantly. He barely hesitated before hurrying to the door, anticipation quickening his steps.

He threw it open just as Clementine appeared, bounding up the steps being tugged by Storm, her coat glossy with water. Inside Storm was free as Emma loosed her leash moving away to shake off the rain. Behind her came Emma, hair dampened, and cheeks flushed with the briskness of the storm. Clementine shook droplets from her sleeves, giving Nick a quick smile before crossing the room with determined purpose, claiming her usual post at the computer— her seat of strategy these last few tense days. Emma, sparing only a brief nod, disappeared down the hallway toward the restroom. Storm followed her, always the obedient subordinate.

Nick lingered a moment, letting the warmth of their arrival settle his nerves. Then, moving to the counter, he poured a cup of coffee—the routine gesture steadying his hands, anchoring him in the familiar. He set the cup down on the table by Clementine, the rise of steam curling between them like a silent greeting.

Outside, the rain tapped its steady rhythm. Inside, the waiting had shifted: answers felt closer now, the air charged with the promise of revelations just through that open door.

Wrapping her hands around the cup to feel the warmth, Clementine looked at Nick, her gaze steady and urgent. "I have a lot to tell you, and first—you need to tell Doc to start taking notes."

"First off, the girls name is Lan Phuong. If you have not heard that, with Emma translating and with her being so run down it was slow. Well, the big surprise is that she was rescued from the Oriental Palace. By the kidnapper. How she could not explain. So, we have proof that they are running the building as a stopping place for human trafficking. Which substantiates what I have been trying to prove through my investigation."

Walking up to them, Emma shaking her hair spraying the air with raindrops. She stopped close; so, she could hear and help Clementine tell Nick what they had found out.

"Just relax Nick, she has it all together, she called DC, and they put all the wheels in motion for you to head up the team to close down that human mill. We need some time to put everything in place. That is unless the surveillance brings up another group of new victims. That is the plan you will be hearing from Clementine's boss. He will be filling you in on all of the details."

As the weight lifted from Nick's thoughts, he felt his shoulders drop and his breathing slow. Relief, fragile but real, swept through him. Both of the victims were going to be fine—the hospital had told Emma that Maya just needed one night of observation before she'd be cleared to leave. The new arrival, though, would need more time to recover, their ordeal leaving wounds that would not heal overnight. Even so, knowing help had come in time was enough to steady Nick, at least for this moment. For the first time in days, he allowed himself a sliver of hope, the kind that flickers quietly at the heart of every rescue.

Just as Nick allowed himself that fragile hope, Doc appeared at his side, the lines of worry eased only slightly from his brow. "Here, Nick. It's Evan," he said, holding out the phone with a quiet gravity. Nick accepted it, the familiar weight settling into his palm as he pressed it to his ear.

"Morning, Evan—sorry, I must have caught you when you were busy." The voice on the other end was brisk, clipped by urgency but threaded with reassurance.

"Yes, I understand," Nick replied, already anticipating the next move. "I'll be right there." He swiped the screen, ending the call, and handed the phone back to Doc, their gazes meeting in a tacit exchange of resolve.

"He's going to meet me at the county jail," Nick announced, feeling the room sharpen around him. "The suspect wants to talk to us. Maybe I can get at least some of our questions answered— especially the ones that have been puzzling us from the start."

As Nick turned to go, the words caught in his throat, and he paused, looking back at Emma. The storm outside seemed to hush for a brief moment, as if offering a space for gratitude to settle.

Walking to Emma, Nick leaned close, lowering his voice so only she could hear.

"I just wanted to stop the train for a small second to tell you thank you for your part in this case. I am sure that it went as smoothly as it could with you, and you have been irreplaceable with Storm. You have added the very best part of this investigation. Your knowledge of the language only added to the swiftness that we have returned the two girls to safety. I would be glad to work with you and Storm any time."

Emma's lips curled into a weary but genuine smile, her eyes shining with relief and maybe a touch of pride. A faint pink rose in her cheeks, and the tension in her shoulders released just a little. "Thank you, Nick. That means... a lot. It really does."

He nodded, the moment suspended between them—just warmth, no need for embellishment. Outside, the rain softened to a gentle patter, almost like applause against the windows. The road ahead was uncertain, but for a heartbeat, gratitude anchored them in the here and now, a quiet affirmation that, together, they had made a difference.

Stepping outside, Nick leaned into the drizzle, the coolness brushing his face and clinging to his hair. Fresh rain carried the scent of wet earth and new beginnings, and beneath the low hum of the clouds, the steady hiss of tires slicing through puddles filled the air. Each passing car pushed water from the street in graceful arcs, washing away the stubborn traces of dirt—much like the case itself, scouring the stain of the past from the lives of the two girls who had been rescued. Nick watched the droplets bead and run down his jacket sleeve, feeling the world scrub itself clean, and for a fleeting moment, he let himself believe in renewal. Even as questions remained, the storm was passing, leaving behind a world ready to be remade.

Slipping into the car, his thoughts raced to the newness that the case was turning. They were going to pursue the thoughts of the Palace being the human mill that Clementine had been chasing for over six months and was stymied.

Nick fastened his seatbelt with hands still trembling from the adrenaline of the morning, the engine's rumble beneath him steady and grounding. The windshield wipers swept away the remnants of rain as he steered into the gray morning light, his mind already pivoting toward the next phase—toward the Palace, that looming presence on the edge of every rumor and report. Clementine's tenacity echoed in his memory, her conviction that the truth was hidden behind those ornate doors, masked by opulence and silence.

Now, with the case shifting in the light of new evidence, Nick felt both the weight of responsibility and a glimmer of possibility. Six months was a long time to be chasing ghosts, but now the path felt tangible, the clues sharpening into a trail he could finally follow. As the city unfolded around him, washed clean by the storm, he found himself gripping the wheel with a renewed sense of purpose. This wasn't just about solving a crime—it was about ending a cycle that had trapped too many in its shadows.

He pressed the accelerator, carrying forward both gratitude and determination, the Palace looming in his mind as both a destination and a riddle. And as he merged onto the open road, Nick was certain: this time, they would not be stymied. This time, they would break through.

Parking the car next to the two Sheriff's cars, Nick noticed the uniformed MHP cruiser tucked against the far wall, its lights still glistening with rain. He stepped out, the remnants of drizzle pattering against his collar, and headed inside.   The lobby was tinged with the sharp aroma of coffee and damp uniforms, the morning's energy vibrating beneath the fluorescent lights.

He was slightly surprised to see Evan standing near the caged counter, posture alert, hand resting on the polished brass of his belt.

"Morning again, Nick," Evan greeted, a wry smile threading through his words. "I got called to testify on a drug bust my partner and I were on. They want us in court by nine o'clock, so here I am early. The captain insisted: when we're in uniform making the arrest, we show up in court in uniform."

Nick nodded, appreciating Evan's attention to protocol. Evan continued, lowering his voice, "I already cleared it with everybody—you can question the perp. He is in holding, waiting on you."

A hum of anticipation rose in Nick's chest as he thanked Evan, the day's second wind already gathering strength. He glanced down the corridor toward the holding cells, the sense of purpose from earlier settling firmly back onto his shoulders. With a brief nod, he made his way past the counter, the click of his boots echoing softly as the building buzzed with the machinery of justice about to unfold.

Stepping to the counter, Nick handed over his identification, the plastic card sliding across the worn laminate beside a stack of intake forms. The officer on duty gave him a quick, searching glance before nodding and reaching for the logbook.

Nick's hands moved with deliberate ease as he unfastened his Glock and, keeping it sheathed in its holster, placed it into the lockbox provided—a ritual both familiar and charged with silent tension. In exchange, he accepted a small, numbered chit: a receipt for trust, for the temporary surrender of authority.

He waited, feeling the stillness of the moment, punctuated by bursts of radio static and the muted bustle of the lobby behind him. The inside deputy regarded him from behind the heavy steel security door, its wired window opaque with the shifting silhouettes of early morning activity. At last, the deputy cracked the door open, metal scraping against metal, and beckoned Nick and Evan inside.

The corridor stretched ahead, institutional and unforgiving, the hush disturbed only by the distant clatter of keys and the sharp scent of disinfectant. Evan fell into step beside Nick, their footfalls echoing in tandem. They passed rows of holding cells, each one humming with its own quiet urgency, until the deputy gestured them through a final door into the interview room.

Inside, the air was taut, the fluorescent hum overhead casting everything in a pale clinical light. The assailant sat shackled at a scarred metal table, eyes shadowed but watchful, hands fidgeting with the cuffed chain. The deputy stationed himself discreetly by the door, a silent sentinel, while Evan settled into the chair opposite the suspect, his expression open but unyielding.

Nick took his place beside Evan, setting his notepad and pen on the table with a measured calm. He could feel the accumulated energy of the day—rain-scrubbed streets, lingering adrenaline, the city's pulse—funneling into this moment. With a steadying breath, he began, his tone gentle but resolute, "Let's talk about what happened. Start from the beginning—this is your chance."

The interview room pulsed with possibility, the machinery of justice turning once more, and Nick felt, despite the weight of the room, the persistent promise of truth hovering just within reach.

The suspect's voice was rough-edged, wary at first but loosening as Nick's steady gaze met his. He leaned forward, shackles clinking, and began to talk.

"I went over there—the palace, you know the one," he said, his words tumbling out with a mix of bravado and regret. "Downstairs, there's the bar. That's where I go when I feel... I don't know, just alone. You get a drink, maybe make small talk, but it's the upstairs that everyone knows about. For a price, you can... well, you can do what you want, more or less. They don't ask too many questions."

He shifted in his seat, his hands tightening on the chain. "It's not the first time I've been there. Sometimes it feels like the only place that doesn't care who you are or what you've done. That night, I just wanted to forget things for a while. That's why I went."

Nick nodded, jotting down a note, not rushing him, letting the words fill the sterile space. The truth, with all its tangled contradictions, began to thread itself through the room.

"When was this?" Nick leaned back trying to shake the smell that was growing in the room. Looking up to the ventilator grate above his head for help.

Nick's pen paused, the ink drying in a tiny pool as he weighed the meaning behind the words. Evan sat motionless, absorbing the admission, his fingers laced together on the cold tabletop. The deputy, alert but impassive, shifted near the door.

The suspect's voice wavered between defensiveness and a strange vulnerability, scraping raw against the room's antiseptic hush.

"She kept saying something over and over. I couldn't make sense of it. That's when I caught the other one—she knows a bit, enough to translate. I just wanted things to calm down, you know? It got out of hand after that. I didn't mean for any of it."

Nick glanced up, his features softening only a fraction. "Who's the other one? The person you brought to your cabin?"

A shadow crossed the man's face, uncertainty flickering in his eyes. He hesitated, chewing on a cracked thumbnail, then shrugged. "Maya. She is the one who I met at the other bar. She's wasn't supposed to get involved but... I didn't know what else to do."

Evan leaned forward, his tone even, "And what happened when she got there? Tell us exactly."

The man's hands stilled on the chain as if he might will himself backward in time. The machinery of truth ground forward, inexorable, as above them, the ventilator exhaled its tired breath, carrying the confession into the fluorescent-lit morning.

Nick stood, the chair scraping faintly against linoleum, and spoke in that measured tone that suggested patience was wearing thin. "Okay, we know that you brought the second one—" he hesitated, deliberately sidestepping her name, "—to the cabin in your truck. But how did you get the first one out of the palace? Did they just let you leave with her?"

A jagged laugh burst from the suspect, its edge echoing oddly in the sterile air. "Oh yeah," he said, almost incredulous at the memory.

"I told the guy behind the bar I was going to take her out to my truck, you know…" His voice trailed off; the meaning left hanging between them like the chemical tang of bleach.

"But I never took her back. That's why I went to the other bar and got the second one." He laughed again, but the sound was hollow, scraping the silence as if trying to carve out some makeshift normalcy.

Nick's jaw tightened fractionally, pen hovering midair. Evan, gaze fixed and unwavering, let the words settle, the implications crystallizing in the humming light. The deputy's hand hovered near their radio, but no one moved—caught in the slow gravity of confession.

Outside, morning crept along the edges of the frosted window, indifferent and pale. Inside, the air was thick with unspoken questions, the ventilator still exhaling its tired, indifferent breath.

Nick's face was stone, unwilling to bend to the immoral ideas the suspect had begun to paint. Eyeing Evan, he stood. Evan, who was already standing, moved toward the door. The deputy stepped to open the door, letting Nick and Evan out of the room. Stopping long enough to retrieve their weapons, the two investigators walked outside.

Outside, Nick stepped close to Evan, their breath fresh in the thin morning air, just out of the tiny raindrops beneath the shelter of the sheriff's stone overhang.

"There you have it," Nick muttered, voice pitched low. "The girl came from upstairs at the palace, but even if I doubt his testimony would hold in court. Still, it's a decent lead. If they're in the human business, there could be others. A raid might shake something loose."

Evan's brow furrowed, the weight of the confession pressing down as he shifted from foot to foot. The ugly pieces slid into place with a reluctant click.

"At least now Clementine will have something—confirmation, however shaky," he said, quietly. "That's more than we had yesterday."

Nick nodded, jaw set, eyes scanning the empty parking lot as if expecting the dawn to deliver new threats.

"It doesn't explain everything, but it gives us reason for what happened to Maya. And if there are more girls—" His voice trailed off, the implication heavy.

Evan glanced sideways at his partner; his perplexity unresolved. The morning felt colder with knowledge, the world outside clinical walls no less sterile. "Let's not wait," he said at last. "If we move tonight, we might get the others out before anyone knows we're coming."

Nick grunted "Yeah, we have a lot to line out before we can do that the right people is on their way. We need to have transportation lined up; we need to secure a place where we can take any victims. That is any there. Like I said maybe not tonight but soon. I'll see you later and again I say to you Good Job." Shaking his hand once again.

Driving back to the lab, Nick left Evan to coordinate at the sheriff's office, which sat just west of the old courthouse, a weathered building whose bricks remembered older sorrows. The day was still brittle, but Nick felt a rare surge of relief—something had finally tilted in their favor.

He didn't go lab; he steered his car toward the city police department. The streets were quiet, early traffic moving with the cautious optimism of a town about to wake up. Nick rehearsed what he would say, weighing how much to reveal, knowing the coming storm would demand frankness and cooperation.

Inside the police department, as though in anticipation. Captain Gordon met him in the foyer, looking every bit as weary as Nick felt. Gordon's shirt was rumpled; his stubbled jaw shadowed with exhaustion—a man pulled from sleep by the weight of responsibilities that refused to let up.

The captain managed a grunt of welcome, eyes sharp despite the fatigue. "Nick. You've got that look—like the world's about to come calling."

Nick offered a terse smile, stepping aside as an officer brushed past with a steaming mug. "You're not wrong. I wanted to give you a heads-up—my department and DHS are about to land here in force. Things are moving fast." He kept his voice cautious , conscious of how helpful the captain had been.

Gordon rubbed his face, sighing into his hand.

"Federal barrage, huh? What set it off?"

Nick met Gordon's gaze, steady and unblinking.

"I know that the other day when I was helped so well by you, I did not have clearance to be free with all of the investigations that has turned up. It seems that you need to talk to Homeland Security about any agent they have working undercover. The patrol is aware of them being here but then again, I didn't mention anything. So, what do you say now that I have brought it up?"

Gordon's eyes narrowed, reading the spaces between Nick's words. A muscle worked at the edge of his jaw.

"That explains the radio silence. And here I thought it was just the feds playing coy."

He let out a slow breath, the kind that gathered the weight of sleepless nights.

"All right, I'll make the call. But you're telling me there's more than just FBI boots on the ground—there's something else we're not seeing?"

"While I am here, I want to thank you again for all of your help. I am sure that all that you gave us made the pieces fall together. It really helped us to bring the missing granddaughter home unharmed, physically anyway. Who knows what happened out there in the woods."

The captain's face showed concern as the words sunk in.

Putting his arm around Nick's shoulder, "Maybe we are better off if we didn't know!"

"You are probably right, thanks again for your help."

Stepping back out into the drizzle, Nick pulled his collar up against the persistent rain. The gray sky pressed low, thick with the kind of damp that seeps into everything—clothes, thoughts, intentions. He lingered a moment at the curb, catching his reflection in a puddle, distorted by each falling drop.

Resolving to head back to the lab, he slid into his car, the interior cool and smelling faintly of wet leather and coffee. The windshield wipers beat a measured rhythm as he eased into the slow current of traffic, headlights smearing silver across the rain-glossed streets.

As he passed the Palace—its sign shining uncertainly in the gloom—he couldn't help but glance toward the parking lot behind the parts store. Two unmarked trooper cars sitting in the shadows, their silhouettes hulking and vigilant, engines quiet beneath a hush of rainfall. Something twitched at the base of his spine: an instinct, a warning, or perhaps just the memory of what had been found, and what might still be hidden.

He tried to shake it off, focusing instead on the task ahead. The lab would be empty except for the hum of computer screens and the faint echo of his own footsteps. He needed to draw up the assignments, map the shifts, and decide who would watch which part of the building, who would keep the late-night vigil by the hour, who would scan the Palace's every arrival and departure.

But as the Palace disappeared in his rearview mirror, Nick couldn't help but wonder if the most important things to watch for were the ones no assignment could cover—the secrets that drifted unseen through the rain, slipping between patrols, waiting for their moment to surface.

The one thought that seemed to persist was the P.A.s office. Nick needed to stop in and find out how the prosecution attorney planned to swear out the warrant. His mind rushed back to the cabin—the handcuffs, the flimsy window sash chain he'd used to secure the victims. The chain had looked new. That detail gnawed at him.

Maybe he should stop by the hardware store in the square. If he could trace that chain back—a recent purchase, perhaps even a receipt—he might be able to establish intent. If the perpetrator had picked up the chain and cuffs beforehand, it would prove he'd meant to restrain the victims, not just in a moment of panic but as part of the plan. Intent to hold them against their will.

He made a mental note to check the store's transaction logs, see if any security footage matched the timeline. The evidence would be circumstantial, but paired with what they'd found at the scene, it could be enough to solidify the case. Outside, the rain showed no sign of relenting, a steady hiss underscoring the urgency that pressed at his thoughts. Nick wiped a palm across his brow, started the engine again, and steered toward the square, where the answers might be waiting among shelves of ordinary hardware and the faint scent of oil and metal.

Nick parked at the edge of the square, wiping rain from his brow as he stepped out into the mist. The sharp scent of wet concrete mingled with the promise of something mechanical as he approached the narrow storefront wedged between a bakery and a shuttered tailor's shop. Its battered green sign swung slightly in the wind; gilded letters barely legible: "Stanley Hardware."

He hesitated a moment beneath the eaves, peering through the fogged glass. Inside, fluorescent light spilled in strips over aisles crowded with ladders, coils of rope, and shelves bristling with bolts and tools. The bell over the door gave a single, startled ring as he entered.

The place was a maze—aisles stitched together with logic only the owner could decipher, every crevice packed with goods: padlocks, paint cans, gardening gloves, lengths of chain arranged with precise care. It smelled of oil, dust, and the faint, metallic tang of years gone by.

He moved slowly, letting his eyes adjust to the dimness, trailing his fingers along the cool metal of a display rack. Toward the back, the shop seemed to loosen up, shelves giving way to a cluttered open space crammed with oddities—fishing gear, radios, even a battered tricycle with a faded red seat.

A movement caught his eye: behind the counter, the clerk turned, neat in a hickory-striped apron, the fabric starched and clean despite the chaos. His face was open and expectant, eager for company or the puzzle of a request.

The sign hanging over the door secured his wants 'Stanley hardware' the tiny place was stuck between the brick buildings. A place that had been put into place out of necessity. Walking in the long rows of items seemed to be there to protect the owner from the entrance of anyone. As Nick walked into the rear portion of the store it opened out into a menagerie of things. The clerk turned his hickory striped apron evident he was ready for work. "Good morning" he sang out "Can I help you?"

Nick was ready with his ID in his hand. "Nick Curtis FBI. I suppose that you are aware that we have arrested the assailant that was detaining the professors granddaughter. I need to know if you remember anyone buying some chain here in the last month. I would like for you to try to remember what kind that he bought."

The clerk began walking toward the rear of the store, his movements brisk but unhurried, the practiced gait of someone who'd threaded these aisles a thousand times. "I keep the chain back in the back— not a big mover, no need to take up the good show spots up front. Come on, I can check the sales book. Don't have one of those new-fangled registers that print off every sale. Know everybody in town."

Nick followed, boots echoing softly against the old wood floor, the air gradually cooling as they moved past the garden tools and into the storeroom gloom. The scent here was sharper, tinged with oil and the sweet, metallic chill of rain seeping through old mortar. Shelves towered over them, stacked with boxes whose labels had faded years ago.

The clerk perched a pair of reading glasses on his nose and thumbed with care through a battered ledger, yellowed pages curling at the corners.

"You say it was about two to three weeks ago..." He muttered, eyes squinting as he ran a callused finger down the columns of neat, spidery script. "Yes, here it is—twenty feet of sash chain and ten screw eye hooks. Paid cash."

He looked up, satisfaction in his voice. "Here, let me show you what kind it was." He reached overhead and lifted down a coil of chain, the links clinking against themselves with a music that was at once ordinary and, in this context, ominous. The chain gleamed in the light; each link precise, flawless, untouched by rust.

"This is the one. Only kind I stock for windows and such—a good strong make. Fellow who bought it, he seemed in a hurry, but polite. Not much of a talker."

Nick's attention sharpened. "Do you remember what he looked like?"

The clerk chewed his lip, thinking.

"Tallish. Maybe a little stooped, wore one of those old army coats. Had a cap pulled low. He didn't say much, just asked for the chain and the hooks. I asked him what he needed it for, just making conversation, but he sort of shrugged it off."

Nick nodded, mind racing ahead to the implications—a deliberate purchase, not just something snatched on a whim.

"Did you see what kind of car he was driving?"

The clerk shook his head apologetically.

"Sorry, can't say as I did. He was on foot, I think. Rainy day, I remember, just like today."

Nick snapped a photo of the chain and made a note of the entry in the ledger.   "Would you be willing to come down to the station, just in case we need you to identify him?"

"Of course," the clerk replied, setting the chain back with a faint rattle. "Anything to help."

Nick thanked him and headed back into the rain, his thoughts as gray and unsettled as the sky. Whatever trail he was following, it was becoming clearer—link by link, the evidence was starting to hold.

As he made his way toward the front of the store, Nick's curiosity snagged on another thread.

"Suppose I needed to replace a set of handcuffs," he ventured, glancing sidelong at the clerk.

"Is there anywhere in town that stocks that sort of thing? I'm guessing that's out of your wheelhouse."

The clerk, moving behind the front counter, gave a small, amiable shrug.   "Oh, sure. If you head across the square, there's a gun shop—Wittel's. John Wittel runs it, and he keeps all kinds of things the police might need. Look for the big sign with the pistol on it. He'll set you right."

Nick nodded, pocketing the information.

"Thanks. Appreciate your help."

"Anything else, glad to help," the clerk replied, a note of genuine goodwill in their voice.

But Nick was already thinking ahead, his mind leaping to the next question, the next lead waiting in the gray haze outside. He stepped out once more into the drizzle, the town's heartbeat steady under the patter of rain, and set his sights across the square—toward Wittel's, and whatever answers might be waiting there.

Seeing that it was only a short walk to the gun shop, and he'd already shrugged on his raincoat, Nick set off at a brisk pace, the steady drizzle beading on his shoulders and rolling down his sleeves. He slipped his phone into his pocket—a small comfort, the knowledge that if anything vital came up, he'd be summoned. For once, he let himself feel a cautious optimism. The pieces were aligning; the case, which had started as nothing but loose ends and damp uncertainty, was taking shape beneath his hands.

He thought of the chain—purchased here, in this unassuming store, not some distant supplier or shadowy source. That detail nagged at him, but in a good way. Maybe, just maybe, it meant their suspect was new to this, that there was no grim trail of victims stretching back through the weeks. He allowed himself to hope: perhaps, this time, there were no bodies buried along this path.

The square was quiet except for the muted rhythm of the rain. Nick's boots splashed through shallow puddles as he crossed toward the gun shop's sign, its painted pistol pointing the way. Each step felt lighter as the sense of possibility bloomed—answers might be ahead, and for the first time in days, the future didn't feel quite so bleak.

Pushing open the door to the gun shop, Nick was relieved to see that the man at the workbench looked thoroughly absorbed in his task. Perched beneath a bright work lamp that seemed to accentuate the gray in his hair, the gunsmith hunched over a pistol clamped tight in a vise. A green shielding visor angled low over sharp eyes lent him a professional air—focused, intent, yet approachable. The delicate tools in his hands gleamed in the steady light as he coaxed life back into the battered firearm.

Nick waited, patient, until the man looked up, pulling the visor aside and revealing a pair of magnifying glasses perched on the bridge of his nose.

"Afternoon," Nick began, stepping closer. "Name's Nick. I was hoping you could help me out with something straightforward."

The man set down his tool and gave a grunt that, in its way, was welcoming. "Depends what you need."

"Mr. Wittel, did you happen to sell any handcuffs recently—to anyone you didn't know was law enforcement? I just need a yes or no."

Wittel's bushy brows rose. He leaned back, the stool creaking beneath him, and gave Nick a once-over—measuring, perhaps, the seriousness in his voice or the badge tucked just out of sight. For a moment, the only sound was the rain tapping at the high windowpanes, and the faint metallic scent of gun oil drifted between them.

"Handcuffs?" he repeated, the word rolling slowly around his mouth. "Don't get asked for those too often by civilians. Let me think."

Turning back to the pistol he smiled You got a badge, do you?"

Nick watched the man work, feeling the tension in the room coil and uncoil with each page turned. The answer might be there—waiting, like a bullet in the chamber, to change the direction of the entire case.

Nick laughed, pulling out his credentials "Nick Curtis FBI, Happy?"

"Sure enough, I knew that I could see your Glock under the coat. Deal only with people I know. So, in answer to your question No I have not sold any cuffs to any one for a while. You the one that freed the Hahn girl?"

"Sure enough," Nick rolled out.

As his eyes returned to the work he was doing, Wittel spoke, his voice quieter but touched with something close to genuine concern.

"Good to see that you found her. She was fine, I hope. Been a friend of ole Pete ever since he went to work over at the college. By the way, I heard that there was another girl with her. You know—small town, hospital grapevine. Have a niece that works in emergency. Know where she came from? No... you wouldn't tell me anyway."

Nick tucked his badge away, a faint smile crossing his lips. "You'd be right about that. But you can trust she's safe."

Wittel nodded, the lines in his face easing as he reached for a rag to wipe his hands.

"Tell the Captain if you see him—his K-38 is ready. Save me a trip to the station, would you?"

"I'll do that," Nick promised, already turning toward the door as the rain outside deepened, the shop's golden light holding the last traces of warmth behind him.

Chapter Sixteen

Glancing at the dashboard clock, Nick wiped a hand over the condensation gathering on the windshield, listening to the insistent patter of rain. The Prosecuting Attorney's office loomed ahead; its brick façade blurred by the steady downpour. He killed the engine, pulled his collar up, and strode through puddles toward the entrance, feeling the weight of the morning settle on his shoulders.

Inside the lot, rain drumming on the roof of his car, he scrolled through his contacts and dialed Emma. She picked up after two rings, her voice warm but alert.   "Morning, Nick. You all right out there?"

"Morning, Emma," he replied, shaking drops off his sleeve. "Need me for anything? I'm at the PA's office, heading in for a meeting. I'll be free as soon as I get finished here. Have you heard anything from the others? Any word from Clementine about the plan?"

There was a pause on the line, the faint click of keyboard keys in the background.

"Not much from Clementine yet—she's been quiet since last night. Matt checked in; said he'd be by the lab after lunch. I'll let you know if anything else comes up. Be careful going in; rumor has it the PA's in a mood today."

Nick chuckled, reminded of a dozen stormy mornings spent in courthouse corridors.

"Aren't they always? I'll call when I'm out." He ended the call, steeled himself against the rain, and slipped through the double doors, boots leaving wet marks on the faded tile, the echo of Emma's cautious optimism still humming in his ear.

Hurrying as the door opened, he stopped as the man started out. "Mr. Springer? Nick Curtis FBI, did I catch you at a bad time." Hesitating, for him to answer.

"Yes, but I am in a hurry!" His face a mask as the rain continued to pour down. "Come on in this shouldn't take long"

Nick wasn't sure that it was him that made him turn around or the pouring rain.

Following him into rear of the building Nick noticed the elderly lady seated behind the fence. She kept her head down as they went into hos private office.

Looking at the brass name plate he could see that his first name was Kent, he sat down. "Kent... may I call you Kent. I think this isn't going to take long, you need to decide what you are going to charge this guy with. I am ready to testify if you think you need me. I can always fly down here."

"Since I have not had time to get the victims in here to talk to them. By the way the woman that was with the coed is still in the hospital. I was on my way over there just now. While I have a chance, I want to say that was a streak of good luck to have a team member who spoke Vietnamese. Good job."

"I can't take credit for that; Emma is a good friend of my wife's and mine it was just the luck of the draw."

Kent leaned back, running a hand through thinning hair, the ceiling light reflecting off the brass nameplate as if to underline his exhaustion.

"Honestly, Nick, the paperwork alone might drown us before the rain does. The press is already sniffing around, and the DA's office is pressing for a quick decision."

Nick nodded, sensing the tangle of complications lying beneath the surface.

"I understand the pressure. But you've got my statement, and the translation from Emma lines up with what was said at the scene. If you need anything clarified, I can coordinate with her—or have her swing by if necessary."

Kent exhaled, tapping a pen against a legal pad.

"Thanks. Between the rain, the politics, and the mess of this case... I'm glad you stopped by."

Nick walked to the door, his mind already racing ahead. I need to call Emma, and if Storm can come too, even better—Lan would surely open up more easily. Slipping past the receptionist in a blur of damp coat and hasty steps, he hurried into the rain, the sky unleashing its confusion in fierce, slanting sheets.

In the shelter of his car, Nick fished out a handkerchief and wiped the rain from his face, feeling the chill settle on his skin. He ran a hand through his hair, trying to tame it, then reached inside his jacket for his phone. Emma's name was at the top of the recent calls. He tapped and after the second ring, her voice, warm and alert, came through the air.

"Hey, Nick, need something?"

"Yeah," he said, starting the engine, the wipers flicking into a rhythm that matched the thud in his chest. "I was going to head over to the hospital to see Lan—try to get some more details from her. Would you come with me? You know her language and if you bring Storm, she might feel even safer."

Emma didn't hesitate. "Of course. I'll bring him. Pick me up?"

"Absolutely. I'll be there in a minute. No need to come out until you see me—I'll stay in the car."

"Sounds good. See you soon."

Nick ended the call, put the car in drive, and nosed into the soaked street. The city blurred beyond the glass, rain and neon bleeding together. As he made his way to the lab to meet Emma and

Storm, he rehearsed the questions in his mind, hoping the storm outside wouldn't mirror the one waiting in the hospital room.

Driving to the lab, it was quiet—so quiet that Nick could hear the patter of rain on the windshield and the soft hum of the engine beneath his thoughts. He glanced at the empty seat beside him, feeling the weight of everything he'd learned. Thank goodness both girls were alive. Yet relief tangled with dread; he couldn't stop thinking about the kind of scars that lingered unseen. Not the bruises and cuts that faded, but those restless wounds that crept into dreams, the kind that yanked you awake at three a.m., heart pounding, struggling to remember where you were. He wondered what it would take for Lan to trust anyone enough to speak, to let someone help her carry even a fragment of that burden.

Storm's presence might help. Sometimes a gentle soul, canine or human, could break through where all the right words failed. Nick hoped that the dog's warm curiosity and unwavering calm would do more than any question he could ask, leaving a trace of comfort where too much sorrow had already settled. He tightened his grip on the wheel as he pulled up to the curb, headlights flashing across the wet sidewalk. In a city where the rain washed everything clean but never seemed to reach the shadows, he knew that healing would not be easy or quick. But maybe, just maybe, tonight would be a beginning.

Driving onto the lot, Nick spotted Emma framed in the open doorway, Storm pressed loyally against her leg, tail wagging in a hopeful blur. As Nick rolled down the window, Storm bounded forward, nose already nudging into the crisp air, eager to bridge the gap between comfort and uncertainty. Nick swung the car close, leaning over to unlatch the passenger door, and grinned as Storm wasted no time jumping into the front seat, her fur damp and warm under his hand as she wriggled in greeting.

Emma scooted in behind her laughing as she closed the door.

Seeing how storm was taking to Nick she laughed out. "When we get this case closed you and Bobbie are going to haft to come visit us in St Louis Storm is going to miss you and her. It seems like she has spent more time with you guys than me!"

As Storm settled down, Nick reached over and rubbed her head gently. "Good girl," he murmured, feeling her heartbeat thrum beneath his palm—a quiet, steady rhythm that somehow made the night's uncertainty a shade more bearable.   He eased out of the lot, tires hissing against the wet asphalt, and flicked a glance at Emma, who was already watching him, her expression brimming with the kind of calm that could only come from years of hard-won empathy.

Once they were rolling through the rain-filled streets, Nick spoke, voice low but certain.

"Emma, I want to make sure that Lan knows exactly what I'm asking. I don't want her to feel boxed in, or pressured. Even in civilian clothes, I'm still just another stranger, and I know she might be afraid." The truth glinted in his words—a genuine desire to build trust, one gentle moment at a time.

He smiled, the corners of his mouth lifting in a weary grin.

"But Storm—having her here is immeasurable. I bet Lan will feel safer just seeing her. Who could feel fear with a sweet furry friend like Storm close by?"

Storm's ears perked at her name, and she leaned against Emma, tail thumping in quiet agreement. The bond between dog and human was simple, honest—no need for explanations or apologies. Nick found himself hoping that tonight, Storm's gentle presence might help bridge the distance that trauma had carved.

Emma nodded, her hand resting lightly on Storm's back. "She's magic, you know. Sometimes, just a nudge or a wag can break through where words can't reach."

The car rolled onward, rain whispering its secrets on the roof, and as Nick watched the city slip past, he clung to that fragile hope: that kindness—four-legged or not—could help carry someone a few steps closer to healing.

Rain streaked the windshield in silvery threads as they pulled into the Phelps County Hospital lot. Emma leaned forward, pointing, her voice urgent but warm with familiarity. "Here—right here, park by the truck at the emergency entrance. They don't have daytime visiting hours, so we'll have to kind of sneak in. The head nurse is a bear. Just follow me."

Nick eased the car into the narrow spot, the glow of the hospital's lights brushing the dashboard in pale yellow. Storm, sensing the shift in mood, lifted her head and pressed her nose against the glass, tail swishing with anticipation. Emma stepped out first, her movements quick and practiced, and Nick followed, badge at the ready but tucked discreetly at his side.

Ducking inside the doors, the cool hospital light washed over them. They were met almost instantly by the security guard—a broad-shouldered man with a gentle gaze who spoke in a hush that matched the mood. "Hello, Emma. How's Storm today?" His words carried a note of quiet complicity, acknowledging the rules they were about to bend.

Emma's answer was easy, her smile reassuring. Storm trotted over and nosed the guard's leg, earning a soft pat on the head. Nick stepped forward, showing his badge with a nod.

"This is Agent Curtis. He's in charge of the case. We just want to stop in for a minute and check on Lan." Emma used Lan's name deliberately, her tone low and respectful, shifting the focus away from the victim's trauma and toward the promise of protection, of gentle concern.

The guard looked from Nick to Emma, then down at Storm, whose presence seemed to diffuse any lingering tension—a living reminder of comfort and constancy. With a brief nod, he gestured toward the corridor, signaling quiet passage. The afternoon outside pressed close, but inside, they moved with purpose, each step drawing them closer to the fragile hope of healing and to Lan, waiting just beyond the next door.

At the nurses' station, Nick paused, letting Emma's easy familiarity pave their way. The nurses exchanged knowing glances at the sight of Storm, but it was Emma's presence—steady, warm, undeniable—that held their attention and, for a crucial moment, granted passage. In a matter of seconds, they moved beyond the threshold, the muted world of the corridor swallowed by anticipation as they approached Lan's private room.

Inside, the sterile hush gave way to something gentler. Storm padded ahead, her paws whispering over the tile, Emma letting the leash slip free. Lan, curled in a half-sleep, instinctively reached for the dog, fingers burying themselves in Storm's fur before her eyes had fully opened.

"Chào em," Emma greeted, her voice soft, the cadence of Lan's language rolling like a lullaby through the room. Storm leaned in, her presence dissolving the last threads of worry from Lan's brow. Emma knelt, arms encircling the girl in a hug that spoke of protection and belonging. Two plastic sacks rustled as Emma placed them on the bed, a promise of normalcy amid the unfamiliar beeps and pale sheets.

For a few moments, the room filled with the quiet, eager conversation of two friends reunited. Emma upended one of the bags, spilling out a small, hopeful cascade of clothing—shirts in sunny colors, soft pants, a hoodie that looked ready to swallow Lan whole. Nick lingered at the threshold, content to watch the exchange from the quiet safety of distance, letting Emma and Lan shape this moment between themselves.

Emma nudged the smaller bag closer and whispered, "Đồ lót," the Vietnamese word for underwear, her voice low and assuring. The corners of Lan's mouth twitched upward; a shy, genuine smile blooming as she pressed her face into Storm's side. In that instant, the room felt safe—wrapped in kindness, laughter, and the steadfast comfort of a dog who understood exactly where she was needed most.

Nick waited, giving the moment space, until Emma and Lan had finished sorting the bright folds of clothing and the air in the room had settled. Then, with a gentleness that matched the hush around them, he stepped closer, his presence careful and unintrusive. He caught Emma's eye, asking silently if Lan was ready.

Emma gave a barely perceptible nod and turned to Lan, her voice a soft bridge. "Nick muốn biết... con đã đến đây bằng cách nào?" she asked, her tone inviting, never pressing.

Lan's hands stilled on Storm's fur. She hesitated, eyes flickering to Nick, then back to Emma, searching for the right words in the safety of her friend's steady presence. After a pause, she spoke, her voice fragile but clear in its truth.

Emma listened closely, then relayed for Nick, her own voice unshaken but laced with sorrow: "Her family paid someone—a man—to bring her to America. They thought she'd have a better life here. But that's not what happened."

Lan's story spilled out in pieces: she had been hidden away, shuttled from place to place, and eventually brought to a restaurant. There, she was made to work—cleaning, cooking, the endless chores that blurred the days together. As she grew older, the work changed. Lan's words faltered. Her hands pressed tighter into Storm's fur.

Emma's voice dropped, barely more than a breath. "She says... as she got older, they made her go with men." Her eyes flicked to Nick, a silent plea for understanding—not just of the facts, but of the weight each word carried. "You know the rest."

Lan's shoulders shook, silent tears threading down her cheeks as she lowered her head. Storm leaned in, anchoring her with quiet warmth, and Emma wrapped her arms gently around Lan's trembling frame. The room felt suspended—grief and comfort mingling in the hush, Nick bearing witness as the last of Lan's secrets found the light. There was nothing left to say for the moment, only the soft cadence of Emma's soothing words, the gentle thump of Storm's tail, and the silent promise that, here, Lan was seen, and safe.

Nick leaned in, his voice a murmur meant just for Emma's ear. "If you want to help her, try on some of the clothes—add a little sweet to the bitter time I brought her—go ahead. I can wait for you in the car. She'll enjoy it." The words brushed past Lan with gentle intent, an offering of respite amid sorrow.

With a quiet step, Nick slipped from the room, closing the door softly behind him so as not to disturb the fragile circle of warmth inside. In the corridor, he paused, the hush of hospital life settling around him, and drew out his phone.   His fingers dialed, the familiar rhythm of Bobbie's number a small comfort.

"Hi babe, have you had lunch yet?" he asked, voice lightening as he spoke. A beat passed—a familiar cadence of affection—and then, "Yes, I'll pick you up. I'm at the hospital with Emma. Oh, sure, I can bring her if you don't mind sharing lunch with a dog." He smiled at the thought, the image of Storm's earnest eyes and wagging tail stitching a thread of joy through his heart.

"Yes, I'll be there in a minute. Okay you say Marion said hello. Tell her hello back, Chào." He ended the call, a quiet resolve settling over him. In the stillness outside Lan's room, Nick lingered a moment, letting the presence of hope and healing take root, before heading for the car—carrying with him the silent promise of care, and the gentle anticipation of reunion.

Settling in the car out of the rain, Nick relaxed as he waited for Emma and Storm. The steady sound of the rain was soothing, a gentle drumbeat against the roof that quieted the worries still circling his mind. For the first time in days, he let himself lean back, breathing in the scent of damp asphalt and rain, and thinking of Bobbie.

He smiled to himself, remembering the two bottles of champagne tucked safely away in the Winnebago—a private promise, a secret kept until the right moment. He'd been holding onto them since the whirlwind drive out to the Ozarks, knowing there would be a need for celebration, for something golden to cut through the gray. The secrecy of the trip, the tension of the case—he was ready, now, to rewrite the memories with her, to make something beautiful out of the uneasy beginnings.

The case was nearly closed, and with that came a gentle reassurance that the future could be shaped, intention by intention, toast by toast. Sometime in the next week, he'd find the right opportunity—a quiet evening, the world pared down to just the two of them and the fizz of promise in a glass—to help her remember this journey differently. Not just as a chapter marked by worry and uncertainty, but as a turning point, a place where hope and healing began to take root.

Nick glanced out the window, watching raindrops chase each other down the glass. He imagined Bobbie's laughter, the spark in her eyes when she realized what he'd planned. The anticipation was a subtle warmth, kindling in his chest as he waited—not just for Emma and Storm, but for the next sweet moment, waiting just on the other side of the rain.

When Emma and Storm finally slipped into the car, the air held the hush of recent rain and a gentle easing of tension. Nick glanced at her in the rearview mirror, a small smile softening his features.

"Thanks for the clothes," he said quietly. "That was a nice touch. Anything to let that little girl wash away the memories of her ordeal—the better."

Emma buckled in, her hand resting lightly on Storm's head as the dog stretched, nosing at Nick's shoulder with eager anticipation.

"It's nothing," Emma murmured, but her eyes were grateful, a hint of relief flickering through them.

Nick continued, "I called Bobbie and all of us are going for lunch. How does pizza sound? I understand there's a small place here—supposedly one of the best around." He turned, the question directed to both Emma and, with a playful tilt of his head, Storm as well.

Storm barked—a sharp, joyous sound—as if she'd caught the word "pizza" and understood every syllable. Emma laughed for the first time that day, the sound bright and genuine, and Nick felt something in his chest unknot.

With the car now alive with a sense of purpose, Nick started the engine, wipers sweeping away the last of the drizzle. He pulled out of the hospital parking lot, the gray world outside beginning to feel a little warmer, a little less heavy. The road ahead was lined with puddles and promise, and as they drove toward the promise of good company and hot pizza, the weight of the past seemed to recede—just enough to let hope, and appetite, in.

Swinging by Doc's house to pick up Bobbie, they pulled in close to the house. Before the engine had even fully settled, Bobbie was already at the door, her face alight with impatience and that infectious, irrepressible joy. She rushed out, barely pausing to tug the front door gently shut behind her, and slid into the back seat with a fluid, practiced ease. Storm's tail thumped a wild rhythm against Emma's arm, and Bobbie immediately reached to scratch the dog's ears, her laugh tumbling out into the soft, rain-washed air.

"Marion said you owe her one—she likes pizza too," Bobbie announced, her eyes sparkling as she relayed the message. The laughter in her tone was bright and unrushed, cutting through any lingering heaviness.

Nick just shook his head, grinning in spite of himself. "She's got good taste. Maybe we'll bring her a slice, if she's lucky." He caught Emma's eye in the rearview mirror; the shared warmth there was something gentle and new.

As the car filled with the mingled scents of wet earth, rain, and the faint trace of hospital antiseptic, it felt—suddenly—like a place of sanctuary. Bobbie, her presence a joy; Storm, always attuned to the mood, laying her head on Emma's knee with a happy sigh; and Emma, quietly steady, her gaze lingering on the road ahead.

The world beyond the windshield was still sodden and silver, but inside, there was laughter, fellowship, and the promise of a meal shared. As Nick steered them away from Doc's house and toward the pizzeria, he felt the narrative shifting—each mile a gentle rewrite, each smile a line of hope added to the story they were all learning to tell together.

The short drive to the pizzeria was quiet, the air thick with the pleasant anticipation of hot food and comfort. Rain still tapped at the windows, soft and persistent, as they hurried inside beneath the awning. After placing their order—two large pies, half loaded with every topping, half pure and simple for Emma and Storm—Nick excused himself, the promise of pizza a pleasant backdrop to the low hum of conversation at the table.

Navigating the narrow hallway at the back of the restaurant, Nick ducked into the men's room, the door swinging shut with a gentle click. He pulled out his phone, hands still damp with rain and found Kerry's number in his contacts. The line rang twice before she picked up.

"Hello, Kerry, I have a question," Nick began, his voice low but steady. "Since we have plenty of people out here to make sure the palace is covered, how about me taking a couple of days off? I'll only be as far away as I can walk in the woods. I'd like to see if I can bag that deer I'm entitled to. Bobbie and I want to take advantage of this beautiful Ozark country. We need to explore some of the woods and relax out here. She was counting on me returning to the position of husband. What do you say?"

The silence on the other end was measured—a familiar, thoughtful pause as Kerry weighed his words. The fluorescent light hummed overhead. Nick ran a hand through his hair, waiting, the sound of laughter and clinking glasses outside muffled by the tiled walls.

"Nick," Kerry replied at last, her voice warm but businesslike, "you've earned it. Just promise me you'll keep your phone on and check in once a day. The world won't fall apart if you take a little time for yourself. And tell Bobbie she's got my blessing to drag you out into the woods—just don't come back empty-handed."

A grin spread across Nick's face. "You have my word. We'll bring you something back if we're lucky."

He ended the call, a weight lifted from his shoulders. For the first time in a long while, the notion of rest—of slow mornings, sun-draped trails, and the simple company of someone who knew him—felt like more than just a dream postponed. Stepping out, Nick caught his reflection in the mirror: tired, perhaps, but hopeful.

He returned to the table, where Bobbie was insisting that Storm deserved her own chair; and Emma watched the gentle chaos with a smile that suggested she'd begun to believe in good days again. As Nick sat, the aroma of baking pizza drifting from the kitchen, he squeezed Bobbie's hand in silent agreement—there would be time to hunt, to rest, to reclaim all the quiet joys waiting in the heart of the Ozarks.

Dinner went well, a quiet satisfaction settling over the table as the rain continued its gentle drumming outside. The pizzeria's warmth was like a comfort, the clatter of plates and laughter of strangers joining their own small world. Storm, ever the opportunist, lay content at Emma's feet, her tail wagging gently each time a morsel "accidentally" found its way to her bowl—a couple of sausage morsels, enough to make her day. Emma kept a watchful eye, reminding Nick and Bobbie that Storm's diet was not to be compromised, her smile both fond and firm.

The pizzas disappeared quickly, each slice a comfort, each bite shared in companionable silence. Nick waited until the last crumbs were swept away, the server clearing their plates before he leaned in, his tone shifting from light to purposeful. He cleared his throat, glancing around at the faces he'd come to cherish.

"I called Kerry a minute ago," he began, the edge of anticipation in his voice. "I am officially on vacation for the next three or four days. That is, unless the surveillance turns up something unexpected. I'll be out in the woods..." He paused, letting the words linger, the promise of freedom and the thrill of the hunt hanging between them.

"Unless I bag that big buck sooner. The rest of the time, I'm under strict orders to spend it with Bobbie—renewing our love, making up for all those days lost to duty."

Bobbie's eyes lit up at his declaration, her laughter warm and genuine. Emma smiled, a subtle nod of approval, her gaze softening as she watched the easy affection between them. Even Storm, sensing the shift, thumped her tail in quiet celebration.

Outside, the rain showed a slight sign of letting up, inside, the table glowed with the promise of days spent in the heart of the woods, of love rekindled, and adventures waiting just beyond the tree line. For the first time in ages, the future felt expansive, threaded with hope and the simple joy of being together.

Finished with lunch, they all wandered out to the car, the rhythm of rain replaced by a gentle hush beneath the clearing sky. Emma took the lead, her stride purposeful and her gaze drawn to the small park tucked off to the side of the street.   Storm,   eager and restless after a morning of short trips in and out of the car, nearly bounced out of her leash, tail wagging high as if she sensed freedom just ahead.

"Hey, Nick," Emma called, pausing at the curb as the sunlight broke through the clouds overhead.

"Storm and I need to stretch our legs after all that sitting—and honestly, I think she's about to burst if she doesn't get a proper walk. There's a little park right there, and the lab is only a couple of blocks away. Why don't we walk? You and Bobbie could get a head start on your vacation, if you don't mind. Storm's not used to so much sitting around."

Bobbie's face lit up, the prospect of time alone with Nick making her eyes sparkle with quiet joy. She wrapped Emma in a spontaneous hug, gratitude blossoming between them.

"Thank you," she murmured, her voice soft but sincere. "I'm sure Storm will appreciate the walk." She punctuated the moment with a playful wink, her delight infectious.

Nick smiled, the last remnants of obligation slipping away as he watched Emma and Storm set off toward the park, Emma's laughter trailing behind her in the freshening breeze. Storm, finally unleashed to her heart's delight, bounded ahead, nose to the damp grass, reveling in the freedom of the open air.

As Emma and Storm disappeared down the tree-lined path, Nick turned to Bobbie, his arm slipping around her shoulders. The world felt wide open—days of woods and wanderings stretched before them, a promise of rest and renewal. Together, they headed toward their car, the first steps of vacation echoing in the clear, rain-washed afternoon, hearts light and hope restored.

Back in the quiet cocoon of the car, Bobbie settled close to Nick, her presence both a comfort and an invitation. She looked at him with a teasing glint, her hand finding his as she leaned in, lowering her voice to a whisper meant only for him.

"I'll make a deal with you," she murmured, laughter dancing at the edge of her words. "I'll pretend not to notice your garlic breath if you promise to do the same for mine. Just kiss me like you did when we were young—when the world seemed new, and every touch was a promise."

The years—every trial, every triumph—seemed to fold away in that moment. Nick's smile was tender, touched with memory, and as he drew her closer, the weight of days melted from his shoulders. She pressed her lips against his, gentle at first, then with all the affection that had weathered storms and seasons.

Outside, the world blurred into a gentle hush of sun and sky. Within, Bobbie's touch traced the familiar line of his jaw, her fingers lingering at his collar.   She unfastened the top button of his shirt, not with haste but with the reverence of rediscovery, as if she were tracing the map of their shared past and the promise of all their tomorrows.

They lingered in that embrace, the years between their first kiss and this quiet reunion collapsing into the present—a space filled with gratitude, laughter, and a love still eager to be renewed. The world beyond the windows faded, leaving only the warmth of their closeness and the bright, steady beat of hope rekindled.

Satisfied to lay next to her heart's content as the car rolled campward, Nick let the gentle rhythm of the road and Bobbie's steady warmth lull him into a rare tranquility. The city faded behind them, replaced by a tapestry of green—rolling hills and dense woodland that marked the outer borders of the Mark Twain Forest.   Here, the Ozarks rose in quiet majesty, a refuge wrapped in untamed beauty, their contours promising shelter from all the noise and complication of the world outside.

As they wound deeper into the park's embrace, the trees thickened, their branches knitting overhead like old friends welcoming them home. They slowed near the ranger's shack, its weathered boards and hand-painted sign standing sentry at the threshold between their past and the possibility of peace.

Nick stepped out, the gravel crunching beneath his boots, and exchanged easy words with the ranger—introducing himself, pointing out Bobbie, explaining with pride that she held the permit to hunt these woods. The formalities were brief, just enough to honor the ritual of entry before Nick returned to his waiting wife to finish driving the short distance to the Winnebago.

Bobbie was already reaching for the door, her fingers steady on the handle. She looked back at Nick, her eyes reflecting the hush and hope of the forest, and together they stepped inside. The little home-on-wheels held the promise of escape—a sanctuary where the weight of the city and the murmurs of crime could not follow. Here, surrounded by the wild cover of the Ozarks, they could forget for a while, let every shadow and sorrow dissolve into the hush of leaves and the gentle, unhurried beat of their own hearts.

Inside, Bobbie kicked off her shoes and curled onto the faded sofa, Nick settling beside her. The world outside was distant now, lost in the sweep of pines and the call of distant birds. Wrapped in each other's company, they let gratitude fill the silence, their thoughts turning to simple joys: the promise of long walks, quiet mornings, and the kind of laughter that blooms only in freedom. In the heart of the forest, they found what they'd needed most—a moment apart, and the space to simply be.

The golden sunlight of the November sky filled the air like an invitation to conspire with their solitude—a kingdom unclaimed, its only subjects the two of them.

Stirred by the lingering warmth and the promise of more private adventure, they set out on foot toward the shower house, the November light filtering through bare branches in shifting mosaics. Their hands joined, fingers entwined, they as the golden hush of afternoon deepened into the soft indigo of early evening, Nick and Bobbie surrendered wholly to the rhythm of their desires, letting the wilderness become both backdrop and confidant to their rediscovered intimacy. The forest, vast and secretive, seemed wandered as if spellbound by youth's old magic, the world falling away until only the crunch of their boots and the hush of their laughter remained.

The hunt had waned; the others had taken their trophies and vanished, leaving Nick and Bobbie the unspoken privilege of being the forest's last storytellers. Each step through the leaf-littered clearing was a gesture of claim—here, in the wild peace, every shadow belonged to them.

At the shower house, its faded exterior softened by twilight, Bobbie paused and cast a mischievous glance at Nick, her voice a low, teasing whisper. "Want to be a little naughty tonight?" she murmured, her lips curving with playful intent. "We could throw caution to the wind and go in together. I can always use a good strong man to scrub my back—especially when the forest is ours alone." The laughter in her eyes was bright, reckless, and full of promise.

Nick grinned, the challenge clear and irresistible. He glanced around, the woods quiet except for the distant flutter of wings—no one else, no interruptions. With a dramatic bow, he offered his arm. "Madam, I accept your scandalous proposition. Lead the way."

Together they slipped inside, their voices echoing softly in the tiled chamber, the mundane transformed into a playground for secret joys. The water steamed, swirling around them as they washed away the remnants of city dust and old cares, laughter blending with the rush of warm spray. Bobbie leaned into Nick's touch, her delight unfurling in the simple intimacy of shared space and gentle hands.

When they emerged, the evening had fallen fully, stars pricking the velvet sky above the silent forest. Returning to their RV, cheeks flushed and hearts light, they found themselves renewed—not only by the thrill of stolen moments, but by the quiet knowledge that, here in the heart of the Ozarks, they had discovered a refuge where love could be both playful and profound, and every day could begin again in freedom.

Searching in the fridge, Bobbie brought out the sliced ham. Looking at Nick, she asked, "I know that you can't really be too hungry after all that pizza you had for lunch, so how about I make us sandwiches and cut off the crusts like they do at the high price parties? I can garnish them with some dip and two varieties of chips. Then later I have some beer nuts to go along with the many beers you're going to want to drink. Just a kind of celebration of the freedom."

Nick laughed, leaning against the counter as the last of the dusk slipped through the RV's small window, gilding Bobbie's hair in a fleeting halo.

"Sounds extravagant," he teased, "The Ozark version of room service." His smile was easy, and the anticipation of a simple meal—transformed by care—felt like its own feast.

Bobbie set about her work, humming as she constructed sandwiches with precise, playful ceremony, stacking them on a chipped plate and placing sprigs of parsley as if the world had nothing but time. Chips crackled into bowls, dip swirled, and beer nuts rattled into an old dish. Outside, the forest settled into nighttime quiet, tender and untroubled.

They ate cross-legged on the sofa, the sandwiches tasting of salt and smoke and laughter. Between bites, stories wove around them, drifting with the scent of pine and the promise of more beer to come. It was a celebration not of extravagance, but of simplicity—of being together, of being hidden away where the rules didn't apply, and every small pleasure was magnified by gratitude.

Later, as the beer bottles clinked and the sky deepened into black velvet, Bobbie reached for Nick's hand, squeezing it in silent thanks. "To freedom," she whispered, and the forest seemed to echo the sentiment, every shadow nodding in agreement.

Chapter Seventeen

The hush of morning lingered, thick and luxurious, wrapping their little world in quiet. No whistle broke the spell—only the gentle rise of light through the forest, streaming across the faded curtains and bathing the RV in a muted gold. Somewhere beyond the trees, the deer wandered unbothered, the world allowed to move at its own easy rhythm.

Nick stretched, still caught in the warmth of the tangled sheets, and found himself gazing at Bobbie. She lay beside him, her smile radiant and unhurried, arms folded behind her head in a gesture of contentment. The thin sheen of her kimono hinted at softness, at secrets kept between lovers and the day. There was an unspoken truce in the air, a shared languor—Bobbie's calm daring Nick to join her in savoring the slow unfolding of the morning.

He brushed a stray lock of hair from her forehead, his fingers lingering in quiet reverence. Outside, the forest was waking: a squirrel chattered somewhere, twigs snapped softly, and the world seemed to tiptoe around their cocoon. Nick didn't speak; words would have felt like an intrusion into the blissful peace.   Instead, he let the gentle rhythm of Bobbie's breathing, the promise in her eyes, draw him deeper into the moment.

No hurry, no agenda—just the two of them, settled in a patchwork nest, letting the Ozarks cradle their freedom. Bobbie's dress, cut in the manner of an old-fashioned housewife, was both modest and mischievous, a playful nod to tradition beneath which something wild and unbound shimmered. She watched Nick with patient amusement, waiting for him to surrender fully to the languid joy she offered.

And so, the morning unfolded, unhurried, as they lay side by side in a world that had, for a few precious hours, forgotten how to rush.

Bobbie's laughter was low and indulgent, her eyes crinkling with that familiar affection, a warmth distilled by years of shared mornings and wordless understanding.

"If you're going to abandon me to the responsibilities of civilization," she teased, "at least promise me you'll be back before I start daydreaming about breakfast in Paris."

Nick grinned, swinging his feet to the floor with the ease of someone whose roots run deep in this place and this moment. Sunlight, bold and insistent, sliced through the curtains, painting golden stripes across the rumpled bed and the curve of Bobbie's shoulder as she turned to gather herself.

As Nick padded over to the small restroom, the hush in the RV shifted, filled now with the soft clatter of cups and the gurgle of water coming to boil. Bobbie moved through the cozy clutter with practiced grace, measuring grounds, listening for the familiar whistle of the kettle, letting the promise of coffee fill the air—a small but sacred ritual of their morning.

The Ozarks stretched beyond their window, vast and inviting, but inside, the world remained tender and intact. The haven they had built was not simply shelter but sanctuary—woven from laughter, glances, and the shared certainty that every ordinary day, when properly savored, was a kind of miracle.

Nick returned, fresh and grinning, his eyes bright with the gentle mischief of a man at peace. "Did Paris call?" he asked, wrapping his arms around Bobbie as she poured steaming coffee into two matching cups.

"No," she whispered, pressing her lips to his cheek. "Ozark mornings are enough for me."

And with that, the quiet magic of their union carried them, lingering in sunlight and steam, into whatever the day would next bring.

Nick's words floated between them, gentle as the morning mist curling along the ridge. Bobbie grinned, her eyes sparkling with anticipation and the promise of shared adventure. "Just let me grab my shoes," she murmured, her voice soft and content, the kind of ease that only comes from knowing you are exactly where you're meant to be.

Nick busied himself for a moment, stacking the toast on a small plate, the golden crusts promising comfort. He set out the last of the orange juice—its brightness glinting in the sun—and made it all feel like a feast. The simple act was a quiet offering, another way to show her that every day together, even with its lists and duties, could feel like a holiday.

The RV glowed with warmth and the unhurried pulse of a day yet to begin. Nick caught Bobbie's hand as she finished lacing her shoes, his thumb tracing lazy circles against her wrist—a silent invitation to linger, to savor the sweetness of this hour. He hesitated over his phone, the device lying face-down on the counter, as if it could steal the magic if touched. The world beyond their haven might clamor for attention, but he resolved to let it wait. For now, the day belonged to them.

They stepped outside into the cool hush of the Ozark morning, sidling close in their matching sweats, their laughter trailing behind them like a string of lights. Dew sparkled on the grass, and the woods beckoned with shadows and secrets. Nick gave Bobbie's hip a playful pat, his words low and beckoning. "I suppose you're ready for our stroll?" he teased.

Bobbie looped her arm through his, her smile serene and sure.

"Lead the way," she replied, letting the rhythm of their footsteps blend with birdsong and the soft rustle of leaves overhead. Together, they wandered into the woods, letting the Ozarks cradle their freedom once more, each step a quiet celebration of simple joys and shared tomorrows.

Following the road that led to the fire roads, Nick held Bobbie's hand, guiding her gently past the tangled weeds that bordered the old county lane. The hush between them felt sacred, and Nick, intent on keeping his world of work at bay, steered their steps toward the Fox hunters' cabin, its weathered timbers tucked deep in the holler across from the road.

Earlier that day, the forensics team had come and gone, their presence marked only by the bright yellow tape fluttering in the breeze—a stark ribbon wound around the cabin's sagging porch. As they neared the fence line, Nick slowed, feeling the pulse of the place, the weight of stories that hung in the morning air.

"I came this way intentionally," he said softly, his voice barely disturbing the quiet,

"So, we wouldn't jump up the big buck that's evaded all the hunters. I just wanted to walk."

He squeezed Bobbie's fingers, the warmth of her palm grounding him. He hoped the yellow tape—garish against the hush of wild grass—had slipped past Bobbie's quick blue gaze, that her morning would remain untroubled.

They lingered at the edge, the cabin's secrets sealed behind its cautionary veil. The woods pressed close, the world both familiar and mysterious. Bobbie glanced at Nick, her expression gentle, sensing the careful distance he kept between their haven and the shadows of duty. With a quiet nod, she let him lead them back toward the sunlit path, their footsteps weaving memory into the soft earth, each stride a silent promise: that together, they would keep finding peace amid the tangled, golden edges of the ordinary.

Reaching the break in the roadway that held the camper shell. The one that had imprisoned Maya Nick hurried past the break walking sideways looking directly at Bobbie. "Not that I am in a hurry; but have you thought about if you would like to be taken out to dinner tonight... Tomorrow, I have got to get after that buck. Of course, if you want to go and act as guide, I will welcome the company. Think about that and decide if tonight you would like to have a sit-down dinner. Maybe a steak cooked on the grill the way you like it."

Bobbie's lips formed a smile as the thought of another treat from her husband crossed her mind.

"Just as long as I don't have to dress up," she said with a sly wink. "I'm beginning to like the feel of these sweats. My shorts from the other night are still dirty. If that wasn't the case, I'd wear them." Her response was light, a gentle tease that sent warmth flickering through Nick's chest. He laughed, the sound low and easy.

Her playfulness was exactly what he needed—a soothe against the heaviness that sometimes threatened to follow him home. They let the conversation fade, the silence companionable as they wandered back toward their RV, hands still entwined. The world around them was waking, the last of the dew vanishing in the golden spill of sun across the clearing.

As they reached their home away from home, Nick paused, pausing just long enough to press a kiss to Bobbie's temple. "Steak it is, then. You can keep the sweats on—just promise you'll save me a dance after." Bobbie chuckled, her eyes bright, and together they stepped inside, letting the quiet promise of the day settle around them like sunlight through the pines.

Outside the RV, Nick paused, sunlight dappling his shoulders as he riffled for his phone—a quiet reminder that some threads of duty tugged at him still. He thumbed in Doc's number, listening to the trilling ring cut through the gentle hush of the morning.

"Hello, Nick—is there a problem, do you need something?" Doc's voice was brisk, familiar as an old shirt.

"No, nothing earth shattering," Nick replied, glancing at Bobbie through the open door, her laughter still lingering in the air. "I was wondering—is there anywhere in the burg where a married man can take his wife for a sit-down dinner? Someplace 'come as you are.' We're in sweats, and neither of us wants to change."

Doc chuckled, a warm rumble that spoke of years in the town and its quirks. "Well, Nick, you know 's Chubb's Diner never turned anybody away, and the steak's just as good whether you're in flannel or a suit. Or there's Joe's Grill by the lake—no dress code, and you can watch the water while you eat. Folks come as they please. You two will fit right in. They are both just out of the campgrounds to the left. Not far at all. "

Nick felt a sigh of relief, that sometimes slips out without notice.

"Thanks, Doc. That's exactly what I needed."

He hung up, the prospect of a simple meal—no fuss, no pretense—settling over him like a smile. Turning to Bobbie, he grinned, "Looks like sweats are on the menu tonight. No one's going to blink twice."

She smiled back, the promise of an easy evening shining in her eyes, and together they stepped into the RV, unhurried, wrapped in ordinary joy.

Bobbie bounced into the RV, her energy infectious, making it impossible for Nick not to follow. She headed straight for the fridge, anticipation brightening her face. A bottle of beer emerged, cold enough to make her shiver as she pressed it to her forehead, sighing with exaggerated relief.

"Me is thirsty. How about you, big hunter man?" she teased, grinning mischievously.

With a swift step, Nick closed the distance between them and gently twisted the bottle out of her hand, pulling her into a hug that was all warmth and laughter. "Sure, I'd like a cold one. Get yourself one—I've got mine now," he quipped, cocking an eyebrow.

Her eyes sparkled with playful challenge.

"Oh, so that's how it is?" She ducked around him, rummaging in the fridge with purpose and producing a second beer, brandishing it like a trophy. Nick let out a low chuckle, the easy rhythm of their banter as comforting as the golden afternoon light still filtering through the RV windows.

They clinked bottles, their grins wide and unguarded, and let themselves sink into the small, perfect moment—the simple pleasure of cool beer, the scent of pine and promise just outside their door, and the knowledge that in this place, and in each other's company, every ordinary day had its own kind of magic.

Soon, they returned to the soft comforts of the couch, the space familiar and inviting, the cushions worn in all the right places. Bobbie, still brushed by a gentle melancholy, inched closer to Nick, her shoulder finding his with quiet intent. The beers glistened in their hands, condensation glimmering like tiny jewels on amber glass.

Nick took a long pull, letting the cold bitterness chase away the past few day's residue of exhaustion; halfway through, he set the bottle aside, satisfied and content. Bobbie, ever the connoisseur, sipped delicately—each taste slow, letting the golden liquid linger, as if each mouthful might reveal some secret hidden in the hops.

She watched Nick out of the corner of her eye, sure that any moment he'd stand and go for another bottle. But for now, silence wrapped around them, gentle and undemanding, the kind that lets two people share a room and a mood without needing words. Outside, the world continued in its quiet way, but here in the glow of the RV, time seemed to soften, stretched and easy, as if it too wanted to savor the flavor of the evening.

Nick stretched his legs out, boots nudging the edge of the faded rug, as he let his gaze wander around the cozy interior—half-listening to the gentle hum of the world just beyond their thin walls. A breeze fluttered through the front door screen, carrying with it the distant call of a mourning dove and the faint, resinous scent of pine. For a moment, there was only their quiet—until Bobbie, restless fingers searching for something more, reached for the little radio perched on the shelf above the kitchenette.

The dial clicked and whined, static giving way to music—a sweet, twanging melody that washed over the room, blending seamlessly with the golden hush. A grin tugged at the corners of Bobbie's lips as she caught the familiar intro, and Nick's brow rose in recognition, lips quirking in silent amusement.

The DJ's voice threaded through the music, both a comfort and a reminder, his words settling gently into the space between them. There was a pause—a soft, vulnerable hush—before Bobbie turned, her expression open, searching Nick's face for understanding.

There was a breathless moment as Bobbie's words, trembling but sure, filled the softly sunlit space.

"I am glad you fooled me with the thoughts that we were going to be down here on just a vacation—I am glad because I could see it in your eyes that you hate to hide behind a lie. Mostly I am glad that you found the coed and she, as well as the other girl, are safe. You know, it is things like this that makes me proud of the job you do, and how well you do it, Nick Curtis. I love you." Her voice faltered, fighting back the tears that threatened to spill, her vulnerability as luminous as the light tracing the dust motes in the air.

Nick didn't answer right away. Instead, he reached for her, his hand gentle at the nape of her neck, thumb brushing a stray lock behind her ear. The beer forgotten, the radio's tune turned distant and thin, and the hush that followed was thick with all the things words could not capture—gratitude, relief, and the fierce, ordinary love that had grown between lines of danger and the quiet aftermath.

"Hey," he whispered, his tone rougher at the edges for all he tried to make it light.

"I didn't do any of it alone. I never do." His gaze caught hers, holding steady.

"You're the reason I can walk back into the world, knowing there's still something good—something worth coming home to."

The tears crested, but Bobbie only smiled through them, all the ache and pride and affection shining on her face. They leaned into each other, the music rising around them, and for a long while, nothing else mattered but the truth spoken between two hearts— quiet, unguarded, and entirely enough.

The time passed slowly, and their second beer was gone when Bobbie stood up, stretching with a little yawn and a half-smile.

"I think I'll use the restroom to freshen up my makeup, and whenever you're ready, I'm sure I'm hungry enough to eat a steak. So, there you are." She walked to the restroom and slipped in behind the door, her laughter trailing soft as she disappeared from sight, leaving Nick alone with the lull of the afternoon and the echo of her warmth.

He gathered the empty bottles, clinking them together in one hand, and stowed them quietly on the counter. As he moved through the little Winnebago, the familiar sounds—the faint whisper of the radio, the muffled rustle of Bobbie's movements—wove a gentle cocoon around him. It was a peace he didn't take for granted.

Drawn by a restless curiosity, Nick drifted toward the open doorway, the old screen door hiding him just enough to remind him where he stood. He leaned his shoulder against the frame, letting the breeze find him. That was when he saw it—a slender, cautious silhouette at the edge of the pines. A buck, antlers polished and gleaming in the low, honeyed light, moved with unhurried grace along the edge of the campground. Nick watched, transfixed by the ease of the animal's presence, the way it paused to nibble at a patch of clover, utterly unbothered by the possibility of a human audience.

For a moment, the world outside and inside the cabin stilled, time bending around the quiet beauty of that wild creature. Nick's thoughts drifted—gratitude for this gentle pause, for the safety hard-won and the ordinary moments given back. He wished Bobbie could see the buck too, but perhaps it was enough for one of them to witness this small wonder. She had seen him in the wild where he was the other day as she had also been alone to witness his beauty.

Quietly, Nick moved back from the doorway, careful not to disturb the hush that lingered in the cabin. He stood waiting, hands in his pockets, listening for the soft click of the restroom door. It wasn't long before Bobbie emerged, freshened and radiant, a little cloud of her perfume preceding her into the narrow passageway.

She paused as they met, her lips curving in a knowing smile. With an effortless gesture, she brushed a quick kiss to his cheek, the delicate scent—warm, floral, and unmistakably hers—clinging to his skin. The brief contact left a shimmer of intimacy between them. "Hmm, you smell good," Nick murmured, the words tumbling out, half-playful, half-reverent, as he slipped past her and into the small, sunlit restroom.

Bobbie lingered for a moment, her laughter low and private, trailing behind her as she returned to the kitchen to set at the table. In the tiny Winnebago, the world was distilled to quiet comforts and the steady rhythm of ordinary rituals—the promise of a meal, the gentle exchange of affection, the silent agreement that, for now, all was well.

Looking at the four empty beer bottles, Bobbie smiled, her fingertips lingering momentarily on the cool glass. She gathered them with a quiet efficiency, opening the cabinet beneath the sink and sliding the bottles neatly into their carton.   Each small action felt deliberate—a gesture of care in the cozy confines of their traveling home.

Settling back into her seat by the window, Bobbie watched the sunlight drift across the tabletop, the gentle hush of the afternoon settling around her like a favorite blanket. She waited, listening for Nick's footsteps, the sound a familiar signal of comfort.

When Nick emerged from the restroom, his face brightened at the sight of her—Bobbie, waiting, content and at ease, her smile lifting the last of the day's tension. There was something in his eyes, a quiet joy, as if the ordinary became extraordinary simply because they shared it. He crossed the small space between them, the room shrinking to just the two of them, and sat down, the Winnebago holding their laughter, their silences, and the promise of a meal still to come.

Walking close to Bobbie, Nick pulled out his phone, thumb hovering for a moment before he offered her a sheepish look.

"Sorry, babe, I just thought of something that needs to be done." He stepped aside, swiping his phone open with practiced ease and dialing Doc's number.

He listened to the low hum of the ring, gaze drifting out the little window where the late sun flickered through the trees.

"Hi Doc, it's Nick. I was by the campsite earlier and the camper was still there. It stood out with all of that yellow police tape wrapped around it."

Doc's voice, faint and staticky, came through the receiver. "What—you say the tow guy picked it up two hours ago? Delivered it to the lab and put it inside so we can really go over the whole thing?" Nick exhaled slowly; tension he hadn't known he was carrying sliding from his shoulders.

"Okay, well, I was a little busy. I was with Bobbie—we went for a walk in the woods." He caught Bobbie's eye, letting a shadow of a grin flicker across his mouth.

"Sorry I bothered you. Have a good night."

He hung up, the phone still warm in his hand, and let the hush settle again. The urgency of the outside world slipped away, replaced by the delicate clockwork of their evening—two hearts, one small home, and the glow of lamplight waiting for the night to gather. Nick slid his phone onto the table and sat beside Bobbie, brushing his knuckles gently against hers.

"Everything's taken care of," he said quietly, and in his voice was the promise that, for now, nothing else mattered but this—her laughter, the meal, the simplicity of togetherness as dusk crept soft against the windows.

Looking at Bobbie, Nick stood up and slid his phone from the table. He moved to the kitchenette, its tiny counter gleaming in the sunlight, and leaned against the wall as he plugged his phone into the charger. For a moment, he watched the little screen flicker to life and then fade into a crescent moon of rest.

"Guess I'll have to go to dinner without this thing to disturb us," he said, his voice playful, a wink tossed in her direction. The world outside—messages, missed calls, digital static—would have to wait.

Bobbie stepped close, warmth enfolding them both as she wrapped her arms around him and pulled him in, her laughter bright and easy.

"Oh, I love you so much," she murmured, the words soft against his ear. "Come on, let's go eat. I can drive—I've still got the rental car."

Nick grinned, letting himself savor the closeness, the simple certainty of her arms around him. They lingered in the hush for a heartbeat more, then slipped on their jackets, shoes nudged from the mat, and headed out into the evening—together, unhurried, ready to leave the phone behind and chase the promise of shared roads and a meal waiting somewhere in the gentle night.

Nick laughed, the sound low and genuine. "No, I will drive—you need to keep your strength. You have to tackle that big steak," he teased, grinning as he plucked the car keys from the dish by the door.

Bobbie rolled her eyes in mock protest but relented, slipping her hand into his as they stepped into the cool dusk. The air hummed with the scent of fresh rain, and the last rays of sunlight painted the treetops gold. The road ahead shimmered with possibility, and as they walked side by side toward the car, their shadows merged and stretched behind them—a pair of silhouettes bound for warmth, laughter, and dinner waiting just out of sight.

Driving out of the campgrounds Nick thought about what Doc had said 'Just drive out on the road from the park and continue on the same road that the lab was on.' Nick drove slowly past the lab turning to the right he passed the donut shop and continued to stay on that road. At the top of the hill his breath he had been holding released. The bright sign on the left jumped out at him Joe's grill.

Pulling in to the lot Nick slowed and turned to Bobbie "Dear, there is no valet so I guess we will be okay to park beside this second pick-up truck."

Bobbie snorted, amusement flashing in her eyes as she unbuckled her seatbelt. "All the better—means nobody's here to judge us for licking the plates clean." She reached into the back seat for her denim jacket, shrugged it on, and grinned at Nick. "Besides, the best places never need linen tablecloths or fancy cars out front."

Nick nodded, his smile softening as he watched her push open the door.   The evening air wrapped around them, gentle and ripe with the smell of lake water, fried onions, and a hint of hickory smoke drifting from the kitchen vents. The neon "Open" sign buzzed a welcome and, as they stepped onto the pavement, the still wet concrete beneath their shoes sounded like the beginning of a small adventure.

He leaned in, voice low. "Well, my dear, shall we risk the culinary reputation of the Ozarks?"

Bobbie arched an eyebrow, laughter dancing in her voice. "Absolutely. If the steak's half as good as the company, we're in for the best night yet."

Outside, in the last glimmer of daylight, their car sat among the pickup trucks, unassuming and content. Inside, Nick and Bobbie let the hush settle again, hungry for whatever joys this simple, perfect evening would serve.

Opening the first door of the alcove they were greeted by the big chalkboard

Proclaiming "Special strip-steak $ 12.95, fries and salad, today's pie blackberry."

Inside they were greeted by a mature lady dressed in a bright white and yellow pinafore, her hair flecked with soft grey amidst sunlit blonde. Her smile was genuine, her voice gentle and reassuring as she welcomed them.

"Evening folks, welcome to Joe's." One hand lingered in her pocket, searching for something unseen as she led them to the small table by the window.

"I'll put you two here at the table looking out over the lake. Must be new in town. Visiting relatives?" She waited until they were settled before pulling out a battered notepad, ready to take their order.

"If you're hungry for a good steak, I'd advise the special. Neil at the butcher's shop ordered them in for me. All his meat is excellent. No alcohol, just soft drinks. No sweet tea—I prefer to add my own sugar. So, will it be two specials?"   Her tone was kindly but a little hurried, her eyes flicking to the growing crowd trickling in through the door like moths to the warm light.

Bobbie met Nick's gaze, her own smile stretching wider, and nodded. "Two specials sound perfect," she said, laughter tucked in her voice. Nick agreed, echoing her choice, "With two Iced teas," He added. his appetite for the night's adventure growing.

As the waitress scribbled down their order and moved to greet the next guests, the lake's reflection shimmered in the window. The promise of a meal—simple, hearty, and served with neighborly charm—settled over them like the comfort of home. In that moment, the world beyond Joe's faded, leaving only the golden hush of evening and the anticipation of good company and steak.

Reaching across the table Nick offered his hands, Bobbie holding the mood reached and joined them. He squeezed them gently a reassuring gesture. Holding hands, they watched out the lake. Surprisingly enjoyed by the setting sun as it shone across the water. They could see the several red and green lights of the boats parked across the lake.

The dusk pressed softly around them, the glimmering lake dancing with the last colors of day. Bobbie held Nick's hand a moment longer, her thumb tracing slow, gentle circles. She let his words linger between them, sweet as the pie promised on the chalkboard and just as fleeting.

"I love you too," she finally whispered, her voice tremulous with the weight of memory. She looked out at the water, its surface now collecting the hues of twilight, and then back at Nick, their joined hands resting atop the faded tablecloth.   "Sometimes I wonder how we managed to circle back to this—how something so small as an evening together could feel so big, so right."

She paused, letting out a quiet laugh, half-mirth, half-tears. The mellow ache of nostalgia softened her expression.

"It's not just luck, you know. You call it engineering, but I think it's more like building—little moments stacked together, just like those boats docked out there, each one moored beside another. We built this, Nick. All of it."

The soft bustle of Joe's echoed behind them—plates clinking, voices rising and falling, the steady rhythm of comfort and belonging. Bobbie's gaze wandered back to the lake, the warmth of Nick's hand grounding her.

"This night isn't just perfect because of what we have," she said quietly,   "it's perfect because of everything we've weathered. I wouldn't trade it for the world."

Outside, the stars began to peek through the velvet sky. For Nick and Bobbie, the hush inside Joe's was a sanctuary—a place where time paused, love settled, and the simple act of holding hands was enough to light the night. Talk was not needed as they enjoyed the moment.

A new young server brought their drinks, dressed in a pinafore of bright orange and white. She seemed almost a younger echo of Joe himself—her face lit with honest warmth, her smile genuine, her voice refined as she set the glasses before them.

"Your food will be here shortly," she announced with a little nod, the syllables carrying just enough cheer to make the whole table glow.

Nick picked up his glass of tea, holding it aloft in a mock toast, his eyes never leaving Bobbie's.

"Here's to many more romantic nights with the girl of my dreams," he said, the words ringing clear and steady in the hush

"The girl I want to spend the rest of my life with."

Bobbie's eyes grew soft as she raised her own glass, the moment threading between them with quiet significance.

"And to the many days when you are gone, and I will miss you, Anxious for your return," she replied, her voice mellow, tinged with both gratitude and longing.

They clinked their glasses gently, the sound delicate as crystal, filled with all the hope and ache of a love that had endured every distance. In the amber glow of Joe's, with the scent of warm biscuits drifting from the kitchen and the lake-light shimmering through the windows, they drank to the present—their hands never far apart, their hearts sheltering a thousand memories and waiting for a thousand more.

Beyond the window, night settled over the water, but inside, the promise of their shared tomorrows burned quietly bright.

The aroma of the sizzling steaks wafted, filling the air. Nick shifted his plate, eager to begin cutting the meat. He ignored the sounds of the diner and the rest of the world as he selected the first bite of the medium-cooked beef. Bobbie grinned at his eagerness to devour the freshly cooked food. Once he had begun chewing the meat, he picked up a hot biscuit, tearing it open. He reached for the case knife and buttered it, watching the steam roll out from the fluffy inside. The butter glistened and melted into the golden bread as he spread it.

Wanting to add a playful flourish to the moment, Nick handed the hot morsel to Bobbie, his eyes twinkling with the delight of small, shared gestures.

She accepted it, her gentle smile a wordless answer to his generous offering.   He picked up another biscuit for himself, savoring its warmth. Around them, the hum of Joe's faded into the background, replaced by the intimate, unspoken language of two people who knew how to turn an ordinary meal into a memory worth holding.

Bobbie's laughter was soft, warm as summer light, and Nick found himself wanting to draw out these moments, stretch them beyond the edges of the night.

To them, every bite was a promise, every passing second another brushstroke on the canvas of their togetherness. Their hands met again over the table—one passing butter, the other returning a smile—each gesture weaving a brighter thread into the story they were writing, right there in the amber-lit hush of Joe's, with the world held gently at bay.

As their laughter settled into a contented hush, the creak of worn floorboards signaled Joe's return. She appeared at their table, her warm hands dusted with flour, her eyes alive with the easy candor of someone who'd poured love into every plate.

"Well, folks, did I steer you wrong?" Joe grinned, her melodious voice carrying a familiarity that made the room feel smaller, cozier.

"How was your dinner? I know I shouldn't ask, but I guess that's just the country in me. Everybody around here is like family. Never met a stranger. Like I said, I don't remember seeing you in here before."

Nick rose, brushing biscuit crumbs from his hands, the gesture half-formal, half at ease.

"I'm Nick Curtis, and this is my wife, Bobbie," he offered, his tone friendly as he gestured to his companion.

"We're down here for the special hunt—Bobbie's already bagged hers. I'll be out trying for mine the rest of our stay. And yes, the food was good—really good."

Bobbie reached out, her palm soft with gratitude and the warmth of a shared evening. She took Joe's flour-dusted hand, squeezing it gently.

"My steak was tender, and the biscuits were scrumptious," she said, her praise honest and unforced, her eyes shining with the simple satisfaction of a meal well-made and well received.

Joe's laughter tumbled out, bright and genuine.

"Well, I surely do appreciate that. It's always nice to have new faces around. Nothing fancy here—just good food and good folks."

As Joe headed back toward the kitchen, Nick and Bobbie exchanged a glance, a silent agreement passing between them: there was something about this little diner, about Joe herself, that made the night feel more than ordinary. The glow of the lamps, the taste of real butter, the hush of the lake—these, too, would linger in their memory, stitched in with the flavor of home and the kindness of strangers who, in the span of a supper, had become friends.

Slowly walking to the cash register they waited for the young server to help them. Sliding a tip across the counter. Nick reached for Bobbie, and they left the sounds and friendly atmosphere of diner behind.

Still holding on to Nick's arm Bobbie pulled close as the evening at the diner by the Lake was replaced with the trip back to the campgrounds. They both slipped into the car with Bobbie glued to Nick as if he might slip away. Laying against his shoulder with a tiny bit of possessiveness. She settled close for the quiet ride.

The headlights cast gentle arcs along the winding road, shadows dancing against the pines as Nick steered them toward their secluded retreat. Bobbie's mind lingered on the warmth of the diner, the ease of conversation, the memory of Joe's laughter echoing softly in her chest. But that sense of belonging had now given way to anticipation—a quiet thrill that tingled beneath her skin.

Their Winnebago was tucked just beyond the bath house, sheltered by a stand of old firs and the hush of the evening. Bobbie felt the comfort of solitude as the world grew dim—only the hush of the forest and the sounds of night insects interrupted the peace. She glanced at Nick, her smile carrying secrets, and reached across the upholstered seats to rest her hand atop his.

"Here, stop here," she said, voice hushed but purposeful. "I have my bathing things in the back seat. I want to get a shower now."

Nick nodded, a half-smile curving his lips as he pulled the car to a gentle stop. The bath house door creaked open, and Bobbie gathered her bag, the familiar weight of her preparations nestled inside—a small mystery she'd carefully planned, a token of romance plucked from shelves on a quiet afternoon with Marion.

In the privacy of the afternoon, she had tucked her new skimpy nightie away, anticipation threading through her thoughts like moonlight through the trees.

Inside the steamy haze of the shower, Bobbie let the day's dust and worries slip away. The scent of pine mingled with warm water, and she breathed deeply, letting the promise of the night settle over her. The evening was hers—hers and Nick's—to savor, to stitch together with laughter and gentle touches, beneath the hush of the woods and the tender hush of stars above.

When she emerged, skin aglow and spirit light, dressed in her previous clothes. Covering her new surprise nightie. She found Nick waiting just outside, eyes alight with the kind of affection that comes from shared adventure and quiet understanding.

Bobbie smiled, the memory of good food and good company now folded into the deeper comfort of being with someone she loved, in a place where the world felt briefly paused—just for them.

Together, they rode back to their RV, the night stretching ahead, slow and sweet, promising more than rest—a renewal of closeness, a celebration of simple joys, wrapped in the magic of a place that felt like home.

Hesitating in the car for a moment, they kissed—softly at first, lingering in the hush as if time itself was theirs to command. Nick's arm slipped around Bobbie, drawing her closer, his warmth radiant in the gentle darkness. He bent to her ear, his breath a tender secret.

"Punkin, it's awhile before we need to go to bed," he murmured, voice wrapped in affection. "I'd like to start a fire in the pit, sit out here for a while. Maybe enjoy the quiet of the evening, and just... enjoy each other."

Bobbie traced her fingers along his jaw, holding him close. "Anything you say. The night is ours."

The rental car door opened with a soft click, and they stepped into the hush of the campground, cool air brushing their faces. Nick rummaged for kindling, stacking it with practiced care, while Bobbie gathered the old woven blanket and the pillows, she'd tucked away for just such a moment. The first match flared golden in Nick's hands, and soon the fire crackled, sending sparks pirouetting into the velvet sky.

They settled by the fire, legs tangled beneath the blanket, the world around them silent but for the occasional whisper of wind in the firs and the distant, contented chirp of crickets. Firelight played over their faces, painting their closeness in amber and shadow.

For a while, they said nothing—there was no need. Bobbie leaned her head against Nick's shoulder, watching the flames dance and the embers drift upward.   The kind of peace that arrives only in wild places, when the day is done and there's nothing left to do but savor the presence of someone you love, settled over them.

And as the fire's glow mingled with the promise of night, their laughter and quiet words stitched the evening into memory, a gentle tapestry of trust, comfort, and something beautifully unspoken.

As the first embers were nestled in the bottom of the firepit Nick extracted himself out of Bobbie's grip. He reached and threw a couple more logs on the fire. Still standing he leaned close "Any chance that you are ready for some of the bubbly. I am sure that it is cold enough for us to share it." Not waiting for her answer, he started for the RV. Stopping briefly to be sure she was ready he waited for her to answer. Her smile was enough, so he continued to the task.

Bobbie's mind was not on drink as she slipped out of her clothes and sat down draping her body with the blanket. The tiny undergarment hid her but just barely. The warmth of the fire felt good as the night air was creeping into the dense forest of their hideaway.

Minute later Nick returned with the bubbly and the red solo cups. Bobbie remained seated as she accepted her cup and Nick poured it full. Bobbie was careful to keep the blanket in place covering her.

Nick continued to stand, smiling down at her, knowing that a mock toast was unnecessary. Drinking some of the glistening liquid as the bubble rose to the top. He walked close to Bobbie and sat down.

"This is nice, it doesn't get any better than this." Turning towards Bobbie.

Her response was immediate dropping the blanket... "You think so?"

 The firelight flickered across the space that led to her. She smiled as his eyes saw the bareness of the night.

In a second, he was close, the place that he remained the rest of the night. Before long the fire had died out and the trip to the Winnebago led to the bedroom and romance.

Chapter Eighteen

The morning came quick as did the rest, a sleep they both enjoyed. Bobbie stirred first it was before Six, her contentment was magnified by the presence of Nick his body sprawled across the bed. His breathing a melody of his love for her. She wanted to remain there and enjoying him. But she knew that her enjoyment could be replaced with a better show of her love by greeting him with hot coffee and breakfast waiting for him.

Quietly she slipped out of the tiny half bed. Slowly she reached for her old chenille robe. Her stepped were measured as she chastely moved to the kitchenette.

Her movement hushed as she filled the coffee pot. Pouring the hopper full she stood in front of the counter hoping to shield the sounds she was creating. Aware that the next steps were going to be hindered by the easy clack of the frying pan as she began to fry the bacon. Her hopes were that the lager billowy chenille bathrobe would shield the sound. She poured out her love in a quiet act.

As the aroma of the bacon drifted to the small part of the RV where Nick was sleeping, he awoke. Reaching across the bed He searched the bed for Bobbie his long arm sifting through the blankets. Turning he could see that his prey had escaped.

Bobbie was all eyes as she was waiting for his waking. "Good morning she sang out. I have coffee ready but there is a toll you have to pay with a kiss."

Rolling out of the bed nick walked to Her as she poured his first cup of that starter liquid that he needed.

Pursing her lips she cautiously held the cup out away from them. As their lips touched it was quick.

Nick took the cup gingerly holding it safely away from them. Taking it close he blew into the dark liquid, as the steam blew away, he sipped a drink. Walking to the table he sat it down. Uttering one word "bathroom", as he stepped to the restroom.

Looking at himself in the small mirror he winked at himself. The thoughts of the day and the hunt was delighting to his thoughts. The fact that Bobbie had gotten up and was serving him breakfast reminded him of his life and how good it was. Today it was going to be even better he would try to make the trip to the Ozarks something special. Maybe if he was even luckier, he would bag that big elusive deer that everyone including himself had seen.

Nick grinned, the warmth of Bobbie's presence dissolving the lingering chill from the splash of water. He took the plate from her tender hands, the aroma of eggs and bacon mingling with the gentle hush of their morning.

"You always know how to make the ordinary feel like a celebration," he murmured, settling into the worn cushions.

 Bobbie hovered nearby; her eyes bright with the kind of happiness that comes only from shared rituals. She set down her own plate, perching at the edge of the table, her robe now falling carelessly open to reveal a faded T-shirt beneath. The sunlight, filtered through the modest curtains, painted their small world in soft gold.

Nick forked a bite, savoring not just the meal but the moment, and Bobbie watched, her smile playing at the corners of her mouth.

"Did you sleep well?" she asked, voice low, as if the morning might shatter if they spoke too loudly.

"Well, enough," Nick replied, his gaze lingering on her,

"But waking up to this... to you... that's what makes the day worth chasing."

She ducked her head, a blush rising, and reached out to tuck a stray lock of hair behind her ear.

"You'd best eat up before it gets cold. I made your favorite, you know. I figured you'd need your strength for whatever you're planning out there today."

Nick raised his mug, the steam curling between them.

"Here's to breakfast, and to luck—maybe today's the day for that elusive deer."

Bobbie winked, her mischief rising again.

"Just remember, no matter what you bag, you'd better come back lonely."

He laughed, the sound filling the little RV with life, and together they faced the promise of the day, their hearts full, the day ahead waiting in quiet anticipation.

Nick quickly dressed, slipping into his camo jacket as he sat to lace up his boots. The quiet shuffle of movement was broken by Bobbie's soft approach. She lingered near, brushing an invisible crumb from the counter.

"I think I'll call Marion and meet her for coffee in a few minutes, if you don't mind," she said, a gentle smile curving her lips.

"We always have so much fun together, and I'd hate to waste the morning here without you. She'll appreciate the company—and I think Doc's tied up with that new case anyway."

Bobbie glanced around the small space, her gaze resting on the nearly empty pantry.

"Besides, we're running low on supplies. I'll stop by the store and restock. We can't have you coming home to an empty cupboard."

Nick grinned, pausing with one boot half-tied.

"You think of everything."

She shrugged, a playful spark in her eyes.

"Someone has to keep this operation running."

Outside, the day was already brightening, the scent of pine and promise drifting through the open window. Bobbie reached for her bag, humming softly, as Nick finished tying his boots and rose to press a quick kiss to her cheek.

"Be safe, you," she said, lingering for a heartbeat at the door.

"You too," he replied, "and give Marion my best."

With that, they parted—each carrying a quiet joy, the day unfolding before them in golden possibility.

Watching as Bobbie drove out of the campground Nick walked towards the spot, he had seen the big buck the night before that place that was just across the way from the campsite. He knew that it would not be long before that big, racked devil would be laying down somewhere in the thick blanket of pine needles to get his daytime sleep.

Walking to the edge he kneeled down and touched the imprint the hoofs had left in the soft ground. His fingers measuring the width of the hoof print. The size brought a grin to his face. He stood he was ready to follow the trail that was easily marked as it crossed the campsite. His thoughts warned him that it was foolish to believe that the buck would sleep in the same place two nights in a row.

There were many spots for the buck could return to but that depended on the area. The presence of the campers and the hunters could have forced him to move. Nick had not seen or heard anyone mention seeing any does or fawns.

His thoughts were getting in the way of his hunt. Telling himself that he needed to shirk his thoughts to getting further into the woods and find a spot and sit down and wait. The time was running short for the deer to be moving, the lack of any other hunters was allowing them to settle down dand go to sleep. The dawn was breaking fast as he walked quietly into the thick brush of the forest.

Minutes later as he reached a small hillside he sat down. He could see from his perch a long ways as the sun began peeking through the trees to the east.

Spending the morning sitting there he saw several fox squirrels bouncing around the ground and scaling up the many trees.

By about ten o'clock he moved into the thickest brush.

As he walked, he noticed that the ground was carpeted with high piles of leaves, their edges curling and brown, the forest floor rich with the scent of last autumn's memory. Kneeling, Nick examined a patch where the leaves had been pressed down—an oval, shallow impression, the telltale sign of something bedding here. He leaned closer, brushing aside a brittle oak leaf to reveal the fresh outlines of tracks stamped in the shaded earth. Maybe a small group had rested here, does and yearlings, their patterns overlapping and tangled. He marked the spot in his memory, thinking he would return tomorrow, earlier, before the sun warmed the forest and set the deer in motion again.

The hours slipped by as Nick followed the wandering prints, each step leading him deeper into the hush and shadow. He moved quietly, attentive to the smallest clue: a snapped twig, the gentle scatter of acorns, the faint shimmer of hair caught on bramble. Now and then, a fox squirrel would chatter overhead, but the deer moved silent as ghosts.

Near midday, he found himself at the edge of a narrow stream, its water clear and quick over the stones. On the muddy bank, tracks etched the surface—some large, broad and deep, others smaller, delicate and hesitant. He crouched, studying the prints: a family, perhaps, drinking under cover of dawn, before vanishing back into the thicket. He drank in the quiet, the timeless rhythm of the woods, and resolved to return, patient and unseen, trusting that the trail would reveal its secrets to those willing to wait.

It was still dark when he settled deep in the cover. His hopes were raised by the many tracks at the edge of the tiny stream. Finding a large oak with several oak sprouts covering the ground around it, he slipped into the small grove. His cover was perfect. The sun was still in the east. It was barely dawn. Looking at his phone he could see that he had twelve minutes before he could legally bag a deer.

Wanting to drink some of the coffee that Bobbie had filled his thermos with, he waited—the smell of the aromatic liquid would give him away. Leaving the thermos lying on the stump, he slowly stretched his leg.

The forest was holding its breath, drenched in the lavender-blue hush of morning. Nick let his eyes adjust to the slow brightening, each minute sharpening the edges of the world. In his shelter, the chill bit through his jacket, but anticipation was a warmer thing. He listened to the small sounds: the distant tap of a woodpecker, the rustle of a field mouse in last year's leaves, the soft sighing of breeze in the oak's limbs above.

He watched the mottled light creep across the ground, the dew shimmering as dawn advanced. His hands rested lightly on his knees, every muscle quiet, mind as still as the air before a songbird's call. The minutes dragged with the weight of ritual. He thought of Bobbie and the comfort in simple things—a thermos of coffee, the promise of warmth, the shared understanding between old friends at the edge of wild places.

A flicker in the brush caught his attention—a shadow, a ripple in the undergrowth. He held his breath, heart slow and steady. The new day was opening around him, every sense stretched taut, hope kindling with every whisper of movement. Twelve minutes more—a hunter's eternity—before the world would shift and the moment arrive.

He heard them first as they trekked thru the quiet forest. As the mothers head broke thru the trees and under-growth Nick could see the doe, she was tall. Following right behind her were two fawns the must be twins. The sun was behind them as the pushed thru the limbs. The sun glinted from their smooth silky coat.   The large Doe was leading a group of six. All of the others were also Does full grown, not a buck in the bunch. Nick was well hidden as they continued their slow walk as the nibbled at the sparse grass. He could see they were headed for the stream. The fawns were stopping and drinking from some of the small puddles that were there from the hard rain three nights ago. As they stopped and drank Nick had only one thought he wished he had brought a camera and could have captured the herd on film.

His smile came out just as sudden as the deer had appeared. He was content to sit and watch as they slowly worked their way to the stream and drank. The Mother would stop and raise her head, sniff the air, and flick her ears, alert to every distant sound and scent. The fawns pressed close, their small muzzles dipping into the silver pools left by rain, tails flicking as water rippled around their legs. When they had drunk their fill, the herd moved on, unconcerned by the unseen visitor. Nick remained still, savoring the simple grace of their passing, the quiet harmony between watcher and wild. In that moment, he needed nothing—not coffee, nor camera, nor trophy— only the peace that lingered in their wake and the gentle promise of the woods at dawn.

His quiet spot seemed to add to the sleepiness that was slowly returning to Nick—the night had been short, stretched thin by the laughter and late hours he and Bobbie had shared with their bottle of bubbly. He let himself relax, stretching his legs flat on the leaf-strewn ground, the crossbow balanced gently atop them.   The hush settled deeper around him, broken only by the sudden entrance of a bushy-tailed fox squirrel bounding down the gnarled oak just across the clearing. Nick watched, fascinated, his eyelids growing heavy as the little creature flicked its tail and darted about, searching for hidden acorns among the roots.

Turning to follow its busy movements, Nick caught the faintest sound, a whisper of motion from the direction the does had come. The minutes slipped by, suspended in the stillness as he cocked his ear, waiting for the forest to reveal what stirred. Then, piercing the streaked morning light, he glimpsed a shape—the proud, sweeping rack of antlers rising above the brush, each tine glinting with dew. A buck, a true ten-point, moved through the undergrowth with measured purpose, following the exact path the herd had traced moments before.

Nick held his breath, heart thudding quietly, every sense heightened. The buck stepped with slow authority, muscles rippling beneath its coat, nose twitching as it sampled the air. It was a rare, magnificent sight, the kind old hunters swap stories about—proof that patience and silence might yet be rewarded. Time seemed to slow as the great animal drew nearer, the woods holding their breath once again, and Nick felt the thrill of the moment, grateful simply to witness such majesty in the wild hush of dawn.

For a long moment, the woods seemed to hold their applause, every leaf and blade of grass trembling with the lingering passage of the buck. Nick let his eyes linger on the empty space where the great animal had vanished, the last curl of vapor fading in the crisp morning air. His hands were steady now, crossbow forgotten, heart full of the quiet exhilaration that comes from being allowed to witness something rare and wild.

He let out a soft breath, only now realizing how tightly he'd held it, and leaned back into the moss and loam. The world was waking in earnest: a flurry of chipmunks rose from the brush, the distant laughter of a woodpecker echoed again through the oaks. Nick rubbed warmth back into his fingers, the memory of the buck's nearness lingering like a half-remembered dream.

He thought of Bobbie, still sleeping perhaps, and of stories waiting to be told back at camp—tales of velvet antlers and the silent promise of dawn. But for now, Nick was content to sit with the hush, listening to the stream's quiet song, letting the peace of the woods settle deep into his bones. The hunt, he realized, was never just about the taking; it was about moments like this—when time stretches, and the wild heart of the world moves close enough to touch.

Reaching for the thermos Nick settled back against the oak. Blowing into the steaming cup he took in a breath. Not happy that the buck had been in such a position as not to allow him a shot. His thoughts rushed to tomorrow he would be sure to position himself in a better position.

Holding the cup with his hands wrapped around it. He watched as the woods came alive; the absence of the buck seemed to call out to the rest of the creatures. Two grey squirrels began chasing each other up and down the elm tree that housed their nest. The chipmunks were joined by a pesky black and white skunk who waddled in and out of view as it moved into the woods.

The last of the menagerie was the ground hog who moseyed from out of nowhere and drank from the stream.

Standing up when his cup was finished and the cup returned to the top of the thermos, he stuffed it into his backpack and began the journey down the path that had taken all of the deer from the stream. He was eager to trail the buck with hopes he could find him laying down and unaware that Nick was tracking him. His cross bow in the ready. Veering off of the path as he slowly crept towards a small break in the woods. Seeing the Blue ribbon that separated the assigned area.

The minutes had rushed away, and the morning sun was heating up the forest. The trip had been a fact-finding mission. The presence of the steam, that was only there because of the hard rain from the yesterdays. By December it would have dried up. The water had been trickling down from the top of the ridge where the campsites were.

Circling the woods just inside the arc of the fire road, Nick pressed deeper, senses tuned to every rustling leaf and broken twig. His boots found purchase on the damp earth; the forest's hush interrupted only by the distant scolding of a jay. He moved with deliberate caution—each step considered; crossbow balanced lightly in his grip.

The woods here grew denser, the trees rising like columns in a cathedral, sunlight filtering through in fractured beams. Nick's eyes scanned for movement, searching the shadowy undergrowth, retracing the path toward the opposite side of the assigned area. It was a quiet sweep, a gentle investigation, hoping to flush out the big buck he'd spied two nights before—a monarch of muscle and antler, grazing in the twilight at the campsite's edge.

The memory was vivid: the broad, mottled back; the massive rack crowned with velvet, heavy and regal. Nick had watched through the pines, breathless, as the animal browsed on wild greenery, oblivious to anything but the evening's feast.   Now, with the sun vaulting higher and the hush of the woods shifting, Nick wondered if luck might bring him face to face with that same magnificent creature once more.

He paused, listening to the layered quiet, then moved on—a silent shadow among birch and maple, his hopes wound tightly around each step. The forest seemed to breathe around him, every living thing stitched together by the invisible threads of anticipation and memory. And as Nick swept the woods, threading his way through bramble and moss, he let possibility lead him onward, deeper into the wild heart of morning.

But fortune had not favored him this morning. The sun, now climbing unimpeded above the treetops, pressed its heat through his layers, bringing a dampness to his back and brow. Nick's throat felt dry, the last of the coffee in his thermos offering little relief from the thirst that crept in with the midday warmth.　　　He　　　paused, debating whether to venture farther, but reason and fatigue converged—he needed more than strong will and hope to outlast the day.

Resigned, he turned for the path that would lead him back toward camp. The RV, with its promise of shade and cool water, seemed a distant oasis as he made his way through the dense hush, boots softened by pine needles and moss. There would be no buck today—only the satisfaction of having tried, and the anticipation of new tales to share with Bobbie. Each step drew him closer to rest, the cool shadows of the campsite, and the comfort of companionship waiting at the end of the trail.

The trip seemed quick as he walked the path of least resistance. Ignoring the thicker brush he trudged toward the higher ground. The forest softened beneath his steady gait, the gentle slope guiding him upward, away from the tangled undergrowth and into a patchwork of streaked sunlight. Ferns nodded at his passing, and the hush of the woods grew deeper, broken only by the occasional whisper of wind threading through the tallest pines.

As Nick ascended, the air felt cooler, touched by a breeze that slipped down from the ridge. He could glimpse, between the trunks, the glimmer of the stream—a silver thread unraveling through the wild. The elevation gave him a view over the budding grasses and the scattered tracks of deer, winding away into shade.　Here, the world seemed quieter, more removed from the urgency of the hunt and the weight of disappointment.

Each step lifted him farther from the fatigue of the morning, the promise of rest growing more tangible as the ground leveled before him. At last, he reached the crest, pausing to catch his breath and drink in the expanse below—the sweep of woodland and the distant shape of the campsite nestled in the woods. Nick allowed himself a moment to enjoy the triumph of the climb, the reward of perspective, drawn homeward by the memory of coffee, cool water, and stories waiting to be told.

Bobbie was outside sitting in a foldup lawn chair enjoying the quiet scene of the world of greenery. She was holding a glass of iced tea. Standing when she saw Nick approaching. Her smile was apparent as she scurried to meet him.

Taking the cold glass of iced tea from her hand, he took a deep breath then gulped down the cold liquid. Then leaned into her and kissed her.

"You are a dear I am dying of thirst. Sorry I would have kissed you first, but my mouth was so dry."

"That's okay I can feel you are sweating. Go ahead and take off those hot clothes there is no one here but us and I have seen you in your birthday suit before. laughing out loudly.

Bobbie grinned, her eyes sparkling with mischief.

"Well, you can't blame a person for wanting to appreciate the view—especially when the woods are so lively with curious eyes." She slipped her arms around his waist, the cold condensation from her glass as it dripped leaving a brief, wet circle on his shirt.

Nick laughed, the fatigue slipping from his shoulders.

"I suppose I'll just have to risk shocking the squirrels and scandalizing the chipmunks," he said, his voice low and playful.

She leaned into him, their laughter mixing with the hush of the forest. "Let them talk," Bobbie whispered. "We've got the place to ourselves, and I, for one, am grateful you hurried back to see me."

Nick pressed his forehead to hers, feeling the coolness of her skin and the warmth of home in her presence. For a moment, the trials of the morning faded, replaced by simple joy—a quiet reunion under the watchful pines, a shared adventure in the wild, and the promise of stories yet to come.

"I ran into the market this morning and grabbed some lunch; I felt like having something cool I made tuna salad it is in the fridge, and we can have it with the sliced vegetables I fixed. Just bring out another lawn chair after you change into something cooler."

"Okay, I'll bring out the TV trays too, when I get changed; you are a dear."

Bobbie was arranging the crisp vegetables on two bright plates when Nick reappeared, his shirt and hair still damp from the quick change. She glanced up, a welcoming smile on her lips, as he settled into the kitchenette, the lightness of his step displaying his contentment.

"I saw a whole family of deer this morning—there were six of them," Nick began, voice colored with fresh wonder. "And there was a big buck trailing after them, must've been a ten-pointer. I could just watch them, you know? No camera, no chance for a shot, but it didn't matter. Just being there, letting the quiet sink in."

Bobbie nodded, pouring a glass of iced tea and handing it to him, her interest piqued. "It's good to slow down. Sometimes just watching is enough."

Nick took a sip, letting the coolness soothe him, then lowered his voice agreeing.   "I can call Doc maybe he and Marion would like to join us for a movie or something, what do you say?"

Bobbie considered, her laughter drifting softly between them like a breeze. "Let's call them later. For now, let's enjoy lunch and the woods. If there's any mystery here, it'll wait for us."

Nick grinned, grateful for the easy companionship, the promise of laughter, and the gentle certainty that, for now, their quiet corner of the world was theirs alone.

Walking out side with the chair and the TV trays he followed Bobbie as she finished fixing the lunch.

Setting the furniture down and opening the TV tray for Bobbie to sit the lunch on them he sat down.

Sitting close under the shaded spot of the trees, they began their lunch, eating quietly as dappled sunlight flickered across their faces. They grinned at each other, sharing a wordless appreciation for the gentle hush that surrounded them, the soft rustle of leaves and the distant chitter of songbirds weaving a tapestry of peace over the hour.

The trip to the Ozarks was beginning to answer the quiet longing Bobbie had carried with her—one she'd hardly dared name. The memory of the sly plotting that had gotten her here faded in the balm of this moment. She watched Nick with a secret delight, noticing how the worry lines had eased from his brow, his shoulders finally settling into the honest ease of someone who had found a pocket of rest in a restless world.

Lunch disappeared by degrees, the crisp vegetables and cool tea leaving only crumbs and a lingering sweetness in their wake. Content, they lingered, unwilling to surrender the gentle enchantment of their tree-hooded oasis. The woods stood sentinel around them, ancient and unhurried, and the sun spilled gold and green across the clearing.

Bobbie closed her eyes and let the quiet soak in. "We could stay here forever," she murmured, voice almost lost to the hush.

Nick smiled, stretching his legs out in front of him, his hand finding hers with the easy certainty of old habit.

"Let's not wish it away, then." And so, in the heart of the Ozarks, they let the afternoon lengthen, savoring the rare gift of time—untouched, unmeasured, and entirely their own.

Unwilling to move or discuss anything serious, Bobbie and Nick watched as the afternoon faded away. Stretched out on the chaise loungers, they sat close, letting the gentle warmth and the hush of their shaded enclave lull them into a brief, contented drowse. It wasn't quite sleep—just the smallest surrender to drowsiness, a rare luxury both found themselves reluctant to resist.

They drifted together in that soft, in-between place where time seemed to slow, their senses attuned to the subtle theater of the clearing: a chipmunk's scamper along a fallen branch, the lazy arc of a butterfly, the distant tap-tap of a woodpecker somewhere deeper in the trees. The sky edged toward amber, and each sigh of the breeze seemed to deepen their peace.

Conversation, when it came, was idle and fragmentary. They shared small observations—a clever bird, a trick of the light—but mostly, they simply basked in the comfort of presence. Nick found himself marveling at how easily the threat of old worries faded here. Even the persistent curiosity about Doc and the unresolved questions that had chased them both across so many clues felt distant now, washed away by the tranquil assurance of togetherness.

As the sun slipped lower, the world around them softened into honeyed shadows. Bobbie squeezed Nick's hand in silent agreement: whatever tomorrow might bring, this—this hush, this ease, this simple nearness—was enough. For now, nothing else mattered.

The light around them deepened as the promise of evening crept in, dappling their faces with shadows. Bobbie stirred, almost reluctantly, breaking the spell of stillness. Stretching her arms overhead and twisting with that languid grace she sometimes wore, she sat up, casting Nick a sidelong glance.

"You have escaped the task of fixing dinner all of the time we have been here," she teased, her tone warm and sly.

"So, I think you need to grill the steaks I bought at Neil's today. I have enough stuff to crank out a salad. You can sneak in a couple of the larger potatoes, and voilà—we'll finish the last bottle of bubbly that we have left."

She gave a little shrug, a mock-serious glint in her eye. "No hurry, you have plenty of time. Just so I can be in charge today, I want you to put off calling anyone connected to the case. Remember, you are still on vacation and that's an order from Kerry."

Nick chuckled, the easy sound rising between them. He reached over, tousling her hair affectionately.

"Yes, ma'am. I know better than to cross Kerry, especially when he's got me outnumbered."

For a moment longer, they let laughter settle over the clearing—a gentle punctuation to the peace they'd found. Then, with the simple choreography of long companionship, they began to gather themselves for the small, golden rituals of evening: preparing food, lighting the grill, letting the world outside wait. The hush of the Ozarks lingered, a quiet promise that—for tonight, at least—there would be no hurry at all.

Nick conceded to Bobbie's gentle command, and the rest of the evening unfolded with the effortless warmth that comes only when people feel entirely at home. Here in the Ozarks, cradled by the hush of trees and the soft, gathering twilight, the world outside their small clearing dissolved. It was as though their little makeshift camp became its own glowing hearth—every bit as familiar and inviting as their living room back home.

Dinner, when it ready, was simple and perfect: fire-kissed steaks, a bright salad, potatoes crisped on the edges and melting within, the last bottle of bubbly opened with a celebratory twist. They lingered at the tiny table in their RV, laughter rolling out in lazy bursts, bubbles rising in a golden ballet within their glasses.

Later, fed and sun-warmed, they sprawled together on the couch, legs entwined, voices subdued into tender murmurs. Through the window, the sky deepened from indigo to velvet, and the last hush of dusk slipped into night. The bottle emptied far too quickly, but neither cared; the closeness, the gentle, unhurried time together was the true celebration.

Eventually, they made their way to the narrow bed, the outside world receding behind a soft click of the door and the hush of fabric against skin. Still playful, they tangled together, exchanging lazy kisses and laughter muffled into pillows. The Ozark night pressed close around them—crickets chanting, a distant owl calling—and they let themselves be carried by the contentment of the moment.   Wrapped in each other's arms, both felt the rare and precious certainty that here, in this quiet corner of the world, they were exactly where they belonged. Sleep came easily, and dreams were gentle

Chapter Nineteen

Nick's pulse hammered in his ears; the room still thick with the residue of dreams as reality rushed in. He was halfway to the door, Glock in hand, before he managed to shake off the last wisps of sleep—the Ozark night suddenly alive with urgency, the gentle hush replaced by Doc's desperate shouts.

He yanked open the RV's thin door, letting in the night air, heavy with the scent of pine and the distant echo of crickets. Doc stood just outside, boots muddy, helmet askew, his SWAT gear streaked with urgency. "Nick, wake up!" Doc barked.

Nick blinked hard, piecing together Doc's words, the adrenaline slicing through the lingering warmth of their evening. "What's going on? What happened?"

Doc stepped inside; urgency etched deep into the lines of his face. "We searched a bread truck behind the Palace. There were five young girls inside. We're about to serve a search warrant on the Palace itself. The team thinks it'll go smoother if you lead the search. Captain Gordon from RPD is outside; wants to represent the city. His idea to bring you in. Got a spare SWAT suit and gear in the car. Want it?"

Nick glanced over his shoulder at Bobbie, who was sitting up, her blanket pulled around her, eyes wide and bright in the dim light. Her voice, still thick with sleep but edged with humor, cut through the tension:

"Kind of late to ask if he wants to go."

He offered her a tight, apologetic smile—one that spoke of promises interrupted, of the world outside their clearing intruding in ways neither could control.

"Duty calls," he murmured.

Outside, the RV was framed by dark figures and flashing lights—the world Bobbie and Nick had tried to keep at bay now pressing in, insistent and inescapable. Nick pulled on the SWAT gear Doc handed him, the familiar weight settling over his shoulders, grounding him in the present. Bobbie's hand found his for just a moment, squeezing it in silent solidarity. A small hug and a kiss as he put on the helmet Bobbie murmured, "Be careful."

As Nick stepped out into the night, leaving the warmth of their sanctuary behind, he felt the old switch flip—the one that turned quiet contentment into determined resolve. The Ozarks seemed to hold their breath as he joined Doc and Captain Gordon, the team gathering for the raid. With the FBI leading, there was hope that justice—finally—would have its day.

Bobbie watched him go, her expression a blend of pride, worry, and fierce affection. The clearing, now lit by the blue and red pulse of emergency lights, was no longer a place apart. It was the threshold to a reckoning that had been waiting at the edge of their peace. As he stepped out of the RV, she looked at her phone four thirty-seven. 'Thinking if it had been one hour later, he would have been in the woods hunting and maybe safer.'

Nick squared his shoulders, ready for whatever the Palace might hold. The night had changed, and so had he. The hush was gone, replaced by the sharp anticipation of what comes next.

As they drove to the Palace Doc was driving and the hour furnished them an empty road. Doc began explaining the whole situation. The used bread truck had pulled in behind the Palace. Doc knew that it was out of character as it was the bread companies day off. He had worked in a bakery when he was younger. He took a chance and him along with the three others. The agents from the two surveillance spots Surrounded it before they could remove the girls. Everything went smooth. Then doc laughed

"They were dumb enough to misspell the name on the truck "Wholesome instead of Holsom only someone who was not familiar or from this area would have done that. I was a dead giveaway."

As Nick listened, he shifted in his seat, the case was coming to an end. He was sure that Clementine would be glad, and Emma plus Storm could rejoice with the knowledge that the girls would be removed from a life that could be torturous.

The trip to the Palace was a blur as they sped through the sleeping town, the Ozarks rolling past in dark silhouettes. Doc kept his eyes on the empty road, every mile bringing them closer to the heart of the crime. When they finally pulled around behind the Palace, Nick noticed right away—the rear seats of two RPD patrol cars glowed under the interior lights, illuminating the confused faces of the girls. They sat quietly, bundled in borrowed jackets, the trauma of the night etched but not overwhelming their expressions.

Outside, officers stood sentinel, their figures tense, rifles slung across chests, alert but measured. The two suspects had already been hauled away, each in a separate sheriff's car, sirens dying in the distance as the county officers took custody. There was a sense of closure, a hush that hovered between exhaustion and relief.

Doc was already moving, his stride purposeful. He was on his way to Nick, eyes flashing with a mixture of pride and concern that spoke of battles won but not yet forgotten. The scene, shadowed in dim lights, felt suspended—a moment of reckoning, a fragile peace hard-earned in the shadow of the Palace.

Nick was ready to do his part in the sweep. As soon as Doc pressed the cool metal keys into his palm—keys taken from the bread truck driver—Nick felt the purpose steady in his nerves. He cocked his rifle and advanced toward the rear of the building, senses sharpened to every sound and flicker of movement. The team split, one trooper circling to cover the front while Nick, Doc, two state troopers, and Captain Gordon lined up behind him, boots thudding on the asphalt driveway in the hush before a storm.

Their target was on the second floor, the rooms with the hasps and locks on the doors. Doc had reassured Nick that the one suspect was in charge and was with the help of the other suspect he was going to transfer the three captives into the make shift jail on the second floor.

Nick slid the key into the basement door's lock, his breath held until a muted click pronounced their entry. He slid the glass door open, the darkness inside thick with the residue of cigarette smoke and alcohol. The group pressed forward—Nick leading, Captain Gordon's presence solid at his back, Doc's hand never far from his sidearm. Each man spread out as they made their way to the stairway leading to the first floor.

The sweep had begun, and with every careful step, the Palace's hold over the night weakened. In the interplay of fear and resolve, Nick and his team moved with the conviction that this, finally, was the night everything would change for the victims.

The uncertainty of what they would encounter they were on the ready. If the man was singly going to deliver the victims to their fate. If would be simple. They could slip in and with the keys to the locked door free any other victims.

But someone had to be involved, someone inside was collecting money for the confinement of these poor girls.

Nick reached the first floor, stepping aside as the others filled the kitchen. The process was slow as they followed Nick, being quiet was essential. Waking any person in the building might cause resistance. Until the innocent subjects they confronted understood what they were doing there they would be resistive, the early hour was against them. Any man that they had roused might still be groggy from sleep.

Nick could see that Doc had made one mistake leaving Emma the only officer who could speak the language had been left out. The thought flashed through his mind. 'Was there time to bring her there?'

Suddenly, the fragile hush fractured—a small boy, no older than six or seven, stumbled into the kitchen, barefoot and half-shrouded in the dawn's uncertain light. He rubbed his eyes, blinking at the strange assembly of uniforms and drawn weapons, the metallic glint reflected in his wide, bewildered gaze. For a split second, he seemed unreal, a ghost conjured by exhaustion and adrenaline.

Then, as the world seemed to tilt on its axis, the boy's face crumpled in terror. He spun and bolted, his cry slicing through the stillness—high, raw, and impossible to forget. The wail echoed down the corridor as he disappeared into the tangle of shadows.

Instinctively, every weapon in the kitchen swiveled to the doorway he'd vanished through, the team's nerves pulled taut as snapped wire. No one moved. Hearts hammered in rhythm with the fading cadence of the child's scream. The line between threat and innocence had never felt so thin.

Nick raised a hand, signaling everyone to hold fire. Nick felt his muscles locked, poised for anything, the world narrowed to the echoing footsteps and the uncertain knowledge of what—who—might come next. The moment seemed suspended, the dawn at the windows painting the kitchen in ghostly gold as they waited for the next revelation of a night that had already changed too much.

As time stood still the team reposition themselves. Two moved and crouched on either side of the doorway. Ready to blindside anyone who entered.

Nick searched for the light switch whispering "No need to do this in the dark" As he settled close by the large commercial stove. The large clock was lighted the only other source of light in the room.

He counted the second as the second hand made it way around the neon lighted face.

They were still as they waited the sounds of an adult was heard coming down the stairway that led to the second-floor bedrooms. The entrance was soon filled with a woman perhaps forty or so. The shock was evident as she stepped into the kitchen.

Her reaction was one of surprise, "What the hell is going on here?" She blurted out. Her speech broken. Still in her night clothes and bleary eyed she reached for the small boy who had followed her back to the kitchen. She rubbed his head a touch of reassurance.

Nick responded, "I am with the FBI, and we believe that you are harboring some victims here against their will."

Before she answered, her eyes flicked over the strangers crowding her kitchen—searching for intent, for mercy, for some thread to grasp. She understood, in that instant, how thoroughly she was ensnared in a web spun from lies and fear.   Her   lips trembled as she struggled with the words, her English halting, the language itself a barrier and a refuge. She was not just complicit; she was captive in her own home, trapped between the secrets she sheltered and the freedom she quietly longed for.

In fractured syllables, she managed, "I will help you. Bad man... still sleeping. I show you." Her voice was barely louder than a whisper, but the hope underneath it rang clear—a plea for deliverance, not just for herself, but for the others she harbored.

Nick stepped forward, a gentler edge to his posture, his hand settling lightly on her shoulder.

"No—you wait here, with one of the officers. We'll handle it from here."

He gestured pointing to the floor. One of his team moved to guide her and the boy away, into a corner safe from whatever waited above.

The kitchen's hush thickened as Nick and the others advanced, their boots soft against the worn floorboards. Each step up the narrow staircase felt loaded with possibility—the light at the top spilled golden onto the landing, illuminating the faded wallpaper, the chipped banister, the promise of answers behind locked doors. With every breath, the air grew heavier, expectation mixing with dread as the team prepared to confront the darkness hidden in this fractured house, knowing the truth they sought might reshape every certainty they'd brought with them.

Doc followed close behind Nick, his steps measured but urgent, drawn by the gravity of the moment and the fragile bond that had formed between them.   This case was no longer just a mission to dismantle lawlessness; for Doc, it had become a rare and personal calling—a chance, perhaps once in a lifetime, to see justice not only served but redeemed.

At the top of the staircase, the team fanned out, their formation a silent promise of resolve. The open bedroom at the far end of the hall beckoned, thick with the uneasy hush of sleep and secrets. Inside lay the man they had come for, his presence unmistakable in the muffled cadence of his breath.

Doc approached, heart thrumming with a mix of fearlessness and protective instinct. With a steady hand, he reached out and shook the man, rousing him from uneasy dreams. The assailant's eyes flashed open, wild and panicked, flickering over the armed figures crowding his room. He bolted upright, fingers clawing blindly for the sheets as if they might shield him from the certainty of his capture.

A trooper stepped forward, voice firm and unwavering, reciting the rights that marked the closing act of every pursuit. The glint of handcuffs sent the man into a fitful protest, his words tumbling out—raw, bewildered, "What is this all about?"

While Nick kept watch, the other trooper and Doc moved through the rest of the room, their search yielding more than just evidence. Two women emerged, shadows of exhaustion on their faces, eyes wide and uncertain. As they rose, they reached for clothing to slip over their nightwear, modest gestures in the midst of chaos and relief. The air in the cramped space was charged with the first notes of hope—a possibility that the nightmare might at last be ending, that the cost of silence and complicity might finally give way to voices unbound.

Outside the bedroom, the team gathered, each person aware that the night's work had drawn them into a story far deeper than they'd anticipated—a story of captivity and courage, sorrow and deliverance, and the fragile beginnings of freedom found at the breaking point of fear.

Nick signaled to the third set of stairs—the ones that vanished into the attic's uncertain gloom. His jaw tightened with intuition: someone was still hiding above. Turning to the Captain, he kept his voice low. "How about you take Doc and check the attic? But be careful—there might be another male up there."

The captain nodded; the wordless weight of the night measured in his eyes. With Doc at his side, he moved toward the last staircase, every floorboard creak a warning in the hush. As they ascended, the air grew thinner, dust motes swirling in the faint spill of morning light. At the upper landing, the attic door loomed—slightly ajar, a wedge of darkness beckoning inside.

Doc exchanged a look with the captain. Together, they slipped through the doorway, senses straining for the sound of breath, a shudder of movement, any flicker in the gloom that might betray a presence. The attic yawned wide and hollow, rafters arching like the ribs of a beast. In the far corner, the outline of a figure trembled—a silhouette barely visible in the dimness, knees drawn up, arms wrapped tight in a silent shield. Eyes glinted, reflecting fear and the faintest hope.

The captain spoke, his tone calm and unwavering. "We're here to help. You don't have to hide anymore." Doc stepped forward, hands open, letting patience and gentleness fill the space between them. The figure remained motionless for a beat—a heartbeat suspended—before finally, quietly, uncoiling from the shadows.

As they led the last survivor down into the promise of dawn, Doc understood that the house's secrets had not only been unearthed but transformed—each captive now reclaimed by the fragile light of freedom, each rescuer marked by the courage it took to walk into the dark and bring another soul home.

While Doc and the Captain were securing the attic, Nick moved with purpose toward the row of doors—each marked by battered hasps and locks, relics of control that had long outlasted their welcome. He paused at the first, adrenaline mixing with routine, and reached up to unfasten the heavy padlock. But before his fingers closed around the cold metal, he felt a presence—a gentle but unmistakable hand on his shoulder.

Startled, he spun, coming face to face with Emma. Her arrival was unexpected, but the steady look in her eyes was anything but unfamiliar.

"Hi boss," she said, a half-grin tugging at her lips. "I thought you might need me. I was at the motel and had just laid down. Then I heard the sirens and stepped out and could see they were coming to the Palace. I decided that maybe the move on it was going on."

Nick's initial surprise gave way to something like relief as he took in the sight of Emma's vest, the bulge beneath her shirt, speaking to readiness and risk, and Storm's familiar form poised at her side. The room's tension softened, edged with gratitude for reinforcements arriving at the very moment uncertainty threatened to tip into chaos.

A quick nod passed between them—no words needed to bridge the gap between what was and what needed to be done.

Together, they turned back to the locked door, the metal clatter of keys and the warm promise of hope echoing through the halls. With Emma and Storm by his side, Nick found resolve settling in his bones; whatever the rooms held, they would not face it alone.

Unlocking the first door, Nick led the way inside. The corners of the dim room cradled a huddled girl, her hair tangled, her eyes wide and sleepless. She must have awoken at the sound of footsteps, the subtle chorus of locks and voices carrying through the old walls. Emma stepped forward, her presence gentle but sure, and spoke to the girl in her own language—a soft stream of syllables that seemed to melt the tension in the air. She explained that they were safe, that the nightmare was over, and that help had finally arrived.

As understanding dawned, the girl's rigid frame loosened; a single, shuddering breath escaped her. Nick, sensing Emma's calming touch was enough, slipped quietly from the room, leaving Emma and Storm to tend to the delicate task. Storm stood sentinel at the door, ears pricked, while Emma helped the girl to her feet and found her some clothes tucked away in a battered dresser. They moved with no urgency, letting safety settle in slow—letting dignity return unhurried.

Nick waited in the hallway, patience etching itself across his features. He would not rush any of the captives. When Emma finally emerged, the girl by her side, one of the troopers was there—ready to guide her down the stairs, each step a journey from fear toward the uncertain, hopeful promise of freedom. The house, once a haven of despair, now echoed with new footsteps—each one carrying a survivor out of the darkness and into the morning.

Nick's mood shifted as he realized that there were three more doors left—a trio of unknowns, each holding its own story. Emma, staunch and eager to free any others trapped within, moved towards the next door. But she halted abruptly, eyes narrowing as she saw that the lock was missing from the hasp. Her hand moved to her holster, weapon drawn, instincts honed by experience. Nick caught her eye and shook his head, a silent "not yet," then eased her away from the threshold. He needed to see the whole picture.

Just then, footsteps creaked on the attic stairs—Doc and the Captain descending, escorting a woman between them. She wore a dress from the old country, its fabric faded but meticulously kept. Her hair was silver, swept back in a tight knot, her face a landscape of lines shaped by decades. She smiled, bowing repeatedly as she scurried to keep pace with her rescuers. Nick noted, with a jolt, that she was old enough to be the grandmother or the mother of the first woman they'd found in the kitchen—a living thread connecting past and present.

Emma was the first to break the hush, moving quickly to the elder. She spoke softly, reassuring her in the language of her origins, her words weaving comfort. The woman's smile trembled but held, gratitude flickering in her gaze as she clung to Emma's hand.

Nick turned his attention back to the unlocked door, tension coiling along his spine. He drew his own weapon, the solid weight grounding him, and gave Doc a nod. Doc moved to his flank, silent and steady. Together, they braced themselves, then Nick yanked open the door, uncertain of what would greet them in the dim beyond.

Inside, the scene unfolded in a tense moment. A man, desperate and sweating, clawed at the window, his intent clear in every frantic movement. On the bed, a young girl recoiled, pulling the covers up to her chin—her wide eyes fixed on the intruders, terror and hope mingling in her gaze.

Nick crossed the room in a swift, measured stride, positioning himself between the man and the gleaming chrome-plated automatic resting on the nightstand. Doc moved in a slow arc to the left, his presence solid and authoritative, weapon pointing—a silent promise of safety and restraint.

The man's bravado faltered. He glanced from the window to the pistol, calculation flickering in his eyes, but found no resolve. His hands, once scrabbling for escape, faltered and rose in surrender as Nick closed the distance. Nick recognized him—a familiar face from the dining room, the one who had seated them with a practiced smile during an earlier visit.

The realization sent a chill through Nick, a reminder that danger could lurk behind the most ordinary masks.

Doc moved in, efficient and unwavering, securing the man's wrists in cuffs before he could muster another futile attempt at flight. Emma, meanwhile, slipped quietly into the room, her focus entirely on the girl trembling beneath the covers. She knelt beside the bed, voice low and soothing, her words gentle bridges back to safety. The girl's fear began to ebb, replaced by cautious trust as Emma spoke and Storm stood guard at the doorway.

For a long moment, time hung suspended—a fragile peace settling with the morning light filtering through the now-still window. The immediate threat had been contained, but the house still held its secrets, and Nick knew there were more doors yet unopened, more stories waiting to be freed from the shadows. But for now, in the quiet aftermath, dignity and hope found a foothold, and the promise of rescue lingered on the air.

Returning to the hallway, Nick fell in beside Doc, his steps echoing quietly as they guided the subdued man toward the staircase. The creak of the old wood beneath their feet was a steady counterpoint to the muted chaos that lingered behind closed doors. At the landing, Nick spared a backward glance—catching sight of Emma and the Captain, their figures framed in the dim light that pooled in the corridor.

Emma's posture radiated purpose. No longer content to play a supporting role, she strode to the third door and gave the lock a sharp jostle, the metallic jangle announcing her intent. The lock held firm. Her gaze flicked to Nick, a silent communication—caution, but not fear. The captain, reading the tension in the way Emma squared her shoulders, mirrored her actions. He crossed to the fourth and final door, his hand wrapping around the lock and rattling it with a practiced twist. This lock, too, resisted, its presence a reassuring sign that whatever lay beyond was contained for the moment.

With the hallway cleared of immediate threats, the air shifted; suspense yielded to a tentative relief, but vigilance remained. Emma stood, the third lock in her hand,—evidence that there was a good chance that it was safe, designed to keep something in. The captain stood waiting, feet planted, eyes keen, every muscle ready for the unknown.

Downstairs, Doc's voice carried faintly as he handed their captive to a deputy, who waited at the foot of the stairs. Nick lingered at the threshold between stories, torn between the stability of the captured threat and the uncertainty of what remained. He watched as Emma stepped back from the door, her face set in concentration and exchanged a nod with the captain. The unsolved riddles of the house pressed in with the hush, the walls seeming to breathe with secrets.

They would need to enter and make sure that inside they would find another helpless girl waiting for her prayers to be answered.

Stepping close to Emma, he handed her the key ring that he had received from the woman in the kitchen. Stepping away as she unlock the lock. Storm was glued to the door her nose pressed against the crack on the bottom of the door.

Emma slipped the lock out of the hasp as the captain pushed to door open. It was the same one girl huddled in the bed with the covers pulled up. Her eyes were almost hidden by the blankets. She waited uncertain as the future. Who were these men and why were they dressed in those black clothes in the middle of the night. Emma rushed in speaking as she moved to reassure that she was safe that they were here to help her. As she understood she reached out to Emma.

Doc slipped in the room beside Nick as Emma stepped close and hugged the girl. Waiting for the captive to gather up some clothing Nick and Doc eased over to the fourth and last door. The lock was closed and locked as they prepared to make entrance to the last room.

As they gathered to the last door their faces began to show signs of relief, they had made it this far and had not fired a shot, plus they had rescued all of these poor girls. The mood in the dimly lit hall way was one of rejoicing.

Once again Emma stepped up and took the keys from Nick, allowing him to move to his position to open the door. As the Captain squared off for the door to be opened, his hand on his Glock. As the door opened, they were surprised to find two young girls sitting on the bed. As Emma stepped in, she stopped as she registered the situation. The two girls were not like the others, one was red haired and the other blond haired. Hinting they were Caucasian.

Nick seeing the girls allowed Emma to move close. "Hi, my name is Emma, and I am a police officer. Are you alright." The tears began as they heard Emma speak. "We are alright." The younger one jumped off of the bed.

Emma stepped close, her eyes shining with a mixture of exhaustion and awe—amazed at the outcome of their surveillance, the sheer number of girls they had saved from despair. The realization settled heavy and profound: here in the heart of the Ozarks, they had uncovered a place built to break lives, to destroy their will to live. Emma and Nick through courage and persistence, had managed to piece together hope instead.

The feeling that swelled within her was ambiguous—was it pride at the triumph or a deeper, collective joy, the kind that blooms when shared burdens are finally lifted? As she watched the girls embrace safety and one another, Emma sensed the world had paused, just for a moment, to witness their rescue.

Nick, reading the storm of emotion in Emma's posture, stepped quietly to her side and wrapped her in a hug—wordless, steady, anchoring. Storm, ever attuned to the pulse of her person's heart, danced in restless circles, tail wagging, her own joy spilling into the charged air.

In the quiet that followed, relief retreated into gratitude. The team understood the gravity of what they'd accomplished—not only had they dismantled the machinery of suffering, but they had also restored something precious to lives once shadowed by fear. In that dim corridor, among fractured hopes made whole, Emma felt herself breathe freely for the first time in days, the taste of victory rich and bittersweet.

Emma felt the strength return to her body, shaking off the urge to tear she hugged Nick back. He was her friend's husband but tonight he was her hero. He had resisted the urge to let his personal wants side track him and quit the case and spend his time in the forest. He had not stopped the case when the coed had been found. It would have been easy to just leave the supposed crime suggested by rumors and the small clues that Clementine had found be disregarded.

Yet, Nick had pressed on with a patience that bordered on stubbornness, following every thread, trusting the instincts that had kept them searching long after others might have walked away.

Emma glanced at him, gratitude simmering beneath her exhaustion—knowing that without his resolve, the hollowed rooms of this house would remain silent, its secrets festering in the dark.

Now, as the rescued girls gathered themselves, reaching for coats and hand-in-hand unity, Emma saw in their faces a fragile hope rekindled. The hallway, once a passage of dread, became a tunnel of possibility. Behind them, Storm's tail thumped in a steady rhythm, a heartbeat of promise that perhaps, at last, the long night had ended.

Emma straightened her shoulders, catching Nick's eye. "We did it," she mouthed softly, the words fragile as spun glass. Nick nodded, his expression gentle and resolute. For this one night, in this battered place, good had made a stand—and won.

The night exploded with joy as all of the captives, still trembling with disbelief and relief, huddled together in the kitchen. The walls, so recently silent witnesses to unspoken pain, now echoed with laughter and the tentative murmur of hopeful voices. No one knew for certain who had orchestrated their imprisonment, and the shadows of the past lingered in unasked questions, but for now, freedom tasted sweet.

The little boy, wide-eyed and silent since his rescue, clung gently to the grandmother who had been found in the attic. She gathered him close, her arms promising comfort and safety, the two of them an island of calm amid the waves of celebration.

Meanwhile, the first woman—her face a mask of denial—and the two men were escorted out, their hands cuffed, the light from the porch casting stark lines across their faces. Emma spoke quietly with the elderly woman, weighing compassion against duty, and together they decided the arrests were necessary.   Justice, Emma knew, was not always gentle, but here it was right—an affirmation that the suffering endured would not be left unchallenged.

As the police led the perpetrators away and the survivors clustered near the warmth of the stove, the kitchen transformed into a sanctuary. Emma lingered near the doorway, her presence steady and reassuring, watching hope take root where fear once ruled. Storm lay on the floor with her eyes closed; the excitement and all of the commotion had drained her. Tonight, the Ozarks had been changed—not by violence or despair, but by the fierce, collective will to do what was right.

As they locked and secured the basement door, the RPD police officer crisscrossed the entrance with the unmistakable bright yellow tape, the words POLICE LINE—DO NOT CROSS glinting in the dull light. He turned to Nick, nodding with quiet professionalism.

"I'll secure the front door next," he said, his tone clipped but warm, the adrenaline of the night's work not yet faded from his eyes.

Captain Gordon stepped forward; hand outstretched. His palm was callused, grip firm, and there was a rare, unguarded pride in his voice. "Now I know why you were asked to join the FBI."

Nick's chuckle was soft and genuine, his fatigue edged with relief. "Why thank you, Captain. And also—Mister Wittel asked me to tell you that your K-38 is ready."

A small nod was enough to tell Nick he had heard him about the gun.

For a moment, the tension that had held the house together seemed to dissolve, replaced by a ripple of laughter and a quiet sense of understanding. In the hush that followed, the officer moved off down the corridor, tape in hand, while the captain lingered with the team, the weight of the night's ordeal settling into memory. Outside the kitchen's glow, the Ozarks were still and expectant, dawn just a rumor in the distance, but inside, hope—hard-won and fragile—blossomed in the warmth of shared triumph.

The empty bread truck loomed in the morning light, making Nick curious. As the rest of the crew returned to their vehicles Nick wandered over to the truck. Emma joined him. Storm followed as the two slid up the door. Turning to Doc Nick held his hand up stopping Emma and Storm.

"Doc... do you have a camera in you trunk?"

Emma's face showed a perplexed sign. "What are you going to do with a camera. There is nothing in there but a few rags and an empty water bottle."

"Exactly." Nick answered. "A few pictures of how those girls were hauled here like so many cattle; would go a long way with the jury. With You finding out where they came from. It would show how little these men have for human life."

Nick reached up and turned on the inside light of the truck. Waiting for Doc to take the pictures of the cargo area of the truck.

Emma walked around back to the rear of the truck and opened the double doors, her flashlight beam slicing through the stale gloom. The narrow, metal-clad interior was barren—no beds, no blankets, nothing but scuffed planks, a crumpled rag, and the lingering reek of neglect. The acrid stench of urine made her recoil, her expression clouding.

"I see what you mean." Emma said pulling Storm back away from the stench.

The team turned towards him as Captain Gordon approached, his presence steadying the last of the night's frayed nerves. He watched Doc snap photo after photo, each flash illuminating the stark reality within the bread truck's hollow shell.

"Do you want them to take the girls to the hospital?" he asked, his tone gentle but firm, the decision heavy with implication.

"I think it would be best. They need to be checked out before we turn them over to DHS." Emma answered.

Nick nodded, fatigue lining his face. Emma glanced at Storm, who had already begun to process the gravity of what they'd uncovered. The captain continued, his voice shaded with concern, "We all agreed that we would let her sleep while we made the sweep. She had pulled a double shift—was here for sixteen hours. Left here around midnight. I told them to let her rest, so she'd be bright if and when we went to rescue the others."

For a moment, the team stood in quiet contemplation, the sour air drifting from the truck mingling with thoughts of those still to be found. Emma pressed her lips together, the flashlight trembling ever so slightly in her hand.

"Hospital first," she murmured, conviction threading through exhaustion. "They deserve care. Every one of them. I can go and act as an interpreter. taking Storm with me will help them relax."

The captain's nod was approval and reassurance in equal measure. As Doc finished with the camera, the first rays of dawn crept across the parking lot, promising that, for today at least, hope had found room to grow.

The team dispersed, footsteps echoing across the damp asphalt as they headed for their cars. Doc motioned for Nick to join him, and together they walked in companionable silence under the peach-tinged morning sky. Nick paused by   Captain   Gordon, gratitude unspoken but understood, before sliding into the passenger seat beside Doc.

As the car's engine came awake, Nick let out a slow breath, the weight of responsibility settling but not crushing. He pictured Bobbie waiting back at the campgrounds, probably still awake beneath the faded porch light, hope and worry tangled together in the quiet hours. The promise of reunion lent him strength as Doc steered them toward Nick's RV, dawn stretching ahead with the fragile promise of new beginnings.

As Doc guided the car past the ranger station, Nick craned his neck to catch a glimpse of the modest building, its porch light flickering in the gentle morning breeze. He broke the companionable silence with a thoughtful comment,

"They brought in a replacement Ranger. I spoke to the doctor and the ranger on the phone earlier. Sounds like he'll be out for a while." Nick's gaze lingered on the station as they rolled by.

"I need to stop in and introduce myself, but not right now. I'll bring Bobbie over and get it done."

Doc nodded, understanding the delicate dance between duty and the small comforts that made up a life in the field.

The Winnebago appeared around the bend, lights glowing in the pale dawn as if the old camper had caught the sun's earliest rays.

Nick smiled, unsurprised. "I am sure that Bobbie has stayed up and made coffee," he mused, warmth seeping into his voice.

"But if you don't mind, I won't invite you in. I think I'm going to sneak on down into the woods and see if the buck is around. By the time I change clothes it'll be after six."

Doc grinned, shifting the car into park. The morning had the crisp scent of dew and pine, and the world felt momentarily suspended between exhaustion and the promise of renewal. Nick stepped out, the promise of strong coffee and Bobbie's welcome giving him a quiet boost. With one last wave to Doc, he headed toward the camper, already picturing the silent woods beyond—the buck's careful watch, the hush that settles as the day begins, and the hopeful comfort of company waiting just inside beneath the golden light.

Chapter Twenty

As Doc's taillights disappeared down the gravel lane, Nick caught sight of the camper's door swinging open. Bobbie stood framed in the golden spill of light, her silhouette familiar and grounding. He hurried his steps, boots thudding softly on the wet grass, and was through the door almost before she could greet him. In one smooth motion, he swept her into a tight embrace, lifting her with a warmth that made the fatigue of the night seem distant.

His kiss was brief but full of silent gratitude, and when their laughter mingled in the small space, the world outside faded away. They navigated easily to the tiny kitchenette, the gentle clatter of mugs and spoons replacing the hush of dawn.

Bobbie eased away with a knowing smile, her hands already reaching for the skillet.

"I'll start you breakfast while you change," she said, eyes twinkling with mischief and affection.

"I suppose you're heading out to try your luck for that big buck again. I saw him a little while ago, right by the edge of the campgrounds. He looks bigger every time, I see him, I swear." She chuckled, the sound bright and reassuring in the early morning hush.

Nick grinned, already shrugging out of his jacket.

"Well, maybe today's the day," he replied, hope and routine twining together as naturally as the steam rising from the fresh coffee Bobbie poured. The promise of a simple breakfast, a morning hunt, and the comfort of her company filled the RV with a quiet joy only found at the edge of wilderness and home.

The air inside the camper turned gentle as the scent of frying eggs mingled with steam from their cups. Bobbie set a plate before Nick and slid into the seat across from him, her gaze soft but intent.

She let the quiet linger, watching the lines of fatigue and exhilaration play across his face.

Nick picked at his breakfast, his appetite slow but steady, feeling Bobbie's curiosity like a pulse in the small space. He knew she sensed something had shifted; a weight eased from his shoulders. For a moment, he busied himself with his fork, but the satisfaction of what they'd accomplished pressed up in his chest, too full to keep silent much longer.

With a spark in his eye, he finally broke the silence. "Would you like to be one of the first to hear some good news?" His voice was low but playful, mischief edging his words.

Bobbie met his gaze, a gentle smile curving her lips. "No, dear, not if you think it'll sound like you're bragging," she teased, but her tone was warm, encouraging.

Nick chuckled, then grew a little more earnest, the reality of the night's events shimmering just beneath his surface calm. "It's not bragging, not really. I just—after everything, I want you to know. We did it, Bobbie. The whole team. Those girls, they're safe now." He paused, the gravity of it settling between them, and for an instant the world seemed hushed in witness.

"Just so you know the whole story. Clemetine has been working on a human slave case for about six months. They were keeping young girls for the sex trade. She had not been able to get the right evidence to break the case. When we came into the picture we began watching the place."

"Stop... wait a minute are you talking about the Tommie's Oriental Palace the place we ate at the first evening?" Her face was questioning.

"Yes, as a matter of fact it is. They had several bedrooms upstairs that they kept them locked in. They were bringing a new group in tonight. We rescued them."

Bobbie's eyes welled with quiet pride, her hand reaching across the table to rest over his. "I always knew you would. I'm just glad you're all home safe. Emma told me about the surveillance. Just not where it was." Her words were a solace, anchoring him, and in that peaceful morning, the burdens of the night felt lighter.

They sat together, letting hope and relief mingle with the dawn, savoring the rare sweetness of a victory shared in the hush before the world caught on.

Standing up as he finished the food Nick accepted the thermos of coffee that she had fixed him for his time in the woods. Stepping to the cabinet where he had stored his crossbow. He took the case out. Laying it on the small bed he took out the cross bow. Slipped out the quiver holding arrows. Leaned in and kissed Bobbie.

Leaving Bobbie in the RV he headed out to the forest. His path led him straight to the place that he and Bobie had seen the big buck. As he walked into the underbrush, he could see signs of the buck and other deer. Following the trail, he continued to follow the signs.

As He continued through the forest the signs became stronger. Stopping next to a large Oak tree. Stepping close almost hugging it wanting to use it as cover. Minute went by as he hid there the lower limbs shielding him from the sun. His camo clothes blending in with the forage.

Minutes went by as he raised his bow to the ready. A yearling maybe seven of eight months old appeared in the sparce vegetation. Seconds later the second fawn appeared. Nicks arm was tiring as he waited. The next deer that sauntered into his sight was a buck. Nick took aim as the eight-point buck stepped out. The trigger was pulled and the buck bolted as it hit home. Running almost at Nick the white tail stumbled and strained as he got up and ran down the hill.

As Nick looked the others were gone, scurrying into the thick brush. Nick cocked his bow and loaded another arrow. Advancing in the direction that the buck had went he hurried. Seeing the trail of blood in the leaves he continued to track the prey. He continued to follow the trail until he could see the bright white tail laying in the high grass of a small field. Keeping his eyes on it but stopping a safe distance from the buck. He waited wanting his heart to stop beating like a jack hammer. Squatting down he waited and watched hoping the buck would lay there.

Continuing to watch for any movement he eased to the animal. He could tell that he had mortally wounded the prize. The arrow was barely visible in just the right place. Its tongue had fallen out of its mouth. Reassuring Nick that it was his. Thinking not as big as Bobbies but a nice size. Now he thought 'this will be a good time to go and check it in and meet the new ranger.'

Reaching into the back pack he pulled out his hunting knife and field-dressed the deer. Making sure that he did not puncture the intestines. He washed his hands off with water from his canteen. Stepping to the stump close by.

Sitting down he unscrewed the cap of the thermos and poured himself a cup of the coffee. Sitting still he waited he felt no hurry to take on the task of dragging the prize back to the campgrounds. Almost just a bit of remorse began to creep in as Nick realizes that now he had no real reason to stay here in the Ozarks. His reason to convince Kerry that he needed to remain there had just evaporated. But then again there was the fact that he needed to finish up all p the paper work and secure a place for all of the girls that they had rescued.

Reaching down he tied the two legs of the deer he started to drag it to the campgrounds. As he worked his way back pulling the prize, the morning sun was tugging at him, the camo's absorbed the heat and the load he was dragging was taking its toll. He continued to stop and rest ever now and then. Reaching the road, he continued to moved towards Bobbie who was sitting out in a lawn chair enjoying the morning.

Bobbie caught sight of Nick trudging up the road, the bright white tail trailing behind him. She sprang from her chair, excitement lifting her out of her morning reverie, and hurried to meet him halfway. "So, did you find a deer that someone left behind for you to poach?" she teased, laughter sparkling in her eyes as she watched him approach, sweat streaking his brow and satisfaction in his stride.

Nick growled playfully, pretending to take offense, "Don't get cute. You're not too big to turn over my knee and paddle that cute little butt of yours," he shot back, but the smile tugging at his lips betrayed his affection. Their laughter mingled with the gentle hum of the waking forest, the moment buoyed by shared joy and the unspoken certainty that, whatever came next, they would face it together.

Nick grinned, dropping the deer's legs to the gravel and rolling his shoulders as the sweat trickled down his neck. "Stop right here and take off those hot clothes. I will get you something cold to drink," Bobbie insisted, already halfway to the RV, her voice brimming with amusement and care.

"Yeah, that sounds good," Nick replied, peeling off the camo jacket, his arms grateful for the relief. "I guess we don't have to go any further—I can drive the car over here and haul it up to the ranger. He'll need to see it and my tag before I take it to the freeze locker."

Bobbie took the jacket from his hands, folding it with a practiced motion. "You can do all of that, but to start, take off the camo pants too. I'll take them with me." She winked and turned toward the RV.

He watched her a moment, the sense of accomplishment mingling with the quiet, aching relief of the hunt's end. The sun had climbed higher, the morning now awash in gold and green. Nick loosened his boots and let himself breathe, knowing that for now, the woods would wait.

Squatting down in the shade of the large oak tree, Nick watched as Bobbie hurried to the RV, her steps light and determined. For a moment, the quiet returned, and he found himself alone with his thoughts—thoughts that circled back, unbidden, to the real reason he was in these woods. The memories of the morning, sharp as the autumn air, replayed in his mind. He realized how the events had unfolded almost beyond his control, how the weight of responsibility and the rhythm of busyness had kept him from the simple act of visiting the ranger.

He felt a pang of regret—had he allowed himself to become too wrapped up in his own tasks, forgetting the importance of seeing him, of making a visit.

Dragging the deer the rest of the way to the car he unlocked the trunk and rolled it in. Closing the trunk lid he looked to the forest. His mind busy.

The question hung in the back of his mind as he resolved that, once the deer was tagged and stowed in the freezer locker, he would make his way to the hospital. He owed it to himself, and to the sense of community that lured him here in the first place, to pay that visit.

Realizing that if he had not been pursuing the assailant the ranger would not have been attacked. With a deep breath, he stood, brushing the dust from his hands, and stole one last glance at the gold-flecked forest before heading toward the next task, determination steadying his steps.

Walking to the RV, Bobbie pushed open the door, glancing back at Nick with a teasing arch of her brow. "Coming in, are you?" she called, her tone still light with the ease of their morning banter.

Nick ducked inside, letting the cool shade envelop him. He hesitated, then sighed, letting a measure of honesty slip into his words. "Yes, I just realized that I've been so busy with things that I haven't even made it a point to go to the hospital and visit the ranger. I might have solved this case, but I've ignored him. What does that say about the human side of me? Before you say anything, I know I've been very busy. But throughout this whole thing, I've more or less ignored that he's in the hospital because of me."

He pulled on a clean dress shirt, his movements slowed by the weight of his admission. "I had plenty of time yesterday. I spent most of the day in the woods."

"Just let me say this. Doc and Emma both have visited the ranger, and I am sure that while Clementine is there with the victims, she will stop in to see him. If you give me a minute I will dress and go with you now. "

"You know what is funny about this whole thing I was turning this whole case over in my mind while I was hunting and decided that if we compare the blood residue on the kidnappers knife with the rangers blood it will prove that he attempted to kill the ranger. That is when I realized that I had not visited him. Yes, you going with me that would be a good idea."

Bobbie decided, with firm resolve, that she would be the one to erase the shadow of Nick's lapse—a simple oversight, really, but not one she would let linger. She knew that Doc had made a point of visiting the ranger, and Nick was well aware of it too; in truth, it should have sufficed, but somehow the omission gnawed at him, as if a small mark had been left on their collective conscience.

Sliding into the front seat, she drew closer to Nick, her mood light and pleasant as the forest rolled past their windows, the drive short but weighted with its own intent. When they reached the ranger shack, Nick turned off the engine, the quiet hum of the car giving way to the hush of the woods. He opened his door, pausing for a moment as Bobbie watched him, her expression gentle but encouraging.

Nick stepped out, pocketing the keys with a familiar motion, and made his way to the rear of the car. He flipped open his credentials, the badge gleaming in the morning light. "Name's Nick Curtis, FBI. I'm here with my wife for the hunt. Bagged my deer this morning—it's in the trunk and the tag's tied on. Let me open up so you can check it."

His tone was measured, blending professional courtesy with the informal warmth of a man who knows his way through red tape. "Just a formality," he added, nodding to the conservation officer. "I know I need to take it in for a proper check."

Bobbie lingered for a moment near the passenger door, watching the exchange with an air of quiet satisfaction. This, she thought, was how you neutralize old regrets: by showing up, by doing what needed to be done, by setting things right in small, tangible ways.

As the officer inspected the tag and the contents of the trunk, Nick stepped forward and extended his hand to the ranger, offering a firm, grateful shake. "Thank you for everything," he said quietly, a weight easing in his chest. After the brief exchange, he closed the trunk with a solid thud and circled around to rejoin Bobbie in the car.

Slipping back behind the wheel, he let out a breath he hadn't realized he'd been holding, glancing at Bobbie with a lighter look. "Seems like a nice guy. Said his name was Kirk Sims," Nick remarked, a small, genuine smile tugging at his lips.

They pulled out onto the quiet roadway, the forest slipping by in gentle shades of green. Nick kept one hand on the wheel, the other entwined with Bobbie's, her gentle squeezes grounding him. Silence settled between them, but it was a companionable quiet—one filled with unspoken understanding. Nick held onto that warmth, certain that once he'd visited the ranger in the hospital, the lingering unease shadowing his day would finally dissipate.

Eliminating the menial tasks of stopping at the state conservation agent and checking the deer, their next order of business was to drop off the carcass at the freezer locker. Stopping at Burger King for a Whopper and a cold drink filled the time before they could be admitted to the hospital at two, when visiting hours would begin.

Nick felt a renewed sense of purpose as he walked into the ranger's room and found Clementine already there. She had briefed the ranger on the sequence of events that led to the young girls' rescue from their captor.

Spotting Bobbie standing quietly in the hall, Clementine offered to step out, inviting Bobbie to come in and meet the ranger and his wife, who was also present. The room was warm with gratitude and relief, a subtle current of derie flowing between those who had played their part in untangling the ordeal. Bobbie entered, her smile gentle, bringing with her the ease of someone who knew when a chapter had truly closed.

Nick pulled out a chair and gestured for Bobbie, but she shook her head with a soft, knowing smile. Instead, she crossed the small room and embraced the ranger's wife—a wordless, gentle hug that carried genuine warmth. Turning back, Bobbie gave Nick a playful wink. "I'll wait in the hall," she whispered just for him. "You can't stay long; he needs his rest, so let him rest and don't ask any questions about the case." She squeezed his hand before slipping out, her quiet confidence lingering in the room.

Nick nodded, understanding, and settled into the chair beside the ranger's bed. He softened his voice, aiming for comfort rather than interrogation. "How are you doing?" he asked, his tone gentle. "I suppose Clementine already filled you in—we raided the palace and rescued several girls trapped inside."

The ranger gave a slow, deliberate nod, his eyes shining with exhaustion but edged with relief.

Even so, Nick noticed the way his friend's hand hovered over his abdomen, a subtle testament to the lingering pain from surgery. The lines of discomfort were etched in his features, but there was resolve there too—a quiet strength that spoke volumes.

"Well," Nick said, rising from his seat, "I can see you need your rest. I won't stay, but I wanted to thank you again for the heads up about the fire roads. That was the small piece we needed—it led us straight to the culprit. Good job." Nick's gratitude was earnest, his words meant to give credit where it was due.

He clasped the ranger's hand, a final gesture of understanding, before slipping out of the room. In the hallway, Bobbie was waiting, her expression soft and patient. Nick gave her a grateful smile, feeling a reassuring sense of closure.

Outside of the rangers room Clementine stepped close and whispered "Not to worry the blood samples were sent to the laboratory days ago we should have the results anytime. I don't know who did what but that is why we have one boss and many team members." Clicking her tongue.

As they moved quietly through the hospital corridors, Clementine leaned close to Nick, her voice low but steady. "I've secured a safe place for the girls," she said, her words quick but soothing.

"Emma volunteered to stay on with them in the interim—she'll be there until the court system steps in. The lab's finishing up the last of the tests, so we'll have every piece of evidence soon."

Nick let out the breath as he realized it was over. The threads of worry that had kept him taut these past days began to unwind.

Clementine continued, "The charges are already at the prosecutor's office. Everything lines up, Nick—kidnapping Maya Hahn, the attempted murder of the ranger, and the sexual misconduct with the girl at the cabin. With all that, there's every chance he'll be convicted on multiple counts."

Outside, the afternoon light felt softer, the world less burdened. Nick looked to Clementine, gratitude and determination mingling in his gaze. For the first time, he allowed himself to believe that justice would find its way through.

Together, they left the hospital behind, stepping into the quiet afternoon with the weight of unfinished business finally falling away.

Bobbie grabbed Nick's hand as all of their worries VANISHED.